His Grace of Osmonde

Frances Hodgson Burnett

His Grace of Osmonde

The present edition is a reproduction of previous publication of this classic work. Minor typographical errors may have been corrected without note; however, for an authentic reading experience the spelling, punctuation, and capitalization have been retained from the original text.

ISBN: 978-1-64799-753-3

CONTENTS

Chap.

I	The Fifth Day Of April, 1676	1
II	"He Is The King"	6
III	Sir Jeoffry Wildairs	13
IV	"God Have Mercy On Its Evil Fortunes"	17
V	My Lord Marquess Plunges Into The Thames	28
VI	"No; She Has Not Yet Come To Court"	33
VII	"'Tis Clo Wildairs, Man—All The County Knows The Vixen"	38
VIII	In Which My Lady Betty Tantillion Writes Of A Scandal	46
IX	Sir John Oxon Lays A Wager At Cribb's Coffee House	53
X	My Lord Marquess Rides To Camylott	59
XI	"It Might Have Been—It Might Have Been!"	65
XII	In Which Is Sold A Portrait	69
XIII	"Your—Grace!"	78
XIV	"For All Her Youth—There Is No Other Woman Like Her"	88
XV	"And 'Twas The Town Rake And Beauty—Sir John Oxon"	93
XVI	A Rumour	96
XVII	As Hugh De Mertoun Rode	106
XVIII	A Night In Which My Lord Duke Did Not Sleep	115
XIX	"Then You Might Have Been One Of Those—"	121
XX	At Camylott	127
XXI	Upon The Moor	134
XXII	My Lady Dunstanwolde Is Widowed	146
XXIII	Her Ladyship Returns To Town	156
XXIV	Sir John Oxon Returns Also	164
XXV	To-Morrow	172
XXVI	A Dead Rose	177
XXVII	"'Twas The Night Thou Hidst The Package In The Wall"	186
XXVIII	Sir John Rides Out Of Town	192
XXIX	At The Cow At Wickben	198
XXX	On Tyburn Hill	207
XXXI	Their Graces Keep Their Wedding Day At Camylott	215
XXXII	In The Turret Chamber—And In Camylott Wood	224

CHAPTER I

The Fifth Day of April, 1676

Upon the village of Camylott there had rested since the earliest peep of dawn a hush of affectionate and anxious expectancy, the very plough-boys going about their labours without boisterous laughter, the children playing quietly, and the good wives in their kitchens and dairies bustling less than usual and modulating the sharpness of their voices, the most motherly among them in truth finding themselves falling into whispering as they gossiped of the great subject of the hour.

"The swallows were but just beginning to stir and twitter in their nests under the eaves when I heard the horses' hoofs a-clatter on the high road," said Dame Watt to her neighbour as they stood in close confab in her small front garden. "Lord's mercy! though I have lain down expecting it every night for a week, the heart of me leapt up in my throat and I jounced Gregory with a thump in his back to wake him from his snoring. 'Gregory,' cries I, "tis sure begun. God be kind to her young Grace this day. There goes a messenger clattering over the road. Hearken to his horse's feet.'"

Dame Bush, her neighbour, being the good mother of fourteen stalwart boys and girls, heaved a lusty sigh, the sound of which was a thing suggesting much experience and fellow-feeling even with noble ladies at such times.

"There is not a woman's heart in Camylott village," said she, "which doth not beat for her to-day—and for his Grace and the heir or heiress that will come of these hours of hers. God bless all three!"

"Lord, how the tiny thing hath been loved and waited for!" said Dame Watt. "'Tis somewhat to be born a great Duke's child! And how its mother hath been cherished and kept like a young saint in a shrine!"

"If 'tis not a great child and a beauteous one 'twill be a wondrous thing, its parents being both beautiful and happy, and both deep in love," quoth motherly Bush.

"Ay, it beginneth well; it beginneth well," said Dame Watt—"a being born to wealth and state. What with chaplains and governors of virtue and learning, there seemeth no way for it to go astray in life or grow to aught but holy greatness. It should be the finest duke or duchess in all England some day, surely."

"Heaven ordains a fair life for some new-born things, 'twould seem," said Bush, "and a black one for others; and the good can no

1

more be escaped than the bad. There goes my Matthew in his ploughboy's smock across the fields. 'Tis a good lad and a handsome. Why was he not a great lord's son?"

Neighbour Watt laughed.

"Because thou wert an honest woman and not a beauty," quoth she.

The small black eyes set deep in Bush's broad red face twinkled somewhat at the rough jest, but not in hearty mirth. She rubbed her hand across her mouth with an awkward gesture.

"Ay," answered she, "but 'twas not that I meant. I thought of all this child is born to—love and wealth and learning—and that others are born to naught but ill."

"Lawk! let us not even speak of ill on such a day," said her neighbour. "Look at the sky's blueness and the spring bursting forth in every branch and clod—and the very skylarks singing hard as if for joy."

"Ay," said Joan Bush, "and look up village street to the Plough Horse, and see thy Gregory and my Will and their mates pouring down ale to drink a health to it—and to her Grace and to my lord Duke, and to the fine Court doctors, and to the nurses, and to the Chaplain, and to old Rowe who waits about to be ready to ring a peal on the church bells. They'll find toasts enough, I warrant."

"That will they," said Dame Watt, but she chuckled good-naturedly, as if she held no grudge against ale drinking for this one day at least.

'Twas true the men found toasts enough and were willing to drink them as they would have been to drink even such as were less popular. These, in sooth, were near their hearts; and there was reason they should be, no nobleman being more just and kindly to his tenants than his Grace of Osmonde, and no lady more deservedly beloved and looked up to with admiring awe than his young Duchess, now being tenderly watched over at Camylott Tower by one of Queen Catherine's own physicians and a score of assistants, nurses, and underlings.

Even at this moment, William Bush was holding forth to the company gathered about the door of the Plough Horse, he having risen from the oaken bench at its threshold to have his pewter tankard filled again.

"'Tis not alone Duke he will be," quoth he, "but with titles and estates enough to make a man feel like King Charles himself. 'Tis thus he will be writ down in history, as his Grace his father hath been before him: Duke of Osmonde—Marquess of Roxholm—Earl of Osmonde—Earl of Marlowell—Baron Dorlocke of Paulyn, and Baron Mertoun of Charleroy."

"Can a man then be six men at once?" said Gregory Watt.

"Ay, and each of him be master of a great house and rich estate. 'Tis so with this one. 'Tis said the Court itself waits to hear the news."

Stout Tom Comfort broke forth into a laugh.

"'Tis not often the Court waits," says he, "to hear news so honest. At Camylott Tower lies one Duchess whom King Charles did not make, thank God, but was made one by her husband."

Will Bush set down his tankard with a smack upon the table before the sitting-bench.

"She had but once appeared at Whitehall when his Grace met her and fell deep in love that hour," he said.

"Was't not rumoured," said Tom Comfort, somewhat lowering his voice, "that He cast glances her way as he casts them on every young beauty brought before him, and that his Grace could scarce hold his tongue—King or no King?"

"Ay," said Will Bush, sharply, "his royal glance fell on her, and he made a jest on what a man's joy would be whose fortune it was to see her violet eyes melt in love—and his Grace went to her mother, the Lady Elspeth, and besought her to let him proffer his vows to the young lady; and she was his Duchess in ten months' time—and Madame Carwell had come from France, and in a year was made Duchess of Portsmouth."

"Heard you not that she too—some three weeks past—?" quoth Comfort, who was as fond of gossip as an old woman.

"Seventeen days gone," put in Bush; "and 'twas dead, by Heaven's mercy, poor brat. They say she loses her looks, and that his Majesty tires of her, and looks already toward other quarters."
And so they sat over their ale and gossiped, they being supplied with anecdote by his Grace's gentleman's gentleman, who was fond of Court life and found the country tiresome, and whose habit it was to spend an occasional evening at the Plough Horse for the pleasure of having even an audience of yokels; liking it the better since, being yokels, they would listen open-mouthed and staring by the hour to his swagger and stories of Whitehall and Hampton Court, and the many beauties who surrounded the sacred person of his most gracious Majesty, King Charles the Second. Every yokel in the country had heard rumours of these ladies, but Mr. Mount gave those at Camylott village details which were often true and always picturesque.

"What could be expected," he would say, "of a man who had lived in gay exile through his first years, and then of a sudden was made a King, and had all the beauties of England kneeling before him—and he with a squat, black, long-toothed Portugee fastened to

3

him for a wife? And Mistress Barbara Palmer at him from his first landing on English soil to be restored—she that was made my Lady Castlemaine."

And then he would relate stories of this beauteous fury, and her tempestuous quarrels with the King, and of how 'twas known his ease and pleasure-loving nature stood in terror of her violence and gave way before it with bribes and promises through sheer weariness.

"'Tis not that he loves her best," said Mr. Mount, snuff-taking in graceful Court fashion, "for he hath loved a dozen since; but she is a shrew, and can rave and bluster at him till he would hang her with jewels, and give him his crown itself to quieten her furies. 'Tis the pretty orange wench and actor woman Nell Gwynne who will please him longest, for she is a good-humoured baggage and witty, and gives him rest."

'Twas not alone Charles who was pleased with Nell Gwynne. All England liked her, and the lower orders best of all, because she was merry and kind of heart and her jokes and open-handedness pleased them. They were deep in the midst of a story of a poor gentleman in orders whom she had rescued from the debtors' prison, when old Rowe, who had been watching the road leading from the park gates, pricked up his ears and left his seat, trembling with excitement.

"'Tis a horse galloping," he cried; and as they all turned to look he flung his cap in the air. "'Tis the messenger," he burst forth, "and he waves his hat in his hand as if he had gone mad with joy. Off go I to the church tower as fast as legs will carry me."

And off he hobbled, and the messenger galloped onward, flourishing his hat as he rode, and giving it no rest till he drew rein before the Plough Horse door, and all gathered about him to hear his news.

"An heir—an heir!" he cried. "'Tis an heir, and as lusty as a young lion. Gerald Walter John Percy Mertoun, next Duke of Osmonde! Hurrah, hurrah, hurrah!"

And at the words all the men shouted and flung up their hats, the landlord with his wife and children ran forth, women rushed out of their cottages and cried for joy—and the bells in the old church's grey tower swung and rang such a peal of gladness as sounded as if they had gone wild in their ecstacy of welcome to the new-born thing.

In all England there was no nobleman's estate adorned by a house more beautiful than was the Tower of Camylott. Through the centuries in which it had stood upon the fair hill which was its site, there had passed no reign in which a king or queen had not been

4

guest there, and no pair of royal eyes had looked from its window quite without envy, upon the richly timbered, far reaching park and the broad lovely land rolling away to the sea. There was no palace with such lands spread before it, and there were few kings' houses as stately and beauteous in their proportions as was this one.

The fairest room in the fair house had ever been the one known as her Grace's White Chamber. 'Twas a spacious room with white panelled walls and large mullioned windows looking forth over green hill and vale and purple woodland melting into the blue horizon. The ivy grew thick about the windows, and birds nested therein and twittered tenderly in their little homes. The Duchess greatly loved the sound, as she did the fragrance of flowers with which the air of the White Chamber was ever sweet, and which was wafted up to it by each wandering breeze from the flower-beds blooming on the terrace below.

In this room—as the bells in the church tower rang their joyous peal—her young Grace lay in her great bed, her new-born child on her arm and her lord seated close to her pillow, holding her little hand to his lips, his lashes somewhat moist as he hung over his treasures.

"You scarce can believe that he is here," the Duchess whispered with a touching softness. "Indeed, I scarce believe it myself. 'Twas not fair of him to keep us waiting five years when we so greatly yearned for his coming. Perhaps he waited, knowing that we expected so much from him—such beauty and such wisdom and such strength. Let us look at him together, love. The physician will order you away from me soon, but let us see first how handsome he is."

She thrust the covering aside and the two heads—one golden and one brown—pressed closer together that they might the better behold the infant charms which were such joy to them.

"I would not let them bind his little limbs and head as is their way," she said. "From the first hour I spoke with his chief nurse, I gave her my command that he should be left free to grow and to kick his pretty legs as soon as he was strong enough. See, John, he stirs them a little now. They say he is of wondrous size and long and finely made, and indeed he seems so to me—and 'tis not only because I am so proud, is it?"

"I know but little of their looks when they are so young, sweet," her lord answered, his voice and eyes as tender as her own; for in sooth he felt himself moved as he had been at no other hour in his life before, though he was a man of a nature as gentle as 'twas strong. "I will own that I had ever thought of them as strange, unbeauteous red things a man almost held in fear, and whose

5

ugliness a woman but loved because she was near angel; but this one—" and he drew nearer still with a grave countenance—"surely it looks not like the rest. 'Tis not so red and crumple-visaged—its tiny face hath a sort of comeliness. It hath a broad brow, and its eyes will sure be large and well set."

The Duchess slipped her fair arm about his neck—he was so near to her 'twas easy done—and her smile trembled into sweet tears which were half laughter.

"Ah, we love him so," she cried, "how could we think him like any other? We love him so and are so happy and so proud."

And for a moment they remained silent, their cheeks pressed together, the scent of the spring flowers wafting up to them from the terrace, the church bells pealing out through the radiant air.

"He was born of love," his mother whispered at last. "He will live amid love and see only honour and nobleness."

"He will grow to be a noble gentleman," said my lord Duke. "And some day he will love a noble lady, and they will be as we have been—as we have been, beloved."

And their faces turned towards each other as if some law of nature drew them, and their lips met—and their child stirred softly in its first sleep.

CHAPTER II

"He is the King"

The bells pealed at intervals throughout the day in at least five villages over which his Grace of Osmonde was lord—at Roxholm they pealed, at Marlowell Dane, at Paulyn Dorlocke, at Mertounhurst, at Camylott—and in each place, when night fell, bonfires were lighted and oxen roasted whole, while there were dancing and fiddling and drinking of ale on each village green.

In truth, as Dame Watt had said, he had begun well—Gerald Walter John Percy Mertoun, Marquess of Roxholm; and well it seemed he would go on. He throve in such a way as was a wonder to his physicians and nurses, the first gentlemen finding themselves with no occasion for practising their skill, since he suffered from no infant ailments whatsoever, but fed and slept and grew lustier and fairer every hour. He grew so finely—perhaps because his young mother had defied ancient custom and forbidden his limbs and body to be bound—that at three months he was as big and strong as an infant of half a year. 'Twas plain he was built for a tall man with broad shoulders and noble head. But a few months had passed before his baby features modelled themselves into promise of marked beauty, and his brown eyes gazed back at human beings, not with infant vagueness, but with a look which had in it somewhat of question and reply. His retinue of serving-women were filled with such ardent pride in him that his chief nurse had much to do to keep the peace among them, each wishing to be first with him, and being jealous of another who made him laugh and crow and stretch forth his arms that she might take him. The Commandress-in-Chief of the nurses was no ordinary female. She was the widow of a poor chaplain—her name Mistress Rebecca Halsell—and she gratefully rejoiced to have had the happiness to fall into a place of such honour and responsibility. She was of sober age, and being motherly as well as discreet, kept such faithful watch over him as few children begin life under.

The figure of this good woman throughout his childhood stood out from among all others surrounding him, with singular distinctness. She seemed not like a servant, nor was she like any other in the household. As he ripened in years, he realised that in his earliest memories of her there was a recollection of a certain grave respect she had seemed to pay him, and he saw it had been not mere deference but respect, as though he had been a man in miniature, and one to whom, despite his tender youth, dignity and reason should be qualities of nature, and therefore might be demanded from him in all things. As early as thought began to form itself clearly in him, he singled out Mistress Halsell as a person to reflect upon. When he was too young to know wherefore, he comprehended vaguely that she was of a world to which the rest of his attendants did not belong. 'Twas not that she was of greatly superior education and manners, since all those who waited upon him had been carefully chosen; 'twas that she seemed to love him more gravely than did the others, and to mean a deeper thing when she called him "my lord Marquess." She was a pock-marked woman (she having taken the disease from her late husband the Chaplain, who had died of that scourge), and in her earliest bloom could have been but plainly favoured. She had a large-boned frame, and but for a good and serious carriage would have seemed awkward. She had, however, the good fortune to be the possessor of a mellow voice, and to have clear grey eyes, set well and deep in her head, and full of earnest meaning.

7

"Her I shall always remember," the young Marquess often said when he had grown to be a man and was Duke, and had wife and children of his own. "I loved to sit upon her knee, and lean against her breast, and gaze up into her eyes. 'Twas my child-fancy that there was deep within them something like a star, and when I gazed at it, I felt a kind of loving awe such as grew within me when I lay and looked up at a star in the sky."

His mother's eyes were of so dark a violet that 'twas his fancy of them that they looked like the velvet of a purple pansy. Her complexion was of roses and lilies, and had in truth by nature that sweet bloom which Sir Peter Lely was kind enough to bestow upon every beauty of King Charles's court his brush made to live on canvas. She was indeed a lovely creature and a happy one, her life with her husband and child so contenting her that, young though she was, she cared as little for Court life as my lord Duke, who, having lived longer in its midst than she, had no taste for its intrigues and the vices which so flourished in its hot-bed. Though the noblest Duke in England, and of a family whose whole history was enriched with services to the royal house, his habits and likings were not such as made noblemen favourites at the court of Charles the Second. He was not given to loose adventure, and had not won the heart of my Lady Castlemaine, since he had made no love to her, which was not a thing to be lightly forgiven to any handsome and stalwart gentleman. Besides this, he had been so moved by the piteous case of the poor Queen, during her one hopeless battle for her rights when this termagant beauty was first thrust upon her as lady of her bedchamber, that on those cruel days during the struggle when the poor Catherine had found herself sitting alone, deserted, while her husband and her courtiers gathered in laughing, worshipping groups about her triumphant rival, this one gentleman had sought by his courteous respect to support her in her humiliated desolation, though the King himself had first looked black and then had privately mocked at him.

"He hath fallen in love with her," the Castlemaine had said afterwards to a derisive group; "he hath fallen deep in love—with her long teeth and her Portuguese farthingale."

"She needs love, poor soul, Heaven knows," the Duke returned, when this speech was repeated to him. "A poor girl taken from her own country, married to a King, and then insulted by his Court and his mistresses! Some man should remember her youth and desolateness, and not forget that another man has broke her heart and lets his women laugh at her misfortunes."

'Twould have been a dangerous speech perhaps had a man of the Court of Henry the Eighth made it, even to a friend, but Charles

8

was too lightly vicious and too fond of gay scenes to be savage. His brutality was such as was carelessly wreaked on hearts instead of heads—hearts he polluted, made toys of, flung in the mire or broke; heads he left on the shoulders they belonged to. But he did not love his Grace of Osmonde, and though his rank and character were such that he could not well treat him with indignity, he did not regret that after his Grace's marriage with the Lady Rosalys Delile he appeared but seldom at Court.

"He is a tiresome fellow, for one can find no fault with him," his Majesty said, fretfully. "Odd's fish! fortune is on his side where my house is concerned. His father fought at Edgehill and Marston Moor, and they tell me died but two years after Naseby of a wound he had there. Let him go and bury himself on his great estates, play the benefactor to his tenantry, listen to his Chaplain's homilies, and pay stately visits to the manors of his neighbours."

His Grace lived much in the country, not being fond of town, but he did not bury himself and his fair spouse. Few men lived more active lives and found such joy in existence. He entertained at his country seats most brilliantly, since, though he went but seldom to London, he was able to offer London such pleasures and allurements that it was glad to come to him. There were those who were delighted to leave the Court itself to visit Roxholm or Camylott or some other of his domains. Men who loved hunting and out-of-door life found entertainment on the estates of a man who was the most splendid sportsman of his day, whose moors and forests provided the finest game and his stables the finest horses in England. Women who were beauties found that in his stately rooms they might gather courts about them. Men of letters knew that in his libraries they might delve deep into the richest mines. Those who loved art found treasures in his galleries, and wide comprehension and finished tastes in their master.

And over the assemblies, banquets, and brilliant hunt balls there presided the woman with the loveliest eyes, 'twas said, in England, Scotland, Ireland, or Wales—the violet eyes King Charles had been stirred by and which had caused him a bitter scene with my Lady Castlemaine, whose eyes were neither violet nor depths of tender purity. The sweetest eyes in the world, all vowed them to be; and there was no man or woman, gentle or simple, who was not rejoiced by their smiling.

"In my book of pictures," said the little Marquess to his mother once, "there is an angel. She looks as you do when you come in your white robe to kiss me before you go down to dine with the ladies and gentlemen who are our guests. Your little shining crown is made of glittering stones, and hers is only gold. Angels wear only golden crowns—but you are like her, mother, only more beautiful."

9

The child from his first years was used to the passing and repassing across his horizon of brilliant figures and interesting ones. From the big mullioned window of his nursery he could see the visitors come and go, he watched the beaux and beauties saunter in the park and pleasaunce in their brocades, laces, and plumed hats, he saw the scarlet coats ride forth to hunt, and at times fine chariots roll up the avenue with great people in them come to make visits of state. His little life was full of fair pictures and fair stories of them. When the house was filled with brilliant company he liked nothing so much as to sit on Mistress Halsell's knee or in his chair by her side and ask her questions about the guests he caught glimpses of as they passed to and fro. He was a child of strong imagination and with a great liking for the romantic and poetic. He would have told to him again and again any rumour of adventure connected with those he had beheld. He was greatly pleased by the foreign ladies and gentlemen who were among the guests—he liked to hear of the Court of King Louis the Fourteenth, and to have pointed out to him those visitors who were personages connected with it. He was attracted by the sound of foreign tongues, and would inquire to which country a gentleman or lady belonged, and would thrust his head out of the window when they sauntered on the terraces below that he might hear them speak their language. As was natural, he heard much interesting gossip from his attendants when they were not aware that he was observing, they feeling secure in his extreme youth. He could not himself exactly have explained how his conception of the difference between the French and English Courts arose, but at seven years old, he in some way knew that King Louis was a finer gentleman than King Charles, that his Court was more elegant, and that the beauties who ruled it were not merry orange wenches, or romping card house-building maids of honour, or splendid viragoes who raved and stamped and poured forth oaths as fishwives do. How did he know it—and many other things also? He knew it as children always know things their elders do not suspect them of remarking, but which, falling upon their little ears sink deep into their tiny minds, and lying there like seeds in rich earth, put forth shoots and press upwards until they pierce through the darkness and flower and bear fruit in the light of day. He knew that a certain great Duchess of Portsmouth had been sent over from France by King Louis to gain something from King Charles, who had fallen in love with her. The meaning of "falling in love" he was yet vague in his understanding of, but he knew that the people hated her because they thought she played tricks and would make trouble for England if she led the King as she tried to do. The common people called her "Madame Carwell," that being their pronunciation of the French name she had borne before she had been made a Duchess. He had once heard his nurses Alison and Grace gossiping together of a great service of gold the King had given her, and which, when it had been on exhibition, had made the people so angry that they had said they would like to see it melted and poured down her throat. "If he must give it," they had grumbled, "he had better have bestowed it upon Madame Ellen."

Hearing this, my lord Marquess had left his playing and gone to the women, where they stood enjoying their gossip and not thinking of him. He stood and looked up at Alison in his grave little way.

"Who is Madame Ellen, Alison?" he inquired.

"Good Lord!" the woman exclaimed, aside to her companion.

"Why do the people like her better than the other?" he persisted.

At this moment Mistress Halsell entered the nursery, and her keen eye saw at once that his young Lordship had put some question to his attendants which they scarce knew how to answer.

"What does my lord Marquess ask, Grace?" she said; and my lord Marquess turned and looked at herself.

"I heard them speak of Madame Ellen," he answered. "They said something about some pretty things made of gold and that the people were angry that they were for her Grace of Portsmouth instead of Madame Ellen. Why do they like her better?"

Mistress Halsell took his hand and walked with him to their favourite seat in the big window.

"It is because she is the better woman of the two, my lord," she said.

"Is the other one bad, then?" he inquired. "And why does his Majesty give her things made of gold?"

"To pay her," answered Mistress Rebecca, looking thoughtfully out of the window.

"For what?" the young Marquess asked.

"For—for that an honest woman should not take pay for."

"Then why does he love her? Is he a bad King?" his voice lowering as he said it and his brown-eyed, ruddy little face grown solemn.

"A quiet woman in a place like mine cannot judge of Kings," she answered; "but to be King is a grave thing."

"Grave!" cried he; "I thought it was very splendid. All England belongs to him; he wears a gold crown and people kneel to kiss his hand. My father and mother kneel to him when they go to the Court."

"That is why it is grave," said Mistress Rebecca. "All the

11

people look to him for their example. Because he is their head they follow him. He can lead them to good or evil. He can help England to be honest or base. He is the King."

The little fellow looked out upon the fair scene spread before him. Many thoughts he could not yet have found words for welled up within him and moved him vaguely.

"He is the King," he repeated, softly; "he is the King!"

Mistress Rebecca looked at him with tender, searching eyes. She had, through her own thoughts, learned how much these small creatures—sometimes dealt with so carelessly—felt when they were too young for phrases, and how much, also, they remembered their whole lives through.

"He is the King," she said, "and a King must think of his people. A Duke, too, must think of his—as his Grace, your father, thinks, never dealing lightly with his great name or his great house, or those of whom he is governor."

The boy climbed upon her knee and sat there, leaning against her as he loved to do. His eyes rested on the far edge of the farthest purple moor, behind which the sun seemed to be slipping away into some other world he knew not of. The little clouds floating in the high blue sky were rosy where they were not golden; a flock of rooks was flying slowly homeward over the tree-tops, cawing lazily as they came. A great and beautiful stillness seemed to rest on all the earth, and his little mind was full of strange ponderings, leading him through labyrinths of dreams he would remember and comprehend the deep meaning of only when he was a man. Somehow all his thoughts were trooping round about a rich and brilliant figure which was a sort of image standing to him for the personality of his Most Sacred Majesty King Charles the Second—the King who was not quite a King, though all England looked to him, and he could lead it to good or evil.

CHAPTER III

Sir Jeoffry Wildairs

It was not common in those days for young gentlemen of quality to love their books too dearly; in truth, men of all ranks and ages were given rather to leaving learning and the effort to acquire it to those who depended upon professions to gain their bread for them. Men of rank and fortune had too many amusements which required no aid from books, which, indeed, were not greatly the fashion. For country gentlemen there was hunting, coursing, cockfights, the exhilarating watching of cudgelling bouts between yokels, besides visiting, and much eating and drinking and smoking of tobacco while jovial, and sometimes not too fastidious stories were told. When a man went up to town he had other pleasures to fill his time, and whether he was a country gentleman making his yearly visit or a fashionable rake and beau, his entertainment was not usually derived from books, a man who spent much time with them being indeed generally regarded as a milksop. But from the time when he lay stretched upon his nursery floor and gazed at pictures and lettering he had not learned to read, the little Marquess had a fondness for books. He learned to read early, and once having learned, was never so full of pleasure as when he had a volume to pore over. At first he revelled in stories of magicians, giants, afrits, and gnomes, but as soon as his tutors took him in hand he wakened every day to some new interest. Languages ancient and modern he learned with great rapidity, having a special fondness for them, and at thirteen could speak French, high Dutch, and Italian excellently well for his years, besides having a scholarly knowledge of Latin and Greek. His tutor, Mr. Fox, an elderly scholar of honourable birth and many attainments, was as proud of his talents and advancement as his female attendants had been of his strength and beauty in his infancy. This gentleman, whose income had been reduced by misfortune, who had lost his wife and children tragically by one illness, and who had come to undertake his pupil an almost brokenhearted man, found in the promise of this young mind a solace he had never hoped to know again.

"I have taught young gentlemen before," he remarked privately to Mistress Halsell—"one at least with royal blood in his veins, though he was not called prince—but my lord Marquess has a fire I have seen in no other. To set him to work upon a new branch of study is like setting a flame to brushwood. 'Tis as though he burned his way to that he would reach." The same fire expressed itself in all he did. He was passionately fond of all boyish sports, and there was no bodily feat he undertook which he did not finally perform better than others of his age performed it. He could leap, run, fence, shoot at a mark; there was no horse he could not ride, and at ten he stood as tall as a boy of fourteen, and was stalwart and graceful into the bargain. Of his beauty there could be no question, it being of an order which marked him in any assembly. 'Twas not only that his features were of so fine a moulding, that his thick hair curled about his brow in splendid rings, and that he had a large deep eye, tawny brown and fearless as a young lion's, but there was in the carriage of his head, the bearing of his body, the very movement of his limbs a thing which stamped him. In truth, it was as if nature, in a lavish mood and having leisure, had built a human creature of her best and launched him furnished forth with her fairest fortunes, that she might behold what he would do. The first time he was taken by his parents to London, there was a day upon which, while walking in the garden of Hampton Court, accompanied by his governor, he found himself stopped by a splendid haughty lady, whom Mr. Fox saluted with some fearfulness when she addressed him. She asked the boy's name, and, putting her hand on his shoulder, so held him that she might look at him well.

"The little Roxholm," she said. "Yes, his mother was the beauty who—"

'Twas as if she checked her speech. She made a quick, imperious movement with her head, and added: "He is all rumour said of him;" and she turned away with such abruptness that the child asked himself how he had vexed her, and wondered also at her manners, he being used only to grace and courtesy.

They were near the end of the terrace which looked upon the River Thames, and she went with her companion and leaned upon the stone balustrades, looking out upon the water with fierce eyes. "The woman who could give him a son like that," she said, "could hold him against all others, and demand what she chose. Squat Catherine herself could do it."

Little Roxholm heard her.

"She is a very handsome lady," he said, innocently, "though she has a strange way. Is she of the Court, and do you know her name?"

"'Tis her Grace the Duchess of Cleveland," answered Mr. Fox, gravely, as they walked away.

He was seven years old at this time, and 'twas during this visit to town that he heard a conversation which made a great impression upon him, opening up as it did new vistas of childish thinking.

Having known but one phase of existence, he was not aware that he had lived the life of a young prince in a fairy tale, and that there were other children whose surroundings were as gloomy as his were fair and bright.

He was one day comfortably ensconced in the deep embrasure of a window, a book upon his knee, when Mistress Halsell and one of the upper servants came into the room upon which his study opened, and presently his ear was attracted by a thing they were speaking of with some feeling.

"As sweetly pretty a young lady as ever one beheld," he heard. "Never saw I a fairer skin or eyes more hyacinth-blue—and her hair trailing to the ground like a mantle, and as soft and fine as silk."

'Twas this which made him stop in his reading. The description seeming so like that of a beauty in a story of chivalry in which knights fought for such loveliness.

"And now," the voice went on, "after but a few years of marriage all her beauty lost so that none would know her! Four poor, weak girl infants she hath given birth to, and her husband, Sir Jeoffry, in a fury at the coming of each, raging that it is not an heir. Before the first came he had begun to slight her, and when 'twas born a girl he well-nigh broke her heart. He is a great, bold, handsome man, and she, poor little lady, hopeless in her worship of him. And the next year there was another girl, and each year since— and Sir Jeoffry spends his time in riot and drinking and ill-living— and she fades away in her wing of the house, scarce ever seen."

"Poor, uncared-for thing, 'twould be happier if God took her, and her children, too," said Mistress Halsell.

"Three have been taken," replied her companion, in a low voice. "Neither she nor they have strength. And ah! to see her in these days—her pretty face grown thin and haggard, the blue of her eyes drenched out with weeping. 'Tis told he once said to her, 'When a woman grows thin and yellow, her husband will go in search of better looks, and none has right to blame him.' 'Twas on a day when she had dressed herself in her best to please him, but a few weeks after her third infant came into the world. And so weak was she, poor lady, and so hurt in spirit, that she gave a little sob and swooned."

The young Marquess read his book no more. He drew down his handsome childish brow and stared straight before him through the window. He was a boy with a fiery spirit, despite his general amiability of demeanour, and, had he lived among tormentors and tyrants and been ill-treated, would have had an ungovernable temper. The thing he had heard filled him with a kind of rage against this big handsome man who treated his lady cruelly and

15

hated her infants. 'Twas all brutal and wicked and unfair, as if one should heartlessly beat a little dog that loved one. The picture brought before him was hideous and made him grow hot. His spirit had never been tamed, he had the blood of fighting men in his veins, and he had read innumerable stories of chivalry. He wished he were big enough to go forth in search of such men as this Sir Jeoffry, and strike them to the earth with his sword.

On such evenings as their Graces did not entertain, he was taken by his governour to spend an hour with his father and mother in the withdrawing-room, where they sat, and on this evening, when he went to them, each of them observed that he spoke less than usual and seemed in a new mood. He had always been filled with a passionate adoration of his mother, and was much given to following her with his eyes; but this night his gaze was fixed upon her in such earnest scrutiny that at last her Grace asked him laughingly what he saw in her looks more than ordinary. He had kept very close to her, and had held her hand, and kissed it more than once since he had been in the room. He lifted it to his lips again now, and pressed an impassioned kiss upon its fairness.

"You were never treated cruelly," he said. "No one would ever dare to speak so to you that you would sob and swoon. If any dared!" and his little hand involuntarily went to his side with a fierce childish gesture which made my lord Duke laugh delightedly.

"'Tis in his blood to draw," he said. "Bravo! Roxholm; bravo!"

His mother looked at his beautiful little face and, seeing a thing in his eyes which women who are mothers detect in the eyes of their offspring when others observe little, put a hand on each of his shoulders and went upon one knee so that she could be on a level with his face and see deeper.

"What," she said, with a tender comprehending warmth, "you have been hearing of some poor lady who is hardly treated, and you cannot endure to think of it, because you are a man even though you are but seven years old;" and she bent forward and kissed him with a lovely passion and her violet eyes bedewed. "Yes, love," she said, "you are a Man. All Osmondes are when they are born, I think. Indeed, John"—with the sweetest laughing look at her lord, who stood worshipping her from his place at the opposite side of the hearth—"I am sure that when you were seven years old, if you had had a little sword, you would have drawn it to defend a woman against a giant, though he had been big enough to have eaten you at one mouthful—and Gerald is like you," proudly. "Gerald is a Man, too."

"'Tis not fair," cried little Roxholm, passionately, "'tis not fair that a big gentleman should be so harsh to a poor lady who loves

16

him, that he should make her cry till the blue goes from her eyes and she is beautiful no longer, and that he should hate her infants because they are not boys. And when she tried to please him he made her sob and swoon away. He should be killed for it—he should be killed."

His father and mother glanced at each other. "Surely," her Grace said, "he must have heard of the wicked Gloucestershire baronet my Lord Dunstanwolde told us stories of—Sir Jeoffry."

"Ay, his name was Sir Jeoffry," cried Roxholm, eagerly. "Sir Jeoffry it was they said."

"Yes," said my lord Duke, "Sir Jeoffry Wildairs, and a rank, heartless brute he is to be the father of helpless girl children."

CHAPTER IV

"God Have Mercy on its Evil Fortunes"

In the constantly changing panorama which passes before the mind of a child, it is certain no picture dawns and fades without leaving some trace behind. The exact images may not be recorded, but the effect produced by their passing will remain and become part of the palimpsest of life and character. The panorama which passed before the mental vision of the boy Marquess during the years of his early youth was not only brilliant but full of great changes, being indeed such a panorama as could not fail to produce strong and formative impressions upon a growing mind. The doings of Charles Stuart's dissolute and brilliant Court he began life hearing stories of; before he had reached ten years of age, King Charles had died and James the Second was ruler of England; in three years more his Majesty had been deserted by all and had fled to the protection of Louis of France, leaving his crown behind him to be offered to and accepted by William of Orange and Mary, his well-beloved wife; but four years later Queen Mary had died of small-pox and left her husband overwhelmed with grief, crying that he had been the happiest of men and was now the most miserable. Kings are not made and deposed, crowned and buried and mourned, without pomps, ceremonials, and the occurring of events which must move even the common mind to observation and reflection. This young mind was of no common mould, it having come into the world active and by nature ready to receive impressions, and from its earliest consciousness had been watched and cultured in such manner as must have enriched even the poorest understanding. As children of ordinary rank are familiar with games, and hear of simple every-day events that happen to their neighbours, this heir to a dukedom was familiar with the game of Courts and rulers and heard daily discussion of Kings and great statesmen—of their rights and wrongs, their triumphs and failures. The changing events made such discussion inevitable, and the boy, being through their wise affection treated almost as the companion of his parents, heard much important conversation which filled him with deep interest and led him into grave thinking which greatly developed his powers of mind. Among the many memories which remained with him throughout his life, and which in his later years he realised, had left a singularly definite image upon his mind, was this small incident of his first hearing of the Gloucestershire baronet whose lady had wept the blue from her eyes in her wretchedness under his brutal neglect and cruelty. The impression doubtless owed much of its vividness to the fact that 'twas made so early as to be the first realising of the existence of a world where misery dwelt as a common thing, where men were coarse and cruel, where women were tyrannised over and treated roughly, and where children were unloved and neglected. Into this world he had previously obtained no glimpse; but, once having realised its existence, he could not easily forget it. Often as time passed he found himself haunted by thoughts of the poor injured lady and her children, and being a creature of strong imagination, there would rise before him mental pictures of what a household might be whose master was a coarse rioter before whom his wife and children cowered in fear.

So it happened in his conversing with Mistress Halsell he broached the subject of the Gloucestershire baronet, and the good woman, seeing that his speech did not arise from idle curiosity, told him what she knew of this most unhappy family.

'Twas an old family and a good one in the matter of lineage, but through the debaucheries of the last baronets its estates had become impoverished and its reputation of an ill savour. It had ever been known as a family noted for the great physical strength and beauty of its men and women. For centuries the men of the house of Wildairs had been the biggest and the handsomest in England. They had massive frames, black eyes, thick hair and beards, and feared neither man nor devil, but openly defied both. They were men who lived wildly, ate and drank hugely, pursued women, were great at all deeds of prowess, and bursting with rough health and lawless high

18

spirits. 'Twas a saying of their house that "a Wildairs who could not kill an ox with a blow and eat half of him when he was roasted, was a poor wight indeed." The present baronet, Sir Jeoffry, was of somewhat worse reputation than any Sir Jeoffry before him. He lived a wild life in the country, rarely going up to town, as he was not fond of town manners and town customs, but liked better hunting, coursing, cock-fighting, bull-baiting, and engaging in intrigues with dairy maids and the poppy-cheeked daughters of his cottagers. He had married a sweet creature of fifteen, whom after their brief honeymoon he had neglected as such men neglect a woman, leaving her to break her heart and lose her bloom and beauty in her helpless mourning for his past passion for her. He was at drawn swords with his next of kin, who despised him and his evil, rough living, and he had set his mind upon leaving sons enough to make sure his title should be borne only by his own offspring. He being of this mind, 'twas not to be wondered at that he had no welcome for the daughters who should have pleased him by being sons. When the first was born he flouted its mother bitterly, the poor young lady, who was but sixteen and a delicate creature, falling into a fit of illness through her grief and disappointment. The coming of the second threw him into a rage, the third into a fury; and the birth of a fourth being announced, he stormed like a madman, would not look at it, and went upon a debauch so protracted and disgraceful as to be the scandal of the county and the subject of gossip for many a day.

From that hour the innocent Lady Wildairs did not raise her head. Her family had rejected her on account of her marriage with a rake so unfashionable and of reputation so coarse. Wildairs Hall, ill kept, and going to ruin through the wasteful living of its spendthrift master, was no place for such guests as were ladies and gentlemen. The only visitors who frequented it were a dozen or so chosen spirits who shared Sir Jeoffry's tastes—hunted, drank, gambled with him, and were as loose livers as himself. My Lady Wildairs, grown thin, yellow, and haggard, shrank into her own poor corner of the big house, a bare west wing where she bore her children in lonely suffering and saw them die, one after the other, two only having the strength to survive. She was her lord's hopeless slave, and at the same time the mere knowledge of her existence was an irritation to him, she being indeed regarded by him as a Sultan might regard the least fortunate of his harem.

"Damn her," he cried once to one of his cronies, a certain Lord Eldershaw, "in these days I hate the sight of her, with her skinny throat and face. What's a woman for, after she looks like that? If she were not hanging about my neck I could marry some fine strapping girl who would give me an heir before a year was out."

If young Roxholm did not hear this special anecdote, he heard others from various sources which were productive in him of many puzzled and somewhat anxious thoughts. "Why was it," he pondered, "that women who had not the happy fortune of his mother seemed at so cruel a disadvantage—that men who were big and handsome having won them, grew tired of them and cast them aside, with no care for their loneliness and pain? Why had God so made them that they seemed as helpless as poor driven sheep? 'Twas not fair it should be so—he could not feel it honest, though he was beset by grave fears at his own contumacy since he had been taught that God ordained all things. Had he ordained this, that men should be tyrants, and base, and cruel, and that women should be feeble victims who had but the power to moan and die and be forgotten? There was my Lord Peterborough, who had fought against Algerine pirates, and at nineteen crowned his young brow with glory in action at Tripoli. To the boyish mind he was a figure so brilliant and gallant and to be adored that it seemed impossible to allow that his shining could be tarnished by a fault, yet 'twas but a year after his marriage with the fair daughter of Fraser of Mearns that he had wearied of his love and gaily sailed for the Algerine coast again. Whether the young Countess had bewailed her lot or not, Roxholm had not chanced to hear, but having had for husband a young gentleman so dazzling and full of fascination, how could she have found herself deserted and feel no heartache and shed no tears? My lord could sail away and fight corsairs, but her poor ladyship must remain behind and do battle only with her heart, gaining no laurels thereby.

The sentiment of the times was not one which rated women high or was fraught with consideration for female weakness. Charles Stuart taught men how women should be regarded, and the beauties of his Court had aided him in such manner as deepened the impression he had produced. A beauty had her few years of triumph in which she was pursued, intrigued with, worshipped, flattered, had madrigals sung in her honour; those years over, no one cared to hear of the remainder of her life. If there were dregs left in her cup, she drank them alone. A woman who had no beauty was often a mere drudging or child-bearing wife, scapegoat for ill-humour and morning headaches; victim, slave, or unnoticed appendage. This the whilom toast Lady Wildairs had become, and there were many like her.

The Earl of Dunstanwolde, who was the nobleman who had spoken to the Duke and Duchess of the Gloucestershire Baronet, was a distant kinsman, and a somewhat frequent visitor both at their Graces' country estates and at their town establishment, Osmonde House. His own estate was near Gloucestershire, and he knew the stories of Wildairs Hall, as did so many others.

This gentleman was somewhat past middle age, and was the owner of such qualities of mind and heart as had won for him the friendship of all thinking persons who knew him. A man of kindly refinement and dignity, familiar with arts and letters, and generous in his actions both to his equals and his inferiors, he was of ancient blood, and had large estates in the country and a great house in town.

But, notwithstanding the honourableness of his position, and the ease of his circumstances, he was not a happy gentleman, having made a love-match in his youth, and lost his passionately worshipped consort at the birth of her first child, who had lived but two hours. He had been so happy in his union that, being of a constant nature, he could not console himself for his bereavement, and had remained a widower, content that his estates and titles should pass to a distant cousin who was the next heir. He was a sad-faced gentleman with delicately cut features, and eyes which looked as if they had beheld sorrow, there being deep lines about them, and also about his mouth.

This nobleman had for Roxholm a great attraction—his voice, his bearing, and his gentle gravity all seemed to convey a thing which reached the boy's heart. On his own part the childless man had from the first felt for his little kinsman a pathetic affection. Had fate been kind, instead of cruel, the son of his own Alice might have so bloomed and grown stalwart and fair. He liked to talk with the child even when he was but a few years old, and as time passed, and he shot up into a handsome, tall lad, their friendship became a singularly close one. When my lord was at Camylott the country people became accustomed to seeing the two ride through the lanes together, the gamekeepers in the park were familiar with the sight of the elder gentleman and the young Marquess walking side by side down unfrequented woodland paths engaged in earnest conversation, his lordship's hand oftenest resting on the young shoulder as they went.

There was a subject of which these two talked often, and with great interest, it being one for which Roxholm had always felt a love, since the days when he had walked through the picture gallery with his nurse, looking up with childish delight at the ladies and gentlemen in the family portraits, asking to be told stories of their doings, and requiring that it be explained to him why they wore costumes which seemed strange to him. Mistress Halsell had been

21

able to tell him many stories of them, as also had his father and mother and Mr. Fox, his governour, and these stories had so pleased him that he had pondered upon them until their heroes and heroines seemed his familiar friends, and made of as firm flesh and real blood as the ladies and gentlemen who were his kinswomen and kinsmen to-day. It had always been his pleasure to remember that the stories to be told of them were such fine ones. There were Crusaders among them who had done splendid deeds; there were men who had fought by the side of their King in battle, and there were those who had done high service for him with brain and spoken word when his power stood in danger of being overthrown. To the boy there seemed indeed to have been no battle either of Church or State, or with enemies in open field in which Mertouns had not fought. Long before the Conquest, Normandy had known their high-strung spirit and fiery valour. At Senlac, Guilbert de Mertoun had stood near William of Normandy when he gave his command to his archers that they should shoot into the air, whereby an arrow sought English Harold for its mark and pierced him through eye and brain, leaving him slain, and William conqueror. This same Guilbert, William had loved for his fierce bravery and his splendid aim in their hunting the high deer, of whom 'twas said the monarch "loved them as if he had been their father;" and when the Domesday Book was made, rich lands were given to him that, as the King said—there should be somewhat worthy of his holding to be recorded therein. It had been a Guilbert de Mertoun who rode with Rufus when he would cross to Normandy to put down insurrection there. These two were alike in their spirit (therefore little Roxholm had ever worshipped both), and when they reached the seashore in a raging storm, and the sailors, from fear, refused to put forth, and Rufus cried, "Heard ye ever of a King who was drowned," 'twas Guilbert who sprang forward swearing he would set sail himself if others would not, and so stirred the cowards with his fierce passionate courage that they obeyed the orders given them and crossed the raging sea's arm in the tempest, Guilbert standing in their midst spurring them with shouts, while the wind so raged that only a man of giant strength could have stood upright, and his voice could scarce be heard above its fury. And 'twas he who was at the front when the insurgents were overpowered. Of this one, of whom 'twas handed down that he was of huge build, and had beard and hair as flaming as Rufus's own, there were legends which made him the idol of Roxholm's heart in his childhood. Again and again it had been his custom to demand that they should be repeated to him—the stories of the stags he had pierced to the heart in one day's hunting in the New Forest—the story of how he was held in worship by his villeins, and of his mercifulness to them in days when nobles had the power of life and death, and to do any cruelty to those in servitude to them.

In Edward the Third's time, when the Black Death swept England, there had lived another Guilbert who, having for consort a lovely, noble lady, they two had hand in hand devoted themselves to battling the pestilence among their serfs and retainers, and with the aid of a brother of great learning (the first Gerald of the house) had sought out and discovered such remedies as saved scores of lives and modified the sufferings of all. At the end of their labours, when the violence of the plague was assuaged, the lovely lady Aloys had died of the fatigues she had borne and her husband had devoted himself to a life of merciful deeds, the history of which was a wondrous thing for an impassioned and romance-loving boy to pore over.

Upon the romances of these lives the imagination of the infant Roxholm had nourished itself, and the boy Roxholm being so fed had builded his young life and its ideals upon them.

It was of these ancestors of his house and of their high deeds he found pleasure and profit in talking to his kinsman and friend, and 'twas an incident which took place during one of my Lord Dunstanwolde's visits to Camylott which led them to this manner of converse.

Roxholm was but eleven years old when in taking a barred gate on a new horse the animal leapt imperfectly and, falling upon his rider, broke a leg and two ribs for him. The injuries were such as all knew must give the boy sharp anguish of body, when he was placed upon a hurdle and carried home. His father galloped to the Tower to break the news to her Grace and prepare her for his coming. My Lord Dunstanwolde walked by the hurdle side, and as he did so, watching the boy closely, he was touched to see that though his beautiful young face was white as death and he lay with closed eyes, he uttered no sound and his lips wore a brave smile.

"Is your pain great, Roxholm?" my Lord asked with tender sympathy.

Roxholm opened his eyes and, still smiling, blushed faintly.

"I think of John Cuthbert de Mertoun," he said in a low voice. "It aids me to hold the torment at bay."

He spoke the words with some shyness, as if feeling that one older than himself might smile at the romantic wildness of his fancy. But this my Lord Dunstanwolde did not, understanding him full well, and lying a hand on his pressed it with warm affection. The story of John Cuthbert was, that a hound suddenly going mad one day while he hunted deep in the forest, it had attacked a poor

23

follower and would have torn his throat had his lord not come to his rescue, pulling the beast from him and drawing its fury upon himself, whereby in his battle with it he was horribly bitten; and when the animal lay dead upon the sward he drew his hunting-knife and cut out the mangled flesh with his own hand, "and winced not nor swouned," as the chronicle recorded with open joy in him.

'Twas while Roxholm lay in bed recovering of his injuries that his kinsman referred to this again, asking him what thoughts he had had of this hero and wherein he had felt them an aid, and the boy's answers and the talk which followed them had been the beginning of many such conversations, his Lordship finding the young mind full of vigour and fine imagination. Often, as they conversed in after times, the older man was moved by the courageous fancies and strong, high ideals he found himself confronting. 'Twas all so brave and beautiful, and there was such tragedy in the thought that life might hold clouds to dull the gold of it. 'Tis but human that those of maturer years who have known sorrow should be reminded of it by the very faith and joyfulness of youth. One of the fine features of the Tower of Camylott was its Long Gallery, which was of such length and breadth and so finely panelled as to be renowned through all the land. At each end the broad windows looked out upon noble stretches of varying hill and tall and venerable forest, and in wet weather, when the house was full the ladies and gentlemen would promenade there, chatting or sometimes playing games to amuse themselves.

In such weather my Lord Dunstanwolde and his young kinsman sometimes paced whole mornings away together, and 'twas on such an occasion that there first entered into Roxholm's life that which later filled and ruled it and was its very self. But at this time he was scarcely fourteen, and 'twas but the first strange chapter of a story he heard, in no way dreaming that 'twas one of which his own deepest pain and highest raptures would be part.

Often as the years passed, my Lord Dunstanwolde looked back upon this December day and remembered how, as they walked to and fro, he had marked for the hundredth time how beautiful and picturesque a figure the boy made in his suit of rich-coloured brocade, his curling, warm brown hair falling on his shoulders in thick, natural curls such as no perruquier could imitate, the bloom of health and out-door life upon his cheek, his handsome, well-opened eye sparkling or melting in kindly warmth as he conversed. He was a tall, straight-limbed lad, and had by this time attained such height and so bore himself that there were but few inches between his noble kinsman and himself, though the years between

24

them were so many, and my Lord Dunstanwolde was of no mean stature.

Outside a heavy rain fell, deluging the earth and drenching such grass as the winter had left, covering with its faded tussocks the sweep of the park lands. The sky was heavy with leaden clouds from which the water fell in sweeping dashes. Having walked for some time, the two stopped before the wide bay window at the east end of the Long Gallery and watched the deluge for a space, marking how the drops splashed upon the terrace, how the birds flew before it, and how the deer huddled together under the stripped trees as if glad of the small shelter their trunks and bare branches could afford.

"Such a day brings back to a man the gloomiest things he knows," said Lord Dunstanwolde after a few moments' silent gazing upon the scene. "I no sooner paused here to look forth at the greyness than there came back to me a hard tale I heard before I left Gloucestershire. 'Twas another tale of Wildairs, Gerald."

"Of Sir Jeoffry?" said Roxholm, with interest. It had happened that some time before Lord Dunstanwolde had heard of the impression made upon him by the story of the poor lady and her brutal lord and master. More than once they had spoken together of Wildairs Hall, and those who rioted, and those who suffered, in it, and Roxholm had learned that, year by year the Gloucestershire baronet's living had grown wilder and more dissolute, until his mad follies had cut him off from the companionship of all reputable persons, and he spent his days in brutal sports, drink, and rough entertainment with a dozen men as little respected as himself. His money he had squandered and gambled away at dice, his estate fell to greater ruin every year, and no heir had come to him, his poor helpmeet having at length given him eight daughters, but two of whom had lived. His rage at this had increased even beyond its first fury as he realised that each new blunder of her ladyship was a new jest for the county. So it was that the boy turned towards his kinsman with interest, for in some manner the mishaps of this wretched family always moved him.

"Of Sir Jeoffry?" he said.

"Of Sir Jeoffry," my Lord Dunstanwolde answered; "but not so much of himself as of his poor lady. At last she is dead."

"Dead!" Roxholm exclaimed. "Dead!" and his voice fell, and he stood a moment and watched the driving rain, full of strange thoughts.

"'Tis happier for her, surely," he said. "I—one cannot feel sorrow for her. How did she die, my lord?"

"As woefully and as neglected as she lived," his lordship

answered. "She had given birth to another female infant, and 'twas plain the poor thing knew her last hour had come. She was alone with the one ignorant woman who was all she had to aid her in her hour of trial. The night before Sir Jeoffry had held a drinking bout with a party of his boon companions, and in the morning, when they were gathered noisily in the courtyard to go forth hunting, the old woman appeared in their midst to acquaint her master of the infant's birth and to bring a message from her mistress, who begged her lord to come to her before he rode forth, saying that she felt strangely ill, and wished greatly to see him." His lordship paused a moment, and a shadow passed swiftly across his countenance, brought there by a sad memory.

Young Roxholm turned towards him and waited with a speaking look for his next words.

"Then—my lord—?" he broke forth inquiringly. Lord Dunstanwolde passed his hand over his forehead.

"He would not go," he answered; "he would not go. He sent a ribald message to the poor soul—cursing the child she had brought into the world, and then he rode away. The servants say that the old woman had left her mistress alone in her chamber and came down to eat and drink. When she went back to her charge the fire had gone out—the room was cold as the grave, and the poor lady lay stone dead, her head fallen upon her wailing infant's body in such manner that, had not the child been stronger than most new-born things and fought for its life, it would have been smothered in its first hour."

The boy Marquess turned suddenly away and took several hurried steps up the Long Gallery. When he returned his forehead was flushed, his eyes sparkled with an inward fire, and his breath came quickly—but he found no words to utter.

"Once," said Lord Dunstanwolde, slowly, "I saw a tender creature die after her travail—but she was beloved to worship, and our hearts stood still in our bosoms as we waited. Mine has truly never seemed to beat since then. Her child—who might, perchance, have aided me to live again, and who would have been my hope and joy and pride, died with her. This poor thing, unwanted, hated, and cast aside to live or die—as if it were the young of some wild creature of the woods—this one, they say, has the strength of ten, and will survive. God have mercy on its evil fortunes."

Young Roxholm stood with folded arms gazing straight before him again into the driving rain. His brow was knit, and he was biting his boyish red lip.

"Is there mercy?" he said in a low voice, at length. "Is there

26

justice, since a human thing can be so cast into the world—and left alone?"

Lord Dunstanwolde put his hand upon his shoulder.

"All of us ask," he said. "None of us knows."

CHAPTER V

My Lord Marquess Plunges into the Thames

A rich young nobleman at the University of Oxford, who, having all the resources of wealth and rank at his disposal, chose in these times to devote himself to scholarly pursuits, made in the minds of his fellow-collegians a singular and eccentric figure; but that one, more splendidly endowed by fortune than any other, should so comport himself, and yet no man find it possible to deride or make coarse jokes on him, was, indeed, unheard of.

Yet, when the young heir of the house of Osmonde entered the University, this was the position he held and which none disputed. There were gay young rakes and ardent young toadies who, hearing of his coming among them, fell into anticipation: the first, of more splendid frolics, the second, of richer harvests; and though each party was disappointed in its expectation, neither found opportunity to display its chagrin according to the customary methods.

It is, indeed, a strange thing, how a man's physical body may be his fortress or his enemy. All the world has at times beheld those whom an insignificant figure and an ill-modelled face handicapped with a severity cruel to the utmost. A great man but five feet high, and awkward of bearing, has always added to his efforts at accomplishing great deeds the weight of an obstacle which he must first remove from about his neck—the obstacle his own poor exterior creates. An eloquent man whose voice is cracked and harsh by nature must be fire itself before he can burn away the barrier between himself and his hearers; a prophet with an ignobly featured countenance and a small, vague eye must needs be a god of wisdom to persuade his disciples that high nobleness can dwell in a temple so mean and poor. The physical body of the young Marquess of Roxholm was a fortress well-nigh impregnable. 'Tis not well to take liberties with a creature who takes none himself, and can strike a blow which would fell an ox, if need be. Besides this, there was in this young man's look and temper a something which, while it forbade idle familiarities, won to itself the pleasurable admiration and affection of all beholders. His eye was full of fire and meaning, of laughter and friendliness; his mouth curved into the finest sweet smile in the world, as also it could curl into a look of scorn which could scathe as finely. He had a keen wit, and could be ironic and biting when he chose, but 'twas not his habit to use his power malevolently. Even those who envied his great fortunes, and whose

28

spite would have maligned him had he been of different nature, were in a measure restrained from their bitterness by a certain powerful composure, which all felt who looked on him and heard him speak.

'Twas this composure and commandingness of bearing which were more marked in him than all else. 'Twas not mere coolness, but a great power over himself and all his weaknesses, which years of self-study had begot in him, the truth being indeed that he himself had early realised in a measure a thing one of the gravest instructors at the University had once said: "Were all the strength of his great body and his fervid mind, all the power of his wealth and rank, all the influence of his beauty and passion turned to evil and dishonourable courses, instead of to more noble things, good God! what a devil he might be—devil enough to ruin half England. What weak woman could resist him; what vicious man help following where he led!"

"'Tis not so easy for a man who will be Duke one day to keep straight courses," Roxholm had once said to Mr. Fox, "as 'tis for a man who must live a narrower life and work for his daily bread. And a man who is six feet three in height has six feet and three inches of evil to do battle with, if he has not six feet three of strength and honesty to fight for him. 'Tis Gerald Mertoun I may live in dread of, if Gerald Mertoun is not my help and stay."

This he said half laughing, half sober, after his first visit to the French Court, which he made with his parents and saw many strange though brilliant things, giving him cause for reflection. Tender as his years were at the time, he was so big and finely built a fellow for his age, and so beautiful to look upon, that there were ladies who even tried their bright eyes upon him as if he had been a man instead of a youth; and he encountered many youngsters of his years who had already done much more than dally on the brink of life, some, indeed, having plunged deep into waters not overclean.

Some of these last regarded him at least as one who neglected his opportunities, but his great laugh at their callow jests and their advice to him was so frank and indifferent a thing that they found it singularly baffling. 'Twas indeed as if a man of ripe years and wisdom had laughed at them with good-nature, because he knew they could not understand the thing experience had taught him.

"Why should I be pleased because a beauty older than my mother laughs and teases me," he said. "I am but a boy, and she knows it full well, and would only play with me to see if I am a fool who can be made a toy. I am too big," stretching his great arms, "to sit at ladies' feet and have my curls stroked as if I were a lap-dog. A fellow such as I should be exercising his body and putting somewhat in his brain. Why should I overdrink and overfeed myself and give my strength to follies? 'Tis not my taste. On my life, I would rather get up at daybreak with a clean tongue and a clear head and go out to leap and ride and fence and toss the bar with well-strung muscles. Some day I shall meet a beauty whom I would be ready for." And he laughed his big, musical, boyish laugh again and his tawny eye sparkled.

At the University there were temptations enough to lead youth to folly, even when it was not such youth as his, and therefore a shining mark. The seed Charles Stuart had sown had flourished and grown rank and strong, so that the great seat of learning was rich with dissolute young fools and madcaps and their hangers-on. But even the most foolish swaggerer of them could not call milksop a man who could outride, outleap, outfence, outhunt him; who could drive the four horses of his coach to London and back at such a pace and in such a manner as made purple-faced old stage-coach drivers shake their heads with glee, and who, in a wrestling-match, could break a man's back at a throw if he chose to be unmerciful. Besides this, he was popular for a score of reasons, being no sanctimonious preacher of his doctrines, but as joyous a liver as any among them and as open-handed and high of spirit.

"'Tis not for me to say how other men should live," was his simple and straightforward creed. "I live as I like best and find best pays me. 'Tis for others to seek out and follow what best pays themselves."

Many a story was told of him which his fellows liked, youth always being elated by any deed of prowess and daring in youth. One of these stories, which was indeed no great one, but picturesque and pretty, took their fancy greatly, and was much related and laughed gaily over, and indeed beloved.

He was a strong and wondrous swimmer, having learned the art in his childhood on the seacoast, being taught by his Grace his father. When at Oxford it was his custom to rise before the rest of the world, and in any weather or season plunge into the river and swim and dive and play in the water like a young river god. He had chosen a favourite swimming-spot and would undress under cover of the trees and then dash out to his pastime, and it so chanced that going there one hot afternoon he fell upon an adventure.

A party of jolly personages of the middle class, who had come up from town on pleasure and rollicking interest, were taking a jaunt upon the river in a wherry. 'Twas a wedding-party, and both males and females, having dined at a tavern, were well filled with ale and in the mood for disporting themselves. The groom and his men friends, being in frolicsome humour and knowing nothing whatever of oarsmanship, were playing great pranks to make the women scream at their daring. The bride, a pretty thing in cherry ribbands, clung to the boat's side in amaze at the heroic swagger of her new lord, but her cheeks, which had matched her ribbands, grew paler at each rock and dip of the boat, and her fear forced little shrieks from her. Her companions shrieked too, but laughingly and in such manner as but spurred the men to greater follies. The sport was at its highest and noisiest when they neared the spot all Oxford knew by this time by the name of "my Lord Marquess's diving hole." At this point the river was broad and deep, and not far below it the water washed over a weir near which was a post bearing a board marked "Danger!" To those who knew the waters and had some skill with their oars there was no peril, but to a crew of drink-filled junketers it was an ill-omened place. The wedding-party was too wild and young and rollicking to observe the sign-board. The men rocked the boat, shouted and sang, the women squealed and laughed and shouted with them; the little bride burst forth weeping, shrieking wildly the next moment as the wherry was overset, and the whole party struggled in the water, the hat, with its cherry-ribbands, floating on the top.

Some distance above there were people walking. Shrieks filled the air and roused all within sight to running and shouting. Poor gasping, choking, deadly faced heads bobbed up a moment on the river's surface and went under struggling.

"Help! Help!" shouted the running people. "God save them all! Good Lord! Good Lord!" And in the midst of it out sprang from among the trees and bushes the great white body of a man, who dashed into the stream and swam like a dolphin.

If he had been clothed the drowning creatures would have had somewhat to drag upon—if he had not been as strong as a giant and cool enough to control them, the poor strangling fools would have so hampered him in their frenzy that they might have dragged him under water with them. But there was a power in him and a freedom from all sense of peril which dominated them all.

"Keep your senses and you are safe," he shouted, swimming and pushing the overturned boat within reach of the men, who struggled together.

His voice rang like a clarion and held in it such encouragement that the poor little bride, who came up gasping near him at that moment, almost took him for a god as he shot to her rescue.

"Your hand on my shoulder; be brave, my girl—be brave," he cried out with such good cheer as would have put heart in any woman and aided her to gather her poor frightened wits and obey him like a child, while even in the midst of her terror, as her little red hands clung to him, she marked, half unconsciously the beauty and vigour of him—his strong white neck like a column, the great corded muscles of his white arms as he clove the water through.

He bore her to the shore and left her safe there, and plunged in again, crying to her, over his shoulder: "I will bring back the others!" And she stood dripping, gazing after him, sobbing and wringing her hands, but filled with wild admiration and amaze.

He shouted orders to the sobered men to hold steady to the wherry and dived to bring back one woman after another to firm land; a boat found in the osiers was put forth above, and in time all were brought to shore, though the bridegroom, who had not come near enough to the wherry, was dragged in looking like a dead man.

The bride flung herself upon his body, shrieking and kissing him. The people who had run up crowded about in senseless excitement and would have kept all air away. But there was one among them who had his wits clear and ordered them off, plainly remembering not for a moment that his brocades and laces lay hid among the trees, and he stood among them as Apollo stands in marble.

"Bring brandy," he commanded the nearest. "Stand back; strip his clothes from him and empty the water from his stomach. Here," to a matron who had come up panting, "take his wife away."

The good woman he addressed dropped a hurried curtsey and hustled off the woman under her wing. She led them into the sun and wrung the water from their garments, while they sobbed and choked and wept.

"Hush thee, wench!" she said to the stricken bride. "Hush thee, little fool; my lord Marquess will put life into him and set him on his feet before thy petticoats are dry, Lord! Lord! what a young man! When built Heaven such another? And he a Duke's son!"

"A Marquess!" cried one of the bride's friends. "A Duke's son!" sobbed the bride.

"Ay, a Duke's son!" the good woman cried, exulting further. "And were he a King's, the nation might be proud of him. 'Tis his young lordship the Marquess of Roxholm."

CHAPTER VI

"No; She has not yet Come to Court"

'Tis but a small adventure for a youth who is a strong swimmer to save a party of cits from drowning in a river, but 'twas a story much repeated, having a picturesqueness and colour because its chief figure Nature had fitted out with all the appointments which might be expected to adorn a hero.

"'Tis a pretty story, too," said a laughing great lady when 'twas talked of in town. "My lord Marquess dashing in and out of the river, bearing in his big white arms soused little citizen beauties and their half-drowned sweethearts, and towering in their midst giving orders—like a tall young god in marble come to life. The handsomest Marquess in Great Britain, and in France likewise, they tell me."

"The handsomest man," quoth the old Dowager Lady Storms, who had a country seat in Oxfordshire and knew more of the tale than any one else. "The handsomest man, say I, for it chanced that I drove by the river at that moment and saw him."

And then—freedom of speech being the fashion in those days and she an old woman—she painted such a picture of his fine looks, his broad shoulders, and the markings of his muscles under his polished skin, as, being repeated and spread abroad, as gossip will spread itself, fixed him in the minds of admirers of manly beauty and built him a reputation in the world of fashion before he had entered it or even left his books.

When he did leave them and quitted the University, it was with honour to himself and family, and also with joy to his Governour and Chaplain Mr. Fox, who had attended him. At his coming of age there were feastings and bonfires in five villages again, and Rowe rang the bells at Camylott Church with an exultant ardour which came near to being his final end, and though seventy years of age, he would give up his post to no younger man, and actually blubbered aloud when 'twas delicately suggested that his middle-aged son should take his place to save him fatigue.

"Nay! nay!" he cried; "I rang their Graces' wedding peal—I rang my lord Marquess into the world, and will give him up to none until I am a dead man."

At the Tower there was high feasting, the apartments being filled with guests from foreign Courts as well as from the English one, and as the young hero of the day moved among them, and among the tenantry rejoicing with waving flags and rural games in the park, as he danced with lovely ladies in the ball-room, and as he made his maiden speech to the people, who went wild with joy over him, all agreed that a noble house having such an heir need not fear for its future renown, howsoever glorious its history might have been in the past.

After he had been presented at Court there seemed nothing this young man might not have asked for with the prospect of getting—a place near the King, a regiment to lead to glory, the hand of the fairest beauty of the greatest fortune and rank. But it seemed that he wanted nothing, for he made no request for any favour which might have brought him place or power or love. The great events at that time disturbing the nation he observed with an interest grave and thoughtful beyond his years. Men who were deep in the problems of statesmanship were amazed to discover the seriousness of his views and the amount of reflection he had given to public questions. Beauties who paraded themselves before him to attract his heart and eye—even sweetly tender ones who blushed when he approached them and sighed when he made his obeisance and retired—all were treated with a like courtesy and grace of manner, but he gave none more reason to sigh and blush, to ogle and languish, than another, the honest truth being that he did not fall in love, despite his youth and the warmth of his nature, not having yet beheld the beauty who could blot out all others for him and reign alone.

"I will not play with love," he said to his mother once as they talked intimately to each other. "I have thought of it—that which should come to a man and be himself, not a part of his being but the very life of him. If it comes not, a man must go unsatisfied to his grave. If it comes—You know," he said, and turned and kissed her hand impulsively, "It came to my father and to you."

"Pray Heaven it may come to you, dear one," she said; "you would know bliss then."

"Yes," he answered, "I should know rapture that would make life Heaven. I do not know what it is I wait for—but when I see it in some woman's eyes I shall know, and so will she."

His mother kissed his ringed hair, smiling softly.

"Till then you wait and think of other things."

"There are so many things for a man to do," he said, "if he would not sit idle. But when that comes it will be first and greatest of all."

At this period all the world talked of the wondrous and splendid Churchill, who, having fought brilliantly for the Stuarts and been made by them first Lord Churchill of Eyemouth, and next

34

Baron Churchill of Sandridge, having, after receiving these advancements, the cold astuteness to see the royal fortunes waver perilously, deserted James the Second with stately readiness and transferred his services to William of Orange. He was rewarded with an earldom and such favour as made him the most shining figure both at the Court of England and in the foreign countries which had learned to regard his almost supernatural powers with somewhat approaching awe.

This man inspired Roxholm with a singular feeling; he in fact exercised over him the fascination he exercised over so many others, but in the case of the young Marquess, wonder and admiration were mixed with other emotions. There were stories so brilliant to be heard of him on all sides, stories of other actions so marvellously ruthless and of things so wondrously mean. Upon a bargain so shameless he had built so wondrous a career—a faithfulness of service so magnificent he had closed with a treachery so base. All greatness and all littleness, all heroism and all crimes, seemed to combine themselves in this one strange being. Having shamelessly sold his youth to a King's mistress, he devoted his splendid maturity to a tender, faithful passion for a beauteous virago, whose displeasure was the sole thing on earth which moved him to pain or fear. In truth 'twas not his genius, his bravery, his victories, which held Roxholm's thought upon him most constantly; 'twas two other things, the first being the marvel of his control over himself, the power with which he held in subjection his passions, his emotions, almost, it seemed, his very thoughts themselves—the power with which he had trained John Churchill to be John Churchill's servant—in peril, in temptation from any weakness to which he did not choose to succumb, in circumstances which, arising without warning, might have caused another man to start, to falter, to change colour, but which he encountered with indomitable calm.

"'Tis that I wish to learn," said the young nobleman in his secret thoughts as he watched him at Court, in the world outside it, among soldiers, statesmen, women, in the society of those greater than himself, of those smaller, of those he would win and of those he would repel. "'Tis that I would learn: to be stronger than my very self, so that naught can betray me—no passion I am tormented by, no anger I would conceal, no lure I would resist. 'Tis a man's self who oftenest entraps him. The traitor once subject, life lies at one's feet."

The second thing which stirred the young observer's interest was the great man's great love. The most parsimonious and mercantile of beings, he had married a poor beauty when fair creatures with fortunes smiled upon him on every side; the most

35

indomitable of spirits, the warrior of whom armies stood in awe, he was the willing subject of a woman whose fiery temper and tempestuous spirit the world knew as well as it knew her beauty and her dominating charm. For some reason he could scarcely have analyzed, it gave Roxholm a strange pleasure to hear anecdotes of the passionate love-letters scrawled on the field—on the eve of battle, the hour after a great encounter and triumph; to know that better than victory to the great conquerer, who could command the slaughter of thousands without the quiver of a muscle or a moment's qualm, were the few lines in a woman's hand which told him he was forgiven for some fancied wrong or missed in some tender hour.

"My Lady Sarah is a handsome creature, and ever was one," 'twas said, "but there are those who are greater beauties, and who have less brimstone in the air about them and less lightning in their eyes."

"But 'twas she who was his own," Roxholm said to himself in pondering it over, "and when their eyes met each knew—and when she is fierce and torments him 'tis as if the fire in his own blood spoke, as if his own voice reproached him—and he remembers their dear hours together, and forgives, and woos her back to him. If she were not his own—if he were not hers, neither could endure it. They would strike each other dead. 'Tis sure nature makes one man for one woman, one woman for one man—as it was in the garden where our first parents loved. Few creatures find their mates, alas; but when they do 'tis Eden over again, in spite of all things—and all else is mean and incomplete.

He did not know that, as he had observed and been attracted by the hero, so the hero had been attracted by himself, though 'twas in a lesser degree, since one man was cold and mature and the other young and warm.

My Lord Churchill had been the most beautiful youth of his time, distinguished for the elegance of his bearing and the perfection of his countenance and form. When, at fifteen, the services of his father in the royal cause had procured for him the place of page in the household of the Duke of York, he had borne away the palm from all others of his age. When, at sixteen, his martial instincts had led to the Prince's obtaining for him a commission in a regiment of the guards, his first appearance in his scarlet and gold lace had produced such commotion among the court beauties as promised to lead to results almost disastrous, since he attracted attention in places too high to reach with safety. But even then his ambitions were stronger than his temptations, and he fled the latter to go to fight the Moors. On his return, more beautiful than ever, the lustre of success in arms added to his ripened charms, the handsomest and wickedest woman in England cast her eyes upon him, and he became the rival of royalty itself. All England knew the story of the founding of his later fortunes, but if he himself blushed for it, none but John Churchill knew—outwardly he was the being whose name was the synonym for success, the lover of the brilliant Castlemaine, the hero of the auxiliary force sent to Louis, the "handsome Englishman" of the siege of Nimeguen for whom Turenne predicted the greatest future a man could dream of.

When Roxholm first had the honour of being presented to this gentleman 'twas at a time when, after a brief period during which the hero's fortunes had been under a cloud, the tide had turned for him and the sun of royal favour shone forth again. Perhaps during certain perilous dark days in the Tower, my Lord Marlborough had passed through hours which had caused him to look back upon the past with some regret and doubting, and when among those who crowded about him when fortune smiled once more—friends, sycophants, place-hunters, and new admirers—he beheld a figure whose youth and physical gifts brought back old memories to him, 'tis possible they awakened in him curious reflections.

"You," he said to Roxholm one day at St. James, "begin the game with all the cards in your hand."

"The game, my lord?" said the youthful Marquess, bowing.

"The game of life," returned the Earl of Marlborough (for so William of Orange had made him nine years before), and his eagle eye rested on the young man with a keen, strange look. "You need not plan and strive for rank and fortune. You were born to them—to those things which will aid a man to gain what he desires, if he is not a flippant idler and has brain enough to create ambitions for him. Most men must spend their youth in building the bridge which is to carry their dreams across to the shore which is their goal. Your bridge was built before you were born. You left Oxford with high honours, they tell me; you are not long of age, you come of a heroic race—what do you think to do, my lord?"

Roxholm met his scrutinizing gaze with that steadiness which ever marked his own. He knew that he reddened a little, but he did not look away.

"I am young to know, my Lord Marlborough," he returned, "but I think to live—to live."

His Lordship slightly narrowed his eyes, and nodded his head.

"Ay," he said, "you will live!"

"There have been soldiers of our house," said Roxholm. "I may fight if need be, perhaps," bowing, "following your lordship to some greater triumph, if I have that fortune. There may be services to the country at home I may be deemed worthy to devote my powers to when I have lived longer. But," reddening and bowing again, "before men of achievement and renown, I am yet a boy."

"England wants such boys," complimented his lordship, gracefully. "The Partition Treaty and the needs of the Great Alliance call for the breeding of them. You will marry?"

"My house is an old one," replied Roxholm, "and if I live I shall be its chief."

My lord cast a glance about the apartment. It was a gala day and there were many lovely creatures near, laughing, conversing, coquetting, bearing themselves with dignity, airiness, or sweet grace. There were beauties who were brown, and beauties who were fair; there were gay charmers and grave ones, those who were tall and commanding, and those who were small and nymph-like.

"There is none here to match you," he said with an imperturbable gravity ('twas plain he was not trifling, but thinking some serious and unusual thoughts). "A man of your build has needs out of the common. No pretty, idle young thing will do. She should have beauty, and that which is more. 'Tis a strange kinship—marriage. No; she has not yet come to court."

"I will wait until she does," Roxholm answered, and his youthful face was as grave as the hero's own, though if triflers had heard their words, they would have taken their talk for idle persiflage and jest.

CHAPTER VII

"'Tis Clo Wildairs, Man—All the County Knows the Vixen."

A month later he went to Warwickshire at my Lord Dunstanwolde's invitation. In that part of the county which borders upon Gloucestershire was his Lordship's seat, which was known as Dunstan's Wolde. 'Twas an ancient and beautiful estate, and his Lordship spent his quiet and secluded life upon it, much beloved by his tenantry, and respected by his neighbours. Since his young wife's death his manner of living had become more secluded year after year; his library, his memories, and the administration of his estates filled his days with quiet occupation.

"Perhaps I am a selfish fellow to ask a young gentleman who is a favourite at Court to come and bury himself with me," he said to Roxholm the night of his arrival, "but you and I have spent many a good quiet hour together, Gerald," laying an affectionate hand upon his broad shoulder. "And if you were my son you would come, I know."

"Think of me as your son," said Roxholm with his fine smile. "A man is the richer for the love of two fathers."

"Oxford has not changed you, Roxholm," said the Earl. "Nor have the Court ladies' flatteries spoiled your kindly manners. We shall be happy together, for awhile at least."

They were indeed happy, spending their days much as they had spent them at Camylott—riding together, taking long sauntering walks, reading old books and new ones, and in these days conversing on maturer subjects. There was indeed much to talk of at this closing of a reign which had been full of struggles with problems affecting not only England but all the European powers. What the Peace of Ryswick had effected, what the death of Charles of Spain would bring, whether Louis would play fairly, how long King William's broken frame would last, what the power of the Marlboroughs would be when the Princess Anne came to the throne—all these things they discussed together, and in their arguments my Lord Dunstanwolde was often roused to the wonder other ripe minds had felt in coming in contact with the activity and daring of this younger one.

"'Tis not possible to hide a handsome young nobleman under a bushel," the Earl said after but a few days had passed. "The neighbours will have you to dine, and dance, and hunt with them, whether it is your will or not. A strapping young fellow must do his duty by the world."

Roxholm performed his duty with propriety and spirit when it was not to be evaded gracefully. He dined with country gentlemen, and listened to their songs and stories until most of them drank themselves under the table, as was the spirited fashion of the time. He answered the questionings of their wives on subjects pertaining to Court fashions and behaviour and,—perhaps somewhat gravely,— danced attendance on the daughters, who most of them, it is true, were used to less courtly manners and voted him in private far too grave and majestic for such a beauty.

"He hath a way of bowing that would give one a fright, were his eyes not so handsome and his smile so sweet," said one lovely ardent hoyden. "Lord! just to watch him standing near with that noble grave look on his face, and not giving one a thought, makes one's heart go pit-a-pat. A man hath no right to be such a beauty—and to be so, and to be a Duke's son, too, is a burning shame. 'Tis wicked that one man should have so much to give to one woman."

'Twas but a week before Roxholm left his kinsman's house, that they spent a day together hunting with a noted pack over the borders of Gloucestershire. The sport was in a neighbourhood where the gentry were hunting-mad, and chased foxes as many days of the week as fortune and weather favoured them.

"'Tis a rough country," said my Lord Dunstanwolde, as they rode forth, "and some of those who hunt are wild livers and no credit to their rank, but there is fine old blood among them, and some of the hardest riders and boldest leapers England knows." Suddenly he seemed to remember something and turned with an exclamation. "Upon my soul!" he said, "till this moment I had forgot. I am too sober an old fogy to hunt with them when I have no young blood near to spur me. Sir Jeoffry Wildairs will be with them—if he has not yet broke his neck."

The country they hunted over proved indeed rough, and the sport exciting. Roxholm had never seen wilder riding and more daring leaps, and it had also happened that he had not yet gone a-hunting with so boisterous and rollicking a body of gentlemen. Their knowledge of dogs, foxes, and horseflesh was plainly absolute, but they had no Court manners, being of that clan of country gentry of which London saw but little. Nearly all the sportsmen were big men and fine ones, with dare-devil bearing, loud voices, and a tendency to loose and profane language. They roared friendly oaths at each other, had brandy flasks on their persons on which they pulled freely, and, their spirits being heightened thereby, exchanged jokes and allusions not too seemly.

Before the fox was found, Roxholm had marked this and observed also that half a dozen more of the best mounted men were the roughest on the field, being no young scapegraces and frolickers, but men past forty, who wore the aspect of reprobate livers and hard drinkers, and who were plainly boon companions and more intimate with each other than with those not of their party.

They seemed to form a band of themselves, which those not of it had an air of avoiding, and 'twas to be seen that their company was looked at askance, and that in the bearing of each member of the group there was a defiance of the general opinion. Roxholm sat on his horse somewhat apart from this group watching it, his kinsman and a certain Lord Twemlow, who was their host for the day, conversing near him.

My Lord Twemlow, who took no note of them, but by the

involuntary casting on them of an occasional glance, when some wild outburst attracted his attention, wore a grave and almost affronted look.

"'Tis the Wildairs cronies," Roxholm heard him say to his Lordship of Dunstanwolde. "I hunt but seldom, purely through disgust of their unseemliness."

"Wildairs!" exclaimed my Lord Dunstanwolde.

"Ay," answered Twemlow, turning his horse slightly and averting his eyes; "and there cometh my reputable kinsman, Sir Jeoffry, even as we speak."

Roxholm turned to look with some stir of feeling in his breast, since this was the man who had so early roused in him an emotion of anger and rebellion. Across the field came pounding a great black horse, a fine big-boned brute; on him rode a tall, heavy man who must once have been of the handsomest, since even yet, in spite of years, bloated face, and careless attire, he retained a sort of dissolute beauty. He was of huge frame and had black eyes, a red mouth, and wore his own thick and curling though grizzled black hair.

He rode with a dare-devil grace, and his cronies greeted him with a shout.

"He has the look of it," thought Roxholm, remembering the old stories; but the next instant he gave a start. Across the field beyond, another rider followed galloping, and at this moment came over the high hedge like a swallow, and, making the leap, gave forth a laughing shout. Roxholm sat and stared at the creature. 'Twas indeed a youthful figure, brilliant and curious to behold in this field of slovenly clad sportsmen. 'Twas a boy of twelve or thereabouts riding a splendid young devil of a hunter, with a skin like black satin and a lovely, dangerous eye. The lad was in scarlet, and no youngster of the Court was more finely clad or fitted, and not one had Roxholm ever set eyes upon whose youthful body and limbs were as splendid in line and symmetry; in truth, the beauty and fire of him were things to make a man lose his breath. He rode as if he had been born upon his horse's back and had never sat elsewhere from his first hour, his flowing-black hair was almost too rich and long for a boy, he had a haughty mouth for a child, though it was a crimson bow and pouting, his complexion matched it, and his black eyes, which were extraordinary big and flashing, had the devil in them.

"Pardi!" the young Marquess cried between his teeth. "What does such a young one in such company?" Never had he beheld a thing which moved him with such strange suddenness of emotion. He could not have explained the reason of his feeling, which was an

41

actual excitement, and caused him to turn in his saddle to watch the boy's every movement as he galloped forward to join the reprobate group.

As they had greeted Sir Jeoffry with a shout of welcome, so they greeted the young newcomer, but in his reception there was more enthusiasm and laughter, as if there were some special cause for gayety in the mere sight of him.

When he drew up in their midst their voices broke forth into a tumult of noisy, frolicsome greeting, to which the lad gave back impudent, laughing answer. In a moment's time he was the centre figure of interest among them, and seemed to dominate them all as if he had been some young potentate instead of a mere handsome lad of twelve.

"If they were a band of barbarians and he their boy chief they could pay him no more court nor joy in him more," Roxholm reflected. "Is it his beauty or—what means it?"

He could not withdraw his eyes from the boy, who sat his fretting hunter among them, sometimes scarcely able to restrain the animal's fiery temper or keep him from lashing out his heels orbiting at the beasts nearest to him. Now he trotted from one man to the other as the group scattered somewhat; now he sat half turned back, his hand on his steed's hind quarters, flinging words and laughter to the outside man.

"Thou'lt have to use scissors again on thy periwig, ecod!" one man cried, banteringly.

"Damme, yes," the youngster rapped out, and he caught a rich lock of his hair and drew it forward to look at it, frowning. "What's a man to do when his hair grows like a girl's?"

The answer was greeted with a shout of laughter, and the boy burst forth with a laugh likewise, showing two rows of ivory teeth. Somehow there was an imperial deviltry about him, an impudent wild spirit which had plainly made him conqueror, favourite, and plaything of the whole disreputable crew.

Men were not fastidious talkers in those times; the cleanest mouthed of them giving themselves plenty of license when they were in spirits. Roxholm had heard broad talk enough at the University, where the young gentlemen indulged in conversation no more restrained than was that of their elders and betters; he had heard the jokes and profanity of both camp and Court since he had left Oxford, and had learned that squeamishness was far from being the fashion. But never had he heard such oath-sprinkled talk or such open obscenity of joking as fell upon his ears this morning in but a brief space. Hearing it in spite of himself, his blood grew hot and his horse began to paw the earth, he, in his irritation, having

42

unknowingly fretted its mouth. And then one of the company, an elderly sportsman with a watery eye, began a story.

"Good God!" Roxholm broke forth to the man nearest to him, one not of the party, but evidently one who found it diverting; "good God! Can they not restrain themselves before a child? Let them be decent for his mere youth's sake! The lad is not thirteen."

The man started and stared at him a moment with open mouth, and then burst into a loud guffaw of laughter.

"The lad!" he cried, roaring and slapping his thigh in his mirth. "'Tis no lad. Didst take it for one? Lord! 'tis Jeoff Wildair's youngest wench. 'Tis Clo—'tis Clo, man. All the county knows the vixen!"

And at that very instant the hounds sprang forth, giving tongue, and the field sprang forward with them, and all was wild excitement: cries of "Tally ho!" ringing, horses plunging, red coats seeming to fly through the air; and my lord Marquess went with the field, his cheek hot, his heart suddenly thumping in his breast with a sense of he knew not what, as his eye, following a slender, scarlet-coated figure, saw it lift its horse for a huge leap over a five-barred gate, take it like a bird, and lead the whole scurrying, galloping multitude.

"Yes," said my Lord Dunstanwolde, as they rode homeward slowly in the evening gray, "'tis the girl infant who was found struggling and shrieking beneath the dead body of her mother, and till to-day I never saw her. Good Heavens! the beauty of the creature—the childish deviltry and fire!"

Each turned and looked into the eyes of the other with a question in his thought, and each man's was the same, though one had lived beyond sixty years and one but twenty-four. A female creature of such beauty, of such temper, bred in such manner, among such companions, by such parents—what fate could be before her? Roxholm averted his eyes.

"Tossed to the wolves," he said; "tossed to the pack—to harry and to slaver over! God's mercy!"

As they rode he heard the story, Lord Twemlow having related such incidents as he naturally knew to my Lord Dunstanwolde. 'Twas a bitter history to Twemlow, whose kinsman the late Lady Wildairs had been, and who was a discreetly sober and God-fearing gentleman, to whom irregular habits and the reckless squandering of fortune were loathly things. And this was the substance of the relation, which was so far out of the common as to be almost monstrous: His disgust at the birth of this ninth girl infant had so inflamed Sir Jeoffry that he had refused even to behold it and had left it to its fate as if it had been an ill-made, blind puppy. But two of

43

her Ladyship's other children had survived their infancy, and of these two their father knew nothing whatever but that they had been called Barbara and Anne, that they showed no promise of beauty, and lived their bare little lives in the Hall's otherwise deserted west wing, having as their sole companion and instructress a certain Mistress Margery Wimpole—a timorous poor relation, who had taken the position in the wretched household to save herself from starvation, and because she was fitted for no other; her education being so poor and her understanding so limited, that no reputable or careful family would have accepted her as governess or companion. Her two poor little charges learned the few things she could teach them, and their meek spiritedness gave her but little trouble. Their dead mother's suffering and their father's rough contempt on the rare occasions when he had chanced to behold them had chastened them to humbleness from their babyhood. There was none who wanted them, none who served or noticed them, and there was no circumstance which could not restrain them, no person who was not their ruler if 'twas his will.

"But the ninth one was not like them," said my Lord. "The blood of the fierce devils who were the chiefs of her house centuries ago woke in her veins at her birth. 'Tis strange indeed, Gerald, how such things break forth—or slumber—in a race. Should you trace Wildairs, as you trace Mertoun through the past, her nature would be made clear enough. They have been splendid devils, some of them—devils who fought, shrieking with ferocious laughter in the face of certain horrible death; devils whose spirit no torture of rack or flame could conquer; beings who could endure in silence horrors almost supernatural; who could bear more, revel more, suffer more, defy more than any other human thing."

"And this child is one of them!" said Roxholm.

He said but little as they rode onward and he listened. There was within him a certain distaste for what seemed to him the unnatural tumult of his feelings. A girl child of twelve rollicking in boys' clothes was not a pleasing picture, but in one sense a tragic one, and certainly not such as should set a man's heart beating and his cheek to flame when he heard stories of her fantastic life and character. On this occasion he did not understand himself; if he had been a sanctimonious youngster he would have reproved his own seeming levity, but he was not so, and frankly felt himself restless and ill at ease.

The name given to her had been Clorinda, and from her babyhood she had been as tempestuous as her sisters were mild. None could manage her. Her baby training left wholly to neglected and loose-living servants, she had spent her first years in kitchens, garrets, and stables. The stables and the stable-boys, the kennels and their keepers, were loved better than aught else. She learned to lisp the language of grooms' and helpers, she cursed and swore as they did, she heard their songs and stories, and was as familiar with profanity and obscene language as other children are with nursery rhymes. Until she was five years old Sir Jeoffry never set eyes upon her. Then a strange chance threw her in his way and sealed her fate.

Straying through the house, having escaped from her woman, the child had reached the big hall, and sate upon the floor playing with a powder-flask she had found. 'Twas Sir Jeoffry's, and he, coming upon her, not knowing her for his own offspring (not that such a knowledge would have calmed his passion), he sprang upon her with curses and soundly trounced her. Either of her sisters Anne or Barbara would have been convulsed with terror, but this one was only roused to a fury as much greater for her size than Sir Jeoffry was bigger than herself. She flew at him and poured forth oaths, she shrieked at him and beat his legs with his own crop, which she caught up from the floor where it lay within reach, she tore at him with tooth and nail, and with such strength and infant fearlessness as arrested him in his frenzy and caused him to burst forth laughing as if he had gone mad.

"From that hour she was a doomed creature," my Lord ended. "What else can a man call the poor beauteous, helpless thing. She is his companion and playmate, and the toy and jest of his comrades. It is the scandal of the county. At twelve she is as near a woman as other girls of fourteen. At fifteen—!" and he stopped speaking.

"'Twould have been safer for her to have died beneath her dead mother's body," said Roxholm, almost fiercely.

"Yes, safer!" said his Lordship. "Yet what a woman!—What a woman!"—and here he broke off speech again.

CHAPTER VIII

In which my Lady Betty Tantillion writes of a Scandal

Scarce two years later, King William riding in the park at Hampton Court was thrown from his horse—the animal stumbling over a mole-hill—and his collar-bone broken. A mole-hill seems but a small heap of earth to send a King to moulder beneath a heap of earth himself, but the fall proved fatal to a system which had long been weakening, and a few days later his Majesty died, commending my Lord Marlborough to the Princess Anne as the guide and counsellor on whose wisdom and power she might most safely rely. Three days after the accession his Lordship was made Captain-General of the English army, and intrusted with power over all warlike matters both at home and abroad. 'Twas a moment of tremendous import—the Alliance shaken by King William's death, Holland panic-stricken lest England should withdraw her protection, King Louis boasting that "henceforth there were no Pyrenees," Whigs and Tories uncertain whether or not to sheath weapons in England, small sovereigns and great ones ready to spring at each other's throats on the Continent. Boldness was demanded, and such executive ability as only a brilliantly daring mind could supply. Without hesitation all power was given into the hands of the man who seemed able to command the Fates themselves. My Lord Marlborough could soothe the fretted vanity of a petty German Prince, he could confront with composure the stupid rancour of those who could not comprehend him, in the most wooden of heavy Dutchmen he could awaken a slow understanding, the most testy royal temper he knew how to appease, and, through all, wear an air of dignity and grace, sometimes even of sweetness.

"What matter the means if a man gains his end," he said. "He can afford to appear worsted and poor spirited, if through all he sees that which he aims at placing itself within his reach."

"The King of Prussia," said Dunstanwolde as they talked of the hero once, "has given more trouble than any of the allies. He is ever ready to contest a point, or to imagine some slight to his dignity and rank. It has been almost impossible to manage him. How think you my Lord Marlborough won him over? By doing that which no other man—diplomat or soldier—would have had the wit to see the implied flattery of, or the composure to perform without loss of dignity. At a state banquet his testy Majesty dropped his napkin and

46

required another. No attendant was immediately at hand. My Lord Marlborough—the most talked of man in Europe, and some say, at this juncture, as powerful as half a dozen Kings—rose and handed his Majesty the piece of linen as simply as if it were but becoming that he should serve as lackey a royalty so important—and with such repose of natural dignity that 'twas he who seemed majestic, and not the man he waited on. Since then all goes with comparative smoothness. If a Queen's favoured counsellor and greatest general so serves him, the little potentate feels his importance properly valued."

"But if one who knows his Lordship had looked straight in his eyes," said Roxholm, "he could have seen the irony within them— held like a spark of light. I have seen it."

When my Lord Marlborough went to the Hague to take command of the Dutch and English forces, and to draw the German power within the confederacy, he took with him more than one young officer notable for his rank and brilliant place in the world, it having become at this period the fashion to go to the wars in the hope that a young Marlborough might lurk beneath any smart brocade and pair of fine shoulders. Among others, his Lordship was attended on his triumphal way by the already much remarked young Marquess of Roxholm, and it was realized that this fortunate young man went not quite as others did, but as one on whom the chief had fixed his attention, and for whom he had a liking.

In truth, he had marked in him certain powers and qualities, which were both agreeable to his tastes and promised usefulness. He had not employed his own powers and charms, physical and mental, from his fifteenth year upward, without having learned the actual weight and measure of their potency, as a man knows the weight and size of a thing he can put into scales and measure with a yardstick. He remembered well hours, when the fact that he was of a beauteous shape and height, and gazed at others with a superb appealing eye, had made that difference which lies between failure and success; he had never forgot one of the occasions upon which the power of keeping silence under provocation or temptation, the ability to control each feature and compel it to calm sweetness, had served him as well as a regiment of soldiers might have served him. Each such experience he had retained mentally for future reference. Roxholm possessed this power to restrain himself, and to keep silent, reflecting, and judging meanwhile, and was taller than he, of greater grace, and unconscious state of bearing; his beauty of countenance had but increased as he grew to manhood.

"I was the handsomest lad at Court in the year '65," his Grace of Marlborough said once (he had been made Duke by this time).

"The year you were born I was the handsomest man in the army, they used to say—but I was no such beauty and giant as you, Marquess. The gods were en veine when they planned you."

"When I was younger," said Roxholm, "it angered me to hear my looks praised so much; I was boy enough to feel I must be unmanly. But now—'tis but as it should be, that a man should have straight limbs and a great body, and a clean-cut countenance. It should be nature—not a thing to be remarked; it should be mere nature—and the other an unnatural thing. 'Tis cruel that either man or woman should be weak or uncomely. All should be as perfect parts of the great universe as are the mountains and the sun."

"'Tis not so yet," remarked my Lord Marlborough, with his inscrutable smile. "'Tis not so yet."

"Not yet," said Roxholm. "But let each creature live to make it so—men that they may be clean and joyous and strong; women that they may be mates for them. They should be as strong as we, and have as great courage."

His Lordship smiled again. They were at the Hague at this time and in his quarters, where he was pleased occasionally to receive the young officer with a gracious familiarity. For reasons of his own, he wished to know him well and understand the strengths and weaknesses of his character. Therefore he led him into talk, and was pleased to find that he frequently said things worth hearing, though they were often new and somewhat daring things to be said by one of his age at this period, when 'twas not the custom for a man to think for himself, but either to follow the licentious follies of his fellows or accept without question such statements as his Chaplain made concerning a somewhat unreasoning Deity, His inflexible laws, and man's duty towards Him. That a handsome youth, for example, should, in a serious voice and with a thoughtful face, announce that beauty should be but nature, and ugliness regarded as a disease, instead of humbly submitted to as the will of God, was, indeed, a startling heresy and might have been regarded as impious, even though so gravely said. Therefore it was my Lord Marlborough smiled.

"I spoke to you of marriage once before," he remarked. "You bring it back to me. Do you care for women?" bluntly.

Roxholm met his eye with his own straight, cool gaze.

"Yes, my Lord," he answered with some grimness, and said no more.

"The one you wait for has not yet come to Court, as I said that day," his Grace went on, and now he was grave again, and had even fallen into a speculative tone. "But it struck me once that I heard of

48

her—though she is no fit companion for you yet—and Heaven knows if she ever will be. The path before her is too full of traps for safety."

Roxholm did not speak. Whether fond of women or not, he was not given to talking of them, and a certain reserve would have prevented his entering upon any discussion of the future Lady Roxholm, whomsoever she might in the future prove to be. He stood in an easy attitude, watching with some vague curiosity the expression of his chief's countenance. But suddenly he found himself checking a slight start, and this was occasioned by his Lordship's next words.

"In the future I shall take pains to hear what befalls her," the Duke said. "In two or three years' time we shall hear somewhat. She will marry a duke—be a King's mistress, or go to ruin in some less splendid and more tragic way. No woman is born into the world with such beauty as they say is hers, and such wild fire in her veins, without setting the world—or herself—in flames. A new Helen of Troy she may be, and yet she is but the ninth daughter of a drunken Gloucestershire baronet."

'Twas here that Roxholm found himself checking his start, but he had not checked it soon enough to escape the observance of the quickest sighted man in Europe.

"What!" he said, "you have heard of her?"

"I have seen her, your Grace," Roxholm answered, "on the hunting field in Gloucestershire."

"Is she so splendid a young creature as they say? Was she in boy's attire, as we hear her rascal father lets her ride with him?"

"I thought her a boy, and had never seen one like her," said Roxholm, and he was amazed to feel himself disturbed as if he spoke not of a child, but of a beauty of ripe years.

"Is she of such height and strength and wondrous development as rumour tells us?" his Grace continued, still observing him as if with interest. "At twelve years old, 'tis told, she is tall enough for eighteen, and can fence and leap hedges and break horses, and that she plays the tyrant over men four times her age."

"I saw her but once, your Grace," replied Roxholm. "She was tall and strong and handsome."

"Go and see her again, my lord Marquess," said the Captain-General, turning to his papers. "But do not wait too long. Such beauties must be caught early."

When he went back to his quarters, my lord Marquess strolled through the quaint streets of the town slowly, and looking upon the ground as he walked. For some reason he felt vaguely depressed, and, searching within himself for a reason, recognised that the slight cloud resting upon his spirits recalled to him a feeling of his early childhood—no other than the sense of restless unhappiness he had felt years ago when he had first overheard the story of the wretched Lady of Wildairs and her neglected children.

"Yes," he said, "'tis almost the same feeling, though then I was a child, and now I am a man. When I saw the girl at the hunt, and rode home afterwards with Dunstanwolde, listening to her story, there was gloom in the air. There is that in it to make a man's spirit heavy. I must not think of her."

But Fate herself was against him. For one thing, my Lord Marlborough had brought back to him, with a few words, with strange vividness the picture of the brilliant young figure in its hunting scarlet, its gallop across the field with head held high, its flying leap over the hedge, and the gay insolence and music of its laugh.

"A child could not have made a man so remember her," he said, impatiently. "She was half woman then—half lovely, youthful devil. There is an ill savour about it all."

When he entered his rooms he found guests waiting him. A pleasure-loving young ensign, whom he had known at Oxford, and two of the lad's cronies. They were a trio of young scapegraces, delighted with any prospect of adventure, and regarding their martial duties chiefly as opportunities to shine in laced coats and cocked hats, and swagger with a warlike air and a military ogle when they passed a pretty woman in the street. It was the pretty woman these young English soldiers had come to do battle with, and hoped to take captive with flying colours and flourish of trumpets.

They were in the midst of great laughter when Roxholm entered, and young Tantillion, the ensign, sprang up to meet him in the midst of a gay roar. The lad had been one of his worshippers at the University, and loved him fondly, coming to him with all sorts of confidences, to pour forth his love difficulties, to grumble at his military duties when they interfered with his pleasures, to borrow money from him to pay his gaming debts.

"He has been with my Lord Marlborough," he cried; "I know he has by his sober countenance! We are ready to cheer thee up, Roxholm, with the jolliest story. 'Tis of the new beauty, who is but twelve years old and has set half the world talking."

"Mistress Clorinda Wildairs of Wildairs Hall in Gloucestershire," put in Bob Langford, one of the cronies, a black-eyed lad of twenty. "Perhaps your Lordship has heard of her, since she is so much gossiped of—Mistress Clorinda Wildairs, who has been brought up half boy by her father and his cronies, and is already the strappingest beauty in England."

"He is too great a gentleman to have heard of such an ill-mannered young hoyden," said Tantillion, "but we will tell him. 'Twas my sister Betty's letter—writ from Warwickshire—set us on," and he pulled forth a scrawled girlish-looking epistle from his pocket and spread it on the table. "Shalt hear it, Roxholm? Bet is a minx, and 'tis plain she is green with jealousy of the other girl—but 'tis the best joke I have heard for many a day."

And forthwith Roxholm must sit down and hear the letter read and listen to their comments thereupon, and their shouts of boyish laughter.

Little Lady Betty Tantillion, who was an embryo coquette of thirteen, had been to visit her relations in Warwickshire, and during her stay among them had found the chief topic of conversation a certain mad creature over the borders of Gloucestershire—a Mistress Clorinda Wildairs, who was the scandal of the county, and plainly the delight of all the tongue-waggers.

"And oh, Tom, she is a grate thing, almost as tall as a woman though she is but twelve years of age," wrote her young Ladyship, whose spelling, by the way, was by no means as correct as her sense of the proprieties. "Her father, Sir Jeoffry, allows her to ride in boys' clothes, which is indecent for a young lady even at her time of life. Brother Tom, how would you like to see your sister Betty astride a hunter, in breeches? Lady Maddon (she is the slender, graceful buty who is called the 'Willow Wand' by the gentlemen who are her servants)—she saith that this girl is a coarse thing and has so little modisty that she is proud to show her legs, thinking men will admire them, but she is mistaken, for gentlemen like a modist woman who is slight and delicate. She (Mistress Clo—as they call her) has big, bold, black eyes and holds her chin in the air and her mouth looks as red as if 'twere painted every hour. Every genteel woman speaks ill of her and is ashamed of her bold ways. And she is not even handsome, Tom, for all their talk, for I have seen her myself and think nothing of her looks. Her breeding is said to be shameful and her langwidge a disgrace to her secks. The gentlemen are always telling tales of her ways, and they laugh and make such a noise when they talk about her over their wine. At our Aunt Flixton's one day, my cousin Gill and me stood behind a tree to hear what was being said by some men who were telling stories of her (which was no wrong because we wished to learn a lesson so that we might not behave like her). Some of their words we did not understand, but some we did and 'twas of a Chaplain (they called him a fat-chopped hipercrit) who went to counsel her to behayve more decent, and she no doubt was impudent and tried to pleas him, for he forgot his cloth and put his arms sudden about her and

51

kist her. And the men roared shameful, for the one who told it said she knocked him down on his knees and held him there with one hand on his shoulder while she boxed his face from side to side till his nose bled in streams, and cried she (Oh, Tom!) 'Damn thy fat head,' each time she struck him 'if that is thy way to convert women, this is my way to convert men.' And he could scarce crawl away weeping, his blood and tears streeming down his face, which shows she hath not a reverence even for the cloth itself. Dere brother Thomas, if you should meet her in England when you come back from the wars, and she is a woman, I do pray you will not be like the other gentlemen and be so silly as to praise her, for such creatures should not be encorragd."

Throughout the reading of the letter uproarious shouts of laughter had burst forth at almost every sentence, and when he had finished the epistle, little Tantillion fell forward, his face on his arms on the table, his mirth almost choking him, while the others leaned back and roared. 'Twas only Roxholm who was not overcome, the story not seeming so comical to him as to the others, and yet there were points at which he himself could not help but laugh.

"'Damn thy fat head,'" shrieked Tom Tantillion, "'If that is thy way to convert women, this is mine to convert men.' Oh, Lord! I think I see the parson!"

"With his fat, slapped face and his streaming eyes and bloody nose!" shouted Langford.

"Serve him damn right!" said Tantillion, sobering and wiping his own eyes. "To put their heads into such hornets' nests would make a lot of them behave more decent." And then he picked up the letter again and made brotherly comments upon it.

"'Tis just like a minx of a girl to think a man cannot see through her spite," he said. "Bet is dying to be a woman and have the fellows ogling her. She is a pretty chit and will be the languishing kind, like the die-away Maddon who is so 'modist.' She is thin enough to be made 'modist' by it. No breeches for her, but farthingales and 'modesty pieces' high enough to graze her chin. 'Some of their words we did not understand'"—reading from the letter, and he looked at the company with a large comprehensive wink. "'Her breeding is disgraceful and her langwidge a disgrace to her secks'—Well, I'll be hanged if she isn't a girl after a man's own heart, if she's handsome enough to dress like a lad, and has the spirit to ride and leap like one—and can slap a Chaplain's face for him when he plays the impudent goat. Aren't you of my opinion, Roxholm, for all you don't laugh as loud as the rest of us? Aren't you of my mind?"

"Yes," said Roxholm, who for a few moments had been gazing at the wall with a somewhat fierce expression.

"Hello!" exclaimed Tantillion, not knowing the meaning of it. "What are you thinking of?"

Roxholm recovered himself, but his smile was rather a grim one.

"I think of the Chaplain," he said, "and how I should like to have dealt with him myself—after young Mistress Wildairs let him go."

CHAPTER IX

Sir John Oxon Lays a Wager at Cribb's Coffee House

This is to be no story of wars and battles, of victories and historic events, such great engines being but touched upon respectfully, as their times and results formed part of the atmosphere of the life of a gentleman of rank who moved in the world affected by them, and among such personages as were most involved in the stirring incidents of their day. That which is to be told is but the story of a man's life and the love which was the greatest power in it—the thing which brought to him the fiercest struggles, the keenest torture, and the most perfect joy.

During the next two years Gerald Mertoun saw some pretty service and much change of scene, making the "grand tour," as it were, under circumstances more exciting and of more moment to the world at large than is usually the case when a gentleman makes it. He so acquitted himself on several occasions that England heard of him and prophesied that if my Lord Marlborough's head were taken off in action there was a younger hero who might fill his place. At the news of each battle, whether it ended in victory or not, old Rowe rang the bells at Camylott, rejoicing that even if the enemy was not routed with great slaughter, my lord Marquess was still alive to fight another day. At Blenheim he so bore himself that the Duke talked long and gravely with him in private, laying before him all the triumphs a career of arms would bring to him.

"Twenty years hence, Roxholm," he said, watching him with

his keen glance as he ever did, "you might take my place, had England such questions to settle as she has to-day. In twenty years I shall be seventy-four. You were hammered from the metal nature cast me in, and you could take any man's place if 'twas your will. I could have taken any man's place I had chosen to take, by God, and so can you. If a man's brain and body are built in a certain way he can be soldier, bishop, physician, financier, statesman, King; and he will have like power in whatsoever he chooses to be, or Fate chooses that he shall be. As statesman, King, or soldier, the world will think him greatest because such things glitter in the eye and make more sound; but the strong man will be strong if Fortune makes him a huckster, and none can hide him. If Louis XV is as great a schemer as the fourteenth Louis has been, you may lead armies if you choose; but you will not choose, I think. You do not love it, Roxholm—you do not love it."

"No," answered Roxholm; "I do not love it. I can fight—any man can fight who has not white blood—and ours has been a fighting house; but mowing men down by thousands, cutting their throats, burning towns, and desolating villages filled with maddened men and shrieking women and children, does not set my blood in a flame as it does the blood of a man who is born for victorious slaughter. I loathe so the slaughter that I hate the victory. No; there are other things I can do better for England, and be happier in doing them."

"I have known that," said the Captain-General, "even when I have seen you sweep by, followed by your men, at your most splendid moment. I have known it most when we have sate together and talked—as 'tis not my way to talk to much older men."

They had so talked together, and upon matters much more important than the world knew. His Grace of Marlborough's years had been given to other things than letters. He could win a great victory with far greater ease than he could pen the dispatch announcing it when 'twas gained. "Of all things," he once said to his Duchess, "I do not love writing." He possessed the faculty of using all men and things that came into his way, and there were times when he found of value the services of a young nobleman whose education and abilities were of the highest, and who felt deeply honoured by his unusual confidence, and was also silent and discreet both through taste and by nature. Older men were oftenest privately envious and ambitious; and a man who has desires for place and power is not to be trusted by one who has gained the highest and is attacked by jealousy on all sides. This man was rich, of high rank, and desired nothing his Grace wished to retain; besides this, his nature was large and so ruled by high honour that 'twas not in him to scheme or parley with schemers. So it befel that, despite his youth, he enjoyed the privilege of being treated as if his years had been as ripe as his intellect. He knew and learned many things. Less was hid from him than from any other man in the army, had the truth been known. When 'twas a burning necessity for the great man to cross to England to persuade her Majesty to change her ministers, Roxholm knew the processes by which the end was reached. He had knowledge of all the feverish fits through which political England passed, in greater measure than he himself was conscious of. His reflections upon the affairs of Portugal and their management, his belief in the importance of the Emperor's reconciliation with the Protestants of Hungary, and of many a serious matter, were taken into consideration and pondered over when he knew it not. In hastening across the Channel to the English Court, in journeying to Berlin to encounter great personages, in hearing of and beholding intrigue, triumphs, disappointments, pomps, and vanities, he studied in the best possible school the art and science of statesmanship, and won for himself a place in men's minds and memories.

When, after Blenheim, he returned to England with a slight wound, his appearance at Court was regarded as an event of public interest, and commented upon with flowery rhetoric in the journals. The ladies vowed he had actually grown taller than before, that his deep eyes had a power no woman could resist, and that there was indeed no gentleman in England to compare with him either for intellect, beauty, or breeding. Her Majesty showed him a particular favour, and it was rumoured that she had remarked that, had one of her many dead infants lived and grown to such a manhood, she would have been a happy woman. Duchess Sarah melted to him as none had ever seen her melt to man before. She had heard many stories of him from her lord, and was prepared to be gracious, but when she beheld him, she was won by another reason, for he brought back to her the day when she had been haughty, penniless Sarah Jennings, and the man who seemed to her almost godlike in his youth and beauty had knelt at her feet.

'Twas most natural that at this time there should be much speculation as to the beauty who might be chosen as his partner in life by a young nobleman of such fortune, a young hero held in such esteem by his country as well as by the world of fashion. Conversation was all the more rife upon the subject because his Lordship paid no special court to any and seemed a heart-free man.

Many suitable young ladies were indeed picked out for him, some by their own friends and families, some—who had not convenient relatives to act for them—by themselves, and each was delicately or with matter-of-fact openness presented to his notice. There were brilliant Court beauties—lovely country virgins of rank and fortune—charming female wits, and fair and bold marauders who would carry on a siege with skill and daring; but the party attacked seemed not so much obdurate as unconscious, and neither succumbed nor ran away. When the lovely Lady Helen Loftus fell into a decline and perished a victim to it at the very opening of her eighteenth year, there was a whisper among certain gossiping elderly matrons, which hinted that only after her acquaintance with the splendid young Marquess had she begun to look frail and large-eyed, and gradually fallen into decay.

"Never shall I forget," said old Lady Storms, "seeing the pretty thing look after him when he bowed and left her after they had danced a minuet together. Her look set me to watching her, and she gazed on him through every dance with her large heaven-blue eyes, and when at last she saw him turn and come towards her again her breast went up and down and her breath fluttered, and she turned from white to red and from red to white with joy. 'Tis not his fault, poor young man, that women will set their hearts on him; 'tis but nature. I should do it myself if I were not seventy-five and a hooked-nosed pock-marked creature. Upon my life, it is not quite a fair thing that a man with all things which all women must want, should be sent forth among us. Usually when a man hath good looks he hath bad manners or poor wit or mean birth, or a black soul like the new man beauty, Sir John Oxon, whom a woman must hate before she hath loved him three months. But this one—good Lord! And with the best will in life, he cannot take all of us."

The new man beauty, Sir John Oxon, was indeed much talked of at this time. Having lived a mad rake's life at the University, and there gained a reputation which had made him the fashionable leader of the wickedest youths of their time, he had fallen heir to his fortune and title just as he left Cambridge and was prepared to launch himself into town life. He had appeared in the world preceded by stories of successful intrigues, daring indeed when connected with the name of a mere youth; but as he was beautiful to behold, and had gayety and grace and a daring wit, such rumours but fixed public attention upon him and made him the topic of the hour. He was not of the build or stateliness of Lord Roxholm, and much younger, but was as much older than his years in sin as the other was in unusual acquirement. He was a slender and exquisitely built youth, with perfect features, melting blue eyes, and rich fair hair which, being so beautiful, he disdained to conceal with any periwig, however elaborate and fashionable. When Roxholm returned to England, this male beauty's star was in the ascendant.

All the town talked of him, his dress, his high play, the various intrigues he was engaged in and was not reluctant that the world of fashion should hear of. The party of young gentlemen who had been led by him at the University took him for their model in town, so that there were a set of beaux whose brocaded coats, lace steenkirks, sword-knots, and carriage were as like Sir John's as their periwigs were like his fair locks, they having been built as similar as possible by their peruquiers. His coach and four were the finest upon the road, his chair and chariot, in the town; he had fought a duel about a woman, and there were those who more than suspected that the wildest band of Mohocks who played pranks at night was formed of half a dozen pretty fellows who were known as the "Jack Oxonites."

He was not a young man whose acquirements were to be praised or emulated, but there were pretty women who flattered him and men of fashion who found pleasure in his society, for a time at least, and many a strange scandal connected itself with his name.

He sang, he told wicked stories, he gambled, and at certain coffee-houses shone with resplendent light as a successful beau and conqueror.

'Twas at a club that Roxholm first beheld him. He had heard him spoken of but had not seen him, and going into the coffee-room one evening with a friend, a Captain Warbeck, found there a noisy party of beaux, all richly dressed, all full of wine, and all seeming to be the guests of a handsome fellow more elegantly attired and wearing a more dashing air than any of them. He was in blue and silver and had fair golden love-locks which fell in rich profusion on his shoulders.

He stood up among the company leaning against the table, taking snuff from a jewelled gold snuff-box with an insolent, laughing grace.

"A quaint jade she must be, damme," he said. "I have heard of her these three years, and she is not yet fifteen. Never were told me such stories of a young thing's beauty since I was man-born. Eyes like stars, flaming and black as jet, a carriage like a Juno, a shape— good Lord! like all the goddesses a man has heard of—and hair which is like a mantle and sweeps upon the ground. In less than a year's time I will go to Gloucestershire and bring back a lock of it— for a trophy." And he looked about him mockingly, as if in triumph.

"She will clout thee blind, Jack, as she clouted the Chaplain," cried one of the company. "No man that lives can tame her. She is the fiercest shrew in England, as she is the greatest beauty."

"She will thrash thee, Jack, as she thrashed her own father

with his hunting crop when she was but five years old," another cried.

The beau in blue and silver flicked the grains of snuff lightly from the lace of his steenkirk with a white jewelled hand and smiled, slowly nodding his fair curled head.

"I know all that," he said. "Every story have I heard, and, egad! they but fire my blood. She is high mettled, but I have dealt with termagants before—and brought them down, by God!—and brought them down! There is a way to tame a woman—and I know it. Begin with a light soft hand and a melting eye—all's fair in love; and the spoils are to the victor. When I come back from Gloucestershire with my lock of raven hair"—he lifted a goblet of wine and tossed it off at a draught—"I shall leave her as such beauties should be left—on her knees." And his laugh rang forth like a chime of silver. Roxholm sprang up with a smothered oath.

"Come!" he said to Warbeck. "Come away, in God's name."

Warbeck had been his fellow-soldier abroad and knew well the dangerous spirit which hid itself beneath his calm. He had seen him roused to fury once before ('twas when in Flanders after a skirmish he found some drunken soldiers stripping a poor struggling peasant woman of her garments, while her husband shrieked curses at them from the tree where he was tied)—and on that occasion he had told himself 'twould be safer to trifle with a mine of powder than with this man's anger. He rose hurriedly and followed him outside. In the street he could scarce keep pace with his great stride, and the curses that broke from him brought back hot days of battle.

"I would not enter into a pot-house brawl with a braggart boy," he cried. "The blackguard, dastard knave! Drag me away, Hal, lest I rush back like a fool and run him through! I have lost my wits. 'Tis the fashion for dandies to pour forth their bestial braggings, but never hath a man made my blood so boil and me so mad to strike him."

"'Tis not like thee so to lose thy wits, Roxholm," Warbeck said, his hand on his arm, "but thou hast lost them this once surely. 'Tis no work for the sword of a gentleman pinking foul-mouthed boasters in a coffee-house. Know you who he is?"

"Damnation, No!" thundered Roxholm, striding on more fiercely still.

"'Tis the new dandy, Sir John Oxon," said Warbeck. "And the beauty he makes his boast on is the Gloucestershire Wildairs handsome madcap—the one they call Mistress Clo."

CHAPTER X

My Lord Marquess rides to Camylott

When he went home my lord sate late over his books before he went to his chamber, yet he read but little, finding his mood disturbed by thoughts which passed through it in his despite. His blood had grown hot at the coffee-house, and though 'twas by no means the first time it had heated when he heard the heartless and coarse talk of woman which it was the habit of most men of the day to indulge in, he realised that it had never so boiled as when he listened to the brutal and significant swagger of Sir John Oxon. His youth and beauty and cruel, confident air had made it seem devilish in its suggestion of what his past almost boyish years might have held of pitiless pleasures and pitiless indifference to the consequences, which, while they were added triumphs to him, were ruin and despair to their victims.

"The laugh in his blue eye was damnable," Roxholm murmured. "'Twas as if there was no help for her or any other poor creature whom he chose to pursue. The base unfairness of it! He is equipped with the whole armament—of lures, of lies, of knowledge, and devilish skill. There are women, 'tis true, who are his equals; but those who are not—those who are ignorant and whose hearts he wins, as 'twould be easy for him to win any woman's who believed his wooing face and voice—Nay, 'twould be as dastardly as if an impregnable fortress should open all its batteries upon a little child who played before it. And he stands laughing among his mocking crew—triumphing, boasting—in cold blood—of what he plans to do months to come. Fate grant he may not come near me often. Some day I should break his devil's neck."

He found himself striding about the room. He was burning with rage against the unfairness of it all, as he had burned when, a mere child, he pondered on the story of Wildairs. To-day he was a man, yet his passion of rebellion was curiously similar in its nature to his young fury. Now, as then, there was naught to be done to help what seemed like Fate. In a world made up of men all more or less hunters of the weak, ready to accept the theory that all things defenceless and lovely are fair game for the stronger, a man whose view was fairer was an abnormality.

"I do not belong to my time," he said, flinging himself into his chair again and speaking grimly. "I am too early—or too late—for it, and must be content to seem a fool."

59

"There is a Fate," he said a little later, having sat a space gazing at the floor and deep in thought—"there is a Fate which seems to link me to the fortunes of these people. My first knowledge of their wretchedness was a thing which sank deep. There are things a human being perhaps remembers his whole life through—and strangely enough they are often small incidents. I do not think there will ever pass from me my memory of the way the rain swept over the park lands and bare trees the day I stood with my Lord Dunstanwolde at the Long Gallery window, and he told me of the new-born child dragged shrieking from beneath its dead mother's body."

Some days later he went to Camylott to pass a few weeks in the country with his parents, who were about to set forth upon a journey to Italy, where they were to visit in state a palace of a Roman noble who had been a friend of his Grace's youth, they having met and become companions when the Duke first visited Rome in making the grand tour. 'Twas a visit long promised to the Roman gentleman who had more than once been a guest of their household in England; and but for affairs of his Grace of Marlborough, which Roxholm had bound himself to keep eye on, he also would have been of the party. As matters stood, honour held him on English soil, for which reason he went to Camylott to spend the last weeks with those he loved, amid the country loveliness.

When my lord Marquess journeyed to the country he took no great cavalcade with him, but only a couple of servants to attend him, while Mr. Fox rode at his side. The English June weather was heavenly fair, and the country a bower of green, the sun shining with soft warmth and the birds singing in the hedgerows and upon the leafy boughs. To ride a fine horse over country roads, by wood and moor and sea, is a pleasant thing when a man is young and hale and full of joy in Nature's loveliness, and above all is riding to a home which seems more beautiful to him than any place on earth. One who has lived twenty-eight years, having no desire unfulfilled, and taking his part of every pleasure that wealth, high birth, and a splendid body can give him, may well ride gaily over a good white road and have leisure to throw back his head to hearken to a skylark soaring in the high blue heavens above him, to smile at a sitting bird's bright eyes peeping timidly at him from under the thick leafage of a hazel hedge, or at the sight of a family of rabbits scurrying over the cropped woodland grass at the sound of his horse's feet, their short white tails marking their leaps as they dart from one fern shelter to the other; and to slacken his horse's pace as he rides past village greens, marking how the little children tumble and are merry there.

So my lord Marquess rode and Mr. Fox with him, for two days at least. In the dewy morning they set forth and travelled between green hedgerows and through pretty tiny villages, talking pleasantly, as old friends will talk, for to the day of his old preceptor's peaceful dying years later at Camylott, the Marquess (who was then a Duke) loved and treated him as a companion and friend, not as a poor underling Chaplain who must rise from table as if dismissed by the course of sweetmeats when it appeared. For refreshments they drew rein at noon before some roadside inn whose eager host spread before them his very best, and himself waited upon them in awful joy. When the sun set, one manservant rode on before to prepare for their entertainment for the night, and when they cantered up to the hostelry, they found the whole establishment waiting to receive and do them honour, landlord and landlady bowing and curtseying on the threshold, maidservants peeping from behind doors and through upper windows, and loiterers from the village hanging about ready to pull forelocks or bob curtseys, as their sex demanded.

"'Tis my lord Marquess of Roxholm, the great Duke of Osmonde's heir," they would hear it whispered. "He has come back from the wars covered with wounds and now rides to pay his respects to their Graces, his parents, at Camylott Tower."

'Twas a pleasant journey; Roxholm always remembered and often spoke of it in after years, for his thought was that in setting out upon it he had begun to journey towards that which Fate, it seemed, had ordained that he should reach—though through dark nights and stormy days—at last.

'Twas on the morning of the fourth day there befel them a strange adventure, and one which had near ended in dark tragedy for one human being at least.

The horse his lordship rode was a beautiful fiery creature, and sometimes from sheer pleasure in his spirit, his master would spur him to a wild gallop in which he went like the wind's self, showing a joy in the excitement of it which was beauteous to behold. When this fourth morning they had been but about an hour upon the road, Roxholm gave to the creature's glossy neck the touch which was the signal 'twas his delight to answer.

"Watch him shoot forward like an arrow from a bow," my lord said to Mr. Fox, and the next instant was yards away.

He flew like the wind, his hoofs scarce seeming to touch the earth as he sped forward, my lord sitting like a Centaur, his face aglow with pleasure, even Mr. Fox's soberer animal taking fire somewhat and putting himself at a gallop, his rider's elderly blood quickening with his.

One side of the road they were upon was higher than the other and covered with a wood, and as Mr. Fox followed at some distance he beheld a parlous sight. At a turn in the way, down the bank, there rushed a woman, a frantic figure, hair flying, garments disordered, and with a shriek flung herself full length upon the earth before my lord Marquess's horse, as if with the intent that the iron hoofs should dash out her brains as they struck ground again. Mr. Fox broke forth into a cry of horror, but even as it left his lips he beheld a wondrous thing, indeed, though 'twas one which brought his heart into his throat. The excited beast's fore parts were jerked upward so high that he seemed to rear till he stood almost straight upon his hind legs, his fore feet beating the air; then, by some marvel of strength and skill, his body was wheeled round and his hoofs struck earth at safe distance from the prostrate woman's head.

My lord sprang from his back and stood a moment soothing his trembling, the animal snorting and panting, the foam flying from his nostrils in his terror at a thing which his friend and master had never done to him before. The two loved each other, and in Roxholm's heart there was a sort of rage that he should have been forced to inflict upon him so harsh a shock.

The woman dragged herself half up from the white dust on which she had lain. She was shuddering convulsively, her long hair was hanging about her, her eyes wild and anguished, and her lips shivering more than trembling.

"Oh, God! Oh, God!" she wailed, and then let herself drop again and writhed, clutching at the white dust with her hands.

"Are you mad?" said Roxholm, sternly, "or only in some hysteric fury? Would you have your brains dashed out?"

She flung out her arms, tearing at the earth still and grinding her teeth.

"Yes—dashed out!" she cried; "all likeness beaten from my face that none might know it again. For that I threw myself before you."

The Marquess gave his horse to the servant, who had ridden to him, and made a sign both to him and Mr. Fox that they ride a little forward.

He bent over the girl (for she was more girl than woman, being scarce eighteen) and put his hand on her shoulder.

"Get up, Mistress," he said. "Rise and strive to calm yourself."

Suddenly his voice had taken a tone which had that in its depths no creature in pain would not understand and answer to. His keen eye had seen a thing which wrung his heart, it seeming to tell so plainly all the cruel story.

"Come, poor creature," he said, "let me help you to your feet."

He put his strong arm about her body, and lifted her as if she had been a child, and finding she was so trembling that she had not strength to support herself, he even carried her to the grass and laid her down upon it. She had a lovely gipsy face which should have been brilliant with beauty, but was wild and wan and dragged with horrid woe. Her great roe's eyes stared at him through big, welling tears of agony.

"You look like some young lord!" she cried. "You have a beautiful face and a sweet voice. Any woman would believe you if you swore a thing! What are women to do! Are you a villain, too— are you a villain, too?"

"No," answered he, looking at her straight. "No, I am not."

"All men are!" she broke forth, wildly. "They lie to us—they trick us—they swear to us—and kneel and pray—and then"—tossing up her arms with a cry that was a shriek—"they make us kneel—and laugh—laugh—and laugh at us!"

She threw herself upon the grass and rolled about, plucking at her flesh as if she had indeed gone mad.

"But for you," she sobbed, "it would be over now, and your horse's hoofs had stamped me out. And now 'tis to do again—for I will do it yet."

"Nay, you will not, Mistress," he said, in a still voice, "for your child's sake."

He thought, indeed, she would go mad then: she so writhed and beat herself, that he blamed himself for his words, and knelt by her, restraining her hands.

"'Tis for its sake I would kill myself, and have my face beaten into the bloody dust. I would kill it—kill it—kill it—more than I would kill myself!"

"Nay, you would not, poor soul," he said, "if you were not distraught."

"But I am distraught," she wailed; "and there is naught but death for both of us."

'Twas a strange situation for a young man to find himself in, watching by the roadside the hysteric frenzy of a maddened girl; but as he had been unconscious on the day he stood, an unclad man, giving the aid that would save a life, so he thought now of naught but the agony he saw in this poor creature's awful eyes and heard in her strangled cries. It mattered naught to him that any passing would have thought themselves gazing upon a scene in a strange story.

There was a little clear stream near, and he went and brought her water, making her drink it and bathe the dust-stains from her face and hands, and the gentle authority with which he made her do

63

these simple things seemed somehow to somewhat calm her madness. She looked up at him staring, and with long, sobbing breaths.

"Who—are you?" she asked, helplessly.

"I am the Marquess of Roxholm," he answered, "and I ride to my father's house at Camylott; but I cannot leave you until I know you are safe."

"Safe!" she said. "I safe!" and she clasped her hands about her knees as she sat, wringing her fingers together. "You do not ask me who I am," she added.

"I need not know your name to do you service," he answered. "But I must ask you where you would go—to rest."

"To Death—from which you have plucked me!" was her reply, and she dropped her head against her held-up knees and broke forth sobbing again. "I tell you there is naught else. If your horse had beat my face into the dust, none would have known where I lay at last. Five days have I walked and my very clothes I changed with a gipsy woman. None would have known." Suddenly she looked up with shame and terror in her eyes, the blood flaming in her face. She involuntarily clutched at his sleeve as if in her horror she must confide even to this stranger. "They had begun to look at me—and whisper," she said. "And one day a girl who hated me laughed outright as I passed—though I strove to bear myself so straightly— and I heard her mock me. 'Pride cometh first,' she said, 'and then the fall. She hath fallen far.'"

She looked so young and piteous that Roxholm felt a mist pass before his eyes.

"Poor child!" he said; "poor child!"

"I was proud," she cried. "It was my sin. They taunted me that he was a gentleman and meant me ill, and it angered me—poor fool—and I held my head higher. He told me he had writ for his Chaplain to come and wed us in secret. He called me 'my lady' and told me what his pride in me would be when we went to the town." She put her hands up to her working throat as if somewhat strangled her, and the awful look came back into her widened eyes. "In but a little while he went away," she gasped—"and when he came back, and I went to meet him in the dark and fell weeping upon his breast, he pushed me back and looked at me, and curled his lip laughing, and turned away! Oh, John!—John Oxon!" she cried out, "God laughs at women—why shouldst not thou?" and her paroxysm began again.

At high noon a wagoner whose cart was loaded with hay drove into the rick yard of a decent farm-house some hours' journey from the turn in the road where my lord Marquess had been so strangely checked in his gallop. An elderly gentleman in Chaplain's garb and bands rode by the rough conveyance, and on a bed made in the hay a woman lay and groaned in mortal anguish.

The good woman of the house this reverend gentleman saw alone and had discourse with, paying her certain moneys for the trouble she would be put to by the charge he commanded to her, himself accompanying her when she went out to the wagon to care for its wretched burden.

Throughout the night she watched by her patient's bedside, but as day dawned she left it for a moment to call the Chaplain to come quickly, he having remained in the house that he might be at hand if need should be, in accordance with his patron's wishes.

"'Tis over, and she is dying," said the good woman. "I fear she hath not her wits, poor soul. All night she hath cried one name, and lies and moans it still."

Mr. Fox followed her into a little cleanly, raftered chamber. He knelt by the bedside and spoke gently to the girl who lay upon the white pillows, her deathly face more white than the clean, coarse linen. 'Twas true she did not see him, but lay staring at the wall's bareness, her lips moving as she muttered the name she had shrieked and wailed at intervals throughout the hours. "John—Oh, John Oxon!" he could barely hear, "God laughs at us—why should not such as thou?"

And when the sun rose she lay stiff and dead, with a dead child in her rigid arm; and Mr. Fox rode slowly back with a grave countenance, to join his lord and patron at the village inn, and tell him all was over.

CHAPTER XI

"It Might Have Been—It Might Have Been!"

The heavenly summer weeks he passed with his beloved parents at Camylott before they set forth on their journey to the Continent remained a sweet memory in the mind of the young Marquess so long as he lived, and was cherished by him most tenderly. In those lovely June days he spent his hours with his father and mother as he had spent them as a child, and in that greater intimacy and closer communion which comes to a son with riper years, if the situation is not reversed and his maturity has not drifted away from such fondness. Both the Duke and Duchess were filled with such noble pride in him and he with such noble love of them. All they had hoped for in him he had given them, all his manly heart longed for they bestowed upon him—tenderness, companionship, sympathy in all he did or dreamed of doing.

After his leave of absence it was his intention to rejoin his Grace of Marlborough on the Continent for a period, since his great friend had so desired, but later he would return and give up his career of arms to devote himself to the interests of his country in other ways, and of this his mother was particularly glad, feeling all a woman's fears for his safety and all her soft dread of the horrors of war.

"I would not have shown you my heart when you went away from England, Gerald," she said. "'Twould not have been brave and just to do so since 'twas your desire to go. But no woman's heart can lie light in her breast when her son is in peril every hour—and I could not bear to think," her violet eyes growing softly dark, "that my son in winning glory might rob other mothers of their joy."

In their rides and talks together he would relate to his father the story of his campaign, describe to him the brilliant exploits of the great Duke, whom he had seen in his most magnificent hours, as only those who fought by his side had seen him; but with her Grace he did not dwell upon such things, knowing she would not be the happier for hearing of them. With her he would walk through the park, sauntering down the avenue beneath the oak-trees, or over the green sward to visit the deer, who knew the sound of her sweet voice, it seemed, and hearing it as she approached would lift their delicate heads and come towards her to be caressed and fed, welcoming her with the dewy lustrousness of their big timorous dark eyes, even the shyest does and little fawns nibbling from her fair and gentle hand, and following her softly a few paces when she turned away. Together she and Roxholm would wander through all the dear places he had loved in his childish years—into the rose gardens, which were a riot of beauty and marvellous colours and the pride and joy of the head gardener, who lived for and among them, as indeed they were the pride of those who worked under his command, not a man or boy of them knowing any such pleasure as to see her Grace walk through their labyrinths of bloom with my lord Marquess, each of them rejoicing in the loveliness on every side and gathering the fairest blossoms as they went, until sometimes they carried away with them rich sheaves of crimson and pink and white and yellow. They loved the high-walled kitchen garden, too, and often visited it, spreading delight there among its gardeners by praising its fine growths, plucking the fruit and gathering nosegays of the old-fashioned flowers which bordered the beds of sober vegetables—sweet peas and Canterbury bells, wall-flowers, sweetwilliams, yellow musk, and pansies, making, her Grace said, the prettiest nosegay in the world. Then they would loiter through the village and make visits to old men and women sitting in the sun, to young mothers with babies in their arms and little mites playing about their feet.

"And you never enter a cottage door, mother," said Roxholm in his young manhood's pride and joy in her, "but it seems that the sun begins to shine through the little window, and if there is a caged bird hanging there it begins to twitter and sing. I cannot find a lady like you"—bending his knee and kissing her white fingers in gay caress. "Indeed, if I could I should bring her home to you to Camylott—and old Rowe might ring his bells until he lost his breath."

"Do you know," she answered, "what your father said to me the first morning I lay in my bed with you in my arm—old Rowe was ringing the bells as if he would go wild. I remember the joyful pealing of them as it floated across the park to come through my open window. We were so proud and full of happiness, and thought you so beautiful—and you are, Gerald, yet; so you are yet," with the prettiest smile, "and your father said of you, 'He will grow to be a noble gentleman and wed a noble lady; and they will be as we have been—as we have been, beloved,' and we kissed each other with blissful tears in our eyes, and you moved in my arm, and there was a tiny, new-born smile on your little face."

"Dear one!" he said, kissing her hand more gravely; "dear one, God grant such sweetness may come to me—for indeed I want to love some woman dearly," and the warm blood mounted to his cheek.

Often in their tender confidences they spoke of this fair one who was to crown his happy life, and one day, having returned from a brief visit in another county, as they sat together in the evening she broke forth with a little sigh in her sweet voice.

"Ah, Gerald," she said, "I saw in Gloucestershire the loveliest strange creature—so lovely and so strange that she gave me an ache in the heart."

"And why, sweet one?" he asked.

"Because I think she must be the most splendid beauteous thing in all the world—and she has been so ill used by Fate. How could the poor child save herself from ill? Her mother died when she was born; her father is a wicked blasphemous rioter. He has so

67

brought her up that she has known no woman all her life, but has been his pastime and toy. From her babyhood she has been taught naught but evil. She is so strong and beautiful and wild that she is the talk of all the country. But, ah, Gerald, the look in her great eyes—her red young mouth—her wonderfulness! My heart stood still to see her. She hurt me so."

My lord Marquess looked down upon the floor and his brow knit itself.

"'Twould hurt any tender soul to see her," he said. "I am but a man—and I think 'twas rage I felt—that such a thing should be cast to ravening wolves."

"You," she cried, as if half alarmed; "you have seen her?"

"'Tis the beauty of Wildairs you speak of surely," he answered; "and I have seen her once—and heard of her often."

"Oh, Gerald," said her Grace, "'tis cruel. If she had had a mother—if God had but been good to her—" she put her hand up to her mouth to check herself, in innocent dread of that her words implied. "Nay, nay," she said, "if I would be a pious woman I must not dare to say such things. But oh! dearest one—if life had been fair to her, she—She is the one you might have loved and who would have worshipped such a man. It might have been—it might have been."

His colour died away and left him pale—he felt it with a sudden sense of shock.

"It was not," he said, hurriedly. "It was not—and she is but fourteen—and our lives lie far apart. I shall be in the field, or at the French or Spanish Courts. And were I on English soil I—I would keep away."

His mother turned pale also. Being his mother she felt with him the beating of his blood—and his face had a strange look which she had never seen before. She rose and went to him.

"Yes, yes, you are right," she exclaimed. "You could not—she could not—! And 'twould be best to keep away—to keep away. For if you loved her, 'twould drive you mad, and make you forget what you must be."

He tried to smile, succeeding but poorly.

"She makes us say strange things—even so far distant," he said. "Perhaps you are right. Yes, I will keep away."

And even while he said it he was aware of a strange tumult in him, and knew that, senseless as it might appear, a new thing had sprung to life in him as if a flame had been lighted. And even in its first small leaping he feared it.

'Twas a week later their Graces set forth upon their journey, and though Roxholm rode with them to Dover, and saw them aboard the packet, he always felt in after years that 'twas in the Long Gallery his mother had bidden him farewell.

They stood at the deep window at the end which faced the west and watched a glowing sunset of great splendour. Never had the earth spread before them seemed more beautiful, or Heaven's self more near. All the west was piled with heaps of stately golden cloud—great and high clouds, which were like the mountains of the Delectable Land, and filled one with awe whose eyes were lifted to their glories. And all the fair land was flooded with their gold. Her Grace looked out to the edge where moor and sky seemed one, and her violet eyes shone to radiance.

"It is the loveliest place in all the world," she said. "It has been the loveliest home—and I the happiest woman. There has not been an hour I would not live again."

She turned and lifted her eyes to his face and put one hand on his broad breast. "And you, Gerald," she said; "you have been happy. Tell me you have been happy, too."

"For twenty-eight years," he said, and folded his hand over hers. "For twenty-eight years."

She bent her face against his breast and kissed the hand closed over her own.

"Yes—yes; you have been happy," she said. "You have said it often; but before I went away I wanted to hear you say it once again," and as she gazed up smiling, a last ray from the sinking sun shot through the window and made a halo about her deep gold hair.

CHAPTER XII

In Which is Sold a Portrait

There are sure more forces in this Universe than Man has so far discovered, and so, not dreaming of them, can neither protect himself against, nor aid them in their workings if he would. Who has not sometimes fancied he saw their mysterious movings and—if of daring mind—been tempted to believe that in some future, even on this earth, the science of their laws might be sought for and explained? Who has not seen the time when his own life, or that of some other, seemed to flow, as a current flows, either towards or

69

away from some end, planned or unplanned by his own mind. At one time he may plan and struggle, and, in spite of all his efforts, the current sweeps him away from the object he strives to attain—as though he were a mere feather floating upon its stream; at another, the tide bears him onward as a boat is borne by the rapids, towards a thing he had not dreamed of, nor even vaguely wished to reach. At such hours, resistance seems useless. We seize an oar, it breaks in the flood; we snatch at an overhanging bough, it snaps or slips our grasp; we utter cries for help, those on the bank pass by not hearing, or cast to us a rope the current bears out of reach. Then we cry "Fate!" and either wring our hands, or curse, or sit and gaze straight before us, while we are swept on—either over the cataract's edge and dashed to fragments, or out to the trackless ocean, to be tossed by wind and wave till some bark sees and saves us—or we sink.

From the time of his mother's speech with him after her return from Gloucestershire, thoughts such as these passed often through Roxholm's mind. "It might have been; it might have been," she had said, and the curious leap of blood and pulse he had felt had vaguely shocked him. It scarcely seemed becoming that so young a creature as this lovely hoyden should so move a man. 'Twas the fashion that girl beauties should be women early, and at Court he had seen young things, wives and mothers when they were scarce older; but this one seemed more than half a boy and—and—! Yet he knew that he had been in earnest when he had said, "I would keep away."

"I know," he had said to himself when he had been alone later; "I know that if the creature were a woman, 'twould be best that I should keep away—'twould be best for any man to keep away from her, who was not free to bear any suffering his passion for her might bring him. The man who will be chief of a great house—whose actions affect the lives of hundreds—is not free, even to let himself be put to the torture"—and he smiled unconsciously the smile which was a little grim.

He had seen and studied many women, and in studying them had learned to know much of himself. He had not been so unconscious of them as he had seemed. Such a man must meet with adventures at any time, and at a period still tainted by the freedom of a dissolute reign, even though 'tis near twenty years past, his life, in his own despite, must contain incidents which would reveal much to the world, if related to it. Roxholm had met with such adventures, little as they were to his taste, and had found at both foreign and English Courts that all women were not non-attacking creatures, and in discovering this had learned that a man must be a stone to resist the luring of some lovely eyes.

"I need not think myself invulnerable," he had thought often. "I can resist because I have loved none of them. Had it chanced otherwise—God have mercy on my soul!"

And now the current of his life for weeks seemed strangely set towards one being. When he returned to London after seeing his parents depart for Italy, he met in his first walk in the city streets his erst fellow-collegian and officer, Lieutenant Thomas Tantillion, in England on leave, who almost hallooed with joy at sight of him, shaking him by the hand as if his arm had been a pump-handle, and then thrusting his own arm through it, and insisting affectionately on dragging him along the street that he might pour forth his renewed protestations of affection and the story of his adventures.

"Never was I more glad to see a man," he said. "I'm damned if we scapegraces have not missed thy good-looking face. Thou art a fine fellow, Roxholm—and good-natured—ay, and modest, too—for all thy beauty and learning. Many a man, with half thou hast, would wear grand Court airs to a rattle-pated rascal like Tom Tantillion. Wilford does it—and he is but a Viscount, and for all his straight nose and fine eyes but five feet ten. Good Lord! he looks down on us who did not pass well at the University, like a cock on a dunghill."

The Marquess laughed out heartily, having in his mind a lively picture of my Lord Wilford, whose magnificence of bearing he knew well.

"Art coming back, Roxholm?" asked Tom next. "When does thy leave expire?"

"I am coming back," Roxholm answered, "but I shall not long live a soldier's life. 'Tis but part of what I wish to do."

"His Grace of Marlborough misses thee, I warrant," said Tom. "'Tis often said he never loved a human thing on earth but John Churchill and his Duchess, but I swear he warmed to thee."

"He did me honour, if 'tis true," Roxholm said, "but I am not vain enough to believe it—gracious as he has been."

At that moment his volatile companion gave his arm a clutch and stopped their walk as if a sudden thought had seized him.

"Where wert thou going, Roxholm?" he asked. "Lord, Lord, I was so glad to see thee, that I forgot."

"What didst forget, Tom?"

Tom slapt his thigh hilariously. "That I had an errand on hand. A good joke, split me, Roxholm! Come with me; I go to see the picture of a beauty, stole by the painter, who is always drunk, and with his clothes in pawn, and lives in a garret in Rag Lane."

He was in the highest spirits over the adventure, and would drag Roxholm with him, telling him the story as they went. The painter, who was plainly enough a drunken rapscallion fellow, in

71

strolling about the country, getting his lodging and skin full of ale, now here, now there, by daubing Turks' Heads, Foxes and Hounds, and Pigs and Whistles, as signs for rustic ale-houses, had seen ride by one day a young lady of such beauty that he had made a sketch of her from memory, and finding where she lived, had hung about in the park to get a glimpse of her again, and having succeeded, had made her portrait and brought it back to town, in the hope that some gentleman might be taken by its charms and buy it.

"He hath drunk himself down to his last groat, and will let it go for a song now," said Tom. "I would get there before any other fellow does. Jack Wyse and Hal Langton both want it, but they have gamed their pockets empty, and wait till necessity forces him to lower his price to their means. But an hour since I heard that he had pawned his breeches and lay in bed writing begging letters. So now is the time to visit him. It was in Gloucestershire he found her—"

He stopped and turned round.

"Hang me! 'Tis the very one Bet wrote of, and I read you the letter. Dost remember it? The vixen who clouted the Chaplain for kissing her."

"Yes," said Roxholm; "I remember."

Tom rattled on in monstrous spirits. "I have had further letters from Bet," he said, "and each is a sermon with the beauty's sins for a text. The women are so jealous of her that the men could not forget her if they would, they scold so everlastingly. Lord, what a stir the hoyden is making!"

They turned into Rag Lane presently, and 'twas dingy enough, being a dirty, narrow place, with high black houses on either side, their windows broken and stuffed with bits of rag and paper, their doorways ornamented with slatternly women or sodden-faced men, while up and down ran squalid, noisy children under the flapping pieces of poor wearing apparel hung on lines to dry.

After some questioning they found the house the man they were in search of lived in, and 'twas a shade dingier than the rest. They mounted a black broken-down stairway till they reached the garret, and there knocked at the door.

For a few moments there was no answer, but that they could hear loud and steady snores within.

"He is sleeping it off!" said Tom, grinning, and whacked loudly on the door's cracked panels, by which, after two or three attacks, he evidently disturbed the sleeper, who was heard first to snort and then to begin to grumble forth drowsy profanities.

"Let us in," cried Tom. "I bring you a patron, sleepy fool."

Then 'twas plain some one tumbled from his bed and shuffled forward to the door, whose handle he had some difficulty in turning.

But when he got the door open, and caught sight of lace and velvet, plumed hats and shining swords, he was not so drunk but that which the sight suggested enlivened and awaked him. He uttered an exclamation, threw the door wide, and stood making unsteady but humbly propitiatory bows.

"Your lordships' pardon," he said. "I was asleep and knew not that such honour awaited me. Enter, your lordships; I pray you enter."

'Twas a little mean place with no furnishings but a broken bedstead, a rickety chair, and an uncleanly old table on which were huddled together a dry loaf, an empty bottle, and some poor daubs of pictures. The painter himself was an elderly man with a blotched face, a bibulous eye, and half unclothed, he having wrapped a dirty blanket about his body to conceal decently his lack of nether garments.

"We come to look at your portrait of the Gloucestershire beauty," said Tom.

"All want to look at it, my Lord," said the man, with a leer, half servile, half cunning. "There came two young gentlemen of fashion yesterday morning, and almost lost their wits at sight of it. Either would have bought it, but both had had ill luck at basset for a week and so could do no more than look, and go forth with their mouths watering."

Tom grinned.

"You painters are all rogues who would bleed every gentleman you see," he said.

"We are poor fellows who find it hard to sell our wares," the artist answered. "'Tis only such as the great Mr. Kneller who do not starve, and lie abed because their shirts and breeches are in pawn. When a man has a picture like to take the fancy of every young nobleman in town, he may well ask its value."

"Let us see it," cried Tom. "To a gentleman it may seem a daub."

The man looked at him slyly.

"'Twould pay me to keep it hid here and exhibit it for a fee," he said. "The gentlemen who were here yesterday will tell others, and they will come and ask to look at it, and then—"

"Show it to us, sir," said Roxholm, breaking in suddenly in his deeper voice and taking a step forward.

He had stood somewhat behind, not being at first in the mood to take part in the conversation, having no liking for the situation. That a young lady's portrait should be stolen from her, so to speak, and put on sale by a drunken painter without her knowledge,

73

annoyed him—and the man's leering hint of its future exhibition roused his blood.

"Show it to us, sir," he said, and in his voice there was that suggestion of command which is often in the voice of a man who has had soldiers under him.

The but half-sober limner being addressed by him for the first time, and for the first time looking at him directly, gave way to a slight hiccoughing start and strove to stand more steady. 'Twas no gay youthful rake who stood before him, but plainly a great gentleman, and most amazing tall and stately. 'Twas not a boy come to look at a peep-show, but might be a possible patron.

"Yes, your lordship," he stammered, bowing shakily, "I—I will bring it forth. Your lordship will find the young lady a wonder." He went swaying across the room, and opened a cupboard in the wall. The canvas stood propped up within, and he took it out and brought it back to them—keeping its face turned away.

"Let me set it in as good a light as the poor place can give," he said, and dragged forth the rickety-legged chair that he might prop it against its back, for the moment looking less drunk and less a vagabond in his eagerness to do his work justice; there lurking somewhere, perhaps, in his besotted being, that love which the artist soul feels for the labour of its dreams.

"In sooth, my lord, 'tis a thing which should have been better done," he said. "I could have done the young lady's loveliness more justice, had I but had the time. First I saw her for scarce more than a moment, and her face so haunted me that I sketched it for my own pleasure—and then I hung about her father's park for days, until by great fortune I came upon her one morning standing under a tree, her dogs at her feet, and she lost in thought—and with such eyes gazing before her—! I stood behind a tree and did my best, trembling lest she should turn. But no man could paint her eyes, my lord," rubbing his head ruefully; "no man could paint them. Mr. Kneller will not—when she weds a Duke and comes to queen it at the Court."

He had managed to keep before the picture as he spoke, and now he stepped aside and let them behold it, glancing from one to the other.

"Damn!" cried Tom Tantillion, and sprang forward from his chair at sight of it.

My lord Marquess made no exclamation nor spoke one word. The painter marked how tall he stood as he remained stationary, gazing. He had folded his arms across his big chest and seemed to have unconsciously drawn himself to his full height. Presently he spoke to the artist, though without withdrawing his eyes from the picture.

"'Tis no daub," he said. "For a thing done hastily 'tis done well. You have given it spirit."

'Twas fairly said. Indeed, the poor fellow knew something of his trade, 'twas evident, and perhaps for once he had been sober, and inspired by the fire of what he saw before him.

She stood straight with her back against a tree's trunk, her hands behind her, her eyes gazing before. She was tall and strong as young Diana; under the shadow of her Cavalier hat, her rich-tinted face was in splendid gloom, it seeming gloom, not only because her hair was like night, and her long and wide eyes black, but because in her far-off look there was gloom's self and somewhat like a hopeless rebellious yearning. She seemed a storm embodied in the form of woman, and yet in her black eyes' depths—as if hid behind their darkest shadows and unknown of by her very self—there lay the possibility of a great and strange melting—a melting which was all woman—and woman who was queen.

"By the Lord!" cried Tom Tantillion again, and then flushed up boyishly and broke forth into an awkward laugh. "She is too magnificent a beauty for an empty-pocketed rascal like me to offer to buy her. I have not what would pay for her—and she knows it. She sets her own price upon herself, as she stands there curling her vermilion lip and daring a man to presume to buy her cheap. 'Tis only a great Duke's son who may make bold to bid." And he turned and bowed, half laughing, half malicious, to Roxholm. "You, my lord Marquess; a purse as full as yours need not bargain for the thing it would have, but clap down guineas for it."

"A great Duke's son!" "My lord Marquess!" The owner of the picture began to prick up his ears. Yes, the truth was what he had thought it.

"The gentleman who owns this picture when the young lady comes up to town that the world may behold her," he said, "will be a proud man."

"No gentleman would have the right to keep it if he had not her permission," said Roxholm—and he said it without lightness.

"Most gentlemen would keep it whether she would or no," answered the painter.

"Catch Langdon or Wyse giving it up," says Tom. "And Wyse said, that blackguard Oxon was coming to see it because he hath made a bet on her in open club, and hearing of the picture, said he would come to see if she were worth his trouble—and buy her to hang in his chambers, if she were—that he might tell her of it when he went to Gloucestershire to lay siege to her. He brags he will persuade her he has prayed to her image for a year."

"What is your price?" said my Lord Roxholm to the painter.

The man set one and 'twas high though 'twould not have seemed so in an age when art was patronised and well paid for in a country where 'twas more generously encouraged than in England in the days of good Queen Anne. In truth, the poor fellow did not expect to get half he asked, but hoped by beginning well to obtain from a Duke's son twice what another gentleman would give him—and he was prepared to haggle, if need be, for two hours.

But my lord Marquess did not haggle. There had come into his countenance the look of a man who has made up his mind to take the thing he wants. He drew forth his purse and paid down the sum in golden guineas and bank-notes, the painter's eyes gloating as they were counted on the table and his head growing giddy with his joy. He would have enough to live drunk for a year, after his own economical methods. A garret—and drink enough—were all he required for bliss. The picture was to be sent forthwith to Osmonde House, and these directions given, the two gentlemen turned to go. But at the door the Marquess paused and spoke again.

"If any should come here before it is sent to me," he said, "remember that 'tis already purchased and not on exhibition."

The artist bowed low a dozen times.

"On my sacred honour, your lordship," he replied, "none shall see it."

Roxholm regarded him for a moment as if a new thought had presented itself to his mind.

"And remember also," he added, "if any should ask you to try to paint a copy from memory—or to lie in wait for the young lady again and make another—'tis better"—and his voice had in it both meaning and command—"'tis far better to please a patron, than a purchaser who has a momentary caprice. Live soberly and do honest work—and bring to me what is worthy of inspection. You need not starve unless 'tis your wish."

"My lord Marquess," cried the man; "your noble lordship," and he made as if he would fall upon his knees.

Roxholm made a gesture towards the picture, still in its place upon the crazy chair.

"I told you that was no daub," he said. "A man who can do that much can do more if he has the spirit."

And his visitors went out and left the artist in his garret, the stormy handsome creature gazing into space on one side, the guineas and bank-notes on the dusty table; and after having reflected upon both for a little space, he thrust his head out of the door and called for his landlady, who having beheld two richly clad gentlemen come from the attic, was inclined to feel it safe to be civil, and answering his summons went up to him, and being called in, was paid her long unpaid dues from the little heap on the table, the seeing of which riches almost blinded her and sent her off willingly to the pawnbroker's to bring back the pledged breeches and coat and linen.

"The tall gentleman with so superb an air," the poor man said, proudly, trembling with triumphant joy, "is my lord Marquess of Roxholm, and he is the heir of the ducal house of Osmonde, and promises me patronage."

When they passed out into the street and were on their way to St. James's Park, Tom Tantillion was in a state of much interested excitement.

"What shall you do with it, Roxholm?" he asked. "Have it set in a rich gold frame and hung up on the gallery at Osmonde House—or in the country? Good Lord! I dare not have carried her to my lodgings if I could have bought her. She would be too high company for me and keep me on my best manners too steady. A man dare not play the fool with such a creature staring at him from the wall. 'Tis only a man who is a hero, and a stately mannered one, who could stay in the same room with her without being put out of countenance. Will she rule in the gallery in town or in the country?"

"She will not be framed or hung, but laid away," answered Roxholm. "I bought her that no ill-mannered rake or braggart should get her and be insolent to her in her own despite when she could not strike him to his knees and box his ears, as she did the Chaplain's—being only a woman painted on canvas." And he showed his white, strong teeth a little in a strange smile.

"What!" cried Tom. "You did not buy her for your own pleasure——?"

The Marquess stopped with a sudden movement.

"On my faith!" he exclaimed, "there is the Earl of Dunstanwolde. He sees us and comes towards us."

77

CHAPTER XIII

"Your—Grace!"

"Come with me, Gerald, to Dunstan's Wolde," said my lord, as they sat together that night in his town-house. "I would have your company if you will give it me until you rejoin Marlborough. I am lonely in these days."

His lordship did not look his usual self, seeming, Roxholm thought, worn and sometimes abstracted. He was most kind and affectionate, and there was in his manner a paternal tenderness and sympathy which the young man was deeply touched by. If it had been possible for him to have spoken to any living being of the singular mental disturbance he had felt beginning in him of late, he could have confessed it to Lord Dunstanwolde. But nature had created in him a tendency to silence and reserve where his own feelings were concerned. As to most human beings there is a consolation in pouring forth the innermost secret thoughts at times, to him there was support in the knowledge that he held all within his own breast and could reflect upon his problems in sacred privacy. At this period, indeed, his feelings were such as he could scarcely have described to any one. He was merely conscious of a sort of unrest and of being far from comprehending his own emotions. They were, indeed, scarcely definite enough to be called emotions, but only seemed shadows hovering about him and causing him vaguely to wonder at their existence. He was neither elated nor depressed, but found himself confronting fancies he had not confronted before, and at times regarding the course of events with something of the feeling of a fatalist. There was a thing it seemed from which he could not escape, yet in his deepest being was aware that he would have preferred to avoid it. No man wishes to encounter unhappiness; he was conscious remotely that this preference for avoidance arose from a vaguely defined knowledge that in one direction there lay possibilities of harsh suffering and pain.

"'Tis a strange thing," he said to himself, "how I seem forbid by Fate to avoid the path of this strange wild creature. My Lord Marlborough brings her up to me at his quarters, I leave them; and going to my own, meet with Tantillion and his letter; I enter a coffee-house and hear wild talk of her; I go to my own house and my mother paints a picture of her which stirs my very depths; I walk in the streets of London and am dragged aside to find myself gazing at her portrait; I leave it, and meet my Lord Dunstanwolde, who prays me to go to Warwickshire, where I shall be within a few miles of her and may encounter her any hour. What will come next?"

That which came next was not unlike what had gone before. On their journey to Warwickshire my Lord Dunstanwolde did not speak of the lovely hoyden, whereat Roxholm somewhat wondered, as his lordship had but lately left her neighbourhood and her doings seemed the county's scandal; but 'tis true that on their journey he conversed little and seemed full of thought.

"Do not think me dull, Gerald," he said; "'tis only that of late I have begun to feel that I am an older man than I thought—perhaps too old to be a fit companion for youth. An old fellow should not give way to fancies. I—I have been giving way."

"Nay, nay, my dear lord," said Roxholm with warm feeling, "'tis to fancy you should give way—and 'tis such as you who are youths' best companions, since you bring to those of fewer years ripeness which is not age, maturity which is not decay. What man is there of twenty-eight with whom I could ride to the country with such pleasure as I feel to-day. You have lived too much alone of late. 'Tis well I came to Warwickshire."

This same evening after they had reached their journey's end, on descending to the saloon before dinner, his guest found my lord standing before the portrait of his lost wife and gazing at it with a strange tender intentness, his hands behind his back. He turned at Roxholm's entrance, and there were shadows in his eyes.

"Such an one as she," he said, "would forgive a man—even if he seemed false—and would understand. But none could be false to her—or forget." And so speaking walked away, the portrait seeming to follow him with its young flower-blue eyes.

'Twas the same evening Lord Twemlow rode over from his estate to spend the night with them, and they were no sooner left with their wine than he broke forth into confidence and fretting.

"I wanted to talk to thee, Edward," he said to Dunstanwolde (they had been boys together). "I am so crossed these days that I can scarce bear my own company. 'Tis that young jade again, and I would invent some measures to be taken."

"Ay, 'tis she again, I swear," had passed through Roxholm's mind as he looked at his wineglass, and that instant his lordship turned on him almost testily to explain.

"I speak of a kinswoman who is the bane and disgrace of my life, as she would be the bane and disgrace of any gentleman who was of her family," he said. "A pretty fool and baby who was my cousin married a reprobate, Jeof Wildairs, and this is his daughter and is a shameless baggage. Egad! you must have seen her on the hunting-field when you were with us—riding in coat and breeches and with her mane of hair looped under her hat."

"I saw her," Roxholm answered—and it seemed to him that as he spoke he beheld again the scarlet figure fly over the hedge on its young devil of a horse—and felt his heart leap as the horse did.

My Lord Dunstanwolde looked grave and pushed his glass back and forth on the mahogany. Glancing at him Roxholm thought his cheek had flushed, as if he did not like the subject. But Twemlow went on, growing hotter.

"One day in the field," he said, "it broke from its loop—her hair—and fell about her like a black mantle, streaming over her horse's back, and a sight it was—and damn it, so was she; and every man in the field shouting with pleasure or laughter. And she snatched her hat off with an oath and sat there as straight as a dart, but in a fury and winding her coils up, with her cheeks as scarlet as her coat and cursing like a young vagabond stable-boy between her teeth."

Dunstanwolde moved suddenly and almost overset his glass, but Roxholm took his up and drained it with an unmoved countenance.

But he could see her sitting in her black hair, and could see, too, the splendid scarlet on her angry cheek, and her eyes flashing wickedly.

"'Tis not decent," cried Lord Twemlow, striking the table with his hand. "If the baggage were not what she is, it would be bad enough, but there is not a woman in England built so. 'Tis well Charles Stuart is not on the throne, or she would outdo any Castlemaine that ever ruled him. And 'tis well that Louis is in France and that Maintenon keeps him sober. She might retrieve her house's fortunes and rule at Court a Duchess; but what decent man will look at her with her Billingsgate and her breeches? A nice lady she would make for a gentleman! Any modest snub-nosed girl would be better. There is scarce a week passes she does not set the country by the ears with some fury or frolic. One time 'tis clouting a Chaplain till his nose bleeds; next 'tis frightening some virtuous woman of fashion into hysteric swooning with her impudent flaming tongue. The women hate her, and she pays them out as she only can. Lady Maddon had fits for an hour, after an encounter with her, in their meeting by chance one day at a mercer's in the county town. She has the wit of a young she-devil and the temper of a tigress, and is so tall, and towers so that she frightens them out of their senses."

My lord Marquess looked at him across the table.

"She is young," he said, "she is beautiful. Is there no man who loves her who can win her from her mad ways?"

"Man!" cried Twemlow, raging, "every scoundrel and bumpkin in the shire is mad after her, but she knows none who are not as bad as she—and they tell me she laughs her wild, scornful laugh at each of them and looks at him—standing with her hands in her breeches pockets and her legs astride, and mocks as if she were some goddess instead of a mere strapping, handsome vixen. 'There is not one of ye,' she says, 'not one among ye who is man and big enough!' Such impudence was never yet in woman born! And the worst on't is, she is right—damn her!—she's right."

"Yes," said my Lord Dunstanwolde with a clouded face. "'Tis a Man who would win her—young and beautiful and strong—strong!"

"She needs a master!" cried Twemlow.

"Nay," said Roxholm—"a mate."

"Mate, good Lord!" cried Twemlow, again turning to stare at him. "A master, say I."

"'Tis a barbaric fancy," said Roxholm thoughtfully as he turned the stem of his glass, keeping his eyes fixed on it as though solving a problem for himself. "A barbaric fancy that a woman needs a master. She who is strong enough is her own conqueror—as a man should be master of himself."

"No gentleman will take her if she does not mend her ways," Lord Twemlow said, hotly; "and with all these country rakes about her she will slip—as more decently bred girls have. All eyes are set upon her, waiting for it. She has so drawn every gaze upon her, that her scandal will set ablaze a light that will flame like a beacon-fire from a hill-top. She will repent her bitterly enough then. None will spare her. She will be like a hare let loose with every pack in the county set upon her to hunt her to her death."

"Ah!"—the exclamation broke forth as if involuntarily from my Lord Dunstanwolde, and Roxholm, turning with a start, saw that he had suddenly grown pale.

"You are ill!" he cried. "You have lost colour!"

"No! No!" his lordship answered hurriedly, and faintly smiling. "'Tis over! 'Twas but a stab of pain." And he refilled his glass with wine and drank it.

"You live too studious a life, Ned," said Twemlow. "You have looked but poorly this month or two."

"Do not let us speak of it," Lord Dunstanwolde answered, a little hurried, as before. "What—what is it you think to do—or have you yet no plan?"

"If she begins her fifteenth year as she has lived the one just past," said my lord, ruffling his periwig in his annoyance, "I shall

81

send my Chaplain to her father to give him warning. We are at such odds that if I went myself we should come to blows, and I have no mind either to be run through or to drive steel through his thick body. He would have her marry, I would swear, and counts on her making as good a match as she can make without going to Court, where he cannot afford to take her. I shall lay command on Twichell to put the case clear before him—that no gentleman will pay her honourable court while he so plays the fool as to let her be the scandal of Gloucestershire—aye, and of Worcestershire and Warwickshire to boot. That may stir his liquor-sodden brain and set him thinking."

"How—will she bear it?" asked his Lordship of Dunstanwolde. "Will not her spirit take fire that she should be so reproved?"

"'Twill take fire enough, doubtless—and be damned to it!" replied my Lord Twemlow, hotly. "She will rage and rap out oaths like a trooper, but if Jeof Wildairs is the man he used to be, he will make her obey him, if he chooses—or he will break her back."

"'Twould be an awful battle," said Roxholm, "between a will like hers and such a brute as he, should her choice not be his."

"Ay, he is a great blackguard," commented Twemlow, coolly enough. "England scarcely holds a bigger than Jeoffry Wildairs, and he has had the building of her, body and soul."

'Twas not alone my Lord Twemlow who talked of her, but almost every other person, so it seemed. Oftenest she was railed at and condemned, the more especially if there were women in the party discussing her; but 'twas to be marked that at such times as men were congregated and talked of her faults and beauties, more was said of her charms than her sins. They fell into relating their stories of her, even the soberest of them, as if with a sense of humour in them, as indeed the point of such anecdotes was generally humorous because of a certain piquant boldness and lawless wild spirit shown in them. The story of the Chaplain, Roxholm heard again, and many others as fantastic. The retorts of this young female Ishmael upon her detractors and assailers, on such rare occasions as she encountered them, were full of a wit so biting and so keen that they were more than any dared to face when it could be avoided. But she was so bold and ingenious, and so ready with devices, that few could escape her. Her companionship with her father's cronies had given her a curious knowledge of the adventures which took place in three counties, at least, and her brain was so alert and her memory so unusual that she was enabled to confront an enemy with such adroitly arranged circumstantial evidence that more than one poor beauty would far rather have faced a loaded cannon than found herself within the immediate

82

neighbourhood of the mocking and flashing eyes. Her meeting in the mercer's shop with the fair "Willow Wand," Lady Maddon, had been so full of spirited and pungent truth as to drive her ladyship back to London after her two hours' fainting fits were over.

"Look you, my lady," she had ended, in her clear, rich girl-voice—and to every word she uttered the mercer and his shopmen and boys had stood listening behind their counters or hid round bales of goods, all grinning as they listened—"I know all your secrets as I know the secrets of other fine ladies. I know and laugh at them because they show you to be such fools. They are but fine jokes to me. My morals do not teach me to pray for you or blame you. Your tricks are your own business, not another woman's, and I would have told none of them—not one—if you had not lied about me. I am not a woman in two things: I wear breeches and I know how to keep my mouth shut as well as if 'twere padlocked; but you lied about me when you told the story of young Lockett and me. 'Twas a damned lie, my lady. Had it been true none would have known of it, and he must have been a finer man—with more beauty and more wit. But as for the thing I tell you of Sir James—and your meeting at——"

But here the fragile "Willow Wand" shrieked and fell into her first fit, not having strength to support herself under the prospect of hearing the story again with further and more special detail.

"I hear too much of her," Roxholm said to himself at last. "She is in the air a man breathes, and seems to get into his veins and fly to his brain." He suddenly laughed a short laugh, which even to himself had a harsh sound. "'Tis time I should go back to Flanders," he said, "and rejoin his Grace of Marlborough."

He had been striding over the hillsides all morning with his gun over his shoulder, and had just before he spoke thrown himself down to rest. He had gone out alone, his mood pleasing itself best with solitude, and had lost his way and found himself crossing strange land. Being wearied and somewhat out of sorts, he had flung himself down among the heather and bracken, where he was well out of sight, and could lie and look up at the gray of the sky, his hands clasped beneath his head.

"Yes, 'twill be as well that I go back to Flanders," he said again, somewhat gloomily; and as he spoke he heard voices on the fall of the hill below him, and glancing down through the gorse bushes, saw approaching his resting-place four sportsmen who looked as fatigued as himself.

He did not choose to move, thinking they would pass him, and as they came nearer he recognised them one by one, having by this time been long enough in the neighbourhood to have learned both names and faces. They were of the Wildairs crew, and one man's

83

face enlightened him as to whose estate he trespassed upon, the owner of the countenance being a certain Sir Christopher Crowell, a jolly drunken dog whose land he had heard was somewhere in the neighbourhood. The other two men were a Lord Eldershawe and Sir Jeoffry Wildairs himself, while the tall stripling with them 'twas easy to give a name to, though she strode over the heather with her gun on her shoulder and as full a game-bag as if she had been a man—it being Mistress Clorinda, in corduroy and with her looped hair threatening to break loose and hanging in disorder about her glowing face. They were plainly in gay humour, though wearied, and talked and laughed noisily as they came.

"We have tramped enough," cried Sir Jeoffry, "and bagged birds enough for one morning. 'Tis time we rested our bones and put meat and drink in our bellies."

He flung himself down upon the heather and the other men followed his example. Mistress Clo, however, remaining standing, at first leaning upon her gun.

My lord Marquess gazed down at her from his ledge and shut his teeth in anger at the mounting of the blood to his cheek and its unseemly burning there.

"I will stay where I am and look at her, at least," he said. "To be looked at does no woman harm, and to look at one can harm no man—if he be going to Flanders."

That which disturbed him most was his realising that he always thought of her as a woman—and also that she was a woman and no child. 'Twas almost impossible to believe she was no older than was said, when one beheld her height and youthful splendour of body and bearing. He knew no woman of twenty as tall as she and shaped with such strength and fineness. Her head was set so on her long throat and her eyes so looked out from under her thick jet lashes, that in merely standing erect she seemed to command and somewhat disdain; but when she laughed, her red lips curling, her little strong teeth gleaming, and her eyes opening and flashing mirth, she was the archest, most boldly joyous creature a man had ever beheld. Her morning's work on the moors had made her look like young Nature's self, her cheek was burnt rich-brown and crimson, her disordered hair twined in big rough rings about her forehead, her movements were as light, alert, and perfect as if she had been a deer or any wild thing of the woods or fields. There was that about her that made Roxholm feel that she must exhale in breath and hair and garments the scent of gorse and heather and fern and summer rains.

As one man gazed at her so did the others, though they were

84

his elders and saw her often, while he was but twenty-eight and had beheld her but once before.

Each man of the party took from his pouch a small but well-filled packet of food and a flask, and fell to upon their contents voraciously, talking as they worked their jaws and joking with Mistress Clo. She also brought forth her own package, which held bread and meat, and a big russet apple, upon she set with a fine appetite. 'Twas good even to see her eat, she did it with such healthy pleasure, as a young horse might have taken his oats or a young setter his supper after a day in the cover.

"Thou'rt not tired, Clo!" cries Eldershawe, laughing, as she fell upon her russet apple, biting into it crisply, and plainly with the pleasure of a hungry child.

"Not I, good Lord!" she answered. "Could shoot over as many miles again."

"When thou'rt fifty years old, wilt not be so limber and have such muscles," said Sir Jeoffry.

"She hath not so long to wait," said the third man, grinning. "Wast not fourteen in November, Clo? Wilt soon be a woman."

She bit deep into her fruit and stared out over the moors below.

"Am not going to be a woman," she said. "I hate them."

"They hate thee," said Eldershawe, with a chuckle, "and will hate thee worse when thou wearest brocades and a farthingale."

"I have watched them," proceeded Mistress Clo. "They cannot keep their mouths shut. If they have a secret they must tell it, whether 'tis their own or another's. They clack, they tell lies, they cry and scream out if they are hurt; but they will hurt anything which cannot hurt them back. They run and weep to each other when they are in love and a man slights them. They have no spirit and no decency." She said it with such an earnest solemnness that her companions shouted with laughter.

"She sits in her breeches—the unruliest baggage in Gloucestershire," cried Eldershawe, "and complains that fine ladies are not decent. What would they say if they heard thee?"

"They may hear me when they will," said Mistress Clo, springing to her feet with a light jump and sending the last of her apple whizzing into space with a boyish throw. "'Tis I who am the modest woman—for all my breeches and manners. I do not see indecency where there is none—for the mere pleasure of ogling and bridling and calling attention to my simpering. I should have seen no reason for airs and graces if I had been among those on the bank when the fine young Marquess we heard of saved the boat-load on the river and gave orders for the reviving of the drowned man—in

85

his wet skin. When 'tis spoke of—for 'tis a favourite story—that little beast Tantillion hides her face behind her fan and cries, 'Oh, Lud! thank Heaven I was not near. I should have swooned away at the very sight.'"

She imitated the affected simper of a girl in such a manner that the three sportsmen yelled with delight, and Roxholm himself gnawed his lip to check an involuntary break into laughter.

"What didst say to her the day she bridled over it at Knepton, when the young heir was there?" said Crowell, grinning. "I was told thou disgraced thyself, Clo. What saidst thou?"

She was standing her full straight height among them and turned, with her hands in her pockets and a grave face.

"My blood was hot," she answered. "I said, 'Damn thee for a lying little fool!' That thou wouldst not!"

And the men who lay on the ground roared till they rolled there, and Roxholm gnawed his lip again, though not all from mirth, for there was in his mind another thing. She did not laugh but stood in the same position, but now looking out across the country spread below.

"I shall love no man who will scorn me," she continued in her mellow voice; "but if I did I would be burned alive at the stake before I would open my lips about it. And I would be burned alive at the stake before I would play tricks with my word or break my promise when 'twas given. Women think they can swear a thing and unswear it, to save or please themselves. They give themselves to a man and then repent it and are slippery. If I had given myself, and found I had been a fool, I would keep faith. I would play no tricks— even though I learned to hate him. No, I will not be a woman."

And she picked up her gun and strode away, and seeing this they rose all three by one accord, as if she were their chieftain, and followed her.

After they were gone my lord Marquess did not move for some time, but lay still among the gorse and bracken at his full length, his hands clasped behind his head. He gazed up into the grey sky with the look of a man whose thoughts are deep and strange. But at last he rose, and picking up his gun, shouldered it and strode forth on his way back to Dunstan's Wolde, which was miles away.

"Yes," he said, speaking aloud to himself, "I will go back and follow his Grace of Marlborough for a while on his campaign—but in two years' time I will come back—to Gloucestershire—and see what time has wrought."

But to Flanders he did not go, nor did my Lord Duke of Marlborough see him for many a day, for Fate, which had so long steadily driven him, had ordained it otherwise. When he reached

Dunstan's Wolde, on crossing the threshold, something in the faces of the lacqueys about the entrance curiously attracted his attention. He thought each man he glanced at or spoke to looked agitated and as if there were that on his mind which so scattered his wits that he scarce knew how to choose his speech. The younger ones stammered and, trying to avoid his eye, seemed to step out of his view as hastily as possible. Those of maturer years wore grave and sorrowful faces, and when, on passing through the great hall upon which opened the library and drawing-rooms he encountered the head butler, the man started back and actually turned pale.

"What has happened?" his lordship demanded, his wonder verging in alarm. "Something has come about, surely. What is it, man? Tell me! My Lord Dunstanwolde—"

The man was not one whose brain worked quickly. 'Twas plain he lost his wits, being distressed for some reason beyond measure. He stepped to the door of the library and threw it open.

"My—my lord awaits your—your lordship—Grace," and then in an uncertain and low voice he announced him in the following strange manner:

"His—lordship—his Grace—has returned, my lord," he said.

And Roxholm, suddenly turning cold and pale himself, and seized upon by a horror of he knew not what, saw as in a dream my lord Dunstanwolde advancing towards him, his face ashen with woe, tears on his cheeks, his shaking hands outstretched as if in awful pity.

"My poor Gerald," he broke forth, one hand grasping his, one laid on his shoulder. "My poor lad—God help me—that I am no more fit to break to you this awful news."

"For God's sake!" cried Gerald, and sank into the chair my lord drew him to, where he sat himself down beside him, the tears rolling down his lined cheeks.

"Both—both your parents!" he cried. "God give me words! Both—both! At Pisa where they had stopped—a malignant fever. Your mother first—and within twelve hours your father! Praise Heaven they were not parted. Gerald, my boy!"

My lord Marquess leaned forward, his elbow sank on his knee, his forehead fell heavily upon his palm and rested there. He felt as if a blow had been struck upon his head, which he moved slowly, seeing nothing before him.

"Both! Both!" he murmured. "The happiest woman in England! Have you been happy? I would hear you say it again— before I leave you! Ay," shaking his head, "that was why the poor fool said, 'Your Grace.'"

CHAPTER XIV

"For all her youth—there is no other woman like her"

They were brought back in state from Italy and borne to their beloved Camylott, to sleep in peace there, side by side; and the bells in the church-tower tolled long and mournfully, and in the five villages in different shires there was not a heart which did not ache—nor one which having faith did not know that somewhere their happy love lived again and was more full of joy than it had been before. And my lord Marquess was my lord Duke; but for many months none beheld him but Lord Dunstanwolde, who came to Camylott with many great people to attend the funeral obsequies; but when all the rest went away he stayed, and through the first strange black weeks the two were nearly always together, and often, through hours, walked in company from one end of the Long Gallery to the other.

Over such periods of sorrow and bereavement it is well to pass gently, since they must come to all, and have so come through all the ages past, to every human being who has lived to maturity; and yet, at the same time, there is none can speak truly for another than himself of what the suffering has been or how it has been borne. None but the one who bears it can know what hours of anguish the endurance cost and how 'twas reached.

My lord Duke looked pale in his mourning garments, and for many months his countenance seemed sharper cut, his eyes looking deeper set and larger, having faint shadows round them, but even Lord Dunstanwolde knew but few of his inmost thoughts, and to others he never spoke of his bereavement.

The taking possession of a great estate, and the first assuming of the responsibilities attached to it, are no small events, and bring upon the man left sole heir numberless new duties, therefore the new Duke had many occupations to attend to—much counselling with his legal advisers, many interviews with stewards, bailiffs, and holders of his lands, visits to one estate after another, and converse with the reverend gentlemen who were the spiritual directors of his people. Such duties gave him less time for brooding than he would have had upon his hands had he been a man more thoughtless of what his responsibilities implied, and, consequently, more willing to permit them to devolve upon those in his employ.

"A man should himself know all things pertaining to his

belongings," the new Duke said to Lord Dunstanwolde, "and all those who serve him should be aware that he knows, and that he will no more allow his dependents to cheat or slight him than he himself will stoop to carelessness or dishonesty in his dealings with themselves. To govern well, a man must be ruler as well as friend."

And this he was to every man in his five villages, and those who had worshipped him as their master's heir loved and revered him as their master.

The great Marlborough wrote a friendly letter expressing his sympathy for him in the calamity by which he had been overtaken, and also his regret at the loss of his services and companionship, he having at once resigned his commission in the army on the occurrence of his bereavement, not only feeling desirous of remaining in England, but finding it necessary to do so.

He spent part of the year upon his various estates in the country, but quarrels of Whigs and Tories, changes in the Cabinet, and the bitter feeling against the march into Germany and the struggles which promised to result, gave him work to do in London and opportunities for the development of those abilities his Grace of Marlborough had marked in him. The air on all sides was heavy with storm—at Court the enemies of Duchess Sarah (and they were many, whether they confessed themselves or not) were prognosticating her fall from her high post of ruler of the Queen of England, and her lord from his pinnacle of fame; there were high Tories and Jacobites who did not fear to speak of the scaffold as the last stage likely to be reached by the greatest military commander the country had ever known in case his march into Germany ended in disaster. There were indeed questions so momentous to be pondered over that for long months my lord Duke had but little time for reflection upon those incidents which had disturbed him by appearing to result from the workings of persistent Fate.

But in a locked cabinet in his private closet there lay a picture which sometimes, as it were, despite himself, he took from its hiding-place to look upon; and when he found himself gazing at the wondrous face of storm, with its great stag's eyes, he knew that the mere sight waked in him the old tumult and that it did not lose its first strange, unexplained power. And once sitting studying the picture, his thought uttered itself aloud, his voice curiously breaking upon the stillness of the room.

"It is," he said, "as if that first hour a deep chord of music had been struck—a stormy minor chord—and each time I hear of her or see her the same chord is struck loud again, and never varies by a note. I swear there is a question in her eyes—and I—I could answer it. Yet, for my soul's sake, I must keep away."

He knew honour itself demanded this of him, for the stories which came to his ears were each wilder and more fantastic than the other, and sometimes spoke strange evil of her—of her violent temper, of her wicked tongue, of her outraging of all customs and decencies, but, almost incredible as it seemed, none had yet proved that her high spirit and proud heart had been subjugated and she made victim by a conqueror. 'Twas this which was talked of at the clubs and coffee-houses, where her name was known by those frequenting them.

"She would be like a hare let loose to be hounded to her death by every pack in the county," my Lord Twemlow had said the night he talked of her at Dunstan's Wolde, and every man agreed with him and waited for the outburst of a scandal, and made bets as to when it would break forth. There were those among the successful heart-breakers whose vanity was piqued by the existence of so invincible and fantastical a female creature, and though my lord Duke did not hear of it, their worlds being far apart, the male beauty and rake, Sir John Oxon, was among them, his fretted pride being so well known among his fellow-beaux that 'twas their habit to make a joke of it and taunt him with their witticisms.

"She is too big a devil," they said, "to care a fig for any man. She would laugh in the face of the mightiest lady-killer in London, and flout him as if he were a mercer's apprentice or a plough-boy. He does not live who could trap her."

With most of them, the noble sport of chasing women was their most exalted pastime. They were like hunters on the chase of birds, the man who brought down the rarest creature of the wildest spirit and the brightest plumage was the man who was a hero for a day at least.

The winter my lord Duke of Marlborough spent at Hanover, Berlin, Vienna, and the Hague, engaged in negotiations and preparations for his campaign, and at Vienna his Grace of Osmonde joined him that they might talk face to face, even the great warrior's composure being shaken by the disappointment of the year. But a fortnight before his leaving England there came to Osmonde's ear rumours of a story from Gloucestershire—'twas of a nature more fantastic than any other, and far more unexpected. The story was imperfectly told and without detail, and detail no man or woman seemed able to acquire, and baffled curiosity ran wild, no story having so whetted it as this last.

"But we shall hear later," said one, "for 'tis said Jack Oxon was there, being on a visit to his kinsman, Lord Eldershawe, who has been the young lady's playmate from her childhood. Jack will come back primed and will strut about for a week and boast of his fortunes whether he can prove them or not."

But this Osmonde did not hear, having already left town for a few days at Camylott, where my Lord Dunstanwolde accompanied him, and at the week's end they went together to Warwickshire, and as on the occasion of Osmonde's other visit, the first evening they were at the Wolde came my Lord Twemlow, more excited than ever before, and he knew and told the whole story.

"Things have gone from bad to worse," he said, "and at last I sent my Chaplain as I had planned, and the man came back frightened out of his wits, having reached the hall-door in a panic and there found himself confronted by what he took to be a fine lad in hunting-dress making his dog practise jumping tricks. And 'twas no lad, of course, but my fine mistress in her boy's clothes, and she takes him to her father and makes a saucy jest of the whole matter, tossing off a tankard of ale as she sits on the table laughing at him and keeping Sir Jeoffry from breaking his head in a rage. And in the end she sends an impudent message to me—but says I am right, the shrewd young jade, and that she will see that no disgrace befalls me. But for all that, the Chaplain came home in a cold sweat, poor fool, and knows not what to say when he speaks of her."

"And then?" said my Lord Dunstanwolde, somewhat anxiously, "is it true—that which we heard rumoured in town——"

Lord Twemlow shook his head ruefully. "Heaven knows how it will end," he said, "or if it is but a new impudent prank—or what she will do next—but the whole country is agog with the story. She bade her father invite his rapscallion crew to her birthnight supper, and says 'tis that they may see her in breeches for the last time, for she will wear them no more, but begin to live a sober, godly, and virtuous life and keep a Chaplain of her own. And on the twenty-fourth night of November, she turning fifteen, they gather prepared for sport, and find her attired like a young prince, in pink satin coat and lace ruffles and diamond buckles and powder; more impudent and handsome than since she was born. And when the drinking sets in heavily, upon her chair she springs and stands laughing at the company of them.

"'Look your last on my fine shape,' she cries, 'for after to-night you'll see no more of it. From this I am a fine lady,' and sings a song and drinks a toast and breaks her glass on the floor and runs away."

At a certain period of my Lord Twemlow's first story, the night he told it, both his Lordship of Dunstanwolde and the then Marquess of Roxholm had made unconscious movements as they heard—this had happened when had been described the falling of the mantle of black hair and the little oaths with which Mistress

Clorinda had sat on her hunter binding it up—and at this point—at this other picture of the audacious beauty and her broken glass each man almost started again—my Lord Dunstanwolde indeed suddenly rising and taking a step across the hearth.

"What a story," he said. "On my soul!"

"And 'tis not the end!" cried Lord Twemlow. "An hour she leaves them talking of her, wondering what she plans to do, and then the door is flung wide open and there she stands—splendid in crimson and silver and jewels, with a diadem on her head, and servants holding lights flaming above her."

My Lord Dunstanwolde turned about and looked at him as if the movement was involuntary, and Lord Twemlow ended with a blow upon the table, his elderly face aflame with appreciation of the dramatic thing he told.

"And makes them a great Court courtesy," he cried, his voice growing almost shrill, "and calls on them all to fall upon their knees, by God! 'for so,' she says, 'from this night all men shall kneel—all men on whom I deign to cast my eyes.'"

His Grace the Duke of Osmonde had listened silently, and throughout with an impenetrable face, but at this moment he put up his hand and slightly swept his brow with his fingers, as if he felt it damp.

"And now what does it mean?" my Lord Twemlow asked them, with an anxious face. "And how will it end? A fortnight later she appeared at church dressed like a lady of the Court, and attended by her sisters and their governess, as if she had never appeared unattended in her life, and prayed, good Lord, with such a majestic seriousness, and listened to the sermon with such a face as made the parson forget his text and fumble about for his notes in dire confusion. 'Twas thought she might be going to play some trick to cause him to break down in the midst of his discourse. But she did not, and sailed out of church as if she had never missed a sermon since she was born."

"Perhaps," said my Lord Dunstanwolde, "perhaps her mind has changed and 'tis true she intends to live more gravely."

"Nay," answered Lord Twemlow, with a troubled countenance. "No such good fortune. She doth not intend to keep it up—and how could she if she would? A girl who hath lived as she hath, seeing no decent company and with not a woman about her—though for that matter they say she has the eye of a hawk and the wit of a dozen women, and the will to do aught she chooses. But surely she could not keep it up!"

"Another woman could not," said Osmonde. "A woman who had not a clear, strong brain and a wondrous determination—a woman who was weak or a fool, or even as other women, could not. But surely—for all her youth—there is no other woman like her."

CHAPTER XV

"And 'twas the town rake and beauty—Sir John Oxon"

That night he lay almost till 'twas morning, his eyes open upon the darkness, since he could not sleep, finding it impossible to control the thoughts which filled his mind. 'Twas a night whose still long hours he never could forget in the years that followed, and 'twas not a memory which was a happy one. He passed through many a curious phase of thought, and more than once felt a pang of sorrow that he was now alone as he had never thought of being, and that if suffering came, his silent endurance of it must be a new thing. To be silent because one does not wish to speak is a different matter from being silent because one knows no creature dear and near enough to hear the story of one's trouble. He realised now that the tender violet eyes which death had closed would have wooed from his reserve many a thing it might have been good to utter in words.

"She would always have understood," he thought. "She understood when she cried out, 'It might have been!'"

He clasped his hands behind his head and lay so, smiling with mingled bitterness and joy.

"It has begun!" he said. "I have heard them tell of it—of how one woman's face came back again and again, of how one pair of eyes would look into a man's and would not leave him, nor let him rest. It has begun for me, too. For good or evil, it has begun."

Until this night he had told himself, and believed himself in the telling, that he had been strangely haunted by thoughts of a strange creature, because the circumstances by which she was encompassed were so unusual and romantic as would have lingered in the mind of any man whether old or young; and this he had been led to feel the more confident of, since he was but one of a dozen men, and indeed each one who knew of her existence appeared to regard her as the heroine of a play, though so far it was to them but

93

a rattling comedy. But from this night he knew a different thing, and realised that he was face to face with that mystery which all men do not encounter, some only meeting with the mere fleeting image of it and never knowing what the reality is—that mystery which may be man's damnation or his heaven, his torture and heart-sickening, or his life and strength and bliss. What his would bring to him, or bring him to, he knew not in the least, and had at times a pang at thought of it, but sometimes such a surge of joy as made him feel himself twice man instead of once.

When he went forth to ride the next day it was with a purpose clear in his mind. Hitherto all he had seen or heard had been by chance, but if he saw aught this morning 'twould be because he had hoped for and gone to meet it.

"Before I cross the sea," was his thought, "I would see her once again if chance so favors me. I would see if there seems any new thing in her face, and if there is—if this is no wild jest and comedy, but means that she has wakened to knowing herself a woman—I shall know when I see her eyes and can carry my thought away with me. Then when I come back—'twill be but a few months at the most—I will ride into Gloucestershire the first week I am on English soil, and I will go to her and ask that I may be her servant until she learns what manner of man I am and can tell me to go—or stay."

If Sir Jeoffry and his crew had dreamed that such a thought worked in the mind of one of the richest young noblemen in England—he a Duke and handsome enough to set any woman's heart beating—as he rode through the Gloucestershire lanes; if they had dreamed that such a thing was within the bounds of human possibility, what a tumult would have been roused among them; how they would have stared at each other, with mouths open, uttering exclamatory oaths of wild amazement and ecstatic triumph; how they would have exulted and drunk each other's healths and their wild playmate's and her splendid fortunes. But, in truth, that such a thing could be, would have seemed to them as likely as that Queen Anne herself should cast a gracious eye upon a poor, fox-hunting, country baronet who was one of her rustic subjects. The riot of Wildairs and its company was a far cry indeed from Camylott and St. James.

If my Lord Twemlow had guessed at the possibility of the strange thing, and had found himself confronting a solution of his carking problem which would flood its past with brilliance and illuminate all its future with refulgent light, casting a glow of splendour even over his own plain country gentleman's existence, how he would have started and flushed with bewildered pride and rubbed his periwig awry in his delighted excitement. If my Lord Dunstanwolde, sitting at that hour in his silent library, a great book open before him, his forehead on his slender veined hand, his thoughts wandering far away, if he had been given by Fate an inkling of the truth which none knew or suspected, or had reason for suspecting, perhaps he would have been the most startled and struck dumb of all—the most troubled and amazed and shocked.

But of such a thing no one dreamed, as, indeed, why should they, and my lord Duke of Osmonde rode over the border into Gloucestershire on his fine beast, and, trotting-up the roads and down the lanes, wore a look upon his face which showed him deep in thought.

'Twas a grey day, unbrightened by any sun. For almost a week there had been rain, and the roads were heavy and the lanes muddy and full of pools of miry water.

It was the intention of my lord Duke to let his horse carry him over such roads and lands as would be in the near neighbourhood of Wildairs, and while he recognised the similarity of his action to that of a school-boy in love, who paces the street before his sweetheart's dwelling, there was no smile at himself, either on his countenance or in his mind.

"I may see her," he said quietly to himself. "I am more like to catch sight of her on these roads than on any other, and, school-boy trick or not, 'twill serve, and if she passes will have won me what I long for—for it is longing, this. I know it now, and own it to myself."

And see her he did, but as is ever the case when a man has planned a thing, it befell as he had not thought of its happening— and 'twas over in a flash.

Down one of the wet lanes he had turned and was riding slowly when he heard suddenly behind him a horse coming at such a sharp gallop that he wheeled his own beast aside, the way being dangerously narrow, that so tempestuous a rider might tear by in safety. And as he turned and was half screened by the bushes, the rider swept past him splashing through the mire and rain-pools so that the muddy water flew up beneath the horses' hoofs—and 'twas the object of his thoughts herself!

She rode her tall young horse and was not clad as he had before beheld her, but in rich riding-coat and hat and sweeping feather. No maid of honour of her Majesty Queen Anne's rode attired more fittingly, none certainly with such a seat and spirit, and none, Heaven knew, looked like her.

These things he marked in a flash, not knowing he had marked them until afterwards, so strong and moving was his sudden feeling that in her nature at that moment there worked some strange new thing—some mood new to herself and angering her. Her brows were bent, her eyes were set and black with shadow. She bit her full lip as she rode, and her horse went like the wind. For but a moment she was through the lane and clattering on the road.

My lord Duke was breathing fast and bit his own lip, but the next second broke into a laugh, turning his horse, whose bridle he had caught up with a sudden gesture.

"Nay," he said, "a man cannot gallop after a lady without ceremony, and command her to stand and deliver as if he were a highwayman. Yet I was within an ace of doing it—within an ace. I have beheld her! I had best ride back to Dunstan's Wolde."

And so he did, at a hot pace; but if he had chanced to turn on the top of the hill he might have seen below him in a lane to the right that two rode together, and one was she whom he had but just seen, her companion a horseman who had leapt a gate in a field and joined her, with flushed cheeks and wooing eyes, though she had frowned—and 'twas the town rake and beauty, Sir John Oxon.

CHAPTER XVI

A Rumour

Through the passing of two years Osmonde's foot did not press English soil again, and his existence during that period was more vivid and changeful than it had ever been before. He saw Ramillies follow Blenheim, great Marlborough attain the height of renown, and French Louis's arrogant ambitions end in downfall and defeat. Life in both camp and Court he knew at its highest tension, brilliant scenes he beheld, strange ones, wicked ones, and lived a life so eventful and full of motion and excitement that there were few men who through its picturesque adventures would have been like to hold in mind one image and one thought. Yet this he did, telling himself that 'twas the thought which held him, not he the thought, it having been proven in the past 'twas one which would not have released him from its dominion even had he been inclined to withdraw himself from it. And this he was not. Nature had so built him, that on the day when he had found himself saying, "In two years' time I will come back to Gloucestershire and see what time has wrought," he had reached a point from which there was no retreating. Through many an hour in time past there had been turmoil in his mind, but in a measure, at least, this ended the uncertainties, and was no rash outburst but a resolve. It had not been made lightly, but had been like a plant which had grown from a seed, long hidden in dark earth and slowly fructifying till at last summer rain and warming sun had caused it to burst forth from its prison, a thing promising full fruit and flower. For long he had not even known the seed was in the soil; he had felt its stirrings before he had believed in its existence, and then one day the earth had broke and he had seen its life and known what its strength might be. 'Twould be of wondrous strength, he knew, and of wondrous beauty if no frost should blight nor storm uproot it.

In its freedom from all tendency to plaything-sentiments and trivial romances, his youth had been unlike the youth of other men. Being man and young, he had known temptation, but had disdained it; being also proud and perhaps haughty in his fastidiousness, and being strong, he had thrust base and light things aside. He had held in his brain a fancy from his boyhood, and singularly enough it had but grown stronger and become more fully formed with his own strength and increase of years. 'Twas a strange fancy indeed to fit the time he lived in, but 'twas his choice. The woman whose eyes held the answer to the question his own soul asked, and whose being asked the question to which his own replied, would bring great and deep joy to him—others did not count in his existence— and for her he had waited and longed, sometimes so fiercely, that he wondered if he was in the wrong and but following a haunting, mocking dream.

"You are an epicure, Osmonde," his Grace of Marlborough said more than once, for he had watched and studied him closely. "Not an anchorite but an epicure."

"Yes," answered Osmonde, "perhaps 'tis that. Any man can love a score of women—most men do—but there are few who can love but one, as I shall, if—" and the words came slowly—"if I ever find her."

"You may not," remarked his Grace.

"I may not," said Osmonde, and he smiled his faint, grim smile.

He could not have sworn when he returned to the Continent that he had found her absolutely at last. Her body he had found, but herself he had not approached nearly enough to know. But this thing he realised, that even in the mad stories he had heard, when they had been divested of their madness, the chief figure in them had always stood out an honest, strong, fair thing, dwarfed by no petty feminine weakness, nor follies, nor spites. Rules she broke, decorums she defied, but in such manner as hurt none but herself. She played no tricks and laid no plots for vengeance, as she might well have done; she but went her daring, lawless way, with her head up and her great eyes wide open; and 'twas her fearless frankness and just, clear wit which moved him more than aught else, since 'twas they which made him feel that 'twas not alone her splendid body commanded love, but a spirit which might mate with a strong man's and be companion to his own. His theories of womankind, which were indeed curiously in advance of his age, were such as demanded great things, and not alone demanded, but also gave them.

"A man and woman should not seem beings of a different race—the one all strength, the other all weakness," was his thought. "They should gaze into each other's eyes with honest, tender human passion, which is surely a great thing, as nature made it. Each should know the other's love, and strength, and honour may be trusted through death—or life—themselves. 'Tis not a woman's love is won by pretty gallantries, nor a man's by flattering weak surrender. Love grows from a greater thing, and should be as compelling—even in the higher, finer thing which thinks—as is the roar of the lion in the jungle to his mate, and her glad cry which answers him."

And therefore, at last he had said to himself that this beauteous, strong, wild thing surely might be she who would answer him one day, and he held his thoughts of her in check no more, nor avoided the speech he heard of her, and indeed, with adroitness which never betrayed itself through his reserve of bearing, at times encouraged it; and in a locked drawer in his apartments, wheresoever he travelled, there lay always the picture with the stormy, yearning eyes.

From young Tantillion he could, without any apparent approach at questioning, hear such details of Gloucestershire life in the neighbourhood of Wildairs as made him feel that he was not far separated from that which his mind dwelt on. Little Lady Betty, having entered the world of fashion, was more voluminous in her correspondence than ever, the more especially as young Langton appeared to her a very pretty fellow, and he being Tom's confidant, was likely to hear her letters read, or at least be given extracts from them. Her caustic condemnation of the fantastical Mistress Clo had gradually lapsed into a doubtful wonder, which later became open amaze not untinged with a pretty spitefulness and resentment.

"'Tis indeed a strange thing, and one to make one suspicious of her, Thomas," she wrote, "with all her bold ways, to suddenly put on such decorum. We are all sure 'tis from some cunning motive, and wait to find out what she will be at next. At first none believed she would hold out or would know how to behave herself, but Lud! if you could see her I am sure, Tom, both you and Mr. Langton would be disgusted by her majestic airs. Being dressed in woman's clothing she is taller than ever, and so holds her chin and her eyes that it makes any modist woman mad. If she was a Duchess at Court she could not be more stately than she now pretends she is (for of course it is pretence, as anyone knows). She has had the vile cunningness to stop her bad langwidg, as if she had never swore an oath in her life (such deseatfulness!). And none can tell where she hath learned her manners, for if you will beleave the thing, 'tis said she never makes a blunder, but can sweep a great curtsey and sail about a saloon full of company as if she was bred to it, and can dance a minuet and bear herself at a feast in a way to surprise you. Lady Maddon says that women who are very vile and undeserving are sometimes wickedly clever, and can pick up modist women's manners wondrously, but they always break out before long and are more indecent than ever; and you may mark my Lady Maddon's words, she says this one will do the same, but first she is playing a part and restraining herself that she may deseave some poor gentleman and trap him into marrying her. It makes Lady Maddon fall into a passion to talk of her, and she will flush quite red and talk so fast, but indeed after I see the creature or hear some new story of her impudent victories, I fall into a passion myself—for, Tom, no human being can put her in her place."

It must be confessed that the attitude of the recipient of these letters was by no means a respectful one, they being read and re-read with broad grins and frequent outbursts of roaring laughter, ending in derisive or admiring comments, even Bob Langton, who had no objection to pretty Lady Betty's oglings and summing of him as a dangerous beau, breaking forth into gleeful grinning himself.

"Hang me if some great nobleman won't marry her," cried Tom, "and a fine lady she'll make, too! Egad, it almost frightens one, for all the joke of it, to think of a woman who can do such things—to be a madder romp than any and suddenly to will that she will change in such a way, and hold herself firm and be beat by naught. 'Tis scarce human. Bet says that her kinsman, my Lord Twemlow, has took her in hand and is as proud of her and as fidgety as some match-making mother. And the county people who would not have spoke to her a year ago, have begun to visit Wildairs and invite her to their houses, for all the men are wild after her, and the best way to make an entertainment a fine thing is to let it be known that she will grace it. Even Sir Jeof and his cronies are taken in because they shine in her glory and are made decent by it."

"They say, too," cried Bob Langton, "that she makes them all behave themselves, telling them that unless their manners are decent they cannot follow her to the fine houses she is bid to—and she puts them through a drill and cuts off their drink and their cursings and wicked stories. And Gloucestershire and Warwickshire and Worcestershire are all agog with it!"

"And they follow her like slaves," added Tantillion, in an ecstacy, "and stand about with their mouths open to stare at her swimming though her minuets with bowing worshippers, and oh! Roxholm—nay, I should say Osmonde; but how can a man remember you are Duke instead of Marquis?—'tis told that in the field in her woman's hat and hunting-coat she is handsomer than ever. Even my Lord Dunstanwolde has rode to the meet to behold her, and admires her as far as a sober elderly gentleman can."

That my Lord Dunstanwolde admired her, Osmonde knew. His rare letters told a grave and dignified gentleman's version of the story and spoke of it with kindly courtesy and pleasure in it. It had proved that the change which had come over her had been the result of no caprice or mischievous spirit but of a reasonable intention, to which she had been faithful with such consistency of behaviour as filled the gossips and onlookers with amazement.

"'Tis my belief," said the kindly nobleman, "that being in truth a noble creature, though bred so wildly, the time came when she realised herself a woman, and both wit and heart told her that 'twas more honourable to live a woman's life and not a madcap boy's. And her intellect being of such vigour and fineness, she can execute what her thought conceives."

Among the gentlemen who were her courtiers there was much talk of the fashionable rake Sir John Oxon, who, having appeared at her birthnight supper, had become madly enamoured of her, and had stayed in the country at Eldershawe Park and laid siege to her with all his forces and with much fervour of feeling besides. 'Twas a thing well known that this successful rake had never lost his heart to a woman in his life before, and that his victims had all been snared by a part played to villanous perfection; but 'twas plain enough that at last he had met a woman who had set that which he called his soul on fire. He could not tear himself away from the country, though the gayeties of the town were at their highest. When in her presence his burning blue eyes followed her every movement, and when she treated him disdainfully he turned pale.

"But she leaves him no room for boasting," related young Tantillion. "He may worship as any man may, but she shows no

100

mercy to any, and him she treats with open scorn when he languishes. He grows thin and pale and is half-crazed with his passion for her."

There is no man who has given himself up to a growing passion and has not yet revealed it, who does not pass through many an hour of unrest. How could it be otherwise? In his absence from the object of his feeling every man who lives is his possible rival, every woman his possible enemy, every event a possible obstacle in the way to that he yearns for. And from this situation there is nothing which can save a man. He need not be a boy or a fool to be tormented despite himself; the wisest and gravest are victims to these fits of heat and cold if they have modesty and know somewhat of the game of chance called Life. What may not happen to a castle left undefended; what may not be filched from coffers left unlocked? This is the history of a man who, despite the lavishness of Fortune and the gifts she had poured forth before him, was of a stately humility. That he was a Duke and of great estate, that he had already been caressed by the hand of Fame and had been born more stalwart and beautiful than nine men of ten, did not, to his mind, make sure for him the love of any woman whom he had not served and won. He was of no meek spirit, but he had too much wit and too great knowledge of the chances of warfare not to know that in love's campaign, as in any other, a man must be on the field if he would wield his sword.

So my lord Duke had his days of fret and restlessness as less fortunate men have them, and being held on the Continent by duties he had undertaken in calmer moments, lay sometimes awake at night reproaching himself that he had left England. Such hours do not make a man grow cooler, and by the time the second year had ripened, the months were long indeed. Well as he had thought he knew himself, there were times when the growth of this passion which possessed him awaked in him somewhat of wonder. 'Twas for one with whom he had yet never exchanged word or glance, a creature whose wild youth seemed sometimes a century away from him. There had been so many others who had crossed his path—great beauties and small ones—but only to this one had his being cried out aloud.

"It has begun," he had said to himself. "I have heard them tell of it—of how one woman's face came back to a man again and again, of how her eyes would look into his and would not leave him or let him rest. It has begun for me, too."

He had grave duties to perform, affairs of serious import to arrange, interviews to hold with great personages and small, and though none might read it in his bearing he found himself ever beholding this face, ever followed by the eyes which would not leave him and which, had they done so, would have left him to the dark. Yet this was hid within his own breast and was his own strange secret which he gave himself up to dwell upon but when he was alone. When he awakened in the morning he lay and thought of it and counted that a day had passed and another begun, and found himself pondering, as all those in his case do, on the events of the future and the incidents which would lead him to them. At night, sometimes in long rides or walks he took alone, he lived these incidents through and imagined he beheld her as she would look when they first met, as she would look when he told her his purpose in coming to her. If he pleased her, his fancy pictured him the warm flash of her large eye, the smile of her mouth, half-proud, half-tender, a look which even when but imagined made his pulses beat.

"I do not know her face well enough," he said, "to picture all the beauteous changes of it, but there will sure be a thousand which a man might spend a life of love in studying."

Among the many who passed hours in his company at this time, there was but one who guessed, even distantly, at what lay at the root of his being, and this was the man who, being in a measure of like nature with his own, had been in the same way possessed when deep passion came to him.

At this period his Grace of Marlborough already felt the tossings of the rising storm in England, and the emotions which his Duchess's letters aroused within him, her anger at the intrigues about her, her tigress love for and belief in him, her determination to defend and uphold him with all the powers of her life and strength and imperial spirit, were, it is probable, moving and stimulating things which put him in the mood to be keen of sight and sympathy.

"There dwells some constant thought in your mind, my lord Duke," he said, on a night in which they sate together alone. "Is it a new one?"

"No," Osmonde answered; "'twould perhaps not be so constant if it were. It is an old thought which has taken a new form. In times past"—his voice involuntarily falling a tone—"I did not realise its presence."

The short silence which fell was broken by the Duke and with some suddenness.

"Is it one of which you would rid yourself?" he asked.

"No, your Grace."

"'Tis well," gravely, "You could not—if you would."

He asked no further question, but went on as if in deep thought, rather reflecting aloud.

"There are times," he said, "when to some it is easy and natural to say that such fevers are folly and unreasonableness—but even to those so slightly built by nature, and of memories so poor, such times do not come, nor can be dreamed of, when they are passing through the furnace fires. They come after—or before."

Osmonde did not speak. He raised his eyes and met those of his illustrious companion squarely, and for a short space each looked into the soul of the other, it so seemed, though not a word was spoke.

"You did not say the thing before," the Duke commented at last. "You will not say it after."

"No, I shall not," answered Osmonde, and somewhat later he added, with flushed cheek, "I thank your Grace for your comprehension of an unspoken thing."

Distant as he was from Gloucestershire there seemed a smiling fortune in the chances by which his thought was fed. What time had wrought he heard as time went on—that her graces but developed with opportunity, that her wit matched her beauty, that those who talked gossip asked each other in these days, not what disgrace would be her downfall, but what gentleman of those who surrounded her, paying court, would be most likely to be smiled upon at last. From young Tantillion he heard such things, from talkative young officers back after leave of absence, and more than once from ladies who, travelling from England to reach foreign gayeties, brought with them the latest talk of the country as well as of the town.

From the old Lady Storms, whom he encountered in Vienna, he heard more than from any other. She had crossed the Channel with her Chaplain, her spaniel, her toady, and her parrot, in search of enlivenment for her declining years, and hearing that her Apollo Belvidere was within reach, sent a message saying she would coax him to come and make love to an old woman, who adored him as no young one could, and whose time hung heavy on her hands.

He went to her because she was a kindly, witty old woman, and had always avowed an affection for him, and when he arrived at her lodgings he found her ready to talk by the hour. All the gossip of the Court she knew, all the marriages being made or broken off, all the public stories of her Grace of Marlborough's bullyings of her Majesty and revilings of Mrs. Masham, and many which were spiced by being private and new. And as she chattered over her dish of chocolate and my lord Duke listened with the respect due her years, he knew full well that her stories would not be brought to a close without reaching Gloucestershire at last—or Warwickshire or Worcester, or even Berks or Wilts, where she would have heard

103

some romance she would repeat to him; for in truth it ever seemed that it must befall so when he met and talked with man or woman who had come lately from England, Ireland, or Wales.

And so it did befall, but this time 'twas neither Gloucestershire, Worcester, Warwick, nor Berks she had visited or entertained guests from, but plain, lively town gossip she repeated apropos of Sir John Oxon, whose fortunes seemed in evil case. In five years' time he had squandered all his inheritance, and now was in such straits through his creditors that it seemed plain his days of fashionable wild living and popularity would soon be over, and his poor mother was using all her wits to find him a young lady with a fortune.

"And in truth she found him one, two years ago," her Ladyship added, "a West Indian heiress, but at that time he was dangling after the wild Gloucestershire beauty and was mad for her. What was her name? I forget it, though I should not. But she was disdainful and treated him so scornfully that at last they quarrelled—or 'twas thought so—for he left the country and hath not been near her for months. Good Lord!" of a sudden; "is not my Lord Dunstanwolde your Grace's distant kinsman?"

"My father's cousin twice removed, your Ladyship," answered Osmonde, wondering somewhat at the irrelevance of the question.

"Then you will be related to the fantastic young lady too," she said, "if his lordship is successful in his elderly suit."

"His lordship?" queried Osmonde; "his lordship of Dunstanwolde?"

"Yes," said the old woman, in great good humour, "for he is more in love than all the rest. Faith, a man must be in love if he will hear 'No' twice said to him when he is sixty-five and then go back to kneel and plead again."

My lord Duke rose from his seat to set upon the table near by his chocolate-cup. Months later he remembered how mad the tale had seemed to him, and that there had been in his mind no shadow of belief in it; even that an hour after it had, in sooth, passed from his memory and been forgotten.

"'Tis a strange rumour, your Ladyship," he said. "For myself I do not credit it, knowing of my lord's early loss and his years of mourning through it."

"'Tis for that reason all the neighbourhood is agog," answered my lady. "But 'tis for that reason I give it credit. These men who have worshipped a woman once can do it again. And this one—Lud! they say, she is a witch and no man resists her."

A few days later came a letter from my Lord Dunstanwolde himself, who had not writ from England for some time, and in the

104

midst of his epistle, which treated with a lettered man's thoughtful interest of the news of both town and country, of Court and State, playhouse and club, there was reference to Gloucestershire and Mistress Clorinda of Wildairs Hall.

"In one of our past talks, Gerald," he wrote, "you said you thought often of the changes time might work in such a creature. You are given to speculative thought and spoke of the wrong the past had done her, and of your wonder if the strength of her character and the clearness of her mind might not reveal to her what the untoward circumstances of her life had hidden, and also lead her to make changes none had believed possible. Your fancies were bolder than mine. You are a stronger man than I, Gerald, though a so much younger one; you have a greater spirit and a far greater brain, and your reason led you to see possibilities I could not picture. In truth, in those days I regarded the young lady with some fear and distaste, being myself sober and elderly. But 'tis you who were right. The change in her is indeed a wondrous one, but that I most marvel at is that I mark in her a curious gentleness, which grows. She hath taken under protection her sister Mistress Anne, a humble creature whose existence none have seemed previously aware of. The poor gentlewoman is timid and uncomely, but Mistress Clorinda shows an affection for her she hath shown to none other. But yesterday she said to me a novel thing in speaking of her—and her deep eyes, which can flash forth such lightnings, were soft as if dew were hid in them—'Why was all given to me,' saith she, 'and naught to her? Since Nature was not fair, then let me try to be so. She is good, she is innocent, she is helpless. I would learn of her. Innocence one cannot learn, and helpless I shall never be, yet would I learn of her.' She hath a great, strange spirit, Gerald, and strange fearlessness of thought. What other woman dare arraign Nature's self, and command mankind to retrieve her cruelties?"

Having finished his reading, my lord Duke turned to his window and looked out upon the night, which was lit to silver by the moon, which flooded the broad square before him and the park beyond it till 'twas lost in the darkness of the trees.

"No other woman—none," he said—and such a tumult shook his soul that of a sudden he stretched forth his arms unknowing of the movement and spoke as though to one close at hand. "Great God!" he said, low and passionate, "you call me, you call me! Let me but look into your eyes—but answer me with yours—and all of Life is ours!"

CHAPTER XVII

As Hugh de Mertoun Rode

When he rode back upon the road which led towards Gloucestershire, 'twas early June again, as it had been when he journeyed to Camylott with Mr. Fox attending. The sky was blue once more, there was the scent of sweet wild things in the air, birds twittered in the hedgerows and skylarks sang on high; all was in full fair leafage and full fair life. This time Mr. Fox was not with him, he riding alone save for his servants, following at some distance, for in truth 'twas his wish to be solitary, and he rode somewhat like a man in a dream.

"There is no land like England," he said, "there are no such meadows elsewhere, no such hedgerows, no such birds, and no such soft fleeced white clouds in the blue sky." In truth, it seemed so to him, as it seems always to an Englishman returning from foreign lands. The thatched cottages spoke of homely comfort, the sound of the village church bells was like a prayer, the rustics, as they looked up from work in the fields to pull their forelocks as he rode by them, seemed to wear kindlier looks upon their sunburnt faces than he had seen in other countries.

"But," he said to himself, and smiled in saying it, "it is because I am a happy man, and am living like one who dreams. Men have ridden before on such errands. Hugh de Mertoun rode so four hundred years gone, to a grey castle in the far north of Scotland, to make his suit to a fair maiden whose beauties he had but heard rumour of and whose face he had never seen. He rode through a savage country, and fought his way to her against axe and spear. But when he reached her she served him in her father's banquet hall, and in years after used to kiss the scars left by his wounds, and sing at her harp the song of his journey to woo her. But he had not known her since the time of her birth, and been haunted by her until her womanhood."

To Dunstan's Wolde in Warwickshire he rode, where he was to be a guest, and sometimes he reproached himself that he was by natural habit of such reserve that in all their converse together he had never felt that he could speak his thoughts to his kinsman on the one subject they had dwelt most upon. During the last two years he had realised how few words he had uttered on this subject even in the days before he had known the reason for his tendency to silence. At times when Dunstanwolde had spoken with freedom and

106

at length of circumstances which attracted the comments of all, he himself had been more frequently listener than talker, and had been wont to sit in attentive silence, making his reflections later to himself when he was alone. After the day on which he had lost himself upon Sir Christopher Crowell's land and, lying among the bracken, had heard the talk of the sportsmen below, he had known why he had been so reticent, and during his last two years he had realised that this reticence had but increased. Despite his warm love for my Lord Dunstanwolde there had never come an hour when he felt that he could have revealed even by the most distant allusion the tenor of his mind. In his replies to his lordship's occasional epistles he had touched more lightly upon his references to the household of Wildairs than upon other things of less moment to him. Of Court stories he could speak openly, of country, town, and letters, with easy freedom, but when he must acknowledge news from Gloucestershire, he sate grave before his paper, his pen idle in his hand, and found but few sentences to indite.

"But later," he would reflect, "I shall surely feel myself more open—and his kind heart is so full of sympathy that he will understand my silence and not feel it has been grudging or ungenerous to his noble friendship."

And even now as he rode to the home of this gentleman whose affection he had enjoyed with so much of appreciation and gratitude, he consoled himself again with this thought, knowing that the time had not yet come when he could unbosom himself, nor would it come until all the world must be taken into his confidence, and he stand revealed an exultant man whose joy broke all bonds for him since that he had dreamed of he had won.

When he had made his last visit to Warwickshire he had thought my lord looking worn and fatigued, and had fancied he saw some hint of new trouble in his eyes. He had even spoke with him of his fancy, trusting that he had no cause for anxiousness and was not in ill-health, and had been answered with a kindly smile, my lord averring that he had no new thing to weary him, but only one which was old, with which he had borne more than sixty years, and which was somewhat the worse for wear in these days—being himself.

He thought of this reply as he passed through the lovely village where every man, woman, and child knew him and greeted him with warmly welcoming joy, and he was pondering on it as he rode through the park gates and under the big beech-trees which formed the avenue.

"Somewhat had saddened him," he thought. "Pray God it has passed," and was aroused from his thinking by a sound of horses' feet, and looking up saw my lord cantering towards him on his brown hackney, and with brightly smiling face.

They greeted each other with joyful affection, as they always did in meeting, and my lord's welcome had a touch of even more loving warmth than usual. He had come out to meet his guest and kinsman on the road, and had thought to be in time to join him earlier and ride with him through the village.

"On my soul, Gerald," he said, gaily, "'tis useless that you should grow handsomer and taller each time you leave us. Surely, there is a time for a man to be content. Or is it that when you are absent one sees gentlemen of proportions so much more modest that when you return we must get used to your looks again. Your sunburn is as becoming as your laurels."

His own worn look had passed. Osmonde had never seen him so well and vigorous, being indeed amazed by his air of freshness and renewed youth. His finely cut, high bred countenance had gained a slight colour, his sweet grey eyes were clear and full of light, and he bore himself more strongly and erect. For the first time within his remembrance of him, my lord Duke observed that he wore another colour than black, though it was of rich, dark shade, being warm, deep brown, and singularly becoming him, his still thick grey hair framing in silver his fine, gentle face.

"And you," Osmonde answered him, marking all these things with affectionate pleasure, "your weariness has left you. I have never seen you look so young and well."

"Young!" said my lord, smiling, "at sixty-eight? Well, in truth, I feel so. Let us pray it may not pass. 'Tis hope—which makes new summer."

They dined alone, and sitting over their wine had cheerful talk. A man is not absent from his native land for two good years, even when they are spent in ordinary travel, without on his return having much to recount in answer to the questionings of his friends; but two years spent in camp and Court during a great campaign may furnish hours of talk indeed.

Yet though their conversation did not flag, and each found pleasure in the other's company, Osmonde was conscious of a secret restlessness. Throughout the whole passing of the repast it chanced not once that the name was mentioned which had so often been spoke before when they had been together; there had been a time when in no talk of the neighbourhood could it well have been avoided, but now, strangely enough, no new incident was related, no reference to its bearer made. This might, perhaps, be because the heroine of that scandal, having begun to live the ordinary life of womankind, there were no fantastic stories to tell, the county

108

having had time to become accustomed to the change in her and comment on it no more. And still there was a singularity in the silence. Yet for my lord Duke himself it was impossible to broach the subject, he being aware that he was not calm enough in mind to open it with a composure which would not betray his interest.

He had come from town under promise to attend that night a birthday ball in the neighbourhood, a young relative coming of age and celebrating his majority. The kinship was not close, but greatly valued by the family of the heir, and his Grace's presence had been so ardently desired, that he, who honoured all claims of his house and name, had given his word.

And 'twas at last through speech of this, and only as they parted to apparel themselves for this festivity, my Lord Dunstanwolde touched upon the thing one man of them, at least, had not had power to banish from his mind throughout their mutual talk.

"Young Colin is a nice, well-meaning lad," said my lord as they passed through the hall to mount the staircase. "He is plain featured and awkward, but modest and of good humour. He will be greatly honoured that the hero of his house should be present on the great night. You are the hero, you know, having been with Marlborough, and bearing still the scar of a wound got at Blenheim, though 'twas 'not as deep as a grave or as wide as a church door.' And with orders on your broad chest and the scent of gunpowder in your splendid periwig you will make a fine figure. They will all prostrate themselves before you, and when you make your state bow to the beauty, Mistress Clorinda—for you will see her—she will surely give you a dazzling smile."

"That I will hope for," answered my lord Duke, smiling himself; but his heart leaped like a live thing in his breast and did not cease its leaping as he mounted the stairway, though he bore himself with outward calm.

When within his room he strode to and fro, his arms folded across his breast. For some time he could not have composed himself to sit down or go to rest. This very night, then, he was to behold her face to face; in but a few hours he would stand before her bowing, and rise from his obeisance to look into the great eyes which had followed him so long—ay, so much longer than he had truly understood. What should he read there—what thought which might answer to his own? It had been his plan to go to my Lord Twemlow and ask that he might be formally presented to his fair kinswoman and her parent. Knowing his mind, he was no schoolboy who would trust to chance, but would move directly and with dignity towards the object he desired. The representatives of her

109

family would receive him, and 'twas for himself to do the rest. But now he need go to no man to ask to be led to her presence. The mere chance of Fortune would lead him there. 'Twas strange how it had ever been so—that Fate's self had seemed to work to this end.

The chamber was a huge one and he had paced its length many times before he stopped and stood in deep thought.

"'Tis sure because of this," he said, "that I have so little doubt. There lies scarce a shadow yet in my mind. 'Tis as if Nature had so ordained it before I woke to life, and I but go to obey her law."

His eye had fallen upon a long mirror standing near, but he did not see what was reflected there, and gazed through and beyond it as if at another thing. And yet the image before him was one which might have removed doubt of himself from any man's heart, it being of such gracious height and manly strength, and, with its beauteous leonine eye and brow, its high bearing, and the richness of its apparel, so noble a picture.

He turned away unseeing, with a smile and half a sigh of deep and tender passion. "May I ride home," he said, "as Hugh de Mertoun did—four hundred years ago!"

When they arrived at their entertainer's house the festivities were at full; brilliant light shone from every window and streamed from the wide entrance in a flood, coaches rolled up the avenue and waited for place before the door, from within strains of music floated out to the darkness of the night, and as the steps were mounted each arrival caught glimpses of the gay scene within: gentlemen in velvet and brocade and ladies attired in all the rich hues of a bed of flowers—crimson, yellow, white and blue, purple and gold and rose.

Their young host met them on the threshold and welcomed them with boyish pride and ardour. He could scarce contain himself for pleasure at being so honoured in his first hospitalities by the great kinsman of his house, who, though but arrived at early maturity, was already spoken of as warrior, statesman, and honoured favourite at Court.

"We are but country gentry, your Grace," he said, reddening boyishly, when he had at length led them up the great stairway to the ball-room, "and most of us have seen little of the world. As for me, I have but just come from Cambridge, where I fear I did myself small credit. In my father's day we went but seldom to town, as he liked horses and dogs better than fine company. So I know nothing of Court beauties, but to-night—" and he reddened a little more and ended somewhat awkwardly—"to-night you will see here a beauty who surely cannot be outshone at Court, and men tell me cannot be matched there."

110

"'Tis Mistress Clorinda Wildairs he speaks of," said Sir Christopher Crowell, who stood near, rubicund in crimson, and he said it with an uncourtly wink; "and, ecod! he's right—though I am not 'a town man.'"

"He is enamoured of her," he added in proud confidence later when he found himself alone for a moment by his Grace. "The youngsters are all so—and men who are riper, too. Good Lord, look at me who have dandled her on my knee when she was but five years old—and am her slave," chuckling. "She's late to-night. Mark the fellows loitering about the doors and on the stairway. 'Tis that each hopes to be the first to catch her eye."

'Twas but a short time afterward my lord Duke had made his way to the grand staircase himself, it being his intention to go to a lower room, and reaching the head of it he paused for a moment to gaze at the brilliant scene. The house was great and old, and both halls and stairway of fine proportions, and now, brilliant with glow of light and the moving colour of rich costumes, presented indeed a comely sight. And he had no sooner paused to look down than he heard near by a murmur of low exclamation, and close at his side a man broke forth in rough ecstacy to his companion.

"Clorinda, by Gad!" he said, "and crowned with roses! The vixen makes them look as if they were built of rubies in every leaf."

And from below she came—up the broad stairway, upon her father's arm.

Well might their eyes follow her indeed, and well might his own look down upon her, burning. The strange compellingness of her power, which was a thing itself apart from beauty, and would have ruled for her had she not possessed a single charm, had so increased that he felt himself change colour at the mere sight of her. Oh! 'twas not the colour and height and regal shape of her which were her splendour, but this one Heaven-born, unconquerable thing. Her lip seemed of a deeper scarlet, the full roundness of her throat rose from among her laces, bound with a slender circlet of glittering stars, her eyes had grown deeper and more melting, and yet held a great flame. Nay, she seemed a flame herself—of life, of love, of spirit which naught could daunt or quell, and on her high-held imperial head she wore a wreath of roses red as blood.

"She will look up," he thought, "she will look up at me."

But she did not, though he could have sworn that which he felt should have arrested her. Somewhat seemed to hold her oblivious of those who were near her; she gazed straight before her as if expecting to see something, and as she passed my lord Duke on the landing, a heavy velvet rose broke from her crown and fell at his very foot.

111

He bent low to pick it up, the blood surging in his veins—and when he raised himself, holding it in his hand, she was moving onward through the crowd which closed behind to gaze and comment on her—and his kinsman Dunstanwolde came forward from an antechamber, his gentle, high bred face and sweet grey eyes glowing with greeting.

Those of reflective habit may indeed find cause for thought in realising the power of small things over great, of rule over important events, of ordinary social observance over the most powerful emotion a man or woman may be torn or uplifted by. He whose greatest longing on earth is to speak face to face to the friend whom ill fortune has caused to think him false, seeing this same friend in a crowded street a hundred yards distant, cannot dash the passers-by aside and race through or leap over them to reach, before it is too late, the beloved object he beholds about to disappear; he cannot arrest that object with loud outcries, such conduct being likely to cause him to be taken for a madman, and restrained by the other lookers-on; the tender woman, whose heart is breaking under the weight of misunderstanding between herself and him she loves, is powerless to attract and detain him if he passes her, either unconscious of her nearness or of intention coldly averting his gaze from her pleading eyes. She may know that, once having crossed the room where she sits in anguish, all hope is lost that they may meet again on this side of the grave. She may know that a dozen words would fill his heart with joy, and that all life would smile to both henceforth, but she cannot force her way to his side in public; she cannot desert without ceremony the stranger who is conversing courteously; she cannot cry out, she may not even speak, it may be that it is not possible that she should leave her place—and he who is her heart's blood approaches slowly—is near—has passed—is gone—and all has come to bitter, cruel end. In my lord Duke of Osmonde's mind there was no thought of anguish or the need for it; he but realised that he had felt an unreasonable pang when she whom he had so desired to behold had passed him by unnoticed. 'Twas after all a mere trick of chance, and recalled to him the morning two years before, when he had heard her horse's feet splashing through the mire of the narrow lane, and had drawn his own beast aside while she galloped past unaware of his nearness, and with the strange, absorbed, and almost fierce look in her eyes. He had involuntarily gathered his bridle to follow her and then had checked his impulse, realising its impetuousness, and had turned to ride homeward with a half smile on his lips but with his heart throbbing hard. But what perchance struck him most to-night, was that her eyes wore a look unlike, yet somehow akin, to that which he had marked and been moved by then—as if storm were hid within their shadows and she herself was like some fine wild thing at bay.

There would have been little becomingness in his hastening after her and his Lordship of Dunstanwolde; his court to her must be paid with grace and considerateness. If there were men who in their eagerness forgot their wit and tact, he was not one of them.

He turned to re-enter the ball-room and approach her there, and on the threshold encountered young Colin, who looked for the moment pale.

"Did you see her?" he asked. "She has but just passed through the room with my Lord Dunstanwolde—Mistress Clorinda," he added, with a little rueful laugh. "In Gloucestershire there is but one 'she.' When we speak of the others we use their names and call them Mistress Margaret or my Lady Betty—or Jane."

"I stood at the head of the stairway as she passed," answered Osmonde.

"It cannot be true," the lad broke forth; "it makes me mad even to hear it spoke—though he is a courtly gentleman and rich and of high standing—but he is old enough to be her grandfather. Though she is such a woman, she is but seventeen, and my lord is near seventy."

Osmonde turned an inquiring gaze upon him, and the boy broke into his confused half-laugh again.

"I speak of my Lord Dunstanwolde," he said. "Twice he has asked her to be his Countess, and all say that to-night she is to give him her answer. Jack Oxon has heard it and is mad enough. Look at him as he stands by the archway there. His eyes are like blue steel and he can scarce hide his rage. But better she should take Dunstanwolde than Jack"—hotly.

The musicians were playing a minuet in the gallery, there was dancing, slow, stately movements and deep obeisance going on in the room, couples were passing to and fro, and here and there groups stood and watched. My lord Duke stood and watched also; a little court had gathered about him and he must converse with those who formed it, or listen with gracious attention to their remarks. But his grace and composure cost him an effort. There came back to him the story old Lady Storms had told in Vienna and which he had not believed and had even forgot. The memory of it returned to him with singular force and clearness. He told himself that still it could not be true, that his young host's repetition of it rose from the natural uneasy jealousy of a boy—and yet the pageant of the brilliant figures moving before him seemed to withdraw themselves as things do in a dream. He remembered my Lord Dunstanwolde's years and his faithfulness to the love of his youth, and there arose

113

before him the young look he had worn when they met in the avenue, his words, "'Tis hope which makes new summer," and the music of the minuet sounded distant in his ears, while as it rang there, he knew he should not forget it to his life's end. Yet no, it could not be so. A gentleman near seventy and a girl of seventeen! And still, to follow the thought honestly, even at seven and sixty years my Lord had greater grace and charm than many a man not half his age. And with that new youth and tenderness in his eyes no woman could shrink from him, at least. And still it could not be true, for Fate herself had driven him to this place—Nature and Fate.

Sir John Oxon stood near the doorway, striving to smile, but biting his lip; here and there his Grace vaguely observed that there seemed new talk among the moving couples and small gathered groups. About the entrance there was a stirring and looking out into the corridor, and in a moment or so more the company parted and gave way, and his Lordship of Dunstanwolde entered, with Mistress Clorinda upon his arm; he, gracefully erect in bearing, as a conqueror returning from his victory.

An exclamation broke from the young Colin which was like a low cry.

"Tis true!" he said. "Yes, yes; 'tis in his eyes. 'Tis done—'tis done!"

His Grace of Osmonde turned towards his kinsman, who he saw was approaching him, and greeted him with a welcoming smile; the red rose was still held in his hand. He stood drawn to his full height, a stately, brilliant figure, with his orders glittering on his breast, his fine eyes deeply shining—waiting.

The company parted before the two advancing figures—his lordship's rich violet velvet, the splendid rose and silver making a wondrous wave of colour, the wreath of crimson flowers on the black hair seeming like a crown of triumph.

Before my lord Duke they paused, and never had the old Earl's gentle, high bred face worn so tenderly affectionate a smile, or his grey eyes so sweet a light.

"My honoured kinsman, his Grace the Duke of Osmonde," he said to her who glowed upon his arm. "Your Grace, it is this lady who is to do me the great honour of becoming my Lady Dunstanwolde."

And they were face to face, her great orbs looking into his own, and he saw a thing which lay hid in their very depths—and his own flashed despite himself, and hers fell; and he bowed low, and she swept a splendid curtsey to the ground.

So, for the first time in their lives, he looked into her eyes.

CHAPTER XVIII

A Night in which my Lord Duke Did Not Sleep

As they rolled over the roads on their way homeward, in the darkness of their coach, my Lord Dunstanwolde spoke of his happiness and told its story. There was no approach to an old lover's exultant folly in his talk; his voice was full of noble feeling, and in his manner there was somewhat like to awe of the great joy which had befallen him. To him who listened to the telling 'twas a strange relation indeed, since each incident seemed to reveal to him a blindness in himself. Why had he not read the significance of a score of things which he could now recall? A score of things?—a hundred! Because he had been in his early prime, and full of the visions and passions of youth, he had not for one moment dreamed that a man who was so far his senior could be a man still, his heart living enough to yearn and ache, his eyes clear to see the radiance others saw, and appraise it as adoringly. 'Twas the common fault of youth to think to lead the world and to sweep aside from its path all less warm-blooded, strong-limbed creatures, feeling their day was done for them, and that for them there was naught left but to wait quietly for the end. There was an ignobleness in it—a self-absorption which was almost dishonour. And in this way he had erred as far as any stripling with blooming cheeks and girlish love-locks who thought that nine and twenty struck the knell of love and life. 'Twas thoughts like these that were passing through his mind as they were driven through the darkness—at least they were the thoughts upon the surface of his mind, while below them surged a torrent into whose darkness he dared not look. He was a man, and he had lost her—lost her! She had become a part of his being—and she had been torn from his side. "Let me but look into your eyes," he had said, and he had looked and read her answering soul—too late!

"I have passed through dark days, Gerald," my lord was saying. "How should I have dared to hope that she would give herself to me? I had been mad to hope it. And yet a man in my case must plead, whether he despairs or not. I think 'twas her gentleness to Mistress Anne which has sustained me. That poor gentlewoman and I have the happiness to know her heart as others do not. Thank God, 'tis so! When to-night I said to her sadly, 'Madam, my youth is long past,' she stopped me with a strange and tender little cry. She put her hand upon my shoulder. Ah, its soft touch, its white, kind caress! 'Youth is not all,' she said. 'I have known younger men who could not bring a woman truth and honourable love. 'Tis not I who give, 'tis not I,' and the full sweet red of her mouth quivered. I—have not yet dared to touch it, Gerald." And his voice was sad as well as reverent. "Youth would have been more bold."

In his dark corner of the coach his Grace checked breath to control a start. In the past he had had visions such as all men have—and all was lost! And to-morrow his kinsman would have gained courage to look his new bliss in the face—the autumn of his days would be warmed by a late glow of the sun, but that long summer which yet lay before himself would know no flame of gold. The years he had spent in training his whole being to outward self-control at least did service to him now, and aided him to calm, affectionate speech.

"You will make her life a happy one, my Lord," he said, "and you will be a joyous man indeed."

Together they conversed on this one subject until their journey was over. When they had passed through the hall and stood at length in the light of the apartment in which it was their custom to sit, Osmonde beheld in my lord's face the freshness and glow he had marked on his arrival, increased tenfold, and now he well understood. In truth, the renewal of his life was a moving thing to see. He stood by the mantel, his arm resting upon it, his forehead in his hand, for a little space in silence and as if lost in thought.

"She is a goddess," he said, "and because she is so, can be humble. Had you but seen her, Gerald, when she spoke. 'Tis not I who give,' she saith. 'You are a great Earl, I am a poor beauty—a shrew—a hoyden. I give naught but this!' and flung her fair arms apart with a great lovely gesture and stood before me stately, her beauty glowing like the sun."

He drew a deep sigh of tenderness and looked up with a faint start. "'Tis not fair I should fatigue you with my ecstasy," he said. "You look pale, Gerald. You are generous to listen with such patience."

"I need no patience," answered my lord Duke with noble warmth, "to aid me to listen to the kinsman I have loved from childhood when he speaks of his happiness with the fairest woman in the world. Having seen her to-night, I do not wonder she is called so by her worshippers."

"The fairest and the noblest," said my Lord. "Great Heaven, how often have I sate alone in this very room calling myself a madman in my despair! And now 'tis past! Sure it cannot be true?"

"'Tis true, my dear Lord," said Osmonde, "for I beheld it."

"Had you been in my place," his lordship said with his grave, kindly look, "you need not have wondered at your fortune. If you had lived in Warwickshire instead of winning laurels in campaign you might have been my rival if you would—and I a hopeless man—and she a Duchess. But you two never met."

My lord Duke held out his hand and grasped his kinsman's with friendly sympathy.

"Until to-night we never met," he said. "'Twas Fate ordained it so—and I would not be your rival, for we have loved each other too long. I must wait to find another lady, and she will be Countess of Dunstanwolde."

He bore himself composedly until they had exchanged the final courtesies and parted for the night, and having mounted the stairs had passed through the long gallery which led him to his apartments. When he opened the door it seemed to his fancy that the wax tapers burned but dimly amid the shadows of the great room, and that the pictured faces hanging on the walls looked white and gazed as if aghast.

The veins were swollen in his temples and throbbed hard, his blood coursed hot and cold alternately, there were drops starting out upon his brow. He had not known his passions were so tempestuous and that he could be prey to such pangs of anguish and of rage. Hitherto he had held himself in check, but now 'twas as if he had lost his hold on the reins which controlled galloping steeds. The blood of men who had been splendid savages centuries ago ran wild within him. His life for thirty years had been noble and just and calm. Being endowed with all gifts by Nature and his path made broad by Fortune, he had dealt in high honour with all bestowed upon him. But now for this night he knew he was a different man, and that his hour had come.

He stood in the centre of the chamber and tossed up his hands, laughing a mad, low, harsh laugh.

"Not as Hugh de Mertoun came back," he said. "Good God! no, no!"

The rage of him, body and soul, made him sick and suffocated him.

"Could a man go mad in such case?" he cried. "I am not sane! I cannot reason! I would not have believed it."

His arteries so throbbed that he tore open the lace at his throat and flung back his head. "I cannot reason!" he said. "I know now how men kill. And yet he is as sweet a soul as Heaven ever made." He paced the great length of the chamber to and fro.

"'Tis not Nature," he said. "It cannot be borne—he to hold her to his breast, and I—I to stand aside. Her eyes—her lovely, melting, woman's eyes!"

Men have been mad before for less of the same torment, and

he whose nature was fire, and whose imagination had the power to torture him by picturing all he had lost and all another man had won, was only saved because he knew his frenzy.

"To this place itself she will be brought," he thought. "In these rooms she will move, wife and queen and mistress. He will so worship her that she cannot but melt to him. At the mere thought of it my brain reels."

He knew that his thoughts were half delirium, his words half raving, yet he could not control them, and thanked chance that his apartment was near none other which was occupied, and that he could stride about and stamp his foot upon the floor, and yet no sound be heard beyond the massive walls and doors. Outside such walls, in the face of the world, he must utter no word, show no sign by any quiver of a muscle; and 'twas the realisation of the silence he must keep, the poignard stabs he must endure without movement, which at this hour drove him to madness.

"This is but the beginning," he groaned. "Since I am his kinsman and we have been friends, I am bound as a man upon the rack is bound while he is torn limb from limb. I must see it all—there will be no escape. At their marriage I must attend them. God save me—taking my fit place as the chief of my house at the nuptials of a well beloved kinsman, I must share in the rejoicings, and be taunted by his rapture and her eyes. Nay, nay, she cannot gaze at him as she would have gazed at me—she cannot! Yet how shall I endure!"

For hours he walked to and fro, the mere sense of restless movement being an aid to his mood. Sometimes again he flung himself into a seat and sat with hidden eyes. But he could not shut out the pictures his fevered fancy painted for him. A man of strong imagination, and who is possessed by a growing passion, cannot fail to depict to himself, and live in, vivid dreams of that future of his hopes which is his chiefest joy. So he had dreamed, sometimes almost with the wild fervour of a boy, smiling while he did it, at his own pleasure in the mere detail his fancy presented to him. In these day-dreams his wealth, the beauty and dignity of his estates, the brilliant social atmosphere his rank assured him, had gained a value he had never recognised before. He remembered now, with torturing distinctness, the happy day when it had first entered his mind, that those things which had been his daily surroundings from his childhood would all be new pleasures to her, all in strong contrast to the atmosphere of her past years. His heart actually leapt at the thought of the smilingness of fortune which had lavished upon him so much, that 'twould be rapture to him to lay at her feet. He had remembered tenderly the stately beauty of his beloved

118

Camylott, the bosky dells at Marlowell Dane, the quaint dignity of the Elizabethan manor at Paulyn Dorlocke, the soft hills near Mertounhurst, where myriads of harebells grew and swayed in the summer breeze as it swept them; and the clear lake in the park at Roxholm, where the deer came to drink, and as a boy he had lain in his boat and rocked among the lily-pads in the early morning, when the great white water-flowers spread their wax cups broad and seemed to hold the gold of the sun. His life had been so full of beauty and fair things; wheresoever his lot had fallen at any time he had had fair days, fair nights, and earth's loveliness to behold. And all he had loved and joyed in, he had known she would love and joy in, too. What a chatelaine she would make, he had thought; how the simple rustic folk would worship her! What a fit setting for her beauty would seem the grand saloons of Osmonde House! What a fit and queen-like wearer she would be for the marvellous jewels which had crowned fair heads and clasped fair throats and arms for centuries! There were diamonds all England had heard rumour of, and he had even lost himself in a lover's fancy of an hour when he himself would clasp a certain dazzling collar round the column of her throat, and never yet had he given himself to the fancy but in his vision he had laid his lips on the warm whiteness when 'twas done, and lost himself in a passionate kiss—and she had turned and smiled a heavenly answering bridal smile.

This he remembered now, clinching his hands until he drove the nails into his palms.

"I have been madder than I thought," he said. "Yes, 'twas madness—but 'twas Nature, too! Good God!" his forehead dropping in his hand and he panting. "I feel as if she had been a year my wife, and another man had torn her from my breast. And yet she has not been mine an hour—nor ever will be—and she is Dunstanwolde's, who, while I wake in torment, dreams in bliss, as is his honest, heavenly right." Even to the torment he had no claim, but in being torn by it seemed but robbing another man. What a night of impotent rage it was, of unreasoning, hopeless hatred of himself, of his fate, and even of the man who was his rival, though at his worst he reviled his frenzy, which could be so base as to rend unjustly a being without blame.

'Twas not himself who hated, but the madness in his blood which for this space ran riot.

At dawn, when the first glimmer of light began to pale the skies, he found himself sitting by the wide-thrown casement still in the attire he had worn the night before. For the first time since he had been born his splendid normal strength had failed him and he was heavy with unnatural fatigue. He sate looking out until the pale tint had deepened to primrose and the primrose into sunrise gold; birds wakened in the trees' broad branches and twittered and flew forth; the sward and flowers were drenched with summer dews, and as the sun changed the drops to diamonds he gazed upon the lovely peace and breathed in the fresh fragrance of the early morn with a deep sigh, knowing his frenzy past but feeling that it had left him a changed man.

"Yes," he said, "I have been given too beauteous and smooth a life. Till now Fate has denied me nothing, and I have gone on my way unknowing it has been so, and fancying that if misfortune came I should bear it better than another man. 'Twas but human vanity to believe in powers which never had been tried. Self-command I have preached to myself, calmness and courage; for years I have believed I possessed them all and was Gerald Mertoun's master, and yet at the first blow I spend hours of the night in madness and railing against Fate. But one thing I can comfort myself with—that I wore a calm face and could speak like a man—until I was alone. Thank God for that."

As he sate he laid his plans for the future, knowing that he must lay out for himself such plans and be well aware of what he meant to do, that he might at no time betray himself to his kinsman and by so doing cast a shadow on his joy.

"Should he guess that it has been paid for by my despair," he said, "'twould be so marred for his kind heart that I know not how he would bear the thought. 'Twould be to him as if he had found himself the rival of the son he loved. He has loved me, Heaven knows, and I have loved him. Tis an affection which must last."

My Lord Dunstanwolde had slept peacefully and risen early. He was full of the reflections natural to a man to whom happiness has come and the whole tenor of whose future life must be changed in its domestic aspect, whose very household must wear a brighter face, and whose entire method of existence will wear new and more youthful form. He walked forth upon his domain, glad of its beauty and the heavenly brightness of the day which showed it fair. He had spent an hour out of doors, and returning to the terrace fronting the house, where already the peacocks had begun to walk daintily, spreading or trailing their gorgeous iridescent plumes, he looked up at his kinsman's casement and gave a start. My lord Duke sate there still in his gala apparel of white and gold brocade, his breast striped by the broad blue ribbon of the Garter, jewelled stars shining on his coat.

"Gerald," he called to him in alarm, "you are still dressed! Are you ill, my dear boy!"

Osmonde rose to his feet with a quickness of movement which

120

allayed his momentary fear; he waved his hand with a greeting smile.

"'Tis nothing," he answered, "I was a little ailing, and after 'twas past I fell asleep in my chair. The morning air has but just awaked me."

CHAPTER XIX

"Then you might have been one of those"

When the Earl and Countess of Dunstanwolde arrived in town and took up their abode at Dunstanwolde House, which being already one of the finest mansions, was made still more stately by its happy owner's command, the world of fashion was filled with delighted furore. Those who had heard of the Gloucestershire beauty by report were stirred to open excitement, and such as had not already heard rumours of her were speedily informed of all her past by those previously enlightened. The young lady who had so high a spirit as to have at times awakened somewhat of terror in those who were her adversaries; the young lady who had made such a fine show in male attire, and of whom it had been said that she could outleap, outfence, and outswear any man her size, had made a fine match indeed, marrying an elderly nobleman and widower, who for years had lived the life of a recluse, at last becoming hopelessly enamoured of one who might well be his youngest child.

"What will she do with him?" said a flippant modish lady to his Grace of Osmonde one morning. "How will she know how to bear herself like a woman of quality?"

"Should you once behold her, madam," said his Grace, "you will know how she would bear herself were she made Queen."

"Faith!" exclaimed the lady, "with what a grave, respectful air you say it. I thought the young creature but a joke."

"She is no joke," Osmonde answered, with a faint, cold smile.

"'Tis plain enough 'tis true what is said—the men all lose their hearts to her. We thought your Grace was adamant"—with simpering roguishness.

"The last two years I have spent with the army in Flanders,"

121

said my lord Duke, "and her Ladyship of Dunstanwolde is the wife of my favourite kinsman."

'Twas this last fact which was the bitterest thing of all, and which made his fate most hard to bear with patience. What he had dreaded had proven itself true, and more. Had my Lord Dunstanwolde been a stranger to him or a mere acquaintance he could have escaped all, or at least the greater part, of what he now must endure. As the chief of his house his share in the festivities attendant upon the nuptials had been greater than that of any other man. As one who seemed through their long affection to occupy almost the place of a son to the bridegroom, it had been but natural that he should do him all affectionate service, show the tenderest courtesy to his bride, and behold all it most tortured him to see. His gifts had been the most magnificent, his words of friendly gratulation the warmest. When they were for a few moments, on the wedding-day, alone, his Lordship had spoken to him of the joy which made him pale.

"Gerald," he said, "I could speak to none other of it. Your great heart will understand. 'Tis almost too sacred for words. Shall I waken from a dream? Surely, 'tis too heavenly sweet to last."

Would it last? his kinsman asked himself in secret, could it? Could one, like her, and who had lived her life, feel an affection for a consort so separated from her youth and bloom by years? She was so young, and all the dazzling of the world was new. What beauteous, high-spirited, country-bred creature of eighteen would not find its dazzle blind her eyes so that she could scarce see aright? He asked himself the questions with a pang. To expect that she should not even swerve with the intoxication of it, was to expect that she should be nigh superhuman, and yet if she should fail, and step down from the high shrine in which his passion had placed her, this would be the fiercest anguish of all.

"Were she mine," he cried, inwardly, "I could hold and guide her with love's hand. We should be lost in love, and follies and Courts would have no power. Love would be her shield and mine. Poor gentleman," remembering the tender worship in my Lord's kind face; "how can she love him as he loves her? But oh, she should—she should!"

If in the arrogance of her youth and power she could deal with him lightly or unkindly, he knew that even his own passion could find no pardon for her—yet if he had but once beheld her eyes answer her lord's as a woman's eyes must answer those of him she loves, it would have driven him mad. And so it came about that to see that she was tender and noble he watched her, and to be sure

122

that she was no more than this he knew he watched her too, calling himself ignoble that Nature so prompted him.

There was a thing she had said to him but a week after the marriage which had sunk deep into his soul and given him comfort.

"From my lord I shall learn new virtues," she said, with a singular smile, which somehow to his mind hid somewhat of pathos. "'New virtues,' say I; all are new to me. At Wildairs we concerned ourselves little with such matters." She lifted her eyes and let them rest upon him with proud gravity. "He is the first good man," she said, "whom I have ever known."

'Twas not as this man observed her life that the world looked on at it, but in a different manner and with a different motive, and yet both the world and his Grace of Osmonde beheld the same thing, which was that my Lord Dunstanwolde's happiness was a thing which grew greater and deeper as time passed, instead of failing him. When she went to Court and set the town on fire with her beauty and her bearing, had her lord been a man of youth and charm matching her own, the grace and sweetness of her manner to him could not have made him a more envied man. The wit and spirit with which she had ruled her father and his cronies stood her in as good stead as ever in the great World of Fashion, as young beaux and old ones who paid court to her might have told; but of her pungency of speech and pride of bearing when she would punish or reprove, my lord knew nothing, he but knew tones of her voice which were tender, looks which were her loveliest, and most womanly, warm, and sweet.

They were so sweet at times that Osmonde turned his gaze away that he might not see them, and when his Lordship, as was natural, would have talked of her dearness and beauties, he used all his powers to gently draw him from the subject without seeming to lack sympathy. But when a man is the idolatrous slave of happy love and, being of mature years, has few, nay, but one friend young enough to tell his joy to with the feeling that he is within reach of the comprehension of it, 'tis inevitable that to this man he will speak often of that which fills his being.

His Lordship's revealings of himself and his tenderness were involuntary things. There was no incident of his life of which one being was not the central figure, no emotion which had not its birth in her. He was not diffuse or fond to weakness, but full of faithful love and noble carefulness.

"I would not weary her with my worship, Gerald," he said one day, having come to Osmonde House to spend an hour in talk with him. "Let me open my heart to you, which is sometimes too full."

On this morning he gave unconscious explanation of many an

123

incident of the past few years. He spoke of the time when he had found himself wakening to this dream of a new life, yet had not dared to let his thoughts dwell upon it. He had known suffering—remorse that he should be faithless to the memory of his youth, in some hours almost horror of himself, and yet had struggled and approached himself in vain. The night of Lord Twemlow's first visit, when my lord Duke (then my lord Marquis) had been at Dunstanwolde, the occasion upon which Twemlow had so fretted at his fair kinswoman and told the story of the falling of her hair in the hunting-field, he had been disturbed indeed, fearing that his countenance would betray him.

"I was afraid, Gerald; afraid," he said, "thinking it unseemly that a man of my years should be so shaken with love—while your strong youth had gone unscathed. Did I not seem ill at ease?"

"I thought that your lordship disliked the subject," Osmonde answered, remembering well. "Once I thought you pale."

"Yes, yes," said my lord. "I felt my colour change at the cruel picture my Lord Twemlow painted—of her hunted helplessness if harm befell her."

"She would not be helpless," said Osmonde. "Nothing would make her so."

Her lord looked up at him with brightened eye.

"True—true!" he said. "At times, Gerald, I think perhaps you know her better than I. More than once your chance speech of her has shown so clear a knowledge. 'Tis because your spirit is like to her own."

Osmonde arose and went to a cabinet, which he unlocked.

"I have hid here," he said, "somewhat which I must show you. It should be yours—or hers—and has a story."

As his eyes fell upon that his kinsman brought forth his lordship uttered an exclamation. 'Twas the picture of his lady, stolen before her marriage by the drunken painter.

"It is herself," he exclaimed, "herself, though so roughly done."

My lord Duke stood a little apart out of the range of his vision and related the history of the canvas. He had long planned that he would do the thing, and therefore did it. All the plans he had made for his future conduct he had carried out without flinching. There had been hours when he had been like a man who held his hand in a brazier, but he had shown no sign. The canvas had been his companion so long that to send it from him would be almost as though he thrust forth herself while she held her deep eyes fixed upon him. But he told the story of the garret and the drunken painter, in well-chosen words.

"'Twas but like you, Gerald," my lord said with gratitude. "Few other men would have shown such noble carefulness for a wild beauty they scarce knew. I—will leave it with you."

"You—will leave it!" answered my lord Duke his pulse quickening. "I did not hope for such generosity."

His lordship smiled affectionately. "Yes, 'tis generous," he returned. "I would be so generous with no other man. Kneller paints her for me now, full length, in her Court bravery and with all her diamonds blazing on her. 'Twill be a splendid canvas. And lest you should think me too ready to give this away, I will tell you that I feel the story of the rascal painter would displease her. She hath too high a spirit not to be fretted at the thought of being the unconscious tool of a drunken vagabond."

"Yes, it will anger her," Osmonde said, and ended with a sudden smiling. "Yet I could not keep hidden the beauties of my kinsman's lady, and must tell him."

So the matter ended with friendly smiles and kindliness, and the picture was laid back within the cabinet until such time as it should be framed and hung.

"Surely you have learned to love it somewhat in your wanderings?" said the older man with trusting nobleness, standing looking at it, his hand on the other's arm. "You could not help it."

"No, I could not help it," answered Osmonde, and to himself he said, "He will drive me mad, generous soul; he will drive me mad."

His one hope and effort was so to bear himself that the unhappy truth should not be suspected, and so well he played his part that he made it harder for himself to endure. It was not only that he had not betrayed himself either in the past or present by word or deed, but that he had been able to so control himself at worst that he had met his kinsman's eye with a clear glance, and chosen such words of response and sympathy, when circumstances so demanded of him, as were generous and gracious and unconcerned.

"There has risen no faintest shadow in his mind," was his thought. "He loves me, he trusts me, he believes I share his happiness. Heaven give me strength."

But there was a time when it was scarce to be avoided that they should be bidden as guests to Camylott, inasmuch as at this splendid and renowned house my Lord of Dunstanwolde had spent some of his happiest hours, and loved it dearly, never ceasing to speak of its stateliness and beauty to his lady.

"It is the loveliest house in England, my lady," he would say, "and Gerald loves it with his whole soul. I think he loves it as well,

125

and almost in such manner as he will some day love her who is his Duchess. Know you that he and I walked together in the noted Long Gallery, on the day I told him the story of your birth?"

My lady turned with sudden involuntary movement and met my lord Duke's eyes (curiously seldom their eyes met, as curiously seldom as if each pair avoided the other). Some strange emotion was in her countenance and rich colour mounted her cheek.

"How was that, my lord?" she asked. "'Twas a strange story, as I have heard it—and a sad one."

"He was but fourteen," said Dunstanwolde, "yet its cruelty set his youthful blood on fire. Never shall I forget how his eyes flashed and he bit his boyish lip, crying out against the hardness of it. 'Is there justice,' he said, 'that a human thing can be cast into the world and so left alone?'"

"Your Grace spoke so," said her ladyship to Osmonde, "while you were yet so young?" and the velvet of her eyes seemed to grow darker.

"It was a bitter thing," said Osmonde. "There was no justice in it."

"Nay, that there was not," my lady said, very low.

"'Twas ordained that you two should be kinsman and kinswoman," said Dunstanwolde. "He was moved by stories of your house when he was yet a child, and he was ever anxious to hear of your ladyship's first years, and later, when I longed for a confidant, though he knew it not, I talked to him often, feeling that he alone of all I knew could understand you."

Her ladyship stood erect and still, her eyes downcast, as she slowly stripped a flower of its petals one by one. My lord Duke watched her until the last flame-coloured fragment fell, when she looked up and gazed into his face with a strange, tragic searching.

"Then you have known me long, your Grace?" she said.

He bowed his head, not wishing that his voice should at that moment be heard.

"Since your ladyship was born," said her lord, happy that these two he loved so well should feel they were not strangers. "Together we both saw you in the hunting-field—when you were but ten years old."

Her eyes were still upon his—he felt that his own gazed into strange depths of her. The crimson had fallen away from her beauteous cheeks and she faintly, faintly smiled—almost, he thought, as if she mocked at somewhat, woefully.

"Then—then you might have been one of those," she said, slow and soft, "who came to the birthnight feast and—and saw my life begin."

126

And she bent down as if she scarce knew what she did, and slowly gathered up one by one the torn petals she had broken from her flower.

"Then you will ask us to come to visit you at Camylott, Gerald?" said my lord later after they had talked further, he speaking of the beauties of the place and the loveliness of the country about it.

"It will be my joy and honour to be your host," Osmonde answered. "Since my parents' death I have not entertained guests, but had already thought of doing so this year, and could have no better reason for hospitality than my wish to place my house at your ladyship's service," with a bow, "and make you free of it—as of every other roof of mine."

CHAPTER XX

At Camylott

A month later the flag floated from Camylott Tower and the village was all alive with rustic excitement, much ale being drunk at the Plough Horse and much eager gossip going on between the women, who had been running in and out of each other's cottages for three days to talk over each item of news as it reached them. Since the new Duke had taken possession of his inheritance there had been no rejoicing or company at the Tower, all the entertaining rooms having been kept closed, and the great house seeming grievously quiet even when his Grace came down to spend a few weeks in it. To himself the silence had been a sorrowful thing, but he had no desire to break it by filling the room with guests, and had indeed resolved in private thought not to throw open its doors until he brought to it a mistress. The lovely presence of the last mistress it had known had been so brightly illuminating a thing, filling its rooms and galleries and the very park and terraces and gardens themselves with sunshine and joyousness. In those happy days no apartment had seemed huge and empty, no space too great to warm and light with homely pleasure. But this fair torch extinguished, apartments large enough for royal banquets, labyrinths of corridors and galleries leading to chambers enough to serve a garrison, seemed all the more desolate for their size and splendour, and in them their owner had suffered a sort of homesickness. 'Twas a strange thing to pass through the beautiful familiar places now that they were all thrown open and adorned for the coming guests, reflecting that the gala air was worn for her who should, Fate willing, have made her first visit as mistress, and realising that Fate had not been willing and that she came but as a guest and Countess of Dunstanwolde. Oh, it was a bitter, relentless thing; and why should it have been—for what wise purpose or what cruel one? And with a maddening clutch about his heart he saw again the tragic searching in her eyes when she had said, "Then you have known me long, your Grace," and afterwards, so soft and strangely slow, "Then you might have been one of those who came to my birthnight feast, and saw my life begin."

He might have been, Heaven knew. Good God, why had he not? Why had he gone back to Flanders? Now it seemed to his mind the folly of a madman, and yet at the time he had felt his duty to his house commanded that he should not give way to the rising tempest of his passion, but should at least wait a space that time might prove that he could justly trust the honour of his name and the fortune of his peoples into this wild, lovely being's hands. Had he been free from all responsibilities, free enough to feel that he risked no happiness but his own, and by his act could wrong none other than himself, he would not have waited to see what time wrought but have staked his future life upon this die. He had denied himself and waited, and here he stood in the Long Gallery, and 'twas thrown open and adorned for the coming of my Lady Dunstanwolde.

"I meant an honest thing," he said, gazing out over his fair domain through a dark mist, it seemed to him. "All my life I have meant honestly. Why should a man's life go wrong because he himself would act right?"

The flag fluttered and floated from the battlements of the tower, the house was beautiful in its air of decorated order and stateliness, glowing masses of flowers lighted every corner, and tall exotic plants stood guard about; the faces of lord and lady, dame and knight, in the pictures seemed to look downward with a waiting gaze. Outside, terraces and parterres were wonders of late summer brilliancy of bloom, and the sunshine glowed over all. On the high road from town at this hour the cavalcades of approaching guests must ride in coach or chariot or on horseback. When the equipage of the Earl and his Countess passed through Camylott village, old Rowe would ring a welcoming peal. But my lord Duke stood still at the window of the Long Gallery where he had said his tender farewell to his beloved mother before she had left her home. He was thinking of a grave thing and feeling that the violet eyes rested upon him again in a soft passion of pity. The thing he thought of was that which, when his eyes met my Lady Dunstanwolde's, made the blood pulse through his veins; 'twas that he had known he should some day see in some woman's eyes, and had told himself would be answer to the question his being asked; 'twas that he had prayed God he might see, ay, and had believed and sworn to himself he should see—in this woman's when he came back to stand face to face with her as lover, if she would. Well, he had come and seen it, and 'twas in the eyes and soul of her who was to be his kinsman's wife. And never since he had been man born had he beheld the faintest glimmering of its glow in any woman's eyes, though they had been like pools of love or stars of Heaven, never yet! Moreover, he knew well that he never should again behold it in any hour to come. Before its fire his soul shook and his body trembled; 'twas a thing which drew him with a power no human being could explain the strength of or describe; had he been weak or evil, and she evil, too, it would have dragged him to her side through crime and hell; he could not have withstood it.

He saw again the sudden pallor of his mother's sweet face, the sudden foreboding in her eyes.

"If you loved her 'twould drive you mad and make you forget what you must be."

"Yes," he cried, putting his hand suddenly to his brow, feeling it damp, "it has driven me mad, I think—mad. I am not the same man! The torture is too great. I could—I could—nay! nay!" with half a shudder. "Let me not forget, mother; let me not forget."

Through this visit he must be a gracious host; a score of other guests would aid him by sharing his attentions; her ladyship, as new wedded bride, would be the central figure of the company. Her lord's love for him and unconsciousness of any suspicion of the truth would put him to the test many a time, but he would keep his word to himself, the vow he made to avoid nearness to her when 'twas to be done with any graciousness, and her eyes he would not meet in more than passing gaze if he could be master of his own.

"If I look straightly at her my own gaze will speak, and she, who is so shrewd of wit and has seen such worship in men's faces, will read and understand, and disdain me, or—disdain me not. God knows which would be worse."

The visit over, he would visit other of his estates, engage himself with friends to be their guests in Scotland, Ireland, and Wales, at their châteaux in France or Spain—everywhere. When he was not thus absorbed he would give himself to a statesman's work at the settling of great questions—the more involved and difficult

129

the better; party enmity would be good for him, the unravelling of webs of intrigue, the baffling of cabals would keep his thoughts in action, and leave him no time for dreams. Yes, to mark out his days thus clearly would help him to stand steady upon his feet—in time might aid in deadening the burning of the wound which would not close. Above all, to Warwickshire he would not go—Dunstan's Wolde must see him no more, and Dunstanwolde House in town he would gradually visit less and less often, until his kinsman ceased to expect the old familiarity, believing his many duties kept him away. In his happiness he would have but little time to miss him seriously, perhaps even to remember that his presence had been once so much less rare a thing.

"'Son,' he once loved to call me," he thought, with a sharp pang. "He is an old man, 'tis true, but Heaven may give him a son of his own."

Even as the thought crossed his mind—as a flame of lightning crosses a black sky—he heard old Rowe begin to ring his peal, and soon—or it seemed soon to him—the first party of arrivals wound through the park, now and then its colours gleaming through an opening in the trees. There were mounted and safely armed servitors riding in attendance to guard the big travelling-coach with its six strong, finely bred horses. In this the Earl and his Countess sate, the lady a little pale, from the fatigue of her journey, perhaps; following them came another vehicle, substantial but less splendid than their own equipage, in it, my lady's two Abigails and the gentleman of his lordship carrying the iron jewel-box secreted in a special hiding-place beneath the seat, for the baffling of highwaymen, if any such were bold enough to attack a party so well attended by sturdy strength and shining arms. When she had stepped forth across the threshold of her town house, attended by subservient lacqueys bowing in line on either side, the Countess had faintly smiled, and when they had entered their coach and the door been closed upon them, she had turned this smile with a sweet archness upon her lord.

"I smile, my Lord," she said, "to think what a great lady your goodness has made of me, and how in these days I ride forth, and how in the past, when I was but Clo Wildairs our old chariot lumbered like a house on wheels, and its leather hung in flaps, and the farm horses pulled it lurching from side to side, and old Bartlemy had grown too portly for his livery and cursed when it split as he rolled in his seat." And her laugh rang out as if it were a chime of bells, and her lord, laughing with her—but for joy in her arch gayety—adored her.

"If any had told the county then that I would one day ride forth like this," says she, "from Dunstanwolde House to pay visit to a Duke at Camylott, who could have believed it? I would not myself. And 'tis you who have given me all, my dear lord," laying her soft hand in his. "You, Edward, and I am full of gratefulness."

What wonder that he was a happy man, he who had hoped for so little and had found so much, since she did not think—as a slighter woman might—that her youth and beauty paid for and outweighed his richest gifts, but was heavenly kind and dutiful and tender, giving him of her brightest humours and prettiest playfulness and gentlest womanly thought, and receiving his offerings, not as her mere right, but as signals of his generousness and tender love for her.

"Look, my lady!" he cried, as they drove up the avenue, "see what a noble house it is; there is no other, in all England, of its size and beauty. And Gerald waits to receive us with no Duchess at his side."

Her ladyship leaned forward to look, and gazed a moment in silence.

"There should be one," she cried, "to reign over such a place, and to be happy in it."

The village saw gayety enough to turn its head in the two weeks that followed. The flag floated from the tower every day, coaches rolled past the village green laden with the county gentry who came to pay their respects, gay cavalcades rode down the avenue and through the big gates to gallop over the country with joyous laughter and talk; at the Plough Horse, Mr. Mount, who had grown too old for service, but had been pensioned and was more fond of fine stories than ever, added to his importance as a gentleman of quality by describing the banquets at the Towers, the richness of the food, the endless courses, the massiveness of the gold plate, the rareness of the wines, and the magnificence of the costumes of the guests.

"There are fine women there," he would say, removing his long churchwarden's pipe from his mouth and waving it to give emphasis. "In my day I have seen King Charles at Hampton Court— my Lady Castlemaine, and Mistress Frances Stewart, who married a Duke and had her eyes put out by smallpox and her face spoiled forever, poor soul; and De Querouaille—the one you will call Carwell, which is not her name, but a French one—and Mazarin— and all could see Nell Gwynne who could pay for a seat in the play-house—so I may well be a judge of women—and have lived gayly myself about the Court. But there is one—this moment at Camylott Towers—there is one," describing a great circle with his pipe as if he

131

writ her name, "and may the devil seize and smite me, if there was ever a lady with such a body and face on earth before."

"'Tis the tall one with the flashing black eyes," cried out Will Bush the first night that he said it. "Me and my dame saw her through the glass of the coach the day they drove over the green with all their servants come to follow them from Lunnon town with pistols and hangers. And what think you? says I to Joan, 'Ecod,' says I, 'there's the woman for our own Duke, and matches him for size and beauty!' And says Joan, staring: 'Lord a mercy, so she is and does!'"

"Village folk," said Mr. Mount with decorum, "are not the ones to take upon themselves the liberty to say who will suit a Duke or who will not suit him. But this I will say to you, that for once you were not so far wrong; I having said the same thing myself. And his Grace is a single man, whom they say loves no woman—and my lady has a husband near seventy years of age. So things go!"

To her husband and lord, this lady seemed for all her powers, the sweetest, frank creature in the world, and indeed in all matters which concerned their united life she was candour itself. But there was a thing in her mind—and 'twas in her thought every day—of which, though she was within his sight almost every waking hour and her head lay upon the pillow by his own, when she slept, he knew nothing. In gaining grace of manner and bearing she had not lost her old quickness of sight and alertness of mind; if any felt that her eyes were less keen, her perception less acute, their error was a grave one. Beneath the majesty of her Ladyship of Dunstanwolde lay all the fire and flaming spirit, the swiftness to deduce and act, which had set Clo Wildairs apart from lesser women. So it was that she had not been three hours at Camylott before she knew that, with regard to herself, my Lord Duke of Osmonde had made some strong resolve. No other than herself could have detected, she knew, but on her first glance at his face she beheld it written there. There are human beings, it is sure, whose natures are so attuned that the thoughts, the griefs, the passions of each are reflected upon the brain of the other; and 'twas thus with these two whom life thrust so far apart from one another and yet forced so near. At their first meeting on the threshold and in the midst of his warm and gracious welcome she read what none other could read, and felt a pang which yet was gladness. 'Twas better so—her strength should aid his own, his greatness should support her. There was no question in her mind, no argument, only a sudden recognition of the truth that up to this time she had scarcely allowed herself mere thought in connection with him, that—after the first hour—when thought had risen she had thrust it back, forbidden its being, denied its presence.

132

"Thought will not help," she had said once, when, as she had sate alone, she had felt hot, passionate tears start to her eyes, and she had flung down her book, risen from her chair, and left the room ten minutes later, riding forth from the court followed by her groom and making for the country roads.

From the earliest days of her marriage she had herself avoided often meeting his gaze. Glances would not help either, but would do harm and betray—between those who are drawn together as by some force of Nature, glances are mad things. They may begin calmly, they may swear that they will so continue, but looks entangle one day and catch fire, and, once alight, the flame cannot extinguish itself, even when it would.

At Camylott each was gracious to the other, he gracious host, she gracious guest and kinswoman, and those who looked on praised each one and honoured, speaking often of their charm and courtly friendliness, which indeed made them seem almost like brother and sister.

"They are a strange pair, those two fine creatures," said the old Dowager Storms one day to her favourite crony, an elderly matron to whom she could safely talk gossip. "But look at them." (They were with the whole party at racquets in the court, and my lord Duke, having made a splendid stroke, glowing and laughing bowed in response to a round of applause.) "Is there a husband at Court—though he were not thirty-five—who has reason to feel as safe as the old Earl Dunstanwolde may—when his wife is guest to such a pretty fellow as he?" nodding her head towards his Grace. "Never in my days saw I a thing so out of nature! 'Tis as though they were not flesh and blood, but—but of some stuff we are not made of. 'Tis but human he should make sly love to her, and her eyes wander after him despite herself wheresoever he goes. All know how a woman's eyes will follow a man, and his hers, but when these look at each other 'tis steadfast honesty that looks out of them—and 'tis scarce to be understood."

CHAPTER XXI

Upon the Moor

Throughout the festivities which followed each other, day by day, my Lady Dunstanwolde was queen of every revel. 'Twas she who led the adventurous party who visited the gipsy encampment in the glen by moonlight, and so won the heart of the old gipsy queen that she took her to her tent and instructed her in the mysteries of spells and potions. She walked among them as though she had been bred and born one of their tribe, and came forth from one tent carrying in her arms a brown infant, and showed it to the company, laughing like a girl and making pretty sounds at the child when it stared at her with great black eyes like her own, and shook at it all her rings, which she stripped from her fingers, holding them in the closed palm of her hand to make a rattle of. She stirred the stew hanging to cook over the camp-fire, and begged a plate of it for each of the company, and ate her own with such gay appetite as recalled to Osmonde the day he had watched her on the moor; and the gipsy women stood by showing their white teeth in their pleasure, and the gipsy men hung about with black shining eyes fixed on her in stealthy admiration. She stood by the fire in the light of the flame, having fantastically wound a scarlet scarf about her head, and 'twas as though she might have been a gipsy queen herself.

"And indeed," she said, as they rode home, "I have often enough thought I should like to be one of them; and when I was a child, and was in a passion, more than once planned to stain my face and run away to the nearest camp I could come upon. Indeed, I think I was always a rebel and loved wild, lawless ways."

When she said it my lord Duke, who was riding near, looked straight before him, with face which had belied his laugh, had any seen it. He was thinking that he could well imagine what a life a man might lead with her, wandering about the thick green woods and white roads and purple moors, tramping, side by side, in the sweet wind and bright sunshine, and even the soft falling rain, each owner of a splendid body which defied the weather and laughed at fatigue. To carry their simple meal with them and stop to eat it joyously together under a hedge, to lie under the shade of a broad branched tree to rest when the sun was hot and hear the skylarks singing in the blue sky, and then at night-time to sit at the door of a tent and watch the stars and tell each other fanciful stories of them, while the red camp-fire danced and glowed in the dark. Of no other

134

woman could he have had such a wild fancy—the others were too frail and delicate to be a man's comrades out of doors; but she, who stood so straight and strong, who moved like a young deer, who could swing along across the moors for a day without fatigue, who had the eye of a hawk and a spirit so gay and untiring—a man might range the world with her and know joy every moment. 'Twas ordained that all she did or said should seem a call to him and should bring visions to him, and there was many an hour when he thanked Heaven she seemed so free from fault, since if she had had one he could not have seen it, or if he had seen, might have loved it for her sake. But she had none, it seemed, and despite all her strange past was surely more noble than any other woman. She was so true—he told himself—so loyal and so high in her honour of the old man who loved her. Had she even been innocently light in her bearing among the men who flocked about her, she might have given her lord many a bitter hour, and seemed regardless of his dignity; but she could rule and restrain all, howsoever near they were to the brink of folly. As for himself, Osmonde thought, all his days he had striven to be master of himself, and felt he must remain so or die; but he could have worshipped her upon his knees in gratitude that no woman's vanity tempted her to use her powers and loveliness to shake him in his hard won calmness and lure him to her feet. He was but man and human, and vaunted himself upon being no more.

There had been for some months much talk in town of the rapid downfall of the whilom favourite of Fashion, Sir John Oxon. But a few weeks before the coming happiness of the old Earl of Dunstanwolde was made known to the world, there had been a flurry of gossip over a rumour that Sir John, whose fortunes were in a precarious condition, was about to retrieve them by a rich marriage. A certain Mistress Isabel Beaton, a young Scotch lady, had been for a year counted the greatest fortune in the market, and besieged by every spendthrift or money-seeker the town knew. Not only was she heiress to fine estates in Scotland, but to wealth-yielding sugar plantations in the West Indies. She was but twenty and had some good looks and an amiable temper, though with her fortune, had she been ugly as Hecate, she would have had more suitors than she could manage with ease. But she was not easily pleased, or of a susceptible nature, and 'twas known she had refused suitor after suitor, among them men of quality and rank, the elegant and decorous Viscount Wilford, among others, having knelt at her feet, and—having proffered her the boon of his lofty manner and high accomplishments —having been obliged to rise a discarded man, to his amazement and discomfort. The world she lived in was

135

of the better and more respectable order, and Jack Oxon had seen little of it, finding it not gay and loose enough for his tastes, but suddenly, for reasons best known to himself and to his anxious mother, he began to appear at its decorous feasts. 'Twas said of him he "had a way" with women and could make them believe anything until they found him out, either through lucky chance or because he had done with them. He could act the part of tender, honest worshipper, of engaging penitent, of impassioned and romantic lover until a woman old and wise enough to be his mother might be entrapped by him, aided as he was by his beauty, his large blue eyes, his merry wit, and the sweetest voice in the world. So it seemed that Mistress Beaton, who was young and had lived among better men, took him for one and found her fancy touched by him. His finest allurements he used, verses he writ, songs he made and sang, poetic homilies on disinterested passion he preached, while the world looked on and his boon companions laid wagers. At last those who had wagered on him won their money, those who had laid against him lost, for 'twas made known publicly that he had won the young lady's heart, and her hand and fortune were to be given to him.

This had happened but a week or two before he had appeared at the ball which celebrated young Colin's coming of age, and also by chance the announcement of the fine match to be made of Mistress Clorinda Wildairs. 'Twas but like him, those who knew him said, that though he himself was on the point of making a marriage, he should burn with fury and jealous rage, because the beauty he had dangled about had found a husband and a fortune. Some said he had loved Mistress Clorinda with such passion that he would have wed her penniless if she would have taken him, others were sure he would have married no woman without fortune, whatsoever his love for her, and that he had but laid dishonest siege to Mistress Clo and been played with and flouted by her. But howsoever this might have been, he watched her that night, black with rage, and went back to town in an evil temper. Perhaps 'twas this temper undid him, and being in such mood he showed the cloven foot, for two weeks later all knew the match was broken off, Mistress Beaton went back to her estates in Scotland, his creditors descended upon him in hordes, such of his properties as could be seized were sold, and in a month his poor, distraught mother died of a fever brought on by her disappointment and shame.

Another story was told in solution of the sudden breaking off the match, and 'twas an ugly one and much believed.

A wild young cousin of the lady's, one given to all the adventures of a man about town, had gone to Tyburn, as was much the elegant fashion, to see a 'hanging. The victim was a girl of sixteen, to suffer for the murder of her infant, and as she went to the gallows she screamed aloud in frenzy the name of the child's father. The young scapegrace looking on, 'twas said, turned pale on hearing her and went into the crowd, asking questions. Two hours later he appeared at his cousin's house and, calling for her guardian, held excited speech with him.

"Mistress Isabel fell like a stone after ten minutes' talk with them," 'twas told, "and looked like one when she got into her travelling-coach to drive away next day. Sir John and his mother had both raged and wept at her door to be let in, but she would see or speak to neither of them."

From that time it seemed that all was over for Sir John. He was far worse than poor and in debt, he was out of fashion, and for a man like himself this meant not only humiliation, but impotent rage. Ladies no longer ogled him and commanded the stopping of their chairs that they might call him to them with coquettish reproaches that he neither came to their assemblies nor bowed and waved hands to them as he sate on the stage at the playhouse; beaux no longer joined him in the coffee-house or on the Mall to ask his opinion of this new beauty or that, and admire the cut of his coat, or the lace on his steenkirk; the new beauty's successes would not be advanced by his opinion—a man whom tradespeople dun from morn till night has few additions to his wardrobe and wears few novelties in lace. Profligacy and defiance of all rules of healthful living had marred his beauty and degraded his youth; his gay wit and spirit had deserted him and left him suspicious and bitter. He had been forced to put down his equipages and change his fashionable lodgings for cheaper ones; when he lounged in the park his old acquaintances failed to see him; when he gambled he lost. Downhill he was going, and there was naught to stop him. For one man in England he had, even in his most flourishing days, cherished a distaste—the man who was five inches taller than himself, who was incomparably handsomer, and whose rank was such, that to approach him as an equal would have savoured of presumption. This man, who was indeed my Lord Duke of Osmonde, had irked him from the first, and all the more when he began to realise that for some reason, howsoever often they chanced to be in the same place, it invariably happened that they did not come in contact with each other, Sir John on no occasion being presented to my lord Duke, his Grace on no occasion seeming to observe his presence near him. At the outset this appeared mere accident, but after a few such encounters ending in nothing, Sir John began to guess that 'twas the result of more than mere chancing, and in time to mark that, though he was not clumsily avoided, or in such manner as would leave any room for complaint, my lord Duke forebore to enter into any conversation in which he took part, or to approach any quarter where he was stationed. Once Sir John had even tried the experiment of addressing an acquaintance who stood near his Grace, meaning to lead up to a meeting, but though the Duke did not move from the place where he stood, in a few moments he had, with ease and naturalness, gathered about him a circle which 'twould have been difficult indeed to enter. Sir John went away livid, and hated and sneered at him from that hour, all the more bitterly, because no hatred was a weapon against him, no sneer could do more than glance from him, leaving no scratch. 'Twas plain enough, the gossips said, that Sir John's passion for her ladyship of Dunstanwolde had not been a dead thing when he paid his court to the heiress; if for a little space he had smothered it from necessity's sake, it had begun to glow again as soon as he had been left a free man, and when my lady came to town and Court, surrounded by the halo of rank and wealth and beauty, the glow had become a flame he could not hide, for 'twas burning in his eyes and his every look spoke of it as if with bitterness.

It scarcely seemed a flame of love; 'twas to be seen so often when he looked fierce and resentful.

"'Tis more than half envy of her," said one wise lady, who had passed through a long life of varied experiences. "'Tis more hate than love. His star having set, it galls him that hers so rises. And as for her, she scarce will deign to see him."

And this was very true, for she had a way of passing him by as if he did not live. And none but herself knew that sometimes, when he stood near, he spoke low to her words she disdained to answer. There were many bitter things she held in mind which were secret from all others upon earth, she thought, but from himself and her who had been Clo Wildairs in days gone by, when, as it now seemed to her, she had been another woman living in another world. There were things she understood which the world did not, and she understood full well the meaning of his presence when she, with the ducal party, came face to face with him at the great ball given in the county town when the guests were gathered at Camylott.

The night was a festal one for the county, the ball being given in honour of a great party movement, his Grace and his visitors driving from Camylott to add to the brilliance of the festivities. The Mayor and his party received them with ceremony, the smaller gentry, who had come attired in their richest, gathered in groups gazing, half admiring, half envious of the more stately splendour of the Court mantua-makers and jewellers. The officers from the garrison assumed a martial air of ease as the cortége advanced up

138

the ballroom, and every man's eyes were drawn towards one tall goddess with a shining circlet set on raven-black braids of hair coiled high, yet twisted tight, as if their length and thickness could only be massed close enough by deftest skill.

"'Tis said 'tis near six feet long," whispered one matron to another; "and a rake at Court wagered he would show a lock of it in town some day, but he came back without it."

Sir John Oxon had come with a young officer, and stood near him as the ducal party approached. The Countess of Dunstanwolde was on his Grace's arm, and Sir John made a step forward. Her ladyship turned her eyes slowly, attracted by the movement of a figure so near her; she did not start nor smile, but let her glance rest quiet on his face and curtsied calmly; my lord Duke bowed low with courtly gravity, and they passed on.

When the ball was at an end, and the party set out on its return to Camylott, the Duke did not set out with the rest, he being at the last moment unexpectedly detained. This he explained with courtly excuses, saying that he would not be long held, and would mount and follow in an hour.

He stood upon the threshold to watch the last chariot leave the courtyard, and then he made his way to a certain supper-room, where a lingering party of officers and guests were drinking. These being of the young and riotous sort, there was much loud talk and laughter and toasting of ladies, sometimes far from respectfully, and Sir John Oxon, who was flushed with wine, was the central figure, and toasted her ladyship of Dunstanwolde with an impudent air.

"'Tis not my lady I drink to," he cried, "but Clo Wildairs—Clo astride a hunter and with her black hair looped under her hat. Clo! Clo!" And with a shout the company drank to the toast.

"There was a lock of that black hair clipt from her head once when she knew it not," Sir John cried next. "'Twas lost, by God, but 'twill be found again. Drink to its finding."

Then my lord Duke stepped forward and, passing the open door, went through the house and out beyond the entrance of the court and waited in a place where any who came forth must pass. He had but gone within to see that Sir John had not yet taken his departure.

There be deeps in the nature of human beings which in some are never stirred, possibilities of heroism, savagery, passion, or crime, and when the hour comes which searches these far secret caverns and brings their best and worst to light, strange things may be seen. On the night, at Dunstanwolde, when he had fought his battle alone, my lord Duke had realised the upheaval in his being of frenzies and lawlessness which were strange indeed to him, and

139

which he had afterwards pondered deeply upon, tracing the germs of them to men whose blood had come down to him through centuries, and who had been untamed, ruthless savages in the days when a man carried his life in his hand and staked it recklessly for any fury or desire.

Now as he stood and waited, his face was white except that on one cheek was a spot almost like a scarlet stain of blood; his eyes seemed changed to blue-black, and in each there was a light which flickered like a point of flame and made him seem not himself, but some new relentless being, for far deeps of him had been shaken and searched once more.

"I wait here like a brigand," he said to himself with a harsh laugh, "or a highwayman—but he shall not pass."

Then Sir John crossed the courtyard and came forward humming, and his Grace of Osmonde advanced and met him.

"Sir John Oxon," he said, and stood still and made a grave bow.

John Oxon started and then stood still also, staring at him, his face flushed and malignant. His Grace of Osmonde was it who had gazed above his head throughout the evening, when all the country world might see!

"Your Grace deigns to address me at last," he said.

"Hitherto there has been no need that either should address the other," answers my lord Duke in a steady voice. "At this moment the necessity arises. Within there"—with a gesture—"I heard you use a lady's name impudently. Earlier in the evening I also chanced to hear you so use it; I was in the ball-room. So I remained behind and waited to have speech with you. Do not speak it again in like manner."

"Must I not!" said Sir John, his blue eyes glaring. "On Clo Wildairs's name was set no embargo, God knows. Is there a reason why a man should be squeamish of a sudden over my Lady Dunstanwolde's? 'Tis but the difference of a title and an old husband."

"And of a man made her kinsman by marriage," said my lord Duke, "who can use a sword."

"Let him use it, by God!" cried Sir John, and insensate with rage he laid his hand upon his own as if he would draw it.

"He will use it and is prepared to do so, or he would not be here," the Duke answered. "We are not two Mohocks brawling in the streets, but two gentlemen, one of whom must give a lesson to the other. Would you have witnesses?"

"Curse it, I care for none!" flamed Sir John. "Let the best man give his lesson now. 'Tis not this night alone I would be even for."

140

The Duke measured him from head to foot, in every inch of sinew.

"I am the better man," he said; "I tell you beforehand."

Sir John flung out a jeering laugh.

"Prove it," he cried. "Prove it. Now is your time."

"There is open moor a short distance away," says his Grace. "Shall we go there?"

So they set out, walking side by side, neither speaking a word. The night was still and splendid, and just upon its turn; the rich dark-blue of the Heavens was still hung with the spangles of the stars, but soon they would begin to dim, and the deepness of the blue to pale for dawn. A scented freshness was in the air, and was just stirring with that light faint wind which so often first foretells the coming of the morning. When, in but a few minutes, the two men stood stript of their upper garments to their shirts, the open purple heath about them, the jewelled sky above, this first fresh scent of day was in their lungs and nostrils. That which stirred John Oxon to fury and at the same time shook his nerve, though he owned it not to himself, and would have died rather, was the singular composure of the man who was his opponent. Every feature, every muscle, every fibre of him seemed embodied stillness, and 'twas not that the mere physical members of him were still, but that the power which was himself, his will, his thought, his motion was in utter quiet, and of a quiet which was deadly in its significance and purpose. 'Twas that still strength which knows its power and will use it, and ever by its presence fills its enemy with impotent rage.

With such rage it filled John Oxon as he beheld it, and sneered. He had heard rumours of the wonders of his Grace's sword-play, that from boyhood he had excelled and delighted in it, that in the army he had won renown, through mere experiments of his skill, that he was as certain of his weapon as an acrobat of his least feat—but 'twas not this which maddened the other man but the look in his steady eye.

"You are the bigger man of the two," he jeered, impudently, "but give me your lesson and shut my mouth on Clo Wildairs—if you can."

"I am the better man," says my lord Duke, "and I will shut it. But I will not kill you."

Then they engaged, and such a fight began as has not been often seen, for such a battle is more of spirit than body, and is more like to be fought alone between two enemies whose antagonism is part of being itself, than to be fought in the presence of others whose nearness would but serve to disturb it.

141

John Oxon had fought duels before, through women who were but his despised playthings, through braggadocio, through drunken folly, through vanity and spite—but never as he fought this night on the broad heath, below the paling stars. This man he hated, this man he would have killed by any thrust he knew, if the devil had helped him. There is no hatred, to a mind like his, such as is wakened by the sight of another's gifts and triumphs—all the more horrible is it if they are borne with nobleness. To have lost all—to see another possess with dignity that thing one has squandered! And for this frenzy there was more than one cause. Clo Wildairs! He could have cursed aloud. My Lady Dunstanwolde! He could have raved like a madman. She! And a Duke here—this Duke would shut his mouth and give him a lesson. He lunged forward and struck wildly; my lord Duke parried his point as if he played with the toy of a child, and in the clear starlight his face looked a beautiful mask, and did not change howsoever furious his opponent's onslaught, or howsoever wondrous his own play. For wondrous it was, and before they had been engaged five minutes John Oxon was a maddened creature, driven so, not only by his own fury, but by seeing a certain thing—which was that this man could kill him if he would, but would not. When he had lost his wits and made his senseless lunge, his Grace had but parried when he might have driven his point home; he did this again and again while their swords clashed and darted. The stamp of their feet sounded dull and heavy on the moor, and John Oxon's breath came short and hissing. As he grew more wild the other grew more cool and steady, and made a play which Sir John could have shrieked out at seeing. What was the man doing? 'Twas as if he would show him where he could strike and did not deign to. He felt his devil's touch in a dozen places, and not one scratch. There he might have laid open his face from brow to chin! Why did he touch him here, there, at one point and another, and deal no wound? Gods! 'twas fighting not with a human thing but with a devil! 'Twas like fighting in a Roman arena, to be played with as a sport until human strength could bear no more; 'twas as men used to fight together hundreds of years ago. His breath grew short, his panting fiercer, the sweat poured down him, his throat was dry, and he could feel no more the fresh stirring of the air of the dawning. He would not stop to breathe, he had reached the point in his insensate fury when he could have flung himself upon the rapier's point and felt it cleave his breastbone and start through his back with the joy of hell, if he could have struck the other man deep but once. The thought made him start afresh; he fought like a thousand devils, his point leaping and flashing, and coming down with a crash; he stamped and gasped and shouted.

142

"Curse you," he cried; "come on!"

"Do I stand back?" said my lord Duke, and gave him such play as made him see the air red as blood, and think he tasted the salt of blood in his dry mouth; his muscles were wrenched with his violence, and this giant devil moved as swift as if he had but just begun. Good God! he was beaten! Good God! by this enemy who would not kill him or be killed. He uttered a sound which was a choking shriek and hurled himself forward. 'Twas his last stroke and he knew it, and my lord Duke struck his point aside and it flew in the air, and Sir John fell backwards broken, conquered, exhausted, but an unwounded man. And he fell full length and lay upon the heather, its purple blooms crushed against his cheek; and the sky was of a sweet pallor just about to glow, and the first bird of morning sprang up in it to sing.

"Damn you!" he gasped. "Damn you," and lay there, his blue eyes glaring, his chest heaving as though 'twould burst, his nostrils dilated with his laboured, tortured puffs of breath. Thereupon, as he lay prostrate, for he was too undone a man to rise, he saw in his Grace of Osmonde's eyes the two points of light which were like ruthless flames and yet burned so still.

And his Grace, standing near him, leaned upon his sword, looking down.

"Do you understand?" he said.

"That you are the better sword—Yes!" shrieked Sir John, and added curses it were useless to repeat.

"That I will have you refrain from speaking that lady's name?"

"Force me to it, if you can," Sir John raved at him. "You can but kill me!"

"I will not kill you," said the Duke, leaning a little nearer and the awful light in his eyes growing intenser—for awful it was and made his pale face deadly. "How I can force you to it I have shown you—and brought you here to prove. For that, I meant that we should fight alone. Myself, I knew, I could hold from killing you, howsoever my blood might tempt me. You, I knew, I could keep from killing me, which I knew you would have done if you could, by foul means if not fair. I would not have it said I was forced to fight to shield that lady's name—so I would have no witness if it could be helped. And you will keep the encounter secret, for I command you."

Sir John started up, leaning upon his elbow, catching his breath, and his wicked face a white flame.

"Curse you!" he shrieked again, blaspheming at a thing he had not dreamed of, and which came upon him like a thunderbolt. "Curse your soul—you love her!"

143

The deadly light danced—he saw it—in his Grace's eyes, but his countenance was a marble mask with no human quiver of flesh in any muscle of it.

"I command you," he went on; "having proved I can enforce. I have the blood of savage devils in me, come down to me through many hundred years. All my life I have kept them at bay. Until late I did not know how savage they were and what they could make me feel. I could do to you, as you lie there, things a man who is of this century, and sane, cannot do. You know I can strike where I will. If you slight that lady's name again I will not kill"—he raised himself from his sword and stood his full height, the earliest gold of the sun shining about him—"I will not kill you, but—so help me God!—I will fight with you once more, and I will leave you so maimed and so disfigured that you can woo no woman to ruin again and jest at her shame and agony with no man—for none can bear to look at you without a shudder—and you will lie and writhe to be given the coup de grace." He lifted the hilt of his sword and kissed it. "That I swear," he said, "by this first dawning of God's sun."

When later my lord Duke returned to the town and got his horse and rode across the moors the shortest road to Camylott, he felt suddenly that his body was slightly trembling. He looked down at his hands and saw they were unsteady, and a strange look—as of a man slowly awakening from a dream—- came over his face. 'Twas this he felt—as if the last two hours he had lived in a dream or had been another man than himself, perhaps some bloody de Mertoun, who had for ages been dry, light dust. The devils which had been awake in him had been devils so awful as he well knew—not devils to possess and tear a man in the days of good Queen Anne, but such as, in times long past, possessed those who slew, and hacked, and tortured, and felt an enemy a prey to be put to peine forte et dure. He drew his glove across his brow and found it damp. This dream had taken hold upon him three hours before, when, standing by chance near a group about John Oxon, he had heard him sneer as the old Earl went by with his lady upon his arm. From that moment his brain had held but one thought—this man should not go away until he had taught him a thing. He would teach him, proving to him that there was a power which he might well fear, and which would show no mercy, not even the mercy mere death would show, but would hold over his vile soul a greater awfulness. But he had danced his minuets and gavottes with my Lady Dunstanwolde as well as with other fair ones, and the country gentry had looked on and applauded him in their talk, telling each other of his fortunes, and of how he had had a wound at Blenheim, distinguished himself elsewhere, and set the world wondering because after his home-

144

coming he took no Duchess instead of choosing one, as all expected. While they had so talked and he had danced he had made his plan, and his devils had roused themselves and risen. And then he had made his excuses to his party and watched the coaches drive away, and had gone back to seek John Oxon. Now he rode back over the moorland, and the day was awake and he was awake too. He rode swiftly through the gorse and heather, scattering the dewdrops as he went, thousands of dewdrops there were, myriads of pinkish purple heath-bells, and some pure white ones, and yellow gorse blossoms which smelt of honey, and birds that trilled, and such a morning fragrance in the air as made his heart ache for vague longing. Ah, if all had been but as it might have been, for there were the fair grey towers of Camylott rising before him, and he was riding homeward—and, oh, God, if he had been riding home to the arms of the most heaven-sweet woman in the world—heaven-sweet not for her mere loveliness' sake, but because she was to him as Eve had been to Adam—the one woman God had made.

His heart swelled and throbbed with thinking it as he rode up the avenue, and its throbbing almost stopped when he approached the garden and saw a tall white figure standing alone by a fountain and looking down. He sprang from his horse and turned it loose to reach its stable, and went forward feeling as if a dream had begun again, but this time a strange, sweet one.

Her long white draperies hung loose about her, so that she looked like some statue; her hands were crossed on her chest and her chin fell upon them, while her eyes looked straight before into the water. She was pale as he had never seen her look before, her lip had a weary curve and droop, and under her eyes were shadows. How young she was—what a girl, for all her height and bearing! and though he knew her years so well he had never thought on her youth before. Would God he might have swept her to his breast, crushing her in his arms and plunging into her eyes, for as she turned and raised them to him he saw tears.

"Your ladyship," he exclaimed.

"My lord has been ill," she said. "He asked for you, and when he fell asleep I came to get the morning air, hoping your Grace might come. I must go back to him. Come, your Grace, with me."

CHAPTER XXII

My Lady Dunstanwolde is Widowed

There was a lady came back to town with the Earl and Countess, on their return from Dunstan's Wolde, to which place they had gone after his lordship's illness at Camylott. This lady was one of the two elder sisters of her ladyship of Dunstanwolde, and 'twas said was her favourite and treated with great tenderness by her. She was but a thin, humble little woman—Mistress Anne Wildairs—and singularly plain and timid to be the sister and chosen companion of one so brilliant and full of fire. She was a pale creature with dull-hued heavy hair and soft dull eyes, which followed her ladyship adoringly whensoever it chanced they were in a room together.

"How can two beings so unlike be of the same blood?" people said; "and what finds my lady in her that she does not lose patience at her plainness and poor spirit?"

What she discovered in her, none knew as she herself did; but my Lord Dunstanwolde understood the tie between them, and so his Grace of Osmonde did, since an occasion when he had had speech with her ladyship upon the subject.

"I love her," she said, with one of her strange, almost passionate, looks. "'Tis thought I can love neither man nor woman. But that I can do, and without change; but I must love a thing not slight nor common. Anne was the first creature to teach me what love meant. Before, I had never seen it. She was afraid of me and often thought I mocked at her, but I was learning from her pureness—from her pureness," she added, saying the words the second time in a lower voice and almost as if to herself. And then the splendid sweet of her smile shone forth. "She is so white—good Anne," she said. "She is a saint and does not know I pray to her to intercede for me, and that I live my life hoping that some day I may make it as fair as hers. She does not know, and I dare not tell her, for she would be made afraid."

To Mistress Anne she seemed in truth a goddess. Until taken under her protection, the poor woman had lived a lonely life, starved of all pleasures and affections. At first—'twas in the days when she had been but Clo Wildairs—her ladyship had begun to befriend her through a mere fanciful caprice, being half-amused, half-touched, to find her, by sheer chance, one day, stolen into her chambers to gaze in delighted terror at some ball finery spread upon

146

a bed. To Mistress Clorinda the frightened creature had seemed a strange thing in her shy fearfulness, and she had for an hour amused herself and then suddenly been vaguely moved, and from that time had been friends with her.

"Perhaps I had no heart then, or 'twas not awake," said her ladyship. "I was but a fierce, selfish thing, like a young she-wolf. Is a young she-wolf honest?" with a half-laugh. "I was that, and feared nothing. I ate and drank and sang and hunted poor beasts for my pleasure, and was as wild as one of them myself. When I look back!"—she flung up a white hand in a strange gesture—"When I look back!"

"Look forward!" said my lord Duke; "'tis the nobler thing."

"Yes," she repeated after him, fixing her great eyes gravely on his face and speaking slowly. "'Tis sure the nobler thing."

And then he heard from her how, day by day, poor Anne had revealed to her things strange—unselfishness, humble and tender love, and sweet patience.

"At first I but wondered," she said, "and sate and would stare at her while she talked. And then I pitied her who was so meek, and then I was angered at Fortune, which had been so careless of her, and being a rebel I began to defy Fate for her and swear I would set its cruelty at naught and make her happy. Always," with quick leap of light in her eyes, "I have hated that they call Fate, and defied it. There is a thing in me," her closed hand on her breast, "which will not be beat down! It will not. If 'tis evil, Heaven help me—for it will not. But Anne"—and she smiled again, her face changing as it always did when she spoke her sister's name—"Anne I began to love and could not help it, and she was the first."

This gentlewoman my lord Duke did not for some time see but on rare occasions, at a distance. In her ladyship's great gilt coach he saw her once or twice—a small, shrinking figure seated by her sister's side, the modest pale brown of her lutestring robe a curious contrast to my lady's velvets and brocades; at the play-house he saw her seated in the Countess' box, at which a score of glasses were levelled, her face lighted with wonder and pleasure at the brighter moments of the tragedy, her soft eyes full of tears when the curtain fell upon the corpse-strewn stage. If Mistress Anne had known that so great a gentleman looked at her gentle face and with an actual tenderness near to love itself, she would indeed have been a startled woman, yet 'twas with a feeling like to this his Grace regarded her, thinking of her in time as a sort of guardian angel. The sweetest words he had ever heard from the lips of her he worshipped with such sad and hopeless passion, were words spoken of Mistress Anne; the sweetest strange smile he had ever seen her wear was

147

worn when she spoke of this meek sister; the sweetest womanly deeds he knew of her performing were thoughtful gentlenesses done for the cherishing and protection of Anne. "Anne was the first creature to teach me what love meant," she said.

"I could have taught you, Heart," was his secret thought; "I could have taught you, but since I might not, God's blessing on this dear soul whose tender humbleness was your first lesson." Yet Mistress Anne he did not encounter in person until the occurring of the sad event which changed for him the whole face of the universe itself, and which took place a year or more after his kinsman's marriage. The resolution his Grace had made the day he waited at Camylott for his guests' arrival, he had kept to the letter, and this often to the wonder of his lordship of Dunstanwolde, who found cause for regret at the rareness of his visits to his lady and himself under their own roof. Other visits my lord Duke had made, as he had planned, passing from one great house to another in Great Britain, or making stay at the estates of his friends upon the continent of Europe. Sometimes he was in Scotland, sometimes in Ireland or Wales, hunting, salmon-fishing, the chief guest at great reunions, everywhere discussed and envied his freedom from any love affair, entanglement, or connection with scandal, always a thing which awakened curiosity.

"The world will have you married, Gerald," said Dunstanwolde. "And 'tis no wonder! My lady and I would find you a Duchess. I think she looks for one for you, but finds none to please her taste. She would have a wondrous consort for you. You do wrong to roam so. You should come to Dunstan's Wolde that she may have you beneath her eye."

But to Dunstan's Wolde he did not go—not even when, in obedience to her lord's commands, the Countess herself besought him with gracious hospitality.

To their town house he went but seldom, pleading as reason, affairs which occupied his time, journeys which removed him to other parts. But to refuse to cross the threshold was impossible; accordingly there were times when he must make visits of ceremony, and on one such occasion he found her ladyship alone, and she conveyed to him her husband's message and his desire that she herself should press his invitation.

'Twas upon a winter afternoon, and when my lord Duke was announced he entered the saloon, to behold my lady sitting by the firelight in a carven gilded chair, her eyes upon the glowing coals, her thoughts plainly preoccupied. On hearing his name she slightly started, and on his entry rose and gave him her soft warm hand, which he did not kiss because its velvet so wooed him that he feared

148

to touch it with his lips. 'Twas not a hand which he could touch with simple courtesy, but must long to kiss passionately, and over and over again, and hold close with whispered words.

"My lord has but just left me," she said. "He will be almost angry at the chance which led him to go before your coming. The last hour of our talk was all of your Grace;" and she sat upright against the high back of her chair. And why was it that, while she sat so straight and still, he felt that she held herself as one who needs support? "The last hour of our talk was all of you," she said again, and oh, the velvet of her eyes was asking him for some aid, some mercy; and his soul leaped in anguish as he saw it. "He says I must beguile you to be less formal with us. Before our marriage, he tells me, your Grace came often to Dunstan's Wolde, and now you seem to desert us."

"No, no!" exclaimed my lord Duke, as if involuntarily, and rose from his seat and stood looking down into the fire.

"I told him you would exclaim so!" said my lady, and her low-pitched voice was a thing to make a man tremble. "I know your Grace loves him—I think any heart must love him——"

My lord Duke turned and looked at her. Their eyes rested on each other and spoke.

"I thank your Ladyship," he said, "that you so understood. I pray you let him not think I could at any time feel less tender of his goodness."

But what his whole being impelled him to, was to throw himself upon his knees before her like a boy, to lay his face upon her little hands which rested open upon her lap, and to cry to her that there were hours when he could bear no more. And could it have been that if he had so done she would have bent her dear head and wept—for her voice, when she answered him, had surely tears in it.

"I will not let him think so," she said. "A heart as full of gentleness and warmth as his must not be chilled. I will use all my power. Your Grace has much to do about the Queen at this time of disturbance and cabal. Her Grace of Marlborough's angers, the intrigues of Harley and St. John, the quarrels of Mrs. Masham, make such a turmoil that you, whom her Majesty loves, must be preoccupied." She laid a hand softly upon her breast. "He will believe all that I say," she said. "His kindness is so great to me."

"He loves you," said my lord Duke, his voice low and grave. "You are so generous and noble a lady to him."

"He is so generous and noble a husband," my Lady Dunstanwolde answered. "He thinks I need but ask a favour to find it granted. 'Twas because he thinks so that he begged me to myself

149

speak with you, to ask you to come to Warwickshire next week when we go there. I—have asked you."

"With most sweet graciousness," my lord Duke answered her. "That I myself will tell him." And then he stepped to her side and lifted the fair hand and kissed it very reverently, and without either speaking another word he turned and went away.

"But I do no wrong," he groaned to himself as he walked in a private room of his own house afterwards. "I do no wrong if I go not near her—if I have no speech with her that is not formal courtesy—if I only look on her when she does not know that I am near. And in seeing her, in the mere beholding of her dear face, there is a poor comfort which may hold a man from madness—as a prisoner shut in a dungeon to perish of thirst, might save himself from death if he found somewhere in the blackness a rare falling drop and could catch it as it fell."

So it befel that many a time he saw her when she was in nowise aware of his nearness. All her incomings and outgoings he found a way to learn, when she left town for the country, and when she returned, what fêtes and assemblies she would attend, at what Court gathering she would shine, at which places it would be possible that he might mingle with the crowd and seem to be but where 'twas natural he should appear, if his presence was observed. To behold her sweep by in her chariot, to feel the heart leap which announced her coming, to catch a view of her crimson cheek, a fleeting glance and bow as she passed by, was at least to feel her in the same world with himself, to know that her pulse was beating still, her deep eyes still alight, her voice still music, and she a creature of love, though not for himself.

His Grace of Marlborough, returning to England after Malplaquet, himself worn with the fierce strain of war, tossed on the changing waves of public feeling, one hour the people's idol the next doubted and reproached, was in such mood as made him keen of perception and of feeling.

"Years mark changes in a man, my lord Duke," he said when first they talked alone, "even before they line his face or pale his bloom of health. Since we met you have seen some hours you had not seen when I beheld you last. And yet"—with ironic bitterness— "you are not battling with intrigues of Court and State, with the ingratitude of a nation and the malice of ladies of the royal bedchamber. 'Tis only the man who has won England's greatest victories for her who must contend with such things as these."

"Mrs. Masham has no enmity against me," said Osmonde. "I have no power she would take from me."

"And no wife she would displace about the throne," his Grace added. "The world waits to behold your Duchess still?"

"'Tis I who wait," said Osmonde, gravely.

There was a pause, and while it lasted, Marlborough gazed at him with a thought dawning in his eye.

"You have seen her," he said at last, in a low voice.

Osmonde remained silent. A moment before he had risen, and so stood. The man who regarded him experienced at the moment a singular thing, feeling that it was singular, and vaguely asking himself why. It was a sudden new realisation of his physical perfection. His tall, great body was so complete in grace and strength, each line and muscle of it so fine a thing. In the workings of such a physical being there could be no flaw. There was such beauty in his countenance, such strength and faithful sweetness in his firm, full mouth, such pure, strong passion in the deeps of his large, kind, human eye. The handsomest and the tallest man in England he might be, but he was something more—a complete noble human thing, to whom it surely seemed that nature should be kind, since he had so honoured and done reverence to the gifts she had bestowed upon him. 'Twas this his illustrious companion saw and was moved by.

"You have seen her," he said, "but—since you wear that look which I can read—something has come between. Had you two bared hearts to each other for but one hour, as 'twas ordained you should, you would stand before me so happy a man that none could pass you by and not turn to behold again the glow of the flame of joy burning within your soul."

My Lord Duke of Osmonde drew a long, deep breath as he listened, looking down upon the ground.

"Yes," he said, "'twould have been so."

But he spoke no further on the subject, nor did his Grace of Marlborough, for suddenly there came to him a certain memory—which was that he had heard that the beautiful wild creature who had set Gloucestershire on fire had made a great marriage, her bridegroom being the Earl of Dunstanwolde, who was the Duke of Osmonde's kinsman. And it was she he himself had felt was born to mate with this man, and had spoke of it in Flanders, finding my lord Duke had seen her at a distance but had not encountered her in any company. And at last it seemed that they had met, but not until she had given herself to another.

That night as he drove homeward after an interview with the Queen at Kensington his coach rolled through a street where was a great house standing alone in a square garden. 'Twas a house well known for its size and massive beauty, and he leaned forward to glance at it, for no other reason than his remembrance that it was the home of his lordship of Dunstanwolde, that fact, in connection with the incident of the morning, wakening in him a vague interest.

"'Tis there she reigns Queen," he said, "with her old lord worshipping at her feet as old lords will at the feet of young wives and beauties. Poor gentleman—though she is kind to him, they say. But if 'twere the other man—Good God!" As he uttered the exclamation he drew back within the coach. 'Twas long past midnight and the lights of Dunstanwolde House were extinguished, but in the dark on the opposite side of the street there walked a tall figure wrapped in a long cloak.

"There is no other gentleman of such inches and so straight," his Grace said. "Good Lord! how a man can suffer in such case, and how we are all alike—schoolboys, scullions, or Dukes—and must writhe and yearn and feel we are driven mad, and can find no help but only to follow and look at her, yards away, or crush to one's lips a rag of ribband or a flower, or pace the night away before her darkened house while she lies asleep. He is the finest man-thing I have ever known—and yet there is no other way for him—and he will walk there half the night, his throat full of mad sobs, which he does not know for sobs, because he is not woman but tortured man."

Many a night the same figure had walked there in the darkness. As his great friend had said, there was no other way. His pain had grown no less, but only more as the months passed by, for it was not the common pain of a man like others. As he was taller, stronger, and had more brain and heart than most, he had greater and keener pangs to do battle with, and in the world he must at intervals be thrown across her path and she across his, and as he had been haunted by talk and rumours of her in the years before he was haunted now. 'Twas but natural all should praise to him his kinsman's wife, sure that he would feel pleasure when he heard her lauded.

Women, especially such as are great ladies, have not at their command, if they hide pain in secret, even the refuges and poor comforts possessed by men. They may not feed their hungry souls by gazing at a distance upon the beloved object of their heavy thoughts; they cannot pace the night through before a dwelling, looking up as they pass at the darkened windows behind which sleeps—or wakes—the creature their hearts cry to in their pain; tears leave traces; faces from which smiles are absent, eyes from which light has fled, arouse query and comment. My lord has a certain privacy and license to be dull or gloomy, but my lady cannot well be either without explaining herself, either by calling in a physician or wearing mourning, or allowing the world to gain some hint of domestic trouble or misfortune.

Her ladyship of Dunstanwolde was surely a happy woman. Having known neither gayety nor luxury in her girlhood, it seemed now that she could give her lord no greater pleasure than to allow him to surround her with both.

"She is more dazzling than they said," my Lord Marlborough thought, watching her at the tragedy one night, "but she carries with her a thought of something she would forget in the gayeties of the world."

The Duke of Osmonde sate in his own box that night and in the course of the play went to his kinsman's for a few moments and paid his respects to her ladyship, who received him graciously. This his Grace of Marlborough beheld but did not mark her soft quick aside to him.

"May I ask your Grace's aid?" she said. "Look at my lord. His kindness to me will not let him own that he is ailing. He will not remain at home from these festivities because he knows I would remain with him. I beg you persuade him that he is wrong and but makes me unhappy. Your Grace will do this?"

"Your Ladyship may trust me," was his answer. 'Twas then that his Grace of Marlborough saw him turn from her with a bow and go to sit by her husband, who, 'twas indeed true, looked this night older than his years, and was of an ivory pallor and worn. 'Twas at this time the Duke marked that there stood upon the stage among the company of men of fashion, idlers, and young fops sitting and lounging there, a man attired in peach-coloured velvet, whose delicacy of bloom, combining itself with the fair curls which fell upon his shoulders, made him look pale and haggard. He was a young man and a handsome one, but had the look of an ill liver, and as he stood in a careless, insolent attitude he gazed steadfastly and with burning eyes at my Lady Dunstanwolde.

"There is somewhat devilish in his air," his Grace thought. "It is some dissolute dandy in love with her and raging against her in his soul. Heaven's grace! how she sits and gazes past his impudent face with her great eyes as if he were not a living thing! She will not see him, and he cannot force her to it, she so holds herself in hand."

My Lord Dunstanwolde gave heed to his kinsman's affectionate appeals and counsellings with the look of a man tenderly moved.

"Has my dear lady asked you to talk with me?" he said. "'Tis but like her generous observance of me. She has cautioned me most tenderly herself, and begs me to leave the gayeties of town and go

153

with her to the country, where she says we will be happy together and she will be my nurse."

"She will be happier with you at Dunstan's Wolde than she can be here, where she is concerned about your health," returned Osmonde. "That I can see plainly. The whirl of town festivities but torments her when she sees you worn and pale."

"Yes," answered my lord with a very tender smile, "I am sure it is true, and there is one lovely young lady with the world at her feet who is heavenly sweet enough to give her youth and bloom willingly to the care of an old husband."

"'Tis to the care of noble tenderness and love she is willing to give herself," said Osmonde. "She is a Woman—a Woman!"

His lordship of Dunstanwolde turned and looked at him with a curious interest.

"Gerald," he said, "'tis singular that you should speak so, though you say so true a thing. Only a few weeks since he and I spoke of yourself, and her own words of you were those: 'He is a Man—he is a Man. Nay, he is as God meant Man should be.' And she added that if men were so, there would be women great enough to be their mates and give the world men like them. And now—you are both right, Gerald; both right. Sometimes I think—" He broke his sentence with a sigh and began quick again. "I will obey you," he said; "after the assembly we hold next week we will go to Dunstan's Wolde. You will be with us that last night, Gerald?"

Osmonde bowed, smiling. 'Twas to be a great assembly, at which Royalty would be entertained, and of such stateliness and ceremony that his absence would have been a thing to be marked.

"Her ladyship has chided me for giving so great an entertainment," said the Earl. "She is very quaint in her play at wifely scolding. Truth is, I am an uxorious husband, and before we leave town would see her a last time all regal and blazing with her newest jewels; reigning over my hospitalities like a Queen. 'Tis a childish thing, no doubt, but perhaps—perhaps—" he broke his sentence again with a sigh which he changed to a smile. "You will be there," he said, "and you will understand the meaning of my weakness."

On the night of this great assembly at Dunstanwolde House, Mr. Hammond, my lord Duke's confidential secretary, and the Comptroller of his household, sate late over his accounts. He was his Grace's attached servant, and having been in his service since he had left the University had had time and opportunity to develop a strong affection for him, and a deep and even intimate interest in his concerns. 'Twas not alone an interest in the affairs of his estate, but in himself and all that touched or moved him. This being the case he also, as well as a greater man, had marked a subtle change in his patron, though wherein its nature lay he could scarcely have described even to himself.

"He is not so calm a creature," he had said to himself, striving to make analysis of what he thought he saw. "He is not so happy. At times when he sits in silence he looks like a man doing battle with himself. Yet what could there be for such as he to combat with?"

He had thought of this very thing when he had seen his Grace pass to his coach which was to bear him to the entertainment at his kinsman's house. The man, who had grown used to silent observance of him, had seen in his face the thing he deplored, while he did not comprehend it.

At midnight he sate in his room, which adjoined his Grace's study, and in which he was ever within call.

"'Tis a thing perhaps none but a woman could understand," he said to himself in quiet thought.

The clock began to strike twelve. One—two—three—four—five—six—

But the rest he did not hear. The coach-wheels were to be heard rolling into the courtyard. His Grace was returning. Mr. Hammond rose from his work, prepared to answer a summons should he hear one. In but a few minutes he was called and entered the adjoining room.

My lord Duke was standing in the centre of the apartment. He looked like a man who had met with a shock. The colour had fled from his countenance, and his eyes were full of pain.

"Hammond," he said, "a great and sudden calamity has taken place. An hour ago my Lord Dunstanwolde was struck down—in the midst of his company—by a fatal seizure of the heart."

"Fatal, your Grace?" Mr. Hammond ejaculated.

"He did not breathe after he fell," was my lord Duke's answer, and his pallor became even more marble-like than before, as if an added coldness had struck him. "He was a dead man when I laid my hand upon his heart."

155

CHAPTER XXIII

Her Ladyship Returns to Town

Upon the awful occasion of his kinsman's sudden death in the midst of the glittering throng of his guests, my lord Duke had spoken for the first time to her ladyship of Dunstanwolde's sister, the gentle Mistress Anne. His Grace had chanced to encounter this lady under such circumstances as naturally led them to address each other, and he being glad to have speech with her on whom his thoughts had dwelt so kindly, had remained in attendance upon her, escorting her through the crowd of celebrities and leading her to the supper-room for refreshment. Had she been wholly a stranger to him, she was one who would have appealed to his heart and touched it, she was so slight and modest a creature, her eyes so soft and loving and her low voice so timid. Such women always moved him and awakened in him that tenderness the weak should always waken in the strong. But Mistress Anne did more; seeming to him, when she spoke of her sister or looked at her, surely the fondest creature Nature had ever made.

"I understand now," his Grace had said to her as they talked, "why her ladyship says that 'twas you who first taught her what love meant."

A soft colour flooded Mistress Anne's whole face as she lifted it to look at him who stood so tall above her smallness.

"Did she so?" she exclaimed. "Did she so?" And her soft dull eyes seemed about to fill with tears.

"Truly she did, madam," he answered with warm feeling, "and added, too, that until you taught her she had never before beheld it."

"I—oh, I am grateful!" said Mistress Anne. "I never dreamed that I—But in these days, she hath a way of always saying that which makes one happy."

"She loves and leans on you," my lord Duke said, and there was sudden emotion in his voice.

"Leans!" cried Mistress Anne with a kind of loving fright; "Anne—on Anne!"

"Yes, yes," he answered. "I have seen it—felt it! Your pardon for my boldness. You will never forget!"

And at that very moment his attention had been caught by the look on his kinsman's face—they chancing to be near his lordship; and he had seen him sway and fall in the midst of a terrified group, which uttered a low simultaneous cry.

After his attendance at the funeral ceremonies, which took place in Warwickshire, his Grace of Osmonde did not return at once to town, but went to Camylott that in the midst of the quiet loveliness he might be alone.

"I must have time to think," he said; "to still my brain which whirls—to teach it to understand."

Oh! the heavenly stillness and beauty of the afternoon when he rode up the avenue on his home-coming! His home-coming! Yes, 'twas that he called it in his thought, and for the first time since his parents' death it seemed so. In the tenderness of his heart and for the sake of his long and true love for his dead kinsman, he scarce dared explain to himself why he now could use this word and could not before—and yet, he felt that in the depths of his being the thought lay that at last he was coming home.

"God forgive me if there is lack of kindness in it," he cried to himself. "Kinsman, forgive me! Nay, you know now and will have pity. I am but man and young, and have so madly loved and been so tortured. Now I may look into her eyes and do no wrong, but only great Love's bidding. My blood beats in my veins—my heart leaps up so and will not be still."

'Twas deep autumn and a day of gold—the sunset burned and flamed and piled the sky with golden mountains such as had heaped upon each other on the evening he had stood with his mother at the Long Gallery window before their last parting; the trees' branches were orange and amber and russet brown, the moors had gold hues on them, and on the terraces the late flowers blooming blazed crimson and yellow as if the summer had burned all paler and less sumptuous colour away. The gables and turrets of the tower rose clear soft grey, or dark with ivy, against a sky of deepest blue, the broad tree-studded acres of the park rolled yellowing green to Camylott village, where white cottages nestled among orchards and fields of corn and were enfolded by wooded hills and rising moorland. Occasional farm-yard sounds were to be heard mingled now and then with voices and laughter of children, rooks cawed in the high tree-tops with a lazy irregularity, and there was an autumn freshness in the ambient air. In the courtyard the fountain played with a soft plashing, and as he rode in some little birds were chirping and fluttering as they drank and flirted the water with their wings. The wide doors were thrown open, showing the beauteous huge hall with its pictures and warm colours, its armour and trophies of the chase; the servants stood waiting to receive him, and as the groom took his horse, Mr. Fox approached to greet him on the threshold. Every face had kindly welcome in it, every object

157

seemed to recall some memory which belonged to his happiest youth—to those years when all had been so warm and fair.

"Yes," he said later, as he stood at the window in the Long Gallery and looked forth. "God grant I have come home."

What hours, what days and nights he spent in the weeks that followed. In truth they were too full of intense feeling to be wholly happy. Many a night he woke trembling from dreams of anguish. There were three dreams which came again and again—one was of the morning when she galloped past him in the narrow lane with the strange look in her eyes, and he never dreamed it without a nightmare sense of mad despair and loss from which his own wild cry to her would wake him; another was of the night she passed him on the stair, and did not see him. Oh, God (for 'twas in this wise the dream always came), she did not see him. She passed him by again. And there was left only the rose lying at his feet. And he should never see her face again! And one was of the night he spent in his room alone at Dunstan's Wolde—the night when he had torn the laces from his throat that he might breathe, and had known himself a frenzied man—while her happy bridegroom to be had slept and dreamed of her.

From such dreams he would waken with an unreasoning terror—a nightmare in itself—a sense that even now, even when both were free and he had seen that in her eyes his soul sought for and cried out to—even now some Fate might come between and tear them apart, that their hearts should never beat against each other—never! And, in truth, cold sweat would break forth on his body and he would spring from his bed and pace to and fro, lighting the tapers that he might drive the darkness from him.

"Naught shall come between!" he would cry. "Naught under God's Heaven—naught on Gods' earth! No man, nor fate, nor devil!"

For he had borne his burden too long, and even for his strength and endurance its heaviness had been too great.

In these weeks of solitude at Camylott he thought much of him who had passed from earth, of the years they had been friends, of the days they had ridden through the green lanes together or walked in the Long Gallery, he himself but a child, the other his mature and affectionate companion. He had loved and been beloved, and now he was gone, leaving behind him no memory which was not tender and full of affectionate reverence.

"Never," was Osmonde's thought, "in all the years we knew each other did I hear him utter a thought which was ungenerous or unjust. You, my lord," he found himself saying aloud one day, "have sure left earth's regrets behind and see with clearer eyes than ours.

A man—loving as you yourself loved, yearning as you yourself yearned—you will but pity with a tender soul."

And he could but remember his last interview with Mistress Anne on his bidding farewell to Dunstan's Wolde after the funeral obsequies.

"'Tis a farewell I bid the place," he had said, "though I may see it again. I came here as a boy, and in the first years of my young manhood, and he was always here to bid me welcome. One of my earliest memories"—they stood in the large saloon together, and he raised his eyes to a picture near them—"one of my first recollections here is of this young face with its blushing cheeks, and of my lord's sorrowful tenderness as he told me that she had died and that his little son—who, had he lived, might have been as myself—had died with her."

Whereupon Mistress Anne, with innocent tears and lowered voice, told him a story of how the night before her lord had been laid to rest, his widow had sat by his side through the slow hours, and had stroked his cold hands and spoken softly to him as if he could feel her lovingness, and on the morning before he left her, she had folded in his clasp a miniature of his young dead wife and a lock of her soft hair and her child's.

"And 'twas, indeed, a tender, strange thing to see and hear," said Anne, "for she said with such noble gentleness, that 'twas the first sweet lady who had been his wife—not herself—and that when she and her child should run to meet him in heaven he would forget that they had ever parted—and all would be well. Think you it will be so, your Grace?" her simple, filled eyes lifted to him appealingly.

"There is no marrying or giving in marriage, 'tis said," answered his Grace, "and she whom he loved first—in his youth—surely——"

Mistress Anne's eyes dwelt upon him in quiet wondering.

"'Tis strange how your Grace and her ladyship sometimes utter the same thoughts, as if you were but one mind," she said. "'No marrying or giving in marriage,' 'twas that she herself said."

Dunstan's Wolde passed into the hands of the next heir, and the countess and her sister went to their father's estate of Wildairs in Gloucestershire, where, during the mourning, they lived in deep seclusion. 'Twas a long mourning, to the wonder of the neighbourhood, who, being accustomed to look upon this young lady as likely to furnish them forth with excitement, had begun at once to make plans for her future and decide what she would do next. Having been rid of her old husband and left an earl's widow with a fine fortune, a town house, and some of the most magnificent jewels in England, 'twas not likely she would long bury herself in an

159

old country house, hiding her beauty in weeds and sad-coloured draperies. She would make her period of seclusion as brief as decency would permit, and after it reappear in a blaze of brilliancy.

But she remained at Wildairs with her sister, Mistress Anne, only being seen on occasions at church, in her long and heavy draperies of black.

"But she is a strange mixture," said my Lord Twemlow's Chaplain, in speaking of her, "and though she hath so changed, hath scarce changed at all. Her black eye can flame as bright as ever under her long widow's veil. She visits the poor with her sister, and gives charities, but she will have no beggarly tricks, and can pick out a hypocrite at his first whining, howsoever clever he may be. One came to her last week with a lying tale of having loved the old Earl Dunstanwolde, and been his pensioner for years. And to see her mark the weak points of his story, and to hear the wit with which she questioned him until he broke down affrighted, was a thing to marvel at.

"'Think you,' she said, 'that I will let knaves trade on my lord's goodness, and play tricks in his name? You shall all see. In the stocks you shall sit and repent it—a warning to other rascals.'"

But in the miserable, long-neglected village of Wildairs she did such deeds as made her remembered to the end of many lives. No village was in worse case than this had been for years, as might well be expected. Falling walls, rotting thatches, dirt and wretchedness were to be seen on all sides; cottages were broken-paned and noisome, men and women who should have been hale were drawn with rheumatism from mouldering dampness, or sodden with drink and idleness; children who should have been rosy and clean and studying their horn books, at the dame school, were little, dirty, evil, brutal things.

"And no blame of theirs, but yours," said my lady to her father.

"Thou didst not complain in days gone by, Clo," said Sir Jeoffry, "but swore at them roundly when they ran in thy horse's way as thou went at gallop through the village, and called the men and women lousy pigs who should be whipt."

"Did I?" said her ladyship, looking at him with large eyes. "Ay, that I did. In those days surely I was mad and blind."

"Wildairs village is no credit to its owner," grumbled Sir Jeoffry. "Wherefore should it be? I am a poor man—I can do naught for it."

"I can," said my Lady Dunstanwolde.

And so she did, but at first when she entered the tumbledown cottages, looking so tall, a black figure in her sweeping draperies

160

and widow's veil, the people were more than half affrighted. But soon she won them from their terror with her own strange power, and they found that she was no longer the wild young lady who had dashed through their hamlet in hunting garb, her dogs following her, and the glance of her black eyes and the sound of her mocking laugh things to flee before. Her eyes had grown kind, and she had a way none could resist, and showed a singular knowledge of poor folks' wants and likings. Her goodness to them was not that of the ordinary lady who felt that flannel petticoats and soup and scriptural readings made up the sum of all requirements. There were other things she knew and talked to them of, as if they were human creatures like herself.

"I can carry to them food and raiment," said Mistress Anne, wondering at her, "but when I try to talk with them I am afraid and have no words. But you, sister—when you sate by that poor distraught young woman yesterday and talked to her of her husband who had met such sudden death—you knew what to say, and in the midst of her agony she turned in her bed and lay and stared at you and listened."

"Yes, I knew," said my lady—her eyes shining. "She is passing through what I might pass through if——! Those two poor souls—rustics, and ignorant, who to greater people seem like cattle—they were man and woman who had loved and mated. They could not have told their joy or the meaning of it. I could—I could! And now her mate is gone—and the world is empty, and she is driven mad. I know, I know! Only another woman who knew could have uttered words she would have listened to."

"What—what did you say?" said Mistress Anne—and almost gasped, for my lady looked so full of tragic truth and passion, and how could she know? being only the widow of an old man whom she had but loved with kindness, as if she had been his daughter? 'Twas not through her loss of my Lord Dunstanwolde she knew. And yet, know she did, 'twas plain.

And her answer was the strangest, daring proof.

"I said to her—almost fiercely, though I spoke beneath my breath, 'He hath not left thee: Thou wouldst not have left him. Thou couldst not. Remember! Think! Thou canst not see him, but thee he sees, and loves—loves, I tell thee, as he did two weeks since. Perhaps he holds thee in his arms and cries to thee to hear him. Perhaps 'tis he who speaks in these words of mine. When we have loved them and they us, death is not strong enough to part us. Love holds too close. Listen? He is here!'"

"Heaven's mercy!" cried gentle Mistress Anne, the tears
161

running down her cheeks. "There seems no Death, when you talk thus, sister—no Death."

"There is none," said my lady, "when Love comes. When Love has come, there is naught else in Nature's universe, for it is stronger than all."

And 'twas as if she were some prophetess who spoke, her face and eyes glowed with such fire and solemness. But Mistress Anne, gazing at her, thrilled to her heart's core, had a strange sense of fear, wondering whence this mood had come, how it had grown, and what it might bring forth in the unknown future.

The custom of the time held that a widowed lady should mourn retired a year, but 'twas near two before her ladyship of Dunstanwolde came forth from her seclusion, and casting her weeds returned to town. And my Lord Duke of Osmonde had come again to Camylott when the news was spread.

He had been engaged in grave business, and having been abroad upon it had, on his return, travelled at once to the country. To Camylott he came because it was his refuge in all unrestful hours or deeply grave ones—the broad, heavenly scene spread out before it soothed him when he gazed through its windows, the waving and rustle of the many huge trees on every side never ceased to bring back to him something of the feeling he had had in his childhood, that they were mighty and mysterious friends who hushed him as a child is hushed to sleep; and so he came to Camylott for a few days' repose before re-entering Court life with its tumults and broils and scheming.

In a certain comfortable suite of rooms which had once been a part of the nurseries there lived at peaceful ease an aged woman who loved his Grace well and faithfully, and had so loved him from his childhood, knowing indeed more of the intimate details of his life and career than he himself imagined. This old gentlewoman was Mistress Rebecca Halsell, the whilom chieftainess of the nursery department, and having failed in health as age drew near her, she had been generously installed a quiet pensioner in her old domain. When the Marquess of Roxholm had returned from his first campaign he had found her living in these apartments—a woman nearing seventy, somewhat bent with rheumatism, and white-haired, but with the grave, clear eyes he remembered, still undimmed.

"I hope to be here still, my lord Marquess," she had said, "when you bring your lady home to us—even perhaps when the nurseries are thrown open again. I have been a happy woman in these rooms since the first hour I entered them and took your lordship from Nurse Alison's arms."

162

She had led a happy life, being surrounded by every comfort, all the servants being her friends, and she spending her days with books and simple work, sitting chiefly at the large window from whence she could see the park, and the avenue where the company came and went, and on days when there was naught else stirring, watch the rookery with its colony of rooks flying to and fro quarrelling or sitting in judgment on affairs of state, settling their big nests, and marrying and giving in marriage.

When his Grace was at the tower he paid her often a friendly visit, and entertained her bravely with stories of camp and Court until, indeed, she had become a wondrous stateswoman, and knew quite well the merits of Marlborough and Prince Eugene, and had her own views of the changing favourites and their bitter struggles to attain their ends. On this occasion of his return, my lord Duke going to give her greeting, found her parting with a friend, a comely country woman who left them courtesying, and Mistress Halsell sate in her armchair with somewhat of a glow in her grave eyes. And after their first exchange of words the room was for a few moments very quiet.

"Your Grace," she said, "before she, who has just left us, came, I sate here and thought of a day many a year ago when you and I sate together, and your Grace climbed on my knee."

"I have climbed there many a time, Nurse Halsell," he said, his brown eye opening, laughing, as it had a trick of doing.

"But this time was a grave one," Mistress Halsell answered. "We talked of grave things, and in my humble way I strove to play Chaplain and preach a sermon. You had heard Grace and Alison gossip of King Charles and Madam Carwell and Nell Gwynne—and would ask questions it was hard to answer."

"I remember well," said my lord Duke, the light of memory in his eye, and he added, as one who reflects, "He is the King—he is the King!"

"You remember!" said Nurse Halsell, her old eyes glowing. "I have never forgot, and your Grace's little face so lost in thought, as you looked out at the sky."

"I have remembered it," said his Grace, "in many a hard hour such as comes in all men's lives."

"You have known some such?" said the old woman, and of a sudden, as she gazed at him, it seemed as if such feeling overswept her as made her forget he was a great Duke and remember only her beauteous nurseling. "Yes, you have known them, for I have sate here at the window and watched, and there have been days when my heart was like to break."

He started and turned towards her. Her deep eyes were full of tears which brimmed over and ran down her furrowed cheeks, and in them he saw a tender and wise knowledge of his nature's self and all its pains—a thing of which, before, he had never dreamed, for how could he have imagined that an old woman living alone could have so followed him with her heart that she had guessed his deepest secret; but this indeed she had, and her next words most touchingly revealed it.

"Being widowed and childless when I came to you," she said, her emotion rising to a passion, "'twas as if you grew to be my own—and in those summer days three years gone, life and love were strong in you—life and love and youth. And her eyes dared not turn to you, nor yours to her—and I am a woman and was afraid—for my man who died and left me widowed was my lover as well as my husband, and soul and body we had been one—so I knew! But as I sate here and saw you as you passed below with your company, I said it to myself again and again, 'He is the King—he is the King!'" And as his Grace rose from his seat, not angered, indeed, gazing at her tenderly, though growing pale, she seized his hand and kissed it, her tears falling.

"If 'tis unseemly," she said, "forgive me, your Grace, forgive me; but I had sate here so long this very morning, and thought but of this thing—and in the midst of my thinking came this woman, and she is from Gloucestershire, and told me of her ladyship of Dunstanwolde—whose chariot passed her on the road, and she goes up to town, and rode radiant and blooming in rich colours, having cast her weeds aside and looking, so the woman said, like a beauteous creature new born, with all of life to come."

CHAPTER XXIV

Sir John Oxon Returns Also

When his Grace of Osmonde returned to town he found but one topic of conversation, and this was of such interest and gave such a fillip to gossip and chatter that fierce Sarah of Marlborough's encounters with Mrs. Masham, and her quarrels with Majesty itself, were for the time actually neglected. Her Grace had engaged in battles royal for so long a time and with such activity that the Court and the world were a little wearied and glad of something new. And here was a most promising event which might be discussed from a thousand points and bring forth pretty stories of past and present, as well as prophecies for the future.

The incomparable and amazing Clorinda, Countess of Dunstanwolde, having mourned in stately retirement for near upon two years (when Fashion demanded but one) and having paid such reverence to her old lord's memory as had seemed almost the building of a monument to his virtues, had cast her sables, left the country, and come up to town to reign again at Dunstanwolde House, which had been swept and garnished.

At Court, and in all the modish houses in the town, one may be sure that the whole story of her strange life was told and retold with a score of imaginative touches. Her baby oaths were resworn, her childish wickedness depicted in colours which glowed, the biographies of the rough old country rakes who had trained her were related, in free translation, so to speak, over many a dish of chocolate and tea, and, these points dwelt on, what more dramatic than to turn upon the singular fortune of her marriage, the wealth, rank, and reputation of the man who had so worshipped her, and the unexpectedness of her grace and decorum the while she bore his name and shared his home with him.

"Had she come up to town," 'twas remarked, "and once having caught him, played the vixen and the shrew, turned his house into a bear-garden, behaved unseemly and put him to shame, none would have been surprised——"

"Many would have been all agog with joy," interrupted old Lady Storms who heard. "She was a woeful disappointment to many a gossiping woman, and a lesson to all the shifty fools who sell themselves to a man, and then trick him out of the price he paid."

At the clubs and coffee-houses the men talked also, though men's tongues do not run as fast as the tongues of womenkind, and their gossip was of a masculine order. She was a finer creature than ever, and at present was the richest widow in England. A man might well lose his wits over her mere self if she had naught but the gown she stood in, but he who got her would get all else beside. The new beaux and the old ones began to buy modish habits and periwigs, adorn themselves with new sword and shoulder knots, and trifle over the latest essences offered in the toyshops.

"Split me," said one splendid fop, "but since my lady returned to town the price of ambergris and bergamot and civet powders has mounted perilously, and the mercers are all too busy to be civil. When I sent my rascal this morning to buy the Secret White Water to Curl Gentlemen's Hair, on my life he was told he must wait for it, since new must be made, as all had been engaged."

One man at that time appeared at the Cocoa Tree and Cribb's with a new richness of garb and a look in his face such as had not been seen there for many a day. In truth, for some time the coffee-houses had seen but little of him, and it had sometimes been said that he had fled the country to escape his creditors, or might be spending his days in a debtors' prison, since he had no acquaintances who would care to look for him if he were missing, and he might escape to France, or be seized and rot in gaol, and none be the wiser.

But on a night even a little before the throwing open of Dunstanwolde House, he sauntered into the Cocoa Tree and, having become so uncommon a sight, several turned to glance at him.

"Egad!" one cried low to another, "'tis Jack Oxon back again. Where doth the fellow spring from?"

His good looks it had been hard for him to lose, they being such as were built of delicately cut features, graceful limbs, and an elegant air, but during the past year he had often enough looked haggard, vicious, and of desperate ill-humour, besides out of fashion, if not out at elbow. Now his look had singularly changed, his face was fresher, his eye brighter, though a little feverish in its light, and he wore a new sword and velvet scabbard, a rich lace steenkirk, and a modish coat of pale violet brocade.

"Where hast come from, Jack?" someone asked him. "Hast been into a nunnery?"

"Yes," he answered, "doing penance for thy sins, having none of my own."

"Hast got credit again, I swear," cried the other, "or thou wouldst not look such a dandy."

Sir John sate down and called for refreshment, which a drawer brought him.

"A man can always get credit," he said, with an ironic, cool little smile, "when his fortunes take a turn."

"Thou look'st as if thine had turned," said his companion. "Purple and silver, and thy ringlets brushed and perfumed like a girl's. In thy eyes 'tis a finer mop than any other man's French periwig, all know."

Sir John looked down on his shoulders at his soft rich fall of curls and smiled. "'Tis finer," he said. "'Tis as fine for a man as a certain beauty's, we once talked of, was for a woman."

The man who talked with him laughed with a half-sneer.

"Thou canst not forget her hair, Jack," he said, "but the lock

166

stayed on her head despite thee. Art going to try again, now she is a widow?"

Sir John looked up from his drink and in his eye there leapt up a devil in spite of himself, for he had meant—if he could—to keep cool.

"Ay," he said, "by God! I am."

So when men talked of Lady Dunstanwolde 'twas not unnatural that, this story having been bruited about, they should talk also of Jack Oxon, and since they talked to each other, the rumour reached feminine ears which pricked themselves at once; and when my lord Duke of Osmonde came to town and went into the world, he also heard discussions of Sir John Oxon. This gentleman who had been missing in the World of Fashion had reappeared, and 'twas believed had returned to life to try his fortunes with my Lady Dunstanwolde. And 'twas well known indeed that he had been the first lover she had known, for the elderly country roisterers had been naught but her playmates and her father's boon companions, and Sir John had appeared at the famous birthnight supper and had been the only town man who had ever seen her in her male attire, and was among those who toasted her when she returned to the banquet-room splendid in crimson and gold, and ordered all to fall upon their knees before her; and Sir John—(he was then in the heyday of his beauty and success) had gone mad with love for her, and 'twas believed that she had returned his passion, as any girl well might, though she was so proud-spirited a creature that none could be quite sure. At least 'twas known that he had laid seige to her, and for near two years had gone often to the country, and many had seen him gaze at her in company when his passion was writ plain in his blue eyes. Suddenly, on his reappearance, since he for some unknown reason wore the look of a man whose fortunes might have changed for the better, there were those among whom the tide took a turn somewhat in Sir John's favour. 'Twas even suggested by a woman of fashion, given somewhat to romance, that perhaps the poor man had fallen into evil ways and lost his good looks and elegant air through thwarted passion, and 'twas thought indeed a touching thing that at the first gleam of hope he should emerge from his retirement almost restored in spirit and bloom.

The occupants of coaches and chairs passing before the entrance to Osmonde House, which was a great mansion situated in a garden, noted but a few days after the world had heard her ladyship was in town, that his Grace had returned also. Lacqueys stood about the entrance, and the Osmonde liveries were to be seen going to and fro in the streets, the Duke was observed to drive to

Kensington and back, and to St. James's, and the House of Parliament, and it was known was given audience by the Queen upon certain secret matters of State. 'Twas indeed at this time that the changes were taking place in her Majesty's councils, and his anticipation of a ministerial revolution had so emboldened King Louis that he had ventured to make private overtures to the royal lady's confidential advisers. "What we lose in Flanders we shall gain in England," Marlborough's French enemy, Torcy, had said. And between the anger and murmurs of a people who had turned to rend a whilom idol, the intrigues and cabals about the throne, the quarrels of her counsellors and ladies of the bedchamber, and the passionate reproaches of the strongest and most indomitable of female tyrants, 'twas small wonder a dull, ease-loving woman, feeling the burden of her royalty all too wearisome and heavy, should turn with almost pathetic insistence to a man young enough to be her son, attractive enough to be a favourite, high enough to be impeccable, and of such clear wit, strength of will and resource, and power over herself and others as seemed to set him apart from all the rest of those who gathered to clamour about her. In truth, my lord Duke's value to her Majesty was founded greatly upon that which had drawn his Grace of Marlborough to him. He wanted nothing; all the others had some desire to gain, secret or avowed. The woman who had so longed for unregal feminine intimacy and companionship that with her favoured attendant she had played a comedy of private life—doffing her queenship and becoming simple "Mrs. Morley," that with "Mrs. Freeman," at least, she might forget she was a Queen—was not formed by Nature to combat with State intrigues and Court duplicities.

"I am given no quiet," the poor august lady said. "These people who resign places and demand them, who call meetings and create a ferment, these ladies who vituperate and clamour like deserted lovers, weary me. Your Grace's strength brings me repose!"

And as the father had felt sympathy and pity for poor Catherine of Braganza in Charles the Second's day, so the son felt pity and gave what support he could to poor bullied and bewildered Queen Anne. To him her queenship was truly the lesser thing, her helpless, somewhat heavy-witted and easily wavering womanhood the greater; and there were those who feared him, for such reasons as few men in his position had been feared before.

His Grace had been but two days in town, and on the morning of the second had driven in his chariot to Kensington, and had an audience upon the private matter already spoken of, and which would in all likelihood take him, despite his wishes, across the Channel and to the French Court. He might be commanded away at the very moment that he wished most to be on English soil, in London itself. For howsoever ardent and long hidden a man's passion, he must, if he be delicate of feeling, await that moment which is ripe for him to speak. And this he pondered on as his chariot rolled through the streets to bear him to make his first visit to her ladyship of Dunstanwolde.

"I have known and dreamed of her almost all her life," he thought. "'Tis but three years since she first saw my face; through the first year she was another man's wife, and these two last his mourning widow. When I behold her to day I shall learn much."

The sun was shining gloriously, and the skies' blue was deep and clear. He looked up at it as he drove, and at the fresh early summer greenness of the huge trees and thick grass in the parks and gardens; and when his equipage rolled into the court at Dunstanwolde House, he smiled to himself for pleasure to see its summer air, with the lacqueys making excuse to stand outside in the brightness of the day, little Nero, the black negro page, sunning himself and his pugs and spaniels on the plot of grass at the front, and the windows thrown open to let in the soft fresh air, while the balconies before the drawing-room casements were filled with masses of flowers—yellow and white perfumed things, sent up fresh from the country and set in such abundance that the balconies bloomed like gardens. The last time he had beheld her, she had stood by her husband's coffin, swathed in long, heavy draperies of black, looking indeed a wonderful tragic figure; and this was in his mind as he walked up the broad staircase, followed by the lacquey, who a moment later flung open the door of the saloon and announced him with solemn majesty.

But oh! the threshold once crossed, the great white-and-gold decorated apartment seemed flooded with sunlight and filled with the fragrance of daffodils and jonquils and narcissus blown in through the open window, and Mistress Anne sate sweet and modest in a fine chair too big for her dear small body; but my lord Duke scarce could see her, for 'twas as if the sun shone in his eyes when there rose from a divan to meet him a tall goddess clad in white and with a gold ribband confining her black hair and her waist, and a branch of yellow-gold flowers in her hand, which looked as if surely she might just have gathered them on the terrace at Camylott.

And she had surely by some magic blotted out the past and had awakened to a present which was like new birth and had no past, for she blushed the loveliest, radiant blush—at sight of him—as if she had been no great lady, but a sweet, glowing girl.

What he said to her, or she to him, he knew no more than any

169

lesser man in his case knows, for he was in a whirl of wonder and strange delight, and could scarce hold in his mind that there was need that he should be sober, this being his first visit to her since she had cast the weeds worn for his own kinsman; and there sate Mistress Anne, changing from red to white, as if through some great secret emotion—though he did not know 'twas at the sight of them standing together, and the sudden knowledge and joy it brought to her, which made her very heart to quake in its tenderness. This—this was the meaning of what she had so wondered at in her sister's mood when they spoke of the poor girl left widowed; this was how she had known, and if so, she must have learned it in her own despite at first, in that year when she had been a bound woman, when they two had been forced to encounter each other, holding their hearts in gyves of iron and making no sound or sign. And the fond creature remembered the night before the marriage when she had passed through a strange scene in her sister's chamber, and one thing she had said came back to her, and now she understood its meaning.

"I love my Lord Dunstanwolde as well as any other man, and better than some, for I do not hate him. Since I have been promised to him"—('twas this which now came back to her)—"I own I have for a moment met another gentleman who might—'twas but for a moment, and 'tis done with."

And this—this had been he, his Grace the Duke of Osmonde—who was so fit a mate for her, and whose brown eyes so burned with love. And she was a free woman, and there they stood at the open window among the flowers—both bound, both free!

Free! She started a little as she said the word in thought again, for she knew a strange wild story none other than herself knew, and her sister, and Sir John Oxon, and they did not suspect she shared their secret. And for long it had seemed to her only some cruel thing she had dreamed; and the wild lovely creature she had watched and stood guard over with such trembling, during a brief season of bewildered anguish, seemed to be a sort of vision also. At the end of but a few short months Mistress Anne had felt this lawless, beauteous being had left the splendid body she had inhabited, and another woman's life had begun in it—another woman's. That woman it was who had wed Lord Dunstanwolde and made him a blissful man, that woman had been since then her sister, her protector, and her friend; 'twas she who had watched by my lord's body, and spoke low words to him, and stroked his poor dead hand; 'twas she who laid his wife's hair and her child's, and the little picture, on his still breast; 'twas she who sate by the widowed girl at

170

Wildairs—and 'twas she, she made glorious by love, who stood and smiled among the window's daffodils.

His Grace and her ladyship were speaking softly together of the flowers, the sunshine, of the town and Court, and of beauteous Camylott. Once my lord Duke's laugh rang out, rich and gay like a boy's, and there was such youth and fire and happiness in his handsome face as made Mistress Anne remember that, as it was with my lady, so it was with him—that because he was so tall and great and stately, the world forgot that he was young.

"But," said the loving woman to herself with a sudden fear, "if he should come back. Nothing so cruel could happen—'tis past and dead and forgiven. He could not—could not come."

Then his Grace went away. My lady spoke sweet and gracious words to him with the laughing, shining eyes of Clo Wildairs at her most wondrous hours, and the Duke holding her hand, bent and kissed it with the tender passion of a hungered man, as he had not dared to dream of kissing it before.

And he went down the staircase a new man, carrying his head as though a crown had been set on it and he would bear it nobly. In his tawny eye there was a smile which was yet solemn though it was deeply bright.

"'Tis the beginning of the world," he said inwardly—"'And the evening and the morning were the first day.' I have looked into her eyes."

And as his chariot rolled through the entrance into the street, another passed it and entered the court, and through the glass he saw a fair man, richly dressed, his bright curls falling soft and thick on his shoulders; and he was arranging the ribband of his sword-knot, and smiling a little with downcast eyes—and it was Sir John Oxon.

CHAPTER XXV

To-morrow

A dozen gentlemen at least, rumour said, would have rejoiced to end for her, by marriage, this lovely lady's widowhood; but there were but two she would be like to choose between, and they were different men indeed. One of them, both her heart and her ambition might have caused her to make choice of, for he combined such qualities and fortunes as might well satisfy either.

"Zounds," said an old beau, "the woman who wants more than his Grace of Osmonde can give—more money, greater estates, and more good looks—is like to go unsatisfied to her grave. She will take him, I swear, and smile like Heaven in doing it."

"But there was a time," said Sir Chris Crowell, who had come to town (to behold his beauty's conquests, as he said) and who spent much time at the coffee-houses and taverns telling garrulous stories of the days of Mistress Clo of Wildairs, "there was a time when I would have took oath that Jack Oxon was the man who would have her. Lord! he was the first young handsome thing she had ever met—and she was but fifteen for all her impudence, and had lived in the country and seen naught but a handful of thick-bodied, red-faced old rakes. And Jack was but four and twenty and fresh from town, and such a beauty that there was not a dairymaid in the country but was heartbroke by him—though he may have done no more than cast his devilish blue eye on her. For he had a way, I tell ye, that lad, he had a way with him that would have took any woman in. A dozen parts he could play and be a wonder in every one of them—and languish, and swear oaths, and repent his sins, and plead for mercy, with the look of an angel come to earth, and bring a woman to tears—and sometimes ruin, God knows!—by his very playing of the mountebank. Good Lord! to see those two at the birthnight supper was a sight indeed. My Lady Oxon she would have been, if either of them had been a fortune. But 'twas Fate—and which jilted the other, Heaven knows. And if 'twas he who played false, and he would come back now, he will find he hath fire to deal with—for my Lady Dunstanwolde is a fierce creature yet, though her eye shines so soft in these days." And he puffed at his churchwarden's pipe and grinned.

Among the men who had been her playmates it would seem that perhaps this old fellow had loved her best of all, or was more given to being demonstrative, or more full of a good-natured vanity

172

which exulted in her as being a sort of personal property to vaunt and delight in; at all events Sir Chris had come to the town, where he had scarce ever visited in all his life before, and had in a way constituted himself a sort of henchman or courtier of her ladyship of Dunstanwolde.

At her house he presented himself when first he came up—short, burly, red-faced, and in his best Gloucestershire clothes, which indeed wore a rustic air when borne to London on the broad back of a country gentleman in a somewhat rusty periwig.

When he beheld the outside stateliness of the big town mansion he grinned with delight; when he entered its doors and saw its interior splendours he stared about him with wondering eyes; and when he was passed from point to point by one tall and gorgeously liveried lacquey after another, he grew sober. When her ladyship came to him shortly after, she found him standing in the middle of the magnificent saloon (which had been rearranged and adorned for her by her late lord in white and golden panels, with decoration of garlands and Cupids and brocades after the manner of the French King Louis Fourteenth), and he was gazing about him still, and now scratching his periwig absently.

"Eh, my lady," he said, making an awkward bow, as if he did not know how to bear himself in the midst of such surroundings; "thy father was right."

Never had he seen a lady clad in such rich stuffs and looking so grand and like a young queen, but her red lips parted, showing her white teeth, and her big black eyes laughed as merrily as ever he had seen them when Clo Wildairs tramped across the moors with him, her gun over her fustian shoulder.

"Was he so?" she cried, taking hold of his thick hand and drawing him towards a huge gold carved sofa. "Come and tell me then when he was right, and if 'twas thou wast wrong."

Sir Chris stared at her a minute, straight at her arch, brilliant face, and then his rueful countenance relaxed itself into a grin.

"Ecod!" he said, still staring hard, "thou art not changed a whit."

"Ecod!" she said, mocking him, "but I am that. Shame on thee to deny it. I am a Countess and have been presented to the Queen, and cast my ill manners, and can make a Court obeisance." And she made him a great, splendid courtesy, sweeping down amidst her rich brocades as if she would touch the floor.

"Lord! Lord!" he said, and scratched his periwig again. "Thou look'st like a Queen thyself. But 'tis thy big eyes are not changed, Clo, that laughed so through the black fringes of them, like stars shining through a bush, and—and thy saucy way that makes a man want to seize hold on thee and hug thee—though—though—" He checked himself, half-frightened, but she laughed out at him with that bell-like clearness he remembered so well, and which he swore afterwards would put heart into any man.

"'Tis no harm that a man should want to seize hold upon a woman," she said; "'tis a thing men are given to, poor souls, and 'tis said Heaven made them so; but let him not be unwary and strive to do it. Town gentlemen know 'tis not the fashion."

Sir Chris chuckled and looked about him again.

"Clo," he said, "since thou hast laughed at me and I am not frightened by thy grandness, as I was at first, I will tell thee. I am going to stay in Lunnon for awhile, and look on at thee, and be a town man myself. Canst make a town man of me, Clo?"—grinning.

"Yes," answered her ladyship, holding her head on one side to look him over, "with a velvet coat and some gold lace, and a fine new periwig scented with orris or jessamine, and a silver-gilt sword and a hat cocked smartly, and a snuff-box, with a lady's picture in it. I will give thee mine, and thou shalt boast of it in company."

He slapped his thigh and laughed till his red face grew purple.

"Nay," he said, "thy father was wrong. He said I was a fool to come, for such as me and him was out of place in town, and fine ladies' drawing-rooms would make us feel like stable-boys. He said I would be heart-sick and shame-faced in twelve hours, and turn tail and come back to Gloucestershire like a whipt dog—but I shall not, I swear, but shall be merrier and in better heart than I have been since I was young. It gets dull in the country, Clo," shaking his head, "when a man gets old and heavy, and 'tis worst when he has no children left to keep him stirring. I have took a good lodging in the town, and I will dress myself like a Court gentleman and go to the coffee-houses and the play, and hear the wits. And I shall watch thy coach-and-six drive by and tell the company I was thy playmate when thou wert Clo Wildairs; and thou art not too fine a lady, even now thou art a Court beauty and a Countess, to be kind to an old fellow from the country."

He strutted away from the mansion, the proudest and happiest man in London, giving his hat a jaunty cock and walking with an air, his old heart beating high with joy to feel that this beautiful creature had not forgot old days and did not disdain him. He went to tailors and mercers and wig-makers and furnished himself forth with fine belongings, and looked a town gentleman indeed when he came to exhibit himself to my lady; and before long the Mall and the park became familiar with his sturdy old figure and beaming country face, and the beauties and beaux and wits began to know him, and that he had been one of Mistress Clorinda Wildairs's companions in her Gloucestershire days, and had now come to town, drawn simply by his worship of her, that he might delight himself by looking on at her triumphs.

There were many who honestly liked his countrified, talkative good nature, and inviting him to their houses made a favourite of him; and there were others who encouraged him, to hear him tell his stories; and several modish beauties amused themselves by coquetting with him, one of these being my Lady Betty Tantillion, who would tease and ogle him until he was ready to lose his wits in his elderly delight. One of her favourite tricks was to pout at him and twit him on his adoration of my Lady Dunstanwolde, of whom she was in truth not too fond; though she had learned to keep a civil tongue in her head, since her ladyship was a match for half a dozen such as she, and, when she chose to use her cutting wit, proved an antagonist as greatly to be feared as in the days when Lady Maddon, the fair and frail "Willow Wand," had fallen into hysteric fits in the country mercer's shop.

"You men always lose your wits when you see her," she would say. "'Tis said Sir John Oxon"—with a malicious little glance at that gentleman, who stood near her ladyship across the room—"'tis said Sir John Oxon lost more, and broke a fine match, and squandered his fortune, and sank into the evilest reputation—all for love of her."

She turned to his Grace of Osmonde, who was near, waving her fan languishing. "Has your Grace heard that story?" she asked. His Grace approached smiling—he never could converse with this young lady without smiling a little—she so bore out all the promise of her school-girl letters and reminded him of the night when he had found her brother, Ensign Tom, and Bob Langley grinning and shouting over her homilies on the Gloucestershire beauty.

"Which one is it?" he said. "Your ladyship has been kind enough to tell me so many."

"'Tis the one about Sir John Oxon and her ladyship of Dunstanwolde," she answered, with a pretty simper. "All Gloucestershire knew how they were in love with each other when she was Mistress Wildairs—until she cast him off for my Lord Dunstanwolde. 'Tis said she drove him to ruin—but now he has come back to her, and all think she will remember her first love and yield to him at last. And surely it would be a pretty romance."

"Jack Oxon was not drove to ruin by her ladyship," cried Sir Chris; "not he. But deep in love with her he was, 'tis sure, and had she been any other woman she must have been melted by him. Ecod!" looking across the room at the two, with a reflective air, "I wonder if she was!"

"But look at his eyes now," said my Lady Betty, giving a side

175

glance at his Grace. "They glow like fire, and wheresoever she moves he keeps them glued on her."

"She doth not keep hers glued on him," said Sir Chris, "but looks away and holds her head up as if she would not see him."

"That is her way to draw him to her," cried Lady Betty. "It drives a man wild with love to be so treated—and she is a shrewd beauty; but when he can get near enough he stands and speaks into her ear—low, that none may listen. I have seen him do it more than once, and she pretends not to hearken, but hears it all, and murmurs back, no doubt, while she seems to gaze straight before her, and waves her fan. I heard him speak once when he did not think me close to him, and he said, 'Have you forgot—have you forgot, Clorinda?' and she answered then, but her words I did not hear." She waved her painted fan with a coquettish flourish. "'Tis not a new way of making love," she said with arch knowingness. "It hath been done before."

"He hath drawn near and is speaking to her now," said Sir Chris, staring wonderingly, "but I swear it does not look like love-making. He looks like a man who threatens."

"He threatens he will fall on his sword if she will not yield," laughed Lady Betty. "They all swear the same thing."

My lord Duke moved forward. He had heard this talk often before during the past weeks, and he had seen this man haunting her presence, and always when he was near or spoke to her a strange look on her face, a look as if she made some struggle with herself or him—and strangest of all, though she was so gracious to himself, something in her eyes had seemed to hold him back from speaking, as if she said, "Not yet—not yet! Soon—but not yet!" and though he had not understood, it had bewildered him, and brought back a memory of the day she had sate in the carven gilded chair and delivered her lord's message to him, and her eyes had pleadingly forbade him to come to Dunstan's Wolde while her words expressed her husband's hospitable desire. His passion for her was so great and deep, 'twas a fathomless pool whose depths were stirred by every breath of her, and so he had even waited till her eyes should say—"Now!"

He had moved towards her this moment, because she had looked up at him, as if she needed he should come nearer. She rose from her seat, leaving Sir John Oxon where he stood. His Grace moved quicker and they met in the crowd, and as she looked up at him, he saw that she had lost a little of her radiant bloom, and she spoke in a low voice like a girl.

"Will your Grace take me to my coach?" she said. "I am not well."

And he led her, leaning on his arm, through the crowd to Mistress Anne, who was always glad to leave any assembly—the more brilliant they, the readier she to desert their throngs—and he escorted them to their coach, and before he left them asked a question gravely.

"Will your ladyship permit me," he said, "to wait on you to-morrow? I would know that your indisposition has passed."

My lady answered him in a low voice from the coach; her colour had come back, and she gave him her hand which he kissed. Then the equipage rolled away and he entered his own, and being driven back to Osmonde House said to himself gravely, over and over again, one word—"To-morrow!"

But within two hours a messenger in the royal liveries came from Kensington and as quickly as horses could carry him my lord Duke was with her Majesty, whom he found agitated and pale, important news from France having but just reached her. Immediate action was necessary, and there was none who could so well bear her private messages to the French Court as could the man who had no interest of his own to serve, whom Nature and experience peculiarly fitted for the direction of affairs requiring discretion, swiftness of perception, self-control, and dignity of bearing. 'Twas his royal Mistress herself who said these things to his Grace, and added to her gracious commands many condescending words and proofs of confidence, which he received with courtly obeisance but with a galled and burning heart.

And on the coming of the morrow he was on his way to Versailles, and my Lady Dunstanwolde, having received news of the sudden exigency and his departure, sate in her chamber alone gazing as into vacancy, with a hunted look in her wide eyes.

CHAPTER XXVI

A Dead Rose

Sovereigns and their thrones, statesmen and their intrigues, favourites and their quarrels—of what moment are they to a man whose heart is on fire and whose whole being resolves itself into but one thought of but one creature? My lord Duke went to France as he was commanded; he had been before at Versailles and Fontainebleau and Saint Germain, and there were eyes which brightened at the sight of his tall form, and there were men who while they greeted him with courteous bows and professions of flattering welcome exchanged side glances and asked each other momentous questions in private. He went about his business with discretion and diplomatic skill and found that he had no reason to despair of its accomplishment, but all his thoughts of his errand, though he held his mind steady and could reason clearly on them, seemed to him like the thoughts of a man in a dream who only in his private moments awakened to the reality of existence.

"'Twas Fate again," he said, "Fate! who has always seemed to stalk in between! If I had gone to her on that 'to-morrow,' I should have poured forth my soul and hers would have answered me. But there shall be another to-morrow, and I swear it shall come soon."

There was but a few hours' journey by land, and the English Channel, between himself and London, and there was much passing to and fro; and though the French Court had stories enough of its own, new ones were always welcome, English gossip being thought to have a special heavy quaintness, droll indeed. The Court of Louis found much entertainment in the Court of Anne, and the frivolities or romances of beauties who ate beef and drank beer and wore, 'twas said, the coquettish commode founded on lovely Fontange's lace handkerchief, as if it were a nightcap.

"But they have a handsome big creature there now, who is amazing," they said with interest at this time. "She was brought up as a boy at the château of her father, and can fight with swords like a man, but is as beautiful as the day and seven feet tall. It would be a pleasure to see her. She is at present a widow with an immense fortune, and all the gentlemen fight duels over her."

Both masculine and feminine members of the Court were much pleased with this lady and found her more interesting and exciting than any of her sister beauties. Naturally many unfounded anecdotes of her were current, and it was said that she fought duels herself. It was not long before it was whispered that the handsome Englishman Monsieur le Duc d'Osmonde, the red blonde giant with the great calm eyes, was one of the two chief pretendants to this picturesque lady's favour. Thus, as was inevitable, my lord Duke heard all the rumours from the English capital in one form or another. Some of them were bitter things for him to hear, for all of them more or less touched upon Sir John Oxon, who seemed to follow her from playhouse to assembly and to dog her very footsteps, while all the world looked on wondering, since her ladyship treated him with such unrelenting coldness and disdain.

His Grace had much to do at this time and did it well, but the days seemed long, and each piece of English gossip he heard recounted added to the length of the twenty-four hours. Then there came a story which created an excitement greater than any other, and was chattered over with a vivacity which made him turn pale.

In London the wonderful Amazon Milady Dunstanwolde had provided the town with a new example of her courage and daring spirit.

"There was a man who owned the most dangerous horse in the country—a monster, a devil." So his Grace heard the history related for the first time in a great lady's salon to breathlessly delighted listeners. "The animal was a horror of vice and temper, but beautiful, beautiful. A skin of black satin, a form incomparable! He has three grooms who take care of him, and all of them are afraid; he bites, he kicks, he rises on his hind legs and falls on those who ride him. None but those three men dare try to manage him. Each one is a wonderful rider and hopes to win or subdue him. It is no use. One morning the first of the three enters his stable and does not come out. He is called and does not answer. Someone goes to look. He is there, but he lies in a heap, kicked to death. A few days later the second one manages to mount the horse, taking him by surprise. At first the animal seems frightened into quietness. Suddenly he begins to run; he goes faster and faster, and all at once stops, and his rider flies over his head and is taken up with a broken neck. His owner, who is a horse dealer, orders him to be shot, but keeps him for a few days because he is so handsome. Who, think you, hears of him and comes to buy him? It is a lady. 'He is the very beast I want,' she says. 'It will please me to teach him there is someone stronger than himself.' Who is it?" asked the narrator, striking her fair hands together in a sort of exultation.

"The Countess of Dunstanwolde!" broke in a voice, and all turned quickly to look at the speaker. It was the Duke of Osmonde.

How did Monsieur le Duc know at once, they asked laughing, and he answered them with a slight smile, though someone remarked later that he had looked pale. He had known that she was a marvellous horsewoman, he had seen her in the hunting-field when she had been a child, he had heard of her riding dangerous animals before. Everyone knew that she was without fear. There was no other woman in England who would dare so much.

He spoke to them in almost ordinary tones, and heard their exclamations of admiration or prophetic fright to the end, but when he had driven homeward and was alone in his own apartment he felt himself cold with dread.

"And I wait here at the command of a Queen," he said, "and

179

cannot be loosed from my duty. And Fate may come between again—again!"—and he almost shuddered the next instant as he heard the sound which broke from his lips, 'twas so like a short, harsh laugh which mocked at his own sharp horror. "'Tis not right that a woman should so play with a man's soul," he cried fiercely; "'tis not fair she should so lay him on the rack!"

But next, manlike, his own anguish melted him.

"She does not know," he said. "If she knew she would be more gentle. She is very noble. Had I spoke with her on that to-morrow, she would have obeyed the commands my love would lay upon her."

"My Lady Dunstanwolde," he heard a day later, "has vowed to conquer her great horse or be killed by it. Each day she fights a battle with it in the park, and all the people crowd to look on. Some say it will kill her, and some she will kill it. She is so strong and without fear."

"To one of her adorers she laughed and said that if the animal broke her neck, she need battle with neither men nor horses again. The name of her horse is Devil, and he is said to look like one. Magnifique!" laughed the man who spoke.

By the third day, his Grace of Osmonde's valet began to look anxious. He had attended his master ten years and had never seen him look as he did in these days. His impression was that his Grace did not sleep, that he had not slept for several nights. Lexton had heard him walking in his room when he ought to have been in bed; one thing was certain, he did not eat his meals, and one thing Lexton had always affirmed was that he had never known a gentleman as fine and regular in his habits as his Grace, and had always said that 'twas because he was so regular that he was such a man as he was—so noble in his build and so clear in his eye, and with such a grand bearing.

At last, turns up in the street young Langton, who had run over to Paris, as he had a habit of doing when he was out of humour with his native land, either because his creditors pressed him, or because some lady was unkind. And he stopped my lord Duke in the Rue Royale, filled to the brim with the excitement of the news he brought fresh from London.

"Has your Grace heard of my Lady Dunstanwolde's breaking of the horse Devil?" he cried. "The story has reached Paris, I know, for I heard it spoke of scarce an hour after my arrival. On Tuesday I stood in Hyde Park and watched the fight between them, and I think, God knows! that surely no woman ever mounted such a beast and ran such danger before. 'Tis the fashion to go out each morning and stand looking on and laying wagers. The stakes run high. At first the odds were all against my lady, but on Tuesday they veered

180

and were against the horse. How they can stand and laugh, and lay bets, Heaven knows!" He was a good-natured young fellow and gave a little shudder. "I could not do it. For all her spirit and her wrists of steel, she is but a woman and a lovely creature, and the horse is so great a demon that if he gets her from his back and beneath his feet—good Lord! it makes me sick to think of it." He shook his shoulders with a shudder again. "What think you," he cried, "I heard Jack Oxon wager? He hath been watching her day after day more fierce and eager than the rest. He turned round one moment when the beast was doing his worst and 'twas life and death between them. And she could hear his words, too, mark you. 'A thousand pounds against fifty,' he says with his sneering laugh; 'a thousand pounds that she is off his back in five minutes and that when she is dragged away, what his heels have left of her will bear no semblance to a woman!'"

"Good God!" broke from the Duke. "This within her hearing! Good God!"

"In my belief 'twas a planned thing to make her lose her nerve," said the young fellow. "'Tis my belief he would gloat over the killing of her, because she has disdained him. Why is there not some man who hath the right to stop her—I—" his honest face reddened— "what am I to dare to speak to such a lady in advice. I know it was an impudence, and felt it one, your Grace, but I plucked up courage to—to—follow her home, and says I, bowing and as red as a turkey-cock, 'My lady, for the Lord's sake give up this awfulness. Think of them that love you. Sure there must be some heart you would tear in two. For God's sake have pity on it wheresoever it be, though I beg your ladyship's pardon, and 'tis impudence, I know.'"

My lord Duke caught his hand and in the passionate gratitude of the grasp he gave it forgot his own strength and that Bob was not a giant also.

"God bless you!" he cried. "God bless you! You are a brave fellow! I—I am her kinsman and am grateful. God bless you, man, and call on Gerald Mertoun for a friend's service when you need it."

And he strode away, leaving Bob Langton staring after him and holding his crushed hand tenderly, but feeling a glow at his heart, for 'tis not every day a careless, empty-pocketed young ensign is disabled by the grasp of a Duke's hand, and given his friendship as the result of a mere artless impulse of boyish good-nature.

His Grace strode homeward and called Lexton to him.

"We go to England within an hour," he said. "We may remain there but a day. Not a moment is to be lost. 'Tis of most serious import."

When he entered Osmonde House, on reaching the end of his

journey, the first person he encountered was Mr. Fox, who had just come in from Hyde Park, where he had spent the morning.

"I have been there each day this week, your Grace," he said, and his lips trembled somewhat as he wiped his brow. "It hath seemed to me all the town hath been there. I—your Grace's pardon—but I could not stay away; it seemed almost a duty. But I would gladly have been spared it. The worst is over." And he wiped his brow again, his thin, clerical countenance pale. "They say the horse is beat; but who knows when such a beast is safe, and at this moment she puts him through his paces, and they all look on applauding."

His Grace had rung the bell. "Bring Rupert," he commanded. "Rupert."

And the beast was brought without delay—as fiery a creature as the horse Devil himself, yet no demon but a spirited brute, knowing his master as his master knew himself; and my lord Duke came forth and flung himself upon him, and the creature sprang forward as if they had been one, and he felt in every nerve that his rider rode with heart beating with passion which was resolute to overleap every obstacle in its way, which had reached the hour when it would see none, hear of none, submit to none, but sweep forward to its goal as though 'twere wind or flame.

A short hour later all the town knew that my Lady Dunstanwolde had sealed her brilliant fate. And 'twas not Sir John Oxon who was conqueror, but his Grace of Osmonde, who, it seemed, had swept down upon her and taken possession of his place by her side as a King might have descended on some citadel and claimed it for his own. Great Heaven! what a thing it had been to behold, and how those congratulated themselves who had indeed beheld it—my lord Duke appearing upon the scene as if by magic, he who had been known to be in France, and who came almost at full gallop beneath the trees, plainly scarce seeing the startled faces turned at the sound of his horse's hoofs, the hats which were doffed at sight of him, the fair faces which lighted, the lovely, hurried courtesies made, his own eyes being fixed upon a certain point on the riding-road where groups stood about and her ladyship of Dunstanwolde sat erect and glowing upon the back of her conquered beast, the black horse Devil!

"Zounds, 'twas like a play!" cried Sir Christopher, gloating over it when 'twas past. "There rides my lady like an empress, Devil going as dainty as a dancing-master, and all the grandees doffing hats to her down the line. And of a sudden one man hears hoofs pounding and turns, and there he comes, my lord Duke of Osmonde, and he sees but one creature and makes straight for her—

and she doth not even hear him till he is close upon her, and then she turns—blushing, good Lord! the loveliest crimson woman ever wore. And in each other's eyes they gaze as if Heaven's gate had opened, and 'twas not earth that was beneath their horses' feet, and both forgot that poor plain flesh and blood stood looking on!"

"Lud!" minced Lady Betty, applauding with her fan. "We must have it made into a play and Mrs. Bracegirdle shall perform it."

"My old heart thumped to see it!" said Sir Chris; "it thumped, I swear!" and he gave his stout side a feeling blow. "All her days I have known her, and it came back to me how, when she was but a vixen of twelve we dubbed her Duchess, and, ecod! the water came into my eyes!"

"Because she was a vixen, or because you called her Duchess?" said my Lady Betty, with her malicious little air.

Sir Christopher stared at her; there was a touch of moisture in his old eyes, 'twas true!

"Nay," he said, bluntly, "because she is such a damned fine woman, and 'tis all come true!"

The words these two had exchanged before the eyes of the world only themselves could know—they had been but few, surely, and yet in ten minutes after their first speech all those who gazed knew that the tale was told. And as they rode homeward together beneath the arching trees and through the crowded streets, their faces wore such looks as drew each passer-by to turn and gaze after them, and to themselves the whole great world had changed; and of a surety, nowhere, nowhere, two hearts beat to such music, or two souls swayed together in such unison.

When they rode into the court at Dunstanwolde House, the lacqueys, seeing them, drew up in state about the entrance.

"Look you," said, in an undertone to his fellow, one of the biggest and sauciest of them, "'tis her Grace of Osmonde who returns, and we may be a great Duke's servants if we carry ourselves with dignity."

They bowed their lowest as the two passed between them, but neither the one nor the other beheld them, scarce knowing that they were present. My lady's sweet, tall body trembled, and her mouth's crimson trembled also, almost as if she had been a child. She could not speak, but looked up, softly smiling, as she led him to a panelled parlour, which was her own chosen and beloved room. And when they entered it, and the door closed, my lord Duke, having no words either, put forth his arms and took her to his heart, folding her close so that she felt his pulsing breast shake. And then he drew her to the gilded chair and made her sit, and knelt down before her, and laid his face upon her lap.

"Let it stay there," he cried, low and even wildly. "Let it stay there—Heart. If you could know—if you could know!"

And then in broken words he told her of how, when she had sate in this same chair before and given him her dead lord's message, he had so madly yearned to throw himself at her feet upon his knees, and hide his anguished face where now it lay, while her sweet hand touched his cheek.

"I love you," she whispered, very low and with a soft, helpless sob in her voice. "I love you," for she could think of no other words to say, and could say no more. And with tears in his lion's eyes he kissed her hands a thousand times as if he had been a boy.

"When I was in France," he said, "and heard of the danger that you ran, my heart rebelled against you. I cried that 'twas not just to so put a man to torture and bind him to the rack. And then I repented and said you did not know or you would be more gentle."

"I will be gentle now," she said, "always, your Grace, always."

"When the sun rose each day," he said, "I could not know it did not rise upon your beauty, lying cold and still, lost—lost to me— this time, forever."

Her fair hand covered her eyes, she shuddering a little.

"Nay, nay," she cried. "I—nay, I could not be lost to you— again. Let us—let us pray God, your Grace, let us pray God!"

And to his heavenly rapture she put forth her arms and laid them round his neck, her face held back that she might gaze at him with her great brimming eyes. Indeed 'twas a wonder to a man to behold how her stateliness had melted and she was like a yearning, clinging girl.

He gazed at her a moment, kneeling so, and all the long years rolled away and he scarce dared to breathe lest he should waken from his dream.

"Ah, Heaven!" he sighed, "there is so much to tell—years, years of pain which your sweet soul will pity."

Ah, how she gazed on him, what longing question there was in her eyes!

He took from his breast a velvet case which might have held a miniature, but did not.

"Look—look," he prayed, "at this. Tis a dead rose."

"A rose!" says she, and then starts and looks up from it to him, a dawning of some thought—or hope—in her face. "A rose!" she uttered, scarcely breathing it, as if half afraid to speak.

"Ah!" he cried, "I pray God you remember. When it fell from your breast that night——"

She broke in, breathless, "The night you came——"

"Too late—too late," he answered; "and this fell at my feet, and

184

you passed by. No night since then I have not pressed it to my lips. No day it has not lain upon my heart through all its darkest hours."

She took it from him—gazed down at it with stormy, filling eyes, and pressing it to her lips, broke into tender, passionate sobbing.

"No night, no day!" she cried. "Poor rose! dear rose!"

"Beloved!" he cried, and would have folded her to his breast, kissing her tears away which were so womanly. But she withdrew herself a little—holding up her hand.

"Wait, your Grace; wait!" she said, as if she would say more, almost as if she was shaken by some strange trouble and knew not how to bear its presence. And, of a sudden, seeing this, a vague fear struck him and he turned a little pale.

But the next moment he controlled himself; 'twas indeed as if he himself called the receding blood back to his heart, and he took her hand and held it in both his own, smiling.

"I have waited so long," he pleaded, caressingly. "I pray you—in Love's name."

And it was but like her, he thought, that she should rise at this and stand before him, her hand laid upon her breast, her great eyes opening upon him in appeal, as if she were some tender culprit standing at judgment bar.

"In Love's name!" she cried, in a low, panting voice. "Oh, Love should give so much. A woman's treasury should be so filled with rich jewels of fair deeds that when Love comes she may pour them at his feet. And what have I—oh, what have I?"

He moved towards her with a noble gesture, and she came nearer and laid one hand upon his breast and one upon his shoulder, her uplifted face white as a lily from some wild emotion, and imploring him—the thought coming to him made him tremble—as some lost, helpless child might implore.

"Is there aught," she panted, "aught that could come between your soul and mine?" And she was trembling, and her voice trembled and her lips, and crystal drops on her lashes which, in quivering, fell. "Think," she whispered; "your Grace, think."

And then a storm swept over him, a storm of love as great as that first storm of frenzy and despair. And he cried out in terror at the thought that Fate might plan some trick to cheat him yet, after the years—the years of lost, lost life, spent as in gyves of iron.

"Great God! No! No!" he cried; "I am a man and you are the life of me! I come to you not as other men, who love and speak their passion. Mine has been a burden hidden and borne so long. It woke at sight of a child, it fed on visions of a girl; before I knew its power

185

it had become my life. The portals of my prison are open and I see the sun. Think you I will let them be closed—be closed again?"

And he would not be withheld and swept her to his breast, and she, lying there, clung to him with a little sobbing cry of joy and gratefulness, uttering wild, sweet, low, broken words.

"I am so young," she said. "Life is so strong; the world seems full of flowers. Sure some of them are mine. My heart beats so—it so beats. Forgive! forgive!"

"Tis from to-day our life begins," he whispered, solemnly. "And God so deal with me, Heart, as I shall deal with you."

CHAPTER XXVII

"'Twas the night thou hidst the package in the wall"

"So," said the fashionable triflers, "'twas the Duke after all, and his Grace flies to France to draw his errand to a close, and when he flies back again, upon the wings of love, five villages will roast oxen whole and drink ale to the chiming of wedding-bells."

"Lud!" said my Lady Betty, this time with her pettish air, this matter not being to her liking, for why should a Duke fall in love with widows when there were exquisite languishing unmarried ladies near at hand. "Tis a wise beauty who sets bells ringing in five villages by marrying a duke, instead of taking a spendthrift rake who is but a baronet and has no estate at all. I could have told you whom her ladyship would wed if she were asked."

"If she were asked! good Lord!" cried Sir Chris Crowell, as red as a turkey-cock. "And this I can tell you, 'tis not the five villages she marries, nor the Duke, but the man. And 'tis not the fine lady he takes to his heart, but our Clo, and none other, and would have taken her in her smock had she been a beggar wench. 'Tis an honest love-match, that I swear!"

Thereupon my Lady Betty laughed.

"Those who see Sir John Oxon's face now," she said, "do not behold a pretty thing. And my lady sees it at every turn. She can go nowhere but she finds him at her elbow glaring."

"He would play some evil trick on her for revenge, I vow," said another lady. "She hath Mistress Anne with her nearly always in these days, as if she would keep him off by having a companion; but 'tis no use, follow and badger her he will."

"Badger her!" blustered Sir Chris. "He durst not, the jackanapes! He is not so fond of drawing point as he was a few years ago."

"'Tis badgering and naught else," said Mistress Lovely. "I have watched him standing by and pouring words like poison in her ear, and she disdaining to reply or look as though she heard."

My Lady Betty laughed again with a prettier venom still.

"He hath gone mad," she said. "And no wonder! My woman, who knows a mercer's wife at whose husband's shop he bought his finery, told me a story of him. He was so deep in debt that none would give him credit for an hour, until the old Earl of Dunstanwolde died, when he persuaded them that he was on the point of marrying her ladyship. These people are so simple they will believe anything, and they watched him go to her house and knew he had been her worshipper before her marriage. And so they gave him credit again. Thence his fine new wardrobe came. And now they have heard the news and have all run mad in rage at their own foolishness, and are hounding him out of his life."

The two ladies made heartless game enough of the anecdote. Perhaps both had little spites of their own against Sir John, who in his heyday had never spoke with a woman without laying siege to her heart and vanity, though he might have but five minutes to do it in. Lady Betty, at least, 'twas known had once had coquettish and sentimental passages with him, if no more; and whether 'twas her vanity or her heart which had been wounded, some sting rankled, leaving her with a malice against him which never failed to show itself when she spoke or heard his name.

A curious passage took place between them but a short time after she had told her story of his tricking of his creditors. 'Twas at a Court ball and was a whimsical affray indeed, though chiefly remembered afterwards because of the events which followed it— one of them occurring upon the spot, another a day later, this second incident being a mystery never after unravelled. At this ball was my Lady Dunstanwolde in white and silver, and looking, some said, like a spirit in the radiance of her happiness.

"For 'tis pure happiness that makes her shine so," said her faithful henchman, old Sir Christopher. "Surely she hath never been a happy woman before, for never hath she smiled so since I knew her first, a child. She looks like a creature born again."

Lady Betty Tantillion engaged in her encounter in an

antechamber near the great saloon. Her ladyship had a pretty way of withdrawing from the moving throng at times to seek comparative seclusion and greater ease. There was more freedom where there would be exchange of wits and glances, not overheard and beheld by the whole world; so her ladyship had a neat taste in nooks and corners, where a select little court of her own could be held by a charming fair one. Thus it fell that after dancing in the ball-room with one admirer and another, she made her way, followed by two of the most attentive, to a pretty retiring-room quite near.

'Twas for the moment, it seemed, deserted, but when she entered with her courtiers, the exquisite Lord Charles Lovelace and his friend Sir Harry Granville, a gentleman turned from a window where he seemed to have been taking the air alone, and seeing them uttered under his breath a malediction.

"To the devil with them!" he said, but the next moment advanced with a somewhat mocking smile, which was scarce hidden by his elaborate bow of ceremony to her ladyship.

"My Lady Betty Tantillion!" he exclaimed, "I did not look for such fortune. 'Tis not necessary to hope your ladyship blooms in health. 'Tis an age since we met."

Since their rupture they had not spoken with each other, but my Lady Betty had used her eyes well when she had beheld him even at a distance, and his life she knew almost as well as if they had been married and she a jealous consort.

But she stood a moment regarding him with an impertinent questioning little stare, and then held up her quizzing-glass and uttered an exclamation of sad surprise.

"Sir John Oxon!" she said. "How changed! how changed! Sure you have been ill, Sir John, or have met with misfortunes."

To the vainest of men and the most galled—he who had been but a few years gone the most lauded man beauty in the town, who had been sought, flattered, adored—'twas a bitter little stab, though he knew well the giver of the thrust. Yet he steeled himself to bow again, though his eyes flashed.

"I have indeed been ill and in misfortune," he answered, sardonically. "Can a man be in health and fortunate when your ladyship has ceased to smile upon him?"

My Lady Betty courtesied with a languid air.

"Lord Charles," she said, with indifferent condescension, "Sir Harry, you have heard of this gentleman, though he was before your day. In his—" (as though she recalled the past glories of some antiquated beau) "you were still at the University."

188

Then as she passed to a divan to seat herself she whispered an aside to Lord Charles, holding up her fan.

"The ruined dandy," she said, "who is mad for my Lady Dunstanwolde. Ask him some question of his wife?"

Whereupon Lord Charles, who was willing enough to join in badgering a man who had still good looks enough to prove a rival had he the humour, turned with a patronising air of civility.

"My Lady Oxon is not with you?" he observed.

"There is none, your lordship," Sir John answered, and almost ground his teeth, seeing the courteous insolence of the joke. "I am a single man."

"Lud!" cried my Lady Betty, fanning with graceful indifference. "'Twas said you were to marry a great fortune, and all were filled with envy. What become, then, of the fair Mistress Isabel Beaton?"

"She returned to Scotland, your ladyship," replied Sir John, his eyes transfixing her. "Ere now 'tis ancient history."

"Fie, Sir John," said Lady Betty, laughing wickedly, "to desert so sweet a creature. So lovely—and so rich! Men are not wise as they once were."

Sir John drew nearer to her and spoke low. "Your ladyship makes a butt of me," he said. And 'twas so ordained by Fate, at this moment when the worst of him seethed within his breast, and was ripest for mad evil, Sir Christopher Crowell came bustling into the apartment, full of exultant hilarity and good wine which he had been partaking of in the banqueting-hall with friends.

"Good Lord!" he cried, having spoke with Lady Betty; "what ails thee, Jack? Thy very face is a killjoy."

"'Tis repentance, perhaps," said Lady Betty. "We are reproaching him with deserting Mistress Beaton—who had even a fortune."

Sir Christopher glanced from Sir John to her ladyship and burst forth into a big guffaw, his convivialities having indeed robbed him of discretion.

"He desert her!" said he. "She jilted him and took her fortune to a Marquis! 'Twas thine own fault, too, Jack. Hadst thou been even a decent rake she would have had thee."

"By God!" cried Sir John, starting and turning livid; and then catching a sight of the delight in my Lady Betty's face, who had set out to enrage him before her company, he checked himself and broke into a contemptuous, short laugh.

"These be country manners, Sir Christopher," he said. "In Gloucestershire bumpers are tossed off early, and a banquet added turns a man's head and makes him garrulous."

"Ecod!" said Sir Christopher, grinning. "A nice fellow he is to twit a man with the bottle. Myself, I've seen him drunk for three days."

Whereupon there took place a singular change in Sir John Oxon's look. His face had been so full of rage but a moment ago that, at Sir Chris's second sally, Lady Betty had moved slightly in some alarm. Town manners were free, but not quite so free as those of the country, and Sir John was known to be an ill-tempered man. If the two gentlemen had quarrelled about her ladyship's own charms 'twould have been a different matter, but to come to an encounter over a mere drinking-bout would be a vulgar, ignominious thing in which she had no mind to be mixed up.

"Lord, Sir Christopher," she exclaimed, tapping him with her fan. "Three days! For shame!"

But though Sir John had started 'twas not in rage. Three days carousing with this old blockhead! When had he so caroused? He could have laughed aloud. Never since that time he had left Wildairs, bearing with him the lock of raven hair—his triumph and his proof. No, 'twas not in anger he started but through a sudden shock of recollection, of fierce, eager hope, that at last, in the moment of his impotent humiliation, he had by chance—by a very miracle of chance—come again upon what he had so long searched for in helpless rage—that which would give power into his hand and vengeance of the bitterest.

And he had come upon it among chatterers in a ball-room through the vinous babbling of a garrulous fool.

"Three days!" he said, and took out his snuff-box and tapped it, laughing jeeringly. And this strange thing my Lady Betty marked, that his white hand shook a little as if from hidden excitement. "Three days!" he mocked.

"No man of fashion now," said Lord Charles, and tapped his snuff-box also, "is drunk for more than two."

But Sir Christopher felt he was gaining a victory before her ladyship's very eyes, which always so mocked and teased him for his clumsiness in any encounter of words, wherefore he pressed his point gleefully.

"Three days!" cries he. "'Twas nearer four."

Sir John turned on him, laughing still, seeming in very truth as if the thing amused him.

"When, when?" he said. "Never, I swear!" and held a pinch of snuff in his fingers daintily, his eyes gleaming blue as sapphires through the new light in them.

"Swear away!" cried Sir Christopher; "thou wast too drunk to remember. 'Twas the night thou hidst the package in the wall."

190

Then he burst forth again in laughter, for Sir John had so started that he forgot his pinch of snuff and scattered it.

"Canst see 'tis no slander, my lady," he cried, pointing at Sir John, who stood like a man who wakes from long sleep and is bewildered by the thoughts which rush through his brain. "I laughed till I was like to crack my sides." Then to Sir John, "Thou hadst but just left Clo Wildairs and I rode with thee to Essex. Lord, how I laughed to watch thee groping to find a place safe enough to put it in. 'I'm drunk,' says thou, 'and I would have it safe till I am sober. 'Twill be safe here,' and stuffed it in the broken plaster 'neath the window-sill. And safe it was, for I'll warrant thou hast not thought of it since, and safe thou'lt find it at the Cow at Wickben still."

Sir John struck one closed hand sudden on the palm of the other.

"It comes back to thee," cried Sir Christopher, with a grimace aside at his audience.

"Ay, it comes back," answers Sir John; "it comes back." And he broke forth into a short, excited laugh, there being in its sound a note of triumph almost hysteric; and hearing this they stared, for why in such case he should be triumphant, Heaven knew.

"'Twas a love-token!" said Lady Betty, simpering, for of a sudden he had become another man—no longer black-visaged, but gallant, and smiling with his old charming, impudent, irresistible air. He bent and took her hand and kissed her finger-tips with this same old enchanting insolence.

"Had your ladyship given it to me," he said, "I had not hid it in a wall, but in my heart." And with a soft glance and a smiling bow he left their circle and sauntered towards the ball-room.

"'Twas the last time I spoke with him," said my Lady Betty, when he was talked of later. "I wonder if 'twas in his head when he kissed my hand—if indeed 'twas a matter he himself planned or had aught to do with. Faith! though he was a villain he had a killing air when he chose."

When her ladyship had played off all her airs and graces upon her servitors she led them again to the ball-room that she might vary her triumphs and fascinations. A minuet was being played, and my Lady Dunstanwolde was among the dancers, moving stately and slow in her white and silver, while the crowd looked on, telling each other of the preparations being made for her marriage, and that my lord Duke of Osmonde was said to worship her, and could scarce live through the hours he was held from her in France.

Among the watchers, and listening to the group as he watched, stood Sir John Oxon. He stood with a graceful air and watched her steadily, and there was a gleam of pleasure in his glance.

"He has followed and gazed at her so for the last half-hour," said Mistress Lovely. "Were I the Duke of Osmonde I would command him to choose some other lady to dog with his eyes. Now the minuet is ending I would wager he will follow her to her seat and hang about her."

And this indeed he did when the music ceased, but 'twas done with a more easy, confident air than had been observed in him for some time past. He did not merely loiter in her vicinity, but when the circle thinned about her he made his way through it and calmly joined her.

"Does he pay her compliments?" said Lord Charles, who looked on at a distance. "Faith, if he does, she does not greatly condescend to him. I should be frozen by a beauty who, while I strove to melt her, did not deign to turn her eyes. Ah, she has turned them now. What has he said? It must have been fire and flame to move her. What's this—what's this?"

He started forward, as all the company did—for her ladyship of Dunstanwolde had risen to her full height with a strange movement and, standing a moment swaying, had fallen at Sir John Oxon's feet, white in a death-like swoon.

CHAPTER XXVIII

Sir John Rides out of Town

Tom Tantillion had not appeared at the ball, having otherwise entertained himself for the evening, but at an hour when most festivities were at an end and people were returning from them, rolling through the streets in their coaches, the young man was sitting at a corner table in Cribb's Coffee-House surrounded by glasses and jolly companions and clouds of tobacco-smoke.

One of these companions had been to the ball and left it early, and had fallen to talking of great personages he had seen there, and describing the beauties who had shone the brightest, among them speaking of my Lady Dunstanwolde and the swoon which had so amazed those who had seen it.

"I was within ten feet of her," says he, "and watching her as a man always does when he is near enough. Jack Oxon stood behind her, and was speaking low over her shoulder, but she seeming to take little note of him and looking straight before her. And of a sudden she stands upright, her black eyes wide open as if some sound had startled her, and the next minute falls like a woman dropping dead, and lies among her white and silver like one carven out of stone. One who knows her well—old Sir Chris Crowell—says she hath never fallen in a swoon before since she was born. Gad! 'twas a strange sight—'twas so sudden." He had just finished speaking, and was filling his glass again, when a man strode into the room in such haste that all turned to glance at him.

He was in riding-dress, and was flushed and excited, and smiling as if to himself.

"Drawer!" he called, "bring me coffee and brandy, and, damme! be in haste."

Young Tantillion nudged his nearest companion with his elbow.

"Jack Oxon," he said. "Where rides the fellow at this time of night?"

"Eh, Jack!" he said, aloud, "art on a journey already, after shining at the Court ball?"

Sir John started, and seeing who spoke, answered with an ugly laugh.

"Ay," said he, "I ride to the country in hot haste. I go to Wickben in Essex, to bring back a thing I once left there."

"'Twas a queer place to leave valuables," said Tom—"a village of tumble-down thatched cottages. Was't a love-token or a purse of gold?"

Sir John gave his knee a sudden joyous slap, and laughed aloud.

"'Twas a little thing," he replied, "but 'twill bring back fortune—if I find it—and help me to pay back old scores, which is a thing I like better." And his grin was so ugly that Tom and his companions glanced aside at each other, believing that he was full of liquor already, and ready to pick a quarrel if they continued their talk. This they were not particularly inclined to, however, and began a game of cards, leaving him to himself to finish his drink. This he did, quickly tossing down both brandy and coffee the instant they were brought to him, and then striding swaggering from the room and mounting his horse, which waited in the street, and riding clattering off over the stones at a fierce pace.

"Does he ride for a wager?" said Will Lovell, dealing the cards.

"He rides for some ill purpose, I swear," said Tom Tantillion.

"Jack Oxon never went in haste towards an honest deed; but to play some devil's trick 'tis but nature to him to go full speed."

But what he rode for they never heard, neither they nor anyone else who told the story, though 'twas sure that if he went to Wickben he came back to town for a few hours at least, for there were those who saw him the next day, but only one there was who spoke with him, and that one my Lady Dunstanwolde herself.

Her ladyship rode out in the morning hoping, 'twas said, that the fresh air and exercise would restore her strength and spirits. She rode without attendant, and towards the country, and in the high road Sir John Oxon joined her.

"I did not know he had been out of town," she said, when the mystery was discussed. "He did not say so. He returned to Dunstanwolde House with me, and we had talk together. He had scarce left me when I remembered that I had forgot to say a thing to him I had wished to say. So I sent Jenfry forth quickly to call him back. He had scarce had time to turn the street's corner, but Jenfry returned, saying he was not within sight."

"Whereupon you sent a note to his lodgings, was't not so?" asked Sir Christopher.

"Yes," answered her ladyship, "but he had not returned there."

"Nor ever did," said Sir Christopher, whenever the mystery was referred to afterwards; "nor ever did, and where he went to from that hour only the devil knows, for no man or woman that one has heard of has ever clapt eyes on him since."

This was, indeed, the mysterious truth. After he entered the Panelled Parlour at Dunstanwolde House it seemed that none had seen him, for the fact was that by a strange chance even the lacquey who should have been at his place in the entrance hall had allowed himself to be ensnared from his duty by a pretty serving-wench, and had left his post for a few minutes to make love to her in the servants' hall, during which time 'twas plain Sir John must have left the house, opening the entrance-door for himself unattended.

"Lord," said the lacquey in secret to his mates, "my gizzard was in my throat when her ladyship began to question me. 'Did you see the gentle, man depart, Martin?' says she. "Twas you who attended him to the door, of a surety.' 'Yes, your ladyship,' stammers I. "Twas I—and I marked he seemed in haste.' 'Did you not observe him as he walked away?' says my lady. 'Did you not see which way he went?' 'To the left he turned, my lady,' says I, cold sweat breaking out on me, for had I faltered in an answer she would have known I was lying and guessed I had broke her orders by leaving my place by the door—and Lord have mercy on a man when she finds he has tricked her. There is a flash in her eye like

194

lightning, and woe betide him it falls on. But truth was that from the moment the door of the Panelled Parlour closed behind him the gentleman's days were ended, for all I saw of him, for I saw him no more."

And there was none who saw him, for from that time he disappeared from his lodgings, from the town, from England, from the surface of the earth, as far as any ever heard or discovered, none knowing where he went, or how, or wherefore.

Had he been a man of greater worth or importance, or one who had made friends, his so disappearing would have aroused a curiosity and excitement not easily allayed; but a vicious wastrel who has lost hold even on his whilom companions in evil-doing, and has no friends more faithful, is like, indeed, on dropping out of the world's sight, to drop easily and lightly from its mind, his loss being a nine days' wonder and nothing more.

So it was with this one, who had had his day of being the fashion and had broken many a fine lady's brittle heart, and, living to be no longer the mode, had seen the fragile trifles cemented together again, to be almost as good as new. When he was gone he was forgot quickly and, indeed, but talked about because her ladyship of Dunstanwolde had last beheld him, and on the afternoon had been entertaining company in the Panelled Parlour when the lacquey had brought back the undelivered note with which Jenfry had waited three hours at the lost man's lodgings in the hope that he would return to them, which he did no more.

"'Tis a good riddance to all, my lady, wheresoever he be gone," said Sir Christopher, sitting nursing his stout knee in the blue parlour a week later (for her ladyship had had a sudden fancy to have the panelled room made wholly new and decorated before the return of his Grace from France). "Tis a good riddance to all."

Then he fell to telling stories of the man, of the creditors he had left in the lurch, having swindled them of their very hearts' blood, and that every day there was heard of some poor tradesman he had ruined, till 'twas a shame to hear it told; and there were worse things—worse things yet!

"By the Lord!" he said, "the ruin one man's life can bring about, the heartbreak, and the shame! 'Tis enough to make even a sinner as old as I, repent, to come upon them face to face. Eh, my lady?" looking at her suddenly, "thou must get back the roses thou hast lost these three days nursing Mistress Anne, or his Grace will be at odds with us every one."

For Mistress Anne had been ailing, and her sister being anxious and watching over her had lost some of her glorious bloom,

195

which was indeed a new thing to see. At this moment the roses had dropped from her cheeks and she smiled strangely.

"They will return," she said, "when his Grace does."

She asked questions of the stories Sir Christopher had told and showed anxiousness concerning the poor people who had been so hardly treated.

"I have often thought," she said, "that so rich a woman as I should set herself some task of good deeds to do. 'Twould be a good work to take in hand the undoing of the wrongs a man who is lost has left behind him. Why should not I, Clo Wildairs, take in hand the undoing of this man's?" And she rose up suddenly and stood before him, straight and tall, the colour coming out on her cheeks as if life flooded back there.

"Thou!" he cried, gazing at her in loving wonder. "Why shouldst thou, Clo?" None among them had ever understood her and her moods, and he surely did not understand this one—for it seemed as if a fire leaped up within her, and she spoke almost wildly.

"Because I would atone for all my past," she said, "and cleanse myself with unceasing mercies, and what I cannot undo, do penance for—that I may be worthy—worthy."

She broke off and drew her hand across her eyes, and ended with a strange little sound, half laugh.

"Perhaps all men and women have been evil," she said, "and some are—some seem fated! And when my lord Duke comes back, I shall be happy—happy—in spite of all; and I scarce dare to think my joy may not be taken from me. Is joy always torn away after it has been given to a human thing—given for just so long, as will make loss, madness?"

"Eh, my lady!" he said, blundering, "thou art fearful, just as another woman might be. 'Tis not like Clo Wildairs. Such thoughts will not make thee a happy woman."

She ended with a laugh stranger than her first one, and her great black eyes were fixed on him as he had remembered seeing her fix them when she was a child and full of some wild fancy or weird sadness.

"'Tis not Clo Wildairs who thinks them," says she; "'tis another woman. 'Twas Clo who knew John Oxon who is gone—and was as big a sinner as he, though she did harm to none but herself. And 'tis for those two—for both—I would have mercy. But I am a strong thing, and was born so, and my happiness will not die, despite—despite whatsoever comes. And I am happy, and know I shall be more; and 'tis for that I'am afraid—afraid."

"Good Lord!" cried Sir Chris, swallowing a lump which rose, he knew not why, in his throat. "What a strange creature thou art!"

His Grace's couriers went back and forth to France, and upon his estates the people prepared their rejoicings for the marriage-day, and never had Camylott been so heavenly fair as on the day when the bells rang out once more, and the villagers stood along the roadside and at their cottage doors, courtesying and throwing up hats and calling down God's blessings on the new-wed pair, as the coach passed by, and his Grace, holding his lady's hand, showed her to his people, seeming to give her and her loveliness to them as they bowed and smiled together—she almost with joyful tears in her sweet eyes.

In her room near the nurseries, at the window which looked out among the ivy, Nurse Halsell sat, watching the equipage as it made its way up the long avenue, and might be seen now and then between the trees, and her old hands trembled in her lap, for very joy. And before the day was done his Grace, knocking on the door gently, brought his Duchess to her.

"And 'twas you," said her Grace, standing close by her chair, and holding the old hand between her own two, which were so white and velvet warm, "and 'twas you who held him in your arms when he was but a little new-born thing, and often sang him to sleep, and were so loved by him. And he played here—" and she looked about the apartment with a tremulous smile.

"Yes," said his Grace, with a low laugh of joyful love, "and now I bring you to her, and 'tis my marriage-day."

Nurse Halsell gazed up at the eyes which glowed above her.

"'Tis what his Grace hath waited long for," she said, "and he would have died an unwedded man had he not reached it at last. 'Tis sure what God ordained." And for a minute she looked straight and steady into the Duchess's face. "A man must come to his own," she said, and bent and kissed the fair hand with passionate love, but her Grace lifted the old face with her palm, and stooped and kissed it fondly—gratefully.

Then the Duke took his wife to the Long Gallery and they stood there, he holding her close against his side, while the golden sun went down.

"Here I stood and heard that you were born," he said, and kissed her red, tender mouth. "Here I stood in agony and fought my battle with my soul the first sad day you came to Camylott." And he kissed her slow and tenderly again, in memory of the grief of that past time. "And here I stand and feel your dear heart beat against my side, and look into your eyes—and look into your eyes—and they are the eyes of her who is mine own—and Death himself cannot take her from me."

CHAPTER XXIX

At the Cow at Wichben

The happiness he had dreamed of was given to him; nay, he knew joy and tenderness even more high and sweet than his fancy had painted. As Camylott had been in his childhood so he saw it again—the most beauteous home in England and the happiest, its mistress the fairest woman and the most nobly loving. As his own father and mother had found life a joyful thing and their world full of warm hearts and faithful friends, so he and she he loved, found it together. The great house was filled once more with guests and pleasures as in the olden time, the stately apartments were thrown open for entertainment, gay cavalcades came and went from town, the forests were hunted, the moors shot over by sportsmen, and the lady who was hostess and chatelaine won renown as well as hearts, since each party of guests she entertained went back to the homes they came from, proclaiming to all her wit and gracious charm.

She rode to hunt and leapt hedges as she had done when she had been Clo Wildairs; she walked the moors with the sportsmen, her gun over her shoulder, she sparkling and showing her white teeth like a laughing gipsy; and when she so walked, the black rings of her hair blown loose about her brow, her cheeks kissed fresh crimson by the wet wind, and turned her eyes upon my lord Duke near her and their looks met, the man who beheld saw lovers who set his own heart beating.

"But is it true," asked once the great French lady who had related the history of the breaking of the horse, Devil, "is it true that a poor man killed himself in despair on her last marriage, and that she lives a secret life of penance to atone—and wears a hair shirt, and peas in her beautiful satin shoes, and does deeds of mercy in the dark places of the big black English city?"

"A man, mad with jealous rage of her, disappeared from sight," said an English lady present. "And he might well have drowned himself from disappointment that she would not wed him and pay his debts; but 'twas more like he fled England to escape his creditors. And 'tis true she does many noble deeds in secret; but if they be done in penance for Sir John Oxon, she is a lady with a conscience that is tender indeed."

That her conscience was a strangely tender thing was a thought which moved one man's heart strongly many a time. Scarce a day passed in which her husband did not mark some evidence of this—hear some word spoken, see some deed done, almost, it seemed, as if in atonement for imagined faults hid in her heart. He did not remark this because he was unused to womanly mercifulness; his own mother's life had been full of gentle kindness to all about her, of acts of charity and goodness, but in the good deeds of this woman, whom he so loved, he observed an eagerness which was almost a passion. She had changed no whit in the brilliance of her spirit; in the world she reigned a queen as she had ever done; wheresoever she moved, life and gayety seemed to follow, whether it was at the Court, in the town, or the country; but in both town and country he found she did strange charities, and seemed to search for creatures she might aid in such places as other women had not courage to dive into.

This he discovered through encountering her one day as she re-entered Osmonde House, returning from some such errand, clad in dark, plain garments, her black hood drawn over her face, being thereby so disguised that but for her height and bearing he should not have recognised her—indeed, he thought, she had not seen and would have passed him in silence.

He put forth his hand and stayed her, smiling.

"Your Grace!" he said, "or some vision!"

She threw the black hood back and her fair face and large black eyes shone out from beneath its shadows. She drew his hand up and kissed it, and held it against her cheek in a dear way which was among the sweetest of her wifely caresses.

"It is like Heaven, Gerald," she said, "to see your face, after beholding such miseries."

And when he took her in his arm and led her to the room in which they loved best to sit in converse together, she told him of a poor creature she had been to visit, and when she named the place where she had found her, 'twas a haunt so dark and wicked that he started in alarm and wonder at her.

"Nay, dear one," he said, "such dens are not for you to visit. You must not go to them again."

She was sitting on a low seat before him, and she leaned forward, the black hood falling back, framing her face and making it look white.

"None else dare go," she said; "none else dare go, Gerald. Such places are so hideous and so noisome, and yet there are those who are born and die there, bound hand and foot when they are born, that they may be bound hand and foot to die!" She rose as if she did not know she moved, and stood up before him, her hand upon her breast.

"'Tis such as I should go," she said, "I who am happy and

199

beloved—after all—after all! 'Tis such as I who should go, and carry love and pity—love and pity!" And she seemed Love's self and Pity's self, and stood transfigured.

"You are a saint," he cried; "and yet I am afraid. Ah! how could any harm you?"

"I am so great and strong," she said, in a still voice, "none could harm me if they would. I am not as other women. And I do not know fear. See!" and she held out her arm. "I am a Wildairs—built of iron and steel. If in a struggle I held aught in my hand and struck at a man—" her arm fell at her side suddenly as if some horrid thought had swept across her soul, like a blighting blast. She turned white and sank upon her low seat, covering her face with her hands. Then she looked up with awed eyes. "If one who was so strong," she said, "should strike at a man in anger, he might strike him dead—unknowing—dead!"

"'Tis not a thing to think of," said his Grace, and shuddered a little.

"But he would think of it," she said, "all his life through and bear it on his soul." And she shuddered, too, and in her eyes was the old look which sometimes haunted them. Surely, he thought, Nature had never before made a woman's eyes so to answer to her lover's and her lord's. They were so warm and full of all a man's soul most craved for. He had seen them flash fire like Juno's, he had seen tears well up into them as if she had been a tender girl, he had seen them laugh like a child's, he had seen them brood over him as a young dove's might brood over her mate, but this look was unlike any other, and was as if she thought on some dark thing in another world—so far away that her mind's vision could scarce reach it, and yet could not refrain from turning towards its shadow.

But this was but a cloud which his love-words and nearness could dispel. This she herself told him on a time when he spoke to her of it.

"When you see it," she said, "come and tell me that you love me, and that there is naught can come between our souls. As you said the day you showed me the dear rose, 'Naught can come between'—and love is more than all."

"But that you know," he answered.

Life is so full of joys for those who love and, being mated, are given by their good fortunes the power to live as their hearts lead them. These two were given all things, it seemed to the world which looked on. From one of their estates to the other they went with the changing seasons, and with them carried happiness and peace. Her Grace, of whom the villagers had heard such tales as made them feel that they should tremble before the proud glance of her dark eyes, found that their last Duchess, whose eyes had been like violets, could smile no more sweetly. This one was somehow the more majestic lady of the two, being taller and having a higher bearing by Nature, but none among them had ever beheld one who was more a woman and seemed so well to understand a woman's heart and ways. Where had she learned it, they wondered among themselves, as others had wondered the year when, as my Lady Dunstanwolde, she had been guest at Camylott, and in the gipsy's encampment had carried, so soft and tenderly, the little gipsy child in her arms. Where had she learned it?

"Gerald," she said once to her husband, and pressed her hand against her heart, "'twas always here—here, lying hid, when none knew it—when I did not know it myself. When I seemed but a hard, wild creature, having only men for friends—I was a woman then, and used sometimes to sit and stare at the red coals of the fire, or the red sun going down on the moors, and feel longings and pities and sadness I knew not the meaning of. And often, suddenly, I was made angry by them and would spring up and walk away that I might be troubled no more. But 'twas Nature crying out in me that I was a woman and could be naught else."

Her love and tenderness for her sister, Mistress Anne, increased, it seemed, hour by hour.

"At Camylott, at Marlowell, at Roxholm, at Paulyn, and at Mertoun," she had said when she was married, "we must have an apartment which is Anne's. She is my saint and I must keep a niche for her in every house and set her in it to be worshipped."

And so it was, to whichsoever of their homes they went, Mistress Anne went with them and found always her own nest warm to receive her.

"It makes me feel audacious, sister," she used to say at first, "to go from one grand house to the other and be led to Mistress Anne's apartments, in each, and they always prepared and waiting as if 'twere I who were a Duchess."

"You are Anne! You are Anne!" said her Grace, and kissed her fondly.

Sometimes she was like a gay and laughing girl, and set all the place alight with her witcheries; she invented entertainments for their guests, games and revels for the villagers, and was the spirit of all. In one of their retrospective hours, Osmonde had told her of the thoughts he had dreamed on, as they had ridden homeward from the encampment of the gipsies—of his fancies of the comrade she would make for a man who lived a roving life. She had both laughed and wept over the story, clinging to his breast as she had told her own, and of her fear of his mere glance at her in those dark days,

201

and that she had not dared to sit alone but kept near her lord's side lest she should ponder and remember what 'twas honest she should forget.

But afterwards she planned, for their fanciful pleasure, rambling long jaunts when they rode or walked unattended, and romanced like children, eating their simple food under broad greenwood trees or on the wide moors with a whole world of heather, as it seemed, rolled out before them.

On such a journey, setting out from London one bright morning, they rode through Essex and stopped by chance at a little village inn. 'Twas the village of Wickben, and on the signboard which hung swinging on a post before the small thatched house of entertainment was painted a brown cow.

None knew 'twas a Duke and his Duchess who dismounted and entered the place. They had made sure that by their attire none could suspect them of being more than ordinary travellers, modest enough to patronise a humble place.

"But Lord, what a fine pair!" said the old fellow who was the landlord. "Adam and Eve may have been such when God first made man and woman, and had stuff in plenty to build them."

He was an aged man and talkative, and being eager for a chance to wag his tongue and hear travellers' adventures, attended them closely. He gave them their simple repast himself in small room, and as he moved to and fro fell to gossiping, emboldened by their friendly gayety of speech and by her Grace's smiling eyes.

"Your ladyship," he began at first, in somewhat awkward, involuntary homage.

"Nay, gaffer, I am no ladyship," she answered, with Clo Wildairs's unceremonious air. "I am but a gipsy woman in good luck for a day, and my man is a gipsy, too, though his skin is fairer than mine. We are going to join our camp near Camylott village. These horses are not ours but borrowed—honestly. Is't not so, John Merton?" And she so laughed at his Grace with her big, saucy eyes, that he wished he had been indeed a gipsy man and could have kissed her openly.

"Art the Gipsies' queen?" asked the old man, bewitched by her.

"Not she," answered his Grace, "but a plain gipsy wench who makes baskets and tells fortunes—for all her good looks. Thou'rt flattering her, old fellow. All the men flatter her."

"'Tis well there are some to flatter me," said her Grace, showing her white teeth. "Thou dost not. But 'tis always so when a poor woman weds a man and tramps by the side of him instead of keeping him at her feet."

202

And then they led their old host on to talk, and told him stories of what gipsies did, and of their living in tents and sleeping in the open, and of the ill-luck which sometimes befel them when the lord of the manor they camped on was a hard man and evil tempered.

"'Tis a Duke who rules over Camylott, is't not?" the old fellow asked.

"Ay," was her Grace's answer, nodding her head. "He is well enough, but his lady—Lord! but they tell that she was a vixen before her marriage a few years gone!"

"I have seen her," said his Grace. "She is not ill to look at, and has done us no harm yet."

"Ay, but she may," says her Grace, nodding wisely again. "Who knows what such a woman may turn out. I have seen him!" She stopped, her elbows on the little round wooden table, her chin on her hands, and gave her saucy stare again. "I'll pay thee a compliment," she said. "He is a big fellow, and not unlike thee—though he be Duke and thou naught but a vagabond gipsy."

Their host had hearkened to them eagerly, and now he put in a question. "Was not she the beauty that was married to an old Earl who left her widow?" he said. "Was not she Countess Dunstanwolde?"

"Ay," answered her Grace, quietly.

"Ecod!" cried the old fellow, "that minds me of a story, and 'twas a thing happened in this very house and room. Look there!"

He pointed with something like excitement to the window. 'Twas but seldom he had chance to tell his story, and 'twas a thing he dearly loved to do, life being but a dull thing at the Cow at Wickben, and few travellers passing that way. A pair so friendly and gay and ready to hearken to his chatter as these two he had not seen for years.

"Look there!" he said. "At that big hole in the wall."

They turned together and looked at it in some wonder that her ladyship of Dunstanwolde should have any connection with it. 'Twas indeed a big hole, and looked as if the plaster of the wall under the sill had been roughly broken and hacked.

"Ay," said the host, "'tis a queer thing and came here in a strange way, being made by a gentleman's sword, and he either wild with liquor or with rage. Never shall I forget hearing his horse's hoofs come tearing over the road, as if some man was riding for his life. I was abed, and started out of my sleep at the sound of it. 'Who's chased by the devil at this time o' night through Wickben village?' says I, and scarce were the words out of my mouth before the horse clatters up to the house and stops. I could hear him

203

panting and heaving as his rider gets off and strides up to bang on the door. 'What dost thou want?' says I, putting my head out of the window. 'Come down and let me in,' answers he; 'I have no time to spare. You have a thing in your house I would find.' 'Twas a gentleman's voice, and I saw 'twas a gentleman's dress he wore, for 'twas fine cloth, and his sword had a silvered scabbard, and his hat rich plumes. 'Come down,' says he, and bangs the door again, so down I went."

"Who was he?" asked her Grace slowly, for he had stopped for breath. She sat quite still as before, her round chin held in her hands, her eyes fixed on him, but there was no longer any laughter in their blackness. "Did he tell his name?"

"Not then," was the answer; "nor did he know I heard when he spoke it, breaking forth in anger. But that is to come later"—with the air of one who would have his tale heard to the most dramatic advantage. "Into this room he strides and to the window straight and looks below the sill. 'Four years ago,' says he, 'there was a hole here in the wall. Was't so or was't not?' and he looks at me sharp and fierce as if he would take me by the throat if I said there had been none. 'Ay, there was a hole there long enough,' I answers him, 'but 'twas mended with new plaster at last. Your lordship can see the patch, for 'twas but roughly done.' Then he goes close to it and stares. 'Ay,' says he, 'there has been a hole mended. Old Chris did not lie.' And on that he turns to me. 'Get out of the room,' he says, 'I have a search to make here. Your wall will want another patch when I am done,' he says. 'But 'twill be made good. Go thy ways.' And he draws out his hanger, and there was sweat on his brow and he breathed fast, as if he was wild with his anxiousness to find what he sought."

"And didst leave him?" asked her Grace, as quiet as before. "For how long?"

The old man grinned.

"Not for long," said he, "nor did I go far. I stood outside, where I could see through the crack o' the door."

The Duchess nodded with an unmoved face.

"He was like a man in a frenzy," the host went on. "He dug at the plaster till I thought his sword would break; he dug as if he were paid for it by the minute. He made a hole bigger than had been there before, and when 'twas made he thrusts his hand in and fumbles about, cursing under his breath. And of a sudden he gives a start and stops and pants for breath, and then draws his hand back, and it was bloody, being scratched by the stone and plaster, but he held somewhat in it, a little dusty package, and he clutches it to his breast and laughs outright. Good Lord, 'twas like a devil's laugh, 'twas so wild and joyful. 'Ha, ha!' cries he, shaking the thing in the air and stamping his foot, 'Jack Oxon comes to his own again, to his own!'"

"Then," says her Grace, more slowly still, "that was his name? I have heard it before."

"I heard it again," said the old story-teller, eager to reach his climax. "And 'tis that ends the story so finely. 'Twas by chance talk of travellers I heard it nigh six months later. The very day after he stood here and searched for his package he disappeared from sight and has not been heard of since. And the last who set eyes on him was my Lady Dunstanwolde, who is now a Duchess at Camylott, where your camp is. 'Twas her name brought the story back to me."

Her Grace rose, catching her breath with a laugh. She turned her face towards the window, as if, of a sudden, attracted by somewhat to be seen outside.

"'Tis a good story," she said, but for a moment the crimson roses on her cheeks had shuddered to whiteness. Why, no man could tell. Her host did not see her countenance—perhaps my lord Duke did not.

"'Tis a good story!" she laughed again.

"And well told," added my lord Duke.

Her Grace turned to them both once more. Through some wondrous exercise of her will she looked herself again.

"As we are in luck to-day," she said, "and it has passed the time, let us count it in the reckoning."

A new, almost wild, fantastic gayety seized her. She flung herself into her playing of the part of a gipsy woman with a spirit which was a marvel to behold. She searched his Grace's pockets and her own for pence, and counted up the reckoning on the table, saying that they could but afford this or that much, that they must save this coin for a meal, that for a bed, this to pay toll on the road. She used such phrases of the gipsy jargon as she had picked up, and made jokes and bantering speeches which set their host cackling with laughter. Osmonde had seen her play a fantastic part before on their whimsical holidays, but never one which suited her so well, and in which she seemed so full of fire and daring wit. She was no Duchess, a man might have sworn, but a tall, splendid, black-eyed laughing gipsy woman, who, to the man who was her partner, would be a fortune every day, and a fortune not of luck alone, but of gay spirit and bravery and light-hearted love.

That night the moon shone white and clear, and in the mid hours my lord Duke waked from his sleep suddenly, and saw the brightness streaming full through the oriel window, and in the fair flood of it his love's white figure kneeling.

205

"Gerald," she cried, clinging to him when he went to her. "'Twas I awaked you. I called, though I did not speak."

"I heard, as I should hear if I lay dead," he answered low.

Her hair was all unbound for the night—her black, wondrous hair which he so loved—and from its billowy cloud her face looked at him wild and white, her mouth quivering.

"Gerald," she said, "look out with me."

Together they looked forth from the wide window into the beauty of the night, up into the great vault of Heaven, where the large silver moon sailed in the blue, the stars shining faintly before her soft brilliance.

"We are Pagans," she said, "poor Pagans who oftenest seem to pray to a cruel thing we do not know but only crouch before in terror, lest it crush us. But when we look up into such a Heaven as this, its majesty and stillness seem a presence, and we dare to utter what our hearts cry out, and know we shall be heard." She caught his hand and held it to her heart, which he felt leap beneath it. "There is no power would harm a woman's child," she cried—"a little unborn thing which has not breathed—because it would wreak vengeance on herself! There is none, Gerald, is there?" And she clung to him, her uplifted face filled with such lovely, passionate, woman's fear and pleading as made him sweep her to his breast and hold her silently—because he could not speak.

"For I have learned to be afraid," she murmured brokenly, against his breast. "And I was kneeling here to pray—to pray with all my soul—that if there were so cruel a thing 'twould kill me now—blight me—take me from you—that I might die in torture—but not bring suffering on my love, and on an innocent thing."

And her heart beat like some terrified caged eaglet against his own, and her eyes were wild with woe. But the wondrous stillness of the deep night enfolded them, as if Nature held them in her great arms which comfort so. And her stars gazed calmly down, even as though their calmness were answering speech.

CHAPTER XXX

On Tyburn Hill

There was none knew her as her husband did—none in the world—though so many were her friends and worshippers. As he loved her he knew her, the passion of his noble heart giving him clearer and more watchful eyes than any other. Truth was, indeed, that she herself did not know how much he saw and pondered on and how tender his watch upon her was.

The dark shadow in her eyes he had first noted, the look which would pass over her face sometimes at a moment when 'twas brightest, when it glowed with tenderest love for himself or with deepest yearning over the children who were given to them as time passed, for there were born to fill their home four sons who were like young gods for strength and beauty, and two daughters as fair things as Nature ever made to promise perfect womanhood.

And how she loved and tended them, and how they joyed in their young lives and worshipped and revered her!

"When I was a child, Gerald," she said to their father, "I was unhappy—and 'tis a hideous thing that a child should be so. I loved none and none loved me, and though all feared my rage and gave me my will, I was restless and savage and a rebel, though I knew not why. There were hours—I did not know their meaning, and hated them—when I was seized with fits of horrid loneliness and would hide myself in the woods, and roll in the dead leaves, and curse myself and all things because I was wretched. I used to think that I was angered at my dogs, or my horse, or some servant, or my father, and would pour forth oaths at them—but 'twas not they. Our children must be happy—they must be happy, Gerald. I will have them happy!"

What a mother they had in her!—a creature who could be wild with play and laughter with them, who was so beauteous that even in mere babyhood they would sit upon her knee and stare at her for sheer infant pleasure in her rich bloom and great, sweet eyes; who could lift and toss and rock them in her strong, soft arms as if they were but flowers and she a summer wind; whose voice was music, and whose black hair was a great soft mantle 'twas their childish delight to coax her to loosen that it might flow about her, billowing, she standing laughing beneath and tossing it over them to hide their smallness under it as beneath a veil. She was their heroine and their young pride, and among themselves they made joyful little boasts that there was no other such lady in all England. To behold her mount her tall horse and gallop and leap hedges and gates, to hear her tell stories of the moorlands and woods, and the game hiding in nests and warrens, of the ways of dogs and hawks and horses, and soldiers and Kings and Queens, and of how their father had fought in battles, and of how big the world was and how full of wonders and of joys! What other children had such pleasures in their lives?

But a few months after their Graces' visit to the Cow at Wickben, young John, who was heir and Marquess of Roxholm, had been born; following each other his two brothers, and later the child Daphne and her sister Anne; last, the little Lord Cuthbert, who was told as he grew older that he was to be the hero of his house in memory of Cuthbert de Mertoun, who had lived centuries ago; and in the five villages 'twas sworn that each son her Grace bore her husband was a finer creature than the last, and that her girl children outbloomed their brothers all.

Among these young human flowers Mistress Anne reigned gentle queen and saint, but softly faded day by day, having been a fragile creature all her life, but growing more so as time passed, despite the peace she lived in and the happiness surrounding her.

In her eyes, too, his Grace had seen a look which held its mystery. They were such soft eyes and so kind and timid he had always loved them. In days gone by he had often observed them as they followed her sister, and had been touched by the faithful tenderness of their look; but after her marriage they seemed to follow her more tenderly still, and sometimes with a vague, piteous wonder, as if the fond creature asked herself in secret a question she knew not how to answer. More and more devout she had grown, and, above all things, craved to aid her Grace in the doing of her good deeds. To such work she gave herself with the devotion of one who would strive to work out a penance.

Her own attendant was one of those whom her sister had aided, and was a young creature with a piteous little story indeed—a pretty, rosy, country child of but seventeen when, after her Grace's marriage, she came to Camylott to serve Mistress Anne.

On her first coming my lord Duke had marked her and the sadness of her innocent, childish face and blue eyes, and had spoken of her to Anne, asking if she had met with some misfortune.

"A pretty, curly-headed creature such as she should be a village beauty and dimpling with smiles," he said, "but the little thing looks sometimes as if she had wept a year. Who has done her a wrong?"

Mistress Anne gave a little start and bent lower over her

embroidery frame, but her Grace, who was in the apartment, answered for her.

"'Twas Sir John Oxon," she answered, "who has wronged so many."

"What!" Osmonde cried, "wrought he the poor thing's ruin?"

"No," the Duchess replied; "but would have done it, and she, poor child, all innocent, believing herself an honest wife. He had so planned it, but Fate saved her!"

"A mock marriage," says the Duke, "and she saved from it! How?"

"Because the day she went to him to be married, as he had told her, he was not at his lodgings, and did not return."

"'Twas the very day he disappeared—the day you saw him?" Osmonde exclaimed.

"Yes," was the answer given, as her Grace crossed the room. "And 'twas because I had seen him that the poor thing came to me with her story—and I cared for her."

She, too, had been sitting at her embroidery frame, and had crossed the room for silks, which lay upon the table near to Mistress Anne. As she laid her hand upon them she looked down and uttered a low exclamation, springing to her sister's side.

"Anne, love!" she cried. "Nay, Anne!"

Mistress Anne's small, worn face had dropped so low over her frame that it at last lay upon it, showing white against the silken roses so gaily broidered there. She was in a dead swoon.

Later Osmonde heard further details of this story—of how the poor child, having no refuge in the great city, had dared at last to go to Dunstanwolde House in the wild hope that her ladyship, who had last seen Sir John, might tell her if he had let drop any word concerning his journey—if he had made one. She had at first hung long about the servants' entrance, watching the workmen who were that day walling in the wing of black cellars my lady had wished to close before she left the place, and at length, in desperation, had appealed to a young stone-mason, with a good-humoured countenance, and he had interceded for her with a lacquey passing by.

"But had I not spoke Sir John's name," the girl said when my lord Duke spoke kindly to her of her story and her Grace's goodness; "had I not spoke his name, the man would not have carried my message. But he said she would see me if I had news of Sir John Oxon. He blundered, your Grace, thinking I came from Sir John himself, and told her Grace 'twas so. And she bade him bring me to her."

Her Grace she worshipped, and would break here into sobs

each time she told the story, describing her fright when she had been led to the apartment where sate the great lady, who had spoke to her in a voice like music and with such strange, deep pity of her grief, and in a passion of tenderness had told the truth to her, taking her, after her swoon, in her own strong, lovely arms, as if she had been no rich Countess but a poor woman, such as she who wept, and one whose heart, too, might have been broke by a cruel, deadly blow.

This poor simple child (who was in time cured of her wound and married an honest fellow who loved her) was not the only one of Sir John Oxon's victims whom her Grace protected. There were, indeed, many of them, and 'twas as though she had made it her curious duty to search them out. When she and her lord lived sumptuously at Osmonde House in town, shining at Court, entertaining Royalty itself at their home, envied and courted by all as the happiest married lovers and the favourites of Fortune, my lord Duke knew that many a day she cast her rich robes and, clad in the dark garments and black hood, went forth to visit strange, squalid places. Since the hour of his first meeting her on her return from such an errand, when they had spoken together, he had never again forbade her to follow the path 'twas plain she had chosen.

"Were I going forth to battle," he had said, "you would not seek to hold me back; and in your battle, for it seems one to me, though I know not what 'tis fought for, I will not restrain you."

"Ay, 'tis a battle," she had said, and seized his hands and kissed them as if in passionate gratitude. "And 'tis a debt—a debt I swore to pay—if that we call God would let me. Perhaps He will not, but were He you—who know my soul—He would."

Yet but a few hours later, when he joined her in the Mall, where she had descended from her coach to walk with the world of fashion and moved among the wits and beaux and leaders of the mode, drawing all round her by the marvel of her spirit and the brilliancy of her gayety and bearing, he hearing her rich laughter and meeting the bright look of her lovely, flashing eyes, wondered if she was the woman whose voice still lingered in his ears and the memory of whose words would not leave his fervent heart.

Their love was so perfect a thing that they had never denied each other aught. Why should they; indeed, how could they? Each so understood and trusted the other that they scarce had need for words in the deciding of such questions as other pairs must reason gravely over. There was no question, only one thought between them, and in his life a thing which grew each hour as he had long since known it would. 'Twas this woman whom he loved—this one— her looks, her ways, her laughter and her tears, her very faults, if she should have them, her past, her present, and her future which seemed all himself.

That—Duchess of Osmonde though she might be—she was known in dark places and moved among the foul evil there, like the sun which strove at rare hours to cleanse and dispel it; that she had in kennels and noisome dens strange friends, was a thing at first vaguely rumoured because the world had ever loved its stories of her, and been ready to believe any it heard and invent new ones when it had tired of the old. But there came a time when through a strange occurrence the rumour was proved, most singularly, to be a truth.

Two gilt coaches, full of chattering fine ladies and gentlemen, were being driven on a certain day through a part of the town not ordinarily frequented by fashion, but the occupants of the coaches had been entertaining themselves with a great and curious sight it had been their delicate fancy to desire to behold as an exciting novelty. This had been no less an exhibition than the hanging of two malefactors on Tyburn Hill—the one a handsome young highwayman, the other a poor woman executed for larceny.

The highwayman had been a favourite and had died gaily, and that he should have been cut off in his prime had put the crowd (among which were several of his yet uncaught companions) in an ill-humour; the poor woman had wept and made a poor end, which had added to the anger of the beholders.

'Twas an evil, squalid, malodorous mob, not of the better class of thieves and tatterdemalions, but of the worst, being made up of cutthroats out of luck, pickpockets, and poor wretches who were the scourings of the town and the refuse of the kennel. 'Twas just the crowd to be roused to some insensate frenzy, being hungry, bitter, and vicious; and when, making ready to slouch back to its dens, its attention was attracted by the gay coaches, with their liveries and high-fed horses, and their burden of silks and velvets, and plumes nodding over laughing, carefree, selfish faces, it fell into a sudden fit of animal rage.

'Twas a woman who began it. (She had been a neighbour of the one who had just met punishment, and in her own hovel at that moment lay hid stolen goods.) She was a wild thing, with a battered face and unkempt hair; her rags hung about her waving, and she had a bloodshot, fierce eye.

"Look!" she screamed out suddenly, high and shrill; "look at them in their goold coaches riding home from Tyburn, where they've seen their betters swing!"

The ladies in the chariots, pretty, heartless fools, started affrighted in their seats, and strove to draw back; their male

211

companions, who were as pretty, effeminate fools themselves and of as little spirit, started also, and began to look pale about the gills.

"Look at them!" shrieked the virago, "shivering like rabbits. A pretty end they would make if they were called to dance at a rope's end. Look ye at them, with their white faces and their swords and periwigs!"

And she stood still, waving her arms, and poured forth a torrent of curses.

'Twas enough. The woman beside her looked and began to shake her fist, seized by the same frenzy; her neighbour caught up her cry, her neighbour hers; a sodden-faced thief broke into a howling laugh, another followed him, the madness spread from side to side, and in a moment the big foul crowd surged about the coaches, shrieking blasphemies and obscenities, shaking fists, howling cries of "Shame!" and threats of vengeance.

"Turn over the coaches! Drag them out! Tear their finery from them! Stuff their mincing mouths with mud!" rose all about them.

The servants were dragged from their seats and hauled from side to side, their liveries were in ribbands, their terrified faces, ghastly with terror and streaming with blood, might be seen one moment in one place, the next in another, sometimes they seemed down on the ground. The crowd roared with rage and laughter at their cries. One lady swooned with terror, one or two crouched on the floor of the coach; the dandies gesticulated and called for help.

"They will kill us! they will kill us!" screamed the finest beau among them. "The watch! the watch! The constables!"

"'Tis worse than the Mohocks," cried another, but his hand so shook he could not have drawn his sword if he had dared.

The next instant the glass of the first coach was smashed and its door beaten open. A burly fellow seized upon a shrieking beauty and dragged her forth laughing, dealing her gallant a mighty clout on the face as he caught her. Blood spouted from the poor gentleman's delicate aquiline nose, and the mob danced and yelled.

"Drag 'em all out!" was roared by the sodden-faced thief. "The women to the women and the men to the men, and then change about." The creatures were like wild beasts, and their prey would have been torn to pieces, but at that moment, from a fellow at the edge of the crowd broke a startled oath.

Someone had made way to him and laid a strong hand on his shoulder, and there was that in his cry which made those nearest turn.

A tall figure in black draperies stood towering above him, and in truth above all the rest of the crowd. 'Twas a woman, and she called out to the mad creatures about her in command.

"Fools!" she cried; "have a care. Do you want to swing at a rope's end yourselves?" 'Twas a fierce voice, the voice of a brave creature who feared none of them; though 'twas a rich voice and a woman's, and so rang with authority that it actually checked the tempest for a moment and made the leaders turn to look.

She made her way nearer and threw back her hood from her face.

"I am Clorinda Mertoun, who is Duchess of Osmonde," she cried to them. "There are many of you know me. Call back your senses, and hearken to what I say."

The ladies afterwards in describing the scene used to quake as they tried to paint this moment.

"There was a cry that was like a low howl," they said, "as if beasts were baffled and robbed of their prey. Some of them knew her and some did not, but they all stood and stared. Good Lord! 'twas her great black eyes that held them; but I shall be affrighted when I think of her, till my dying day."

'Twas her big black eyes and the steady flame in them that held the poor frenzied fools, perchance as wolves are said to be held by the eye of man sometimes; but 'twas another thing, and on that she counted. She looked round from one face to the other.

"You know me," she said to one; "and you, and you, and you," nodding at each. "I can pick out a dozen of you who know me, and should find more if I marked you all. How many here are my friends and servants?"

There was a strange hoarse chorus of sounds; they were the voices of women who were poor bedraggled drabs, men who were thieves and cutthroats, a few shrill voices of lads who were pickpockets and ripe for the gallows already.

"Ay, we know thee! Ay, your Grace! Ay!" they cried, some in half-sullen grunts, some as if half-affrighted, but all in the tones of creatures who suddenly began to submit to a thing they wondered at.

Then the woman who had begun the turmoil suddenly fell down on her knees and began to kiss her Grace's garments with hysteric, choking sobs.

"She said thou wert the only creature had ever spoke her fair," she cried. "She said thou hadst saved her from going distraught when she lay in the gaol. Just before the cart was driven away she cried out sobbing, 'Oh, Lord! Oh, your Grace!' and they thought her praying, but I knew she prayed to thee."

The Duchess put her hand on the woman's greasy, foul shoulder and answered in a strange voice, nodding her head, her black brows knit, her red mouth drawn in.

213

"'Tis over now!" she said. "'Tis over and she quiet, and perchance ere this she has seen a fair thing. Poor soul! poor soul!"

By this time the attacked party had gained strength to dare to move. The pretty creature who had been first dragged forth from the coach uttered a shriek and fell on her knees, clutching at her rescuer's robe.

"Oh, your Grace! your Grace!" she wept; "have mercy! have mercy!"

"Mercy!" said her Grace, looking down at the tower of powdered hair decked with gewgaws. "Mercy! Sure we all need it. Your ladyship came—for sport—to see a woman hang? I saw her in the gaol last night waiting her doom, which would come with the day's dawning. 'Twas not sport. Had you been there with us, you would not have come here to-day. Get up, my lady, and return to your coach. Make way, there!" raising her voice. "Let that poor fellow," pointing to the ashen-faced coachman, "mount to his place. Be less disturbed, Sir Charles," to the trembling fop, "my friends will let you go free."

And that they did, strangely enough, though 'twas not willingly, the victims knew, as they huddled into their places, shuddering, and were driven away, the crowd standing glaring after them, a man or so muttering blasphemies, though none made any movement to follow, but loitered about and cast glances at her Grace of Osmonde, who waited till the equipages were well out of sight and danger.

"'Twas wasted rage," she said to those about her. "The poor light fools were not worth ill-usage."

The next day the Duke heard the tale, which had flown abroad over the town. His very soul was thrilled by it and that it told him, and he went to her Grace and poured forth to her a passion of love that was touched with awe.

"I could see you!" he cried, "when they told the story to me. I could see you as you stood there and held the wild beasts at bay. 'Twas that I saw in your child-eyes when you rode past me in the hunting-field; 'twas that fire which held them back, and the great sweet soul of you which has reached them in their dens and made you worshipped of them."

"'Twas that they know me," she answered; "'twas that I have stood by their sides in their blackest hours. I have seen their children born. I have helped their old ones and their young through death. Some I have saved from the gallows. Some I have—" she stopped and hung her head as if black memories overpowered her.

He knew what she had left unfinished.

214

"You have been—to comfort those who lie in Newgate—at their last extremity?" he ended for her.

"Ay," she answered. "The one who will show kindness to them in those awful hours they worship as God's self. There was a poor fellow I once befriended there"—she spoke slowly and her voice shook. "He was condemned—for taking a man's life. The last night—before I left him—he knelt to me and swore—he had meant not murder. He had struck in rage—one who had tortured him with taunts till he went raving. He struck, and the man fell—and he had killed him! And now must hang."

"Good God!" cried my lord Duke. "By chance! In frenzy! Not knowing! And he died for it?"

"Ay," she answered, her great eyes on his and wide with horror, "on Tyburn Tree!"

CHAPTER XXXI

Their Graces Keep their Wedding Day at Camylott

"She came to Court at last, my Lord Duke," said his Grace of Marlborough. "She came at last—as I felt sure 'twas Fate she should."

'Twas at Camylott he said this, where he had come in those days which darkened about him when, royal favour lost, the acclamations of a fickle public stilled, its clamour of applause almost forgot and denied by itself, his glory as statesman, commander, warrior seemed to sink beneath the horizon like a sunset in a winter sky. His splendid frame shattered by the stroke of illness, his heart bereaved, his great mind dulled and saddened, there were few friends faithful to him, but my Lord Duke of Osmonde, who had never sought his favour or required his protection, who had often held views differing from his own and hidden none of them, was among the few in whose company he found solace and pleasure.

"I see you as I was," he would say. "Nay, rather as I might have been had Nature given me a thing she gave to you and

215

withheld from John Churchill. You were the finer creature and less disturbed by poor worldly dreams."

So more than once he came to be guest at Camylott, and would be moved to pleasure by the happiness and fulness of life in the very air of the place, by the joyousness of the tall, handsome children, by the spirit and sweet majesty of the tall beauty their mother, by the loveliness of the country and the cheerful air of well-being among the villagers and tenantry. But most of all he gave thought to the look which dwelt in the eyes of my Lord Duke and the woman who was so surely mate and companion as well as wife to him. When, though 'twas even at the simplest moment, each looked at the other, 'twas a heavenly thing plain to see.

Upon one of their wedding-days he was at Camylott with them. 'Twas but a short time before the quiet death of Mistress Anne, and was the tenth anniversary of their Graces' union.

At Camylott they always spent their anniversary, though upon their other domains the rejoicings which made Camylott happy were also held. These festivities were gay and rustic, including the pealing of church bells, the lighting of bonfires, rural games, and feastings; but they were most noted for a feature her Grace herself had invented before she had yet been twelve months a wife, and 'twas a pretty fancy, too, as well as a kind thought.

She had talked of it first to her husband one summer afternoon as they walked together in the gold glow of sunset through Camylott Woods. 'Twas one of many happy hours shared with her which he remembered to his life's end, and could always call up in his mind the deep amber light filtering through the trees, the thick green growth of the ferns and the scent of them, the moss under foot and on the huge fallen trunk they at last sate down upon.

"To every man, woman, and child we rule over," she said, "on that day we will give a wedding gift. As the year passes we will discover what each longs for most, and that thing we will give. So on that heavenly day each one shall have his heart's desire—in memory," she added, with soft solemnity.

And he echoed her.

"In memory!" For neither at that time nor at any other did either of them forget those hours they had lived apart and how Fate had seemed to work them ill, and how they had been desolate and hungered.

So on each morning of the wedding-day, while the bells were ringing a peal, the flag flying from the Tower, the park prepared for games and feasting, a crowd of ruddy countenances, clean smocks, petticoats, and red cloaks flocked on the terrace from which the gifts were given.

216

'Twas from his invalid-chair within the library window that the once great Commander sate and saw this sight; her Grace standing by her husband at a long table, giving each gift with her own hand and saying a few words to each recipient with a bright freedom 'twas worth any man's while to see.

The looker-on remembered the histories he had heard of the handsome hoyden whose male attire had been the Gloucestershire scandal, the Court beauty who in the midst of her triumphs had chosen to play gentle consort to an old husband, the Duchess who shone in the great world like the sun and who yet doffed her brocades and jewels to don serge and canvas and labour in Rag Yard and Slaughter Alley to rescue thieves and beggars and watch the mothers of their hapless children in their throes. Ay, and more yet, to sit in the black condemned-cell at Newgate and hold the hand and pour courage into the soul of a shuddering wretch who in the cold grey of morning would dangle from a gallows tree.

"'Tis a strange nature," he thought, "and has ever been so. It has passed through some strange hours and some dark ones. Yet to behold her——"

There had come to her side a young couple, the woman with a child in her arms courtesying blushingly, her youthful husband grinning and pulling his forelock.

Her Grace took the infant and cuddled and kissed it, while its father and mother glowed with delight.

"'Tis a fine boy, Betty," she said. "'Tis bigger than the last one, Tom. His christening finery is in the package here, and I will stand sponsor as before."

"Mother," said young John at her elbow, "may I not stand sponsor, too?"

She laughed and pulled his long love-locks.

"Ay, my lord Marquess," she answered, "if his parents are willing to take such a young one."

Mistress Anne sate by their guest, he holding her in great favour. As the people came for their gifts she told him their names and stories. Through weakness she walked about but little in these days, and the failing soldier liked her company, so she often sate near him in her lounging-chair and with gentle artfulness lured him into reminiscences of his past campaigns. She was very frail to-day, and in her white robe, and with her large eyes which seemed to have outgrown her face, she looked like the wraith of a woman rather than a creature of flesh and blood.

"Those two her Grace rescued," she said, as Betty and Tom Beck retired; "the one from woe, the other from cruel wickedness. He had betrayed the poor child and deserted her, and 'twas her

Grace who touched his heart and woke manhood in it, and made them happy man and wife."

Then came an old woman leading a girl and boy, both fair and blooming and with blue eyes and fair curling locks.

"Are they both well and both happy, dame?" the Duchess asked. "Yes, that they are, I see. And I know they are both good."

She took the girl's face in both hands and smiled into it as she might have smiled at a flower, and then kissed her tenderly. She gave her a little new gown and a pretty huswife stocked with implements to make it. She put her hand on the boy's shoulder and looked at him as his mother would have looked had she been tender of him.

"For you, Robin," she said, "there are books. I know 'tis books and learning you long for, and you shall have them. His Grace's Chaplain has promised me to teach you."

The boy clasped the books under his arm, hugging them against his breast, and when her Grace turned to the next newcomer he seized a fold of her robe and kissed it.

"Who are those children?" the Captain-General asked. "They do not look like rustics."

"Those two she rescued also," answered Mistress Anne in a low voice. "She found them in a thieves' haunt being trained as pickpockets. They are the cast-off offspring of a gentleman who lived an evil life."

"Was she told his name?"

"Yes," Mistress Anne said, lower still; "'twas a gentleman who was—lost. Sir John Oxon."

The mystery of this gentleman's disappearance was a thing forgotten, but Mistress Anne's hearer recalled it, and that the man had left an evil reputation, and that 'twas said that in the first bloom of his youth he had been among the worshippers of the Gloucestershire beauty, and there passed through the old Duke's mind a vague wonder as to whether the Duchess remembered girlish sentiments the hoyden had lived through and forgot.

It seemed the man's name being once drawn from the past was not to be allowed to rest, for later in the day he heard of him again, and curiously indeed.

There came in the afternoon from town a sturdy, loud-voiced country gentleman, with a red, honest face and a good-humoured eye, and he was so received by the family—by his Grace, who shook him warmly by the hand, by the Duchess, who gave him both hers to kiss, and by the young ones, who cried out in rejoicing over him— that their distinguished guest perceived him to be an old friend who was, as it were, an old comrade.

218

And so it proved, for 'twas soon revealed to him by the gentleman himself (whose name was Sir Christopher Crowell, and whose estate lay on the borders of Warwickshire and Gloucestershire) that he had been one of the boon companions of her Grace's father, Sir Jeoffry Wildairs, and he had known her from the time she was five years old, and had been first made the comrade and plaything of a band of the worst rioters in three counties.

"Ay!" he cried, exultantly, for he seemed always exultant when he spoke of her Grace, who was plainly his idol. "At seven she would toss off her ale, and sing and swear as wickedly as any man among us, and had great black eyes that flashed fire when we crossed her, and her hair hung below her waist, and she was the most beauteous child-devil and the most lawless, that man or woman ever clapt eyes on. And to behold her now! to behold her now!" And then he motioned towards the little Anne, who was flashing-eyed, and long-limbed, and a brown beauty. "'Tis my Lady Anne who is most like her," he said; "but Lord! she hath been treated fair by Fortune, and loved and cherished, and is a young queen already."

Later, when the night had fallen and was thick with stars, and the festal lights were twinkling like other stars among the trees of the park, and from the happy crowds at play there floated the sounds of laughter and joyful voices, their Graces and their guests sate or walked upon the terrace amid the night-scents of flowers and watched the merriment going on below them and talked together.

"Ay," broke forth old Sir Christopher, "you two happy folk light joyful fires, and make joyful hearts wheresoever you go."

'Twas at this moment two of the other country guests—they being old Gloucestershire comrades also—stayed their sauntering before her Grace to speak to her.

"Eldershawe and me have just been saying," broke forth one of them, chuckling, "how this bringeth back old times, though 'tis little like them. We three were of the birthnight party—Eldershawe, Chris, and me. Thou dost not forget old friends, Clo, and would not, wert thou ten times a Duchess."

"Nay, not I," answered her Grace. "Not I."

"There be not many of us left," said Sir Christopher, ruefully. "Thy poor old Dad is under sod, and others with him. Two necks were broke in hunting, the others died of years or drink."

"But one we know naught of, egad!" said my Lord Eldershawe, "and he was my kinsman."

"Lord, yes," cried out the other; "Jack Oxon! Jack, who came among us all curls and essences and brocades and lace. Thou'st not forgot Jack Oxon, Clo, for the fellow was wild in love with thee."

"No, I have not forgotten Sir John," she answered, and turned aside a little to break a rose from a bush near her and hold it to her face.

"Nay, that she hath not," cried Sir Christopher, "that I can swear to. I saw the boy and girl to-day, Clo, and, Lord! how they are like to him."

"Yes, they are like him," she answered, gravely.

"The two thou show'dst me playing 'neath the trees?" said Eldershawe. "Ay, they are like enough."

"And but for her Grace would have been brought up a hang-dog thief and a poor drab, with all their beauty," went on Sir Christopher. "Ecod, thou hast done well, Clo, the task 'twas thy whim to take upon thyself."

"What generous deed was that?" asked my lord Duke of Osmonde, drawing near.

"The task of undoing the wrongs a villain had done, if 'twere so there could be undoing of them," answered the old fellow. "A woman rich as I," said she, "should set herself some good work to do. This shall be mine—to live John Oxon's life again and make it bring forth good instead of evil."

Her Grace sate motionless and so did Mistress Anne, who had sunk back in her chair, and in the starlit darkness had grown more white, and was breathing faint and quickly. In the park below the people laughed as merry-makers will, in gay bursts, and half a dozen voices broke forth into a snatch of song. 'Twas a good background for Sir Christopher, who was well launched upon a subject that he loved and had not often chance to hold forth upon, as her Grace was not fond of touching upon it.

"Ten years hath she followed his wicked footsteps and I have followed with her," he rambled on. "I am not squeamish, Lord knoweth! and have no reason to be; but had I known, when I began to aid in the searching, what mire I should have to wade through, ecod! I think I should have said, 'Let ill alone.'"

"But you did not, old friend," said the Duchess's rich, low voice; "you did not."

Lady Betty and her swains had sauntered near and joined the circle, attracted by the subject which waked in them a new interest in an old mystery.

"You have been her Grace's almoner, Sir Christopher," said her ladyship. "That accounts for the stories I have heard of your charities. They were her Grace's good deeds, not your own."

"She knew I would sweep the kennel for her on hands and knees if she would have me," said Sir Chris, "and at the first of it she knew not the ill quarters of the town as I did, and bade me make search for her and ask questions. But 'twas not long before she found her way herself and learned that a tall, strong beauty can do more to reach hearts than a red-faced old man can. Lord, how they love and fear her! And among the honest folk Jack Oxon wronged—poor tradesmen he ruined by his trickery, and simple working-folk who lost their all through him—they would kiss the dust her shoe hath trod. His debts she hath paid, his victims she hath rescued, the wounds he dealt she hath healed and made sound flesh, and for ten years she hath done it!"

Her Grace rose to her feet, the rose uplifted in a listening gesture. From the park below there floated up the lilting music of a dance, a light, unrustic measure played by their own musicians.

"The dancing begins," she said. "Hark! the dancing begins."

Mistress Anne put out her hand and caught at her sister's dress and held a fold of its richness in her trembling hand, though her Grace was not aware of what she did.

"How sweet the music sounds," the poor gentlewoman said, nervously. "How sweet it sounds."

My Lady Betty Tantillion held up her hand as the Duchess, a moment since, had held the rose.

"I have heard that tune before," she cried.

"And I," said Lord Charles.

"And I," Sir Harry Granville echoed.

Lady Betty broke into a shiver.

"Why," she cried, "how strange—at just this moment. We danced to it at the ball at Dunstanwolde House the very night 'twas made known Sir John Oxon had disappeared."

The Duchess held the rose poised in her hand and slowly bent her head.

"Yes," she said, "'tis the very tune."

She stood among them—my lord Duke remembered it later—the centre figure of a sort of circle, some sitting, some standing—his Grace of Marlborough, Mistress Anne, Osmonde himself, the country gentlemen, my Lady Betty and her swains, and others who drew near. She was the centre, standing in the starlight, her rose held in her hand.

"Lord, 'twas a strange thing," said Sir Christopher, thoughtfully, "that a man could disappear like that and leave no trace—no trace."

"Has—all enquiry—ceased?" her Grace asked, quietly.

"There was not much even at first, save from his creditors," said Lord Charles, with a laugh.

"Ay, but 'twas strange," said old Sir Christopher. "I've thought and thought what could have come of him. Why, Clo, thou wast the one who saw him last. What dost thou think?"

In the park below there was a sudden sweet swelling of the music: the dancers had joined in with their voices.

"Yes," said the Duchess, "'twas I who saw him last." And for a few seconds all paused to listen to the melody in the air. But Sir Christopher came back to his theme.

"What sort of humour was the man in?" he asked. "Did he complain of 's lot?"

Her Grace hesitated a second, as one who thought, and then shook her head.

"No," she answered, and no other word.

"Did he speak of taking a journey?" said Lady Betty.

And the Duchess shook her head slow again, and answered as before, "No."

And the music swelled with fresh added voices, and floated up gayer and more sweet.

"Was he dressed for travel?" asked Lord Charles, he being likely to think first of the meaning of a man's dress.

"No," said her Grace.

And then my lord Duke drew near behind her, and spoke over her shoulder.

"Did he bid you any farewell?" he said.

She had not known he was so close, and gave a great start and dropped her rose upon the terrace. Before she answered, she stooped herself and picked it up.

"No," she said, very low. "No; none."

"Then," his Grace said, "I will tell you what I think."

"You!" said my Lady Betty. "Has your Grace thought?"

"Often," he answered. "Who has not, at some time? I—knew more of the man than many. More than once his life touched mine."

"Yours!" they cried.

He waved his hand with the gesture of a man who would sweep away some memory.

"Yes," he said; "once I saw the end of a poor soul he had maddened, and 'twas a cruel thing." He turned his face towards his wife.

"The morning that he left your Grace," he said, "'tis my thought he went not far."

"Not far?" the party exclaimed, but the Duchess joined not in the chorus.

"Between Dunstanwolde House and his lodgings," he went on, "lie some of the worst haunts in London. He was well known there, and not by friends but by enemies. Perchance some tortured creature who owed him a bitter debt may have lain in wait and paid it."

The Duchess turned and gazed at him with large eyes.

"What—" she said, almost hoarsely, "what do you mean?"

"There were men," he answered, gravely—"husbands, fathers, and brothers—there were women he had driven to despair and madness, who might well have struck him down."

"You mean," said her Grace, almost in a whisper, "you mean that he—was murdered?"

"Nay," he replied, "not murdered—struck a frenzied blow and killed, and it might have been by one driven mad with anguish and unknowing what he did."

Her Grace caught her breath.

"As 'twas with the poor man I told you of," she broke forth as if in eagerness, "the one who died on Tyburn Tree?"

"Yes," was his answer.

"Perhaps—you are right," she said, and passed her hand across her brow; "perhaps—you—are right."

"But there was found no trace," Sir Christopher cried out; "no trace."

"Ah!" said my lord Duke, slowly, "that is the mystery. A dead man's body is not easy hid."

The Duchess broke forth laughing—almost wildly. The whole group started at the sound.

"Nay, nay!" she cried. "What dark things do we talk of! Sir Christopher, Sir Christopher, 'twas you who set us on. A dead man's body is not easy hid!"

"'Tis enough to make a woman shudder," cried Lady Betty, hysterically.

"Yes," said her Grace. "See, I am shuddering—I, who am built of Wildairs iron and steel." And she held out her hands to them—her white hands—and indeed they were trembling like leaves.

The evil thing they had spoke of had surely sunk deep into her soul and troubled it, though she had so laughed and lightly changed the subject of their talk, for in the night she had an awful dream, and her lord, wakened from deep slumber—as he had been once before—started up to behold her standing in the middle of the chamber—a tall white figure with its arms outflung as if in wild despair, while she cried out in frenzy to the darkness.

"I have killed thee—I have killed thee," she wailed, "though I meant it not—even hell itself doth know. Thou art a dead man—and this is the worst of all!"

"'Tis a dream," he cried aloud to her and clutched her in his warm, strong arms. "'Tis a dream—a dream! Awake!—Awake!—Awake!"

223

And she awoke and fell upon her knees, sobbing as those sob who are roused from such a horror.

"A dream!—a dream!—a dream!" she cried. "And 'tis you awake me! You—Gerald—Gerald!—And I have been ten years—ten years your wife!"

CHAPTER XXXII

In the Turret Chamber—and in Camylott Wood

When the great soldier returned to Blenheim Castle, his Grace of Osmonde bore him company and having spent a few days in his society at that great house returned to town, from whence he came again to Camylott.

He reached there on a heavenly day, which seemed to him more peaceful and more sweet than any day the summer had so far brought, though it had been a fair one. Many days had been bright and full of flower-scent and rustling of green leaves, and overarched by tender blueness with white clouds softly floating therein, but this one, as he rode, he thought held something in its beauty which seemed to make the earth seem nearer Heaven and Heaven more fair to lifted mortal eyes. He thought this as his horse bore him over the white road, he thought it as he rode across the moor, 'twas in his mind as he passed through the village and saw the white cottages standing warm and peaceful in the sunshine, with good wives at the doors or at their windows, and children playing on the green, who stopped and bobbed courtesies to him or pulled their forelocks, grinning.

Joan Bush was at her gate and stepped out and dipped a courtesy with appealing civility.

"Your Grace," she said, "if I might make so bold—poor Mistress Anne—" And having said so much checked herself in much confusion. "I lose my wits," she said; "your Grace's pardon. Your Grace has been, to town and but now comes back, and will not know. But we so love the kind gentlewoman—" and she mopped her eyes.

"You mean that Mistress Anne is worse?" he said.

"The poor lady fell into a sudden strange swoon but an hour ago," she answered. "My Matthew, who was at the Tower of an errand said she came in from the flower-garden and sank lifeless. And the servants who carried her to her chamber say 'twas like death. And she hath been so long fading. And we know full well the end must come soon."

My lord Duke rode on. A fulness tightened his throat and he looked up at the blue sky.

"Poor Anne! Kind Anne!" he said. "Pure heart! I could think 'twas for the passing of her soul the day was made so fair."

At the park gates the woman from the lodge stood at her door and made her obeisance tearfully. She was an honest soul to whom her Grace's sister seemed a saint from Heaven.

"What is the last news?" said my lord Duke, speaking more from kindness than aught else.

"That the dear lady lies in her bed in the Turret chamber and her Grace watches with her alone. Oh, my lord Duke, God calls another angel to Himself this day!"

The very air was still with a strange stillness. The Tower itself rose white and clear against the blue as though its battlements and fair turrets might be part of the Eternal City. This strange fancy passed through his Grace's mind as he rode towards it. The ivy hung thick about the window of Anne's chamber in the South Tower. 'Twas a room she loved and had spent long, peaceful days in, and had fitted as a little shrine. Her lovingness had taught her to feed the doves from it, and they had grown to be her friends and companions, and now a little cloud of them flew about and lighted on the turrets and clung to the festoons of ivy, and flew softly about as if they were drawn to the place by some strange knowledge and waited for that which was to come to pass. Two or three sate upon the deep window-ledge and cooed as if they told those not so near what they could see inside the quiet room.

On the terrace below the elder children stood John and Gerald and Daphne and Anne. They waited too, as the doves did, and their young faces were lifted that they might watch the window, and they were very sweet and gravely tender and unafraid and fair.

When their father drew near them 'twas the child Daphne who spoke, putting her hand in his and meeting his eyes with a lovely look.

"Father," she said, "we think that Mother Anne lies dying in her room. We are not afraid; mother has told us that to die is only as if a bird was let to fly out into the blue sky. And mother is with her, and we are waiting because we think—perhaps—we are not sure—

but perhaps we might see her soul fly out of the window like a white bird. It seems as if the doves were waiting too."

My lord Duke kissed her and passed on.

"You may see it," he said, gently. "Who knows—and if you see it, sure it will be white."

And he went quietly through the house and up the staircase leading to Anne's tower-chamber, and the pretty apartment her Grace had prepared for her so lovingly to spend quiet hours in when she would be alone. This apartment led into the chamber, but now it was quite empty, for the Duchess was with her sister, who lay on the bed in the room within, where the ivy hung in festoons about the high window, which seemed to look up into the blue sky itself and shut out all the earth below and only look on Heaven.

To enter seemed like entering some sacred shrine where a pure saint lay, and upon the threshold his Grace lingered, almost fearing to go in and break upon the awful tenderness of this last hour, and the last words he heard the loving creature murmuring, while the being she had so worshipped knelt beside her.

"'Twas love," he heard, "'twas love. What matter if I gave my soul for you?"

He drew back with a quick sad beat of the heart. Poor, tender soul—poor woman who had loved and given no sign—and only in her dying dared to speak.

And then there came a cry—and 'twas the voice of her he loved—and he stood spellbound. 'Twas a cry of anguish—of fear—of horror and dismay. 'Twas her voice as he had heard it ring out in the blackness of her dream—her dear voice harsh with woe and broken into moaning—her dear voice which he had heard murmuring love to him—crooning over her children—laughing like music! And the torrent of words which she poured forth made his blood cold, and yet as they fell upon his ear he knew—yes, now he knew—revealed no new story to him, even though it had been until that hour untold. No, 'twas not new, for through many an hour when he had marked the shadow in her eyes he had vaguely guessed some fatal burden lay upon her soul—and had striven to understand.

"And then I struck him with my whip," he heard, "knowing nothing, not seeing, only striking like a goaded, dying thing. And he fell—he fell—and all was done."'

None heard or saw my lord Duke when, later, he passed out from the empty room. He went forth into the fair day again, and through the Park and into Camylott Wood. The deep amber light was there, and the gold-green stillness, and he passed onward till he reached the great wood's depths, and stood beneath an oak-tree's broad-spread branches, leaning his back against the huge rough trunk, his arms folded.

This was her secret burden—this. And Nature had so moulded him that he could look upon it with just, unflinching eyes, his soul filled with a god-like, awful pity.

In a walled-in cellar in the deserted Dunstanwolde House lay, waiting for the call of Judgment Day, a handful of evil dust which once had been a man—one whose each day of life from his youth upward had seemed, as it had passed, to leave black dregs in some poor fellow-creature's cup. One frantic, unthinking blow struck in terror and madness had ended him and all his evil doing, but left her standing frenzied at the awfulness of the thing which had fallen upon her soul in her first hour of Heaven. And all her being had risen in revolt at this most monstrous woe of chance, and in her torture she had cried out that in that hour she would not be struck down.

"Of ending his base life I had never thought," he had heard her wail, "though I had thought to end my own. But when Fate struck the blow for me, I swore that carrion should not taint my whole life through."

To atone for this she had lived her life of passionate penance. Remembering this, she had prayed Heaven strike and blight her, in fear that she herself should blight the noble and the innocent things she loved. And while she had thought she bore the burden all alone, the gentle sister, who had so worshipped her, had known her secret and borne it with her silently. In dying she had revealed it, with trembling and piteous love, and this my lord Duke had heard, and her pure words as she had died.

"Anne! Anne!" the anguished voice had cried. "Must he know—my Gerald? Must I tell him all? If so I must, I will—upon my knees!"

"Nay, tell him not," was faintly breathed in answer. "Let God tell him—who understands."

"'Tis in myself," my lord Duke said at last, through his shut teeth, "'tis in myself to have struck the blow, and had I done it and found him lie dead before me—in her dear name I swear, and in a new shriven soul's presence, for sure the pure thing is near—I would have hid it as she has done; for naught should have torn her from me! And for her sin, if sin it is counted, I will atone with her; and as she does her penance, will do mine. And if, at the end of all things, she be called to Judgment Bar, I will go with her and stand by her side. For her life is my life, and her soul my soul, her sentence my sentence; and being her love I will bear it with her, and pray Him who judges to lay the burden heavier upon me than upon her."

And he went back to the Tower and up the stairway to the turret-chamber, and there Mistress Anne lay still and calm and sweet as a child asleep, and flowers and fair chaplets lay all about her white bed and on her breast and in her small, worn hands, and garlanded her pillow. And the setting sun had sent a shaft of golden glory through the window to touch her hair and the blossoms lying on it.

And her sister stood beside her and looked down. And a new peace was on her face when she laid her cheek upon her husband's breast as he enfolded her.

"She is my saint," she said. "To-day she has taken my sins in her pure hands to God and has asked mercy on them."

"And so having done, dear Heart," he answered her, "she lies amid her flowers, and smiles."

But of that he had overheard he said no word. And if as time passed there came some sacred hour when, their souls being one, there could be no veil not rent away by Love and Nature, and the secret each had kept was revealed to the other, 'twas surely so revealed as but to draw them closer and fill them with higher nobleness, for no other human creature heard of it or guessed.

So it befel that one man met his deserts by chance, and none were punished, and only good grew out of his evil grave. And should there be a Power who for strange, high reasons calls forth helpless souls from peaceful Nothingness to relentless Life, and judges all Life does and leaves undone, 'tis surely sate to trust its honesty and justice.